Praise for *Harry Curry: Counsel of Choice*

'Immensely readable with an accessible style and
excellent dialogue with shades of *Rumpole* and *Rake*'
Bookseller + Publisher

'A well-written, entertaining book' *Sydney Morning Herald*

'a thrilling debut ... Harry Curry is one class act ... the novel
features dialogue par excellence ... I can't wait to read the next
Harry Curry' *Calvet's Book of the Week*

'An enjoyable, refreshingly Australian read that also
provides a fascinating look at the country's legal system'
Australian Penthouse

'both engaging and diverting' *Adelaide Advertiser*

'certain to strike a chord with readers who enjoy a good
legal stoush ... an entertaining and absorbing frolic'
Sunday Tasmanian

Stuart Littlemore QC is an Australian barrister and former journalist and television presenter. He was the writer and host of the ABC's *Media Watch* program from its inception in 1989 until 1997. His first book of Harry Curry stories, *Harry Curry: Counsel of Choice*, was published in 2011.

Stuart Littlemore

HARRY CURRY

The Murder Book

HarperCollins*Publishers*

HarperCollins_Publishers_

First published in Australia in 2012
by HarperCollins_Publishers_ Australia Pty Limited
ABN 36 009 913 517
harpercollins.com.au

HarperCollins_Publishers_
Level 13, 201 Elizabeth Street, Sydney NSW 2000, Australia
31 View Road, Glenfield, Auckland 0627, New Zealand
A 53, Sector 57, Noida, UP, India
77–85 Fulham Palace Road, London W6 8JB, United Kingdom
2 Bloor Street East, 20th floor, Toronto, Ontario M4W 1A8, Canada
10 East 53rd Street, New York NY 10022, USA

National Library of Australia Cataloguing-in-Publication data:

Littlemore, Stuart.
Harry Curry : the murder book / Stuart Littlemore.
978 0 7322 9343 7 (pbk.)
Subjects: Lawyers – Australia – Fiction.
Short stories, Australian.
A823. 4

Cover design by Darren Holt, HarperCollins Design Studio
Cover images: Barrister by Tamara Voninski / Fairfax Syndication (FXJ139124); Court house by
Claver Carroll / Getty Images (128098690); all other images by shutterstock.com
Author photograph by Kezia Littlemore
Typeset in Stempel Garamond LT Std 11/18pt by Kirby Jones
Printed and bound in Australia by Griffin Press
The papers used by HarperCollins in the manufacture of this book are a natural, recyclable
product made from wood grown in sustainable plantation forests. The fibre source and
manufacturing processes meet recognised international environmental standards, and carry
certification.

5 4 3 2 1   12 13 14 15

For Nancy Curry, the little girl on the verandah
(with windmills on her shoes)

Contents

I wish I loved the Human Race;
I wish I loved its silly face;
I wish I liked the way it walks;
I wish I liked the way it talks
And when I'm introduced to one,
I wish I thought 'What Jolly Fun!'

Walter Alexander Raleigh

No discount for mass murder

These are the facts. They're bad enough without embellishment.

Adrian Flowers was born to a fifteen-year-old girl and brought up by his grandparents in a rundown house on a few dusty acres outside Shellharbour, a bit south of Wollongong. The house was crowded with not just his mother and grandparents, but also his three knuckle-dragging uncles, who brutalised the little boy even before he could walk.

Adrian, when he got to Shellharbour Primary, was further bullied and beaten. He was a soft target — lonely, inarticulate, weedy, uncared-for and with a girly name. His mother had long gone — good luck to her — and his idea of 'home' didn't imply any comfort or warmth or affection or belonging. It was just where he went when there wasn't anywhere else.

On his eighth birthday, a hot day in January, Adrian was driven a few kilometres, grudgingly, in the family's FJ Holden ute to Shellharbour village and its little beach, enclosed within a breakwater. While his grandparents drank shandies in the pub and watched horse races on TV, the boy was left to fend for himself on the beach, clad in his singlet and underpants. Observing the children of the Macedonian steelworkers from Port Kembla splashing happily in the gentle swell, he walked in and kept walking until the water was over his head. Adrian stood, looking up at the sunlight dappling the surface for perhaps a minute. A watching mother dragged him out and laid him face down on the wet sand to cough up the saltwater he'd breathed in. Adrian didn't mention it when his grandparents collected him an hour later.

The bullying that he endured at primary school continued at Warilla High until the boy turned fourteen. Then a growth spurt took over his body and transformed him into the biggest boy in his class. The work his grandfather forced on him — digging the vegetable garden, cutting and carrying firewood, cleaning and stacking second-hand bricks for resale — developed his arms and his chest and his sense of personal power. The Police Boys Club taught him to box. To the strapping and determined youth, boxing wasn't about self-defence. His priority was to learn to attack, pitilessly. After a couple of bouts in which Adrian dismayed his instructors with his savagery, he was asked not to come back to the club. He didn't mind. The Police Boys had served its purpose.

With chilling efficiency, Adrian systematically cornered and beat senseless every Warilla boy who had ever bullied him, sometimes taking on two at a time. Then it was his uncles' turn. The sixteen-year-old showed no mercy to the men, aged in their late twenties and early thirties, and forever after they regarded him with surly fear. He continued to sleep on the verandah of his grandparents' house, to which he had been despatched as an infant, and never spoke more than he needed to. The household was afraid of him.

Unlikely as it may seem, there was one teacher who saw something in the young brute and went out of his way to encourage his biology studies. When Adrian confided that he wanted to train as a nurse, the teacher took him, in his own time, for a job interview at Wollongong Hospital, and helped him get a start there as a porter. After two years hard graft on the wards, and on the strength of a good reference from his supervisor, Adrian was hired by the Ambulance Service as a trainee paramedic. His ambition was to learn to fly a helicopter and work in marine rescue. He'd been attracted by the television coverage of rescues at sea of the crews of stricken Sydney-to-Hobart racers in a terrible storm. In the meantime, he was transferred to the Moruya ambulance station, further down the coast.

Three days before Christmas 1989, Adrian was woken in his flat above a real estate agency in the main street of Moruya by his clock radio, turning itself on in time for the 8 a.m. news. What he heard was that, an hour earlier, two tourist coaches had collided on the Princes Highway near Bodalla, and it was feared there had been 'significant loss of life'. He was off duty that day, but immediately dressed in his Ambulance Service uniform and, unshaven and unshowered, rode his motorbike the twenty kilometres south to the accident site. He was waved past the police barricades to be confronted by a ragged, jagged explosion of shattered glass and twisted metal — two big, shiny, aluminium-bodied buses fused into one.

Steam and smoke and weeping rose in the air, and water, oil and diesel were splashing onto the road from beneath the buses' engines. The crash was ringed with ambulances, police vehicles and fire engines. On the fringes, the residents of nearby homes, some still in their dressing gowns, were gawping and chattering and getting in the way, except for a practical few who were shuttling back and forth with mugs of tea for the rescue workers and the walking wounded. Ambulances were leaving with their sirens on low growl, ferrying the injured to Batemans Bay Hospital. The bodies of the dead were placed in a respectful line on the grass verge outside the closest house's fence, where blue and white agapanthus flowers were nodding heedlessly.

Adrian parked his bike and strode to the ambulance officer with most pips on his epaulettes. 'You can go in and get people out of the blue bus,' he was directed. 'Most of them are dead.'

It was hard to get into the bus. The access door was useless: jammed shut, a body wedged behind it. The driver, Adrian thought, glimpsing a uniform soaked in blood. He used a domestic ladder that had been placed on the opposite side of the bus to climb through one of the side windows, broken glass snagging at his trousers and the skin of his thighs. Firemen, police and other ambulance officers were already in the bus, trying to help the living. Someone was crying softly; an old man, perhaps. On the back seat lay three girls in bloodstained summer frocks. They all looked to be about fourteen, but it was impossible to tell as they had been neatly decapitated by a dislodged window. Adrian sighed and for a moment averted his eyes, looking over the torsos to a bright blue summer-morning sky. The girls' dresses were around their waists, exposing their underwear. Without really thinking, he pulled down each dress to cover them to the knees. Then he carried the first girl to the smashed-out window and called to a fireman to take the body from him. She seemed so light.

Adrian remained at the scene for three hours, lifting and carrying, until the last of the injured had been taken to hospital, and the bodies of the fifteen who had died at the scene had been photographed, covered again with blue plastic tarpaulins, and attended to by the Bodalla clergyman who had been there almost from the start. Adrian had a quick word with the incident commander, climbed back on his bike and rode to Moruya Heads, where he took off his clothes and walked into the surf. He stayed in the water, rubbing wet sand into his face and hands, until he stopped crying. Then he went home and got back into bed.

About six months later, Adrian injured his back lifting a survivor out of a car wreck and was invalided out of the Ambulance Service. He never forgave them for that.

Twenty years later, two forensic psychiatrists disagreed about the significance of Adrian's experience at the Bodalla bus crash. One refused to support a diagnosis of post-traumatic stress disorder. Neither thought it explained his sociopathy. They agreed, though, that his personality disorder was linked to his difficult childhood at Shellharbour.

For Adrian, his dreams of a career in marine rescue smashed beyond repair, fell among thieves — and worse. He found a job serving summonses for solicitors and insurance companies, who rightly assumed that his fearsome bulk and habitual scowl would ensure that those presented with the unwelcome documents would not put up a fight. He drank in the back bars of south-western Sydney pubs with like-minded people, and crooked policemen. He was violent, and was paid for it. He received and resold stolen goods. He funded and took part in robberies. He invested in a brothel. He financed drug dealing. He did some really bad things, that no one knew about. He murdered five people.

Long after the last of the killings, on a mild October morning, Adrian Flowers was on a drug run from Adelaide to Sydney. The boot of his Commodore was crammed with orange garbage bags full of cannabis and two smaller clear plastic bags of methyl amphetamine powder. On the Sturt Highway, about three kilometres east of Mildura, a police breath test unit was still being set up when an eager probationer jumped the gun and waved at Adrian to pull over. The sergeant in charge, who was in no hurry, was about to countermand the direction, but decided to let the process take place.

The hand-held breath analyser was pointed through the open window of the Commodore, and Adrian was ordered to count to five. Negative. Standing back to allow the car to move away, the probationer noticed that one of the back tyres was almost flat. 'Hang on, mate,' he called, 'you're going to have to change that. You've got a spare, haven't you?'

And that's how it all fell apart.

By the time David Surrey, solicitor, was able to clear his desk in his office in Goulburn and pick up a flight to Mildura via Adelaide, Adrian was almost halfway through a six-hour video-recorded interview with detectives that initially covered the drug ring he was running with, then progressed to a confession to all five of his killings. The police were incredulous, as Harry Curry would be when Surrey provided him with the police brief for his opinion, instructing the barrister to plead his client guilty to the lot. It turned out that all the homicide detectives had ever had on Adrian Flowers were some insufficient suspicions about two of the deaths.

And those are the facts.

The Sydney detectives worked through the crimes with Adrian in the Mildura police station, taking them in chronological order, starting with the deaths of Edgar O'Brien and Carmen Yee in a McMansion at Kellyville. O'Brien had been found on the floor of his bedroom, with numerous gunshot wounds in his face. Ms Yee was on the bed, tied up and shot several times in the head.

'Tell us about that. About what happened at Kellyville.'

Detective Sergeant Thompson straightened the papers in front of him as Detective Constable Madden scribbled a detail in his notebook.

'Okay.' Adrian took off his incongruous John Lennon glasses and cleaned them carefully with a khaki handkerchief. 'I was doing repossessions for finance companies, and that's how I met him. O'Brien. And we drank in the same pub at Mount Pritchard. Not that we were ever mates. Anyway, I found out that he'd hired some heavies to bash my mate and put him in hospital. Dave Morris. So I decided to kill him.' He replaced his glasses and focused on Thompson's face.

'Did you do it on your own?'

'No. Frank Peters came up from Canberra to help me. I picked him up at the airport in my car — I had a white Valiant in those days, you can check — and we went to Campbelltown.'

'What was that for?'

'To get the gun. Dean Bates cut down a .22 for me, and he sold me that and a silencer and numberplates for the car.'

'What happened next?' DS Thompson wanted to keep the narrative flowing.

'We put the plates on the car. Me and Frankie drove to the house at Kellyville. It was night-time. We went to the front door, and the Asian bird opened it. She was going to have a bath. She was the only one there. We tied her up and put a hankie in her mouth, and put her on the bed. While we waited for O'Brien to come home, we went through the house and took anything worthwhile. There wasn't much.'

'Do you remember what time he got home?'

'No. Maybe half an hour or an hour after we tied her up.'

'Go on.'

7

'We heard his key in the door, and we waited for him to come in. He was carrying two bottles of oysters.'

'Okay. What happened when he entered the house?'

'He walked in … he saw me standing in the hallway and stopped. Yeah, he stepped inside, just inside the door, and stopped.'

'What were you doing at this time?'

'Shooting him.'

'Where?'

'Can't remember much after this, 'cause it's a blur. But I remember, if I remember correctly, I hit him in the middle of the forehead. He fell down straight away. The bottles of oysters smashed on the floor.'

'Okay. And what happened after that?'

'I didn't know if he was dead. We dragged him into the bedroom. It's the only time Frank touched him. Then I shot, shot, shot, shot. We ransacked the place a bit more, made a mess, and left.'

'What do you mean, "shot, shot, shot, shot"? What does that mean?'

'I shot him and her. Shot them both.'

The two policemen pushed back their chairs and looked at Adrian. What they saw was a big, calm man. Huge in the chest and shoulders. Perched on his nose were almost comical round glasses that he took off from time to time and placed on the formica table. He was dressed like a shop assistant in an old-time hardware store: short sleeves, pen in his pocket, KingGee blue drill trousers. Boots, well polished. They dimly recognised his detailed confession as a sort of catharsis, as did the man under arrest. A halt was called, the regulation words about suspending the process were spoken into the video and audio recorders, and

Adrian was taken back to a cell. Phone calls were made, instant coffee was drunk, and a series of questions was mapped out on a word processor for the next round.

David Surrey arrived during the break in a taxi from the airport and asked to see his client before the interview resumed. DS Thompson didn't want to lose the flow of the confession, but agreed to a short delay. He was convinced that no solicitor was going to stop this man's account, and he was right. Surrey's conference with his client, an armed constable standing outside the door, simply served to make it clear to him that Adrian wanted to spell out everything he'd done. He wasn't interested in his right to silence.

'But why tell them all this?' Surrey asked. 'You don't have to.'

'Because they already know.' He assumed, wrongly, that they did.

A disconcerted and frustrated solicitor was permitted to sit with his client as the interview resumed, and the police satisfied themselves that the recorders were working. 'You'll get an audio and video copy of all of it,' they assured Surrey. They didn't really mind this solicitor in his Harris tweed jacket and RM Williams boots, who resembled nothing so much as a grazier trying his hand at a second job to tide his family over in the drought. He was a cut above the spivs they usually dealt with around the fringes of the criminal courts.

'Can we move on to Killara? I've got the file here.' Thompson opened a manila folder and started reading. 'This is six years after the Kellyville matter. This is the short facts from the divisional detectives: Mrs Robbins was found in her bedroom by her husband. She had been gagged tightly around her mouth, her feet bound, in effect, hamstrung, and her body was found covered with blood, lying beside the bed. The curtain had been torn and there was the appearance of a struggle having taken place. The autopsy revealed that she had been stabbed a considerable number of times with a small-bladed object or knife, there being one puncture wound to her lung, and blood in the trachea that was the probable cause of death. That and the tight gag around her mouth.'

Thompson looked up from the file. 'What can you tell me about that?'

Surrey put his hand on Adrian's arm, but quickly withdrew it at a look from his client. 'You did understand the caution — that you're not obliged to say anything, and that anything you do say can be used to prosecute you?'

The big man merely nodded without looking at Surrey, then started to speak, directing his words at the two policemen on the other side of the table. At first, he kept glancing at a milky ring made on the tabletop by a takeaway coffee cup, but as he settled into his speech, his eyes came up, unblinking.

'I was told that Mick Robbins was a multimillionaire, and that he kept a lot of money on him, or at home. I watched the house for a few nights so that I knew who lived there — just him and his missus — and I went back there a couple of afternoons later. As far as I could see, there was no one home.'

'How did you get in?'

'They'd left the garage door open, and there was a house key in the glovebox of the Mercedes in the garage. The car wasn't locked either. I got a screwdriver off the bench and opened the door with the key. I went through the house, looking for money and valuables. I went through the drawers, and was looking under the carpets for a safe. Then I went down the hall and through a bedroom door and the lady was there, with scissors in her hand.'

'You said you thought there was no one there.'

'That's right. I'd only surmise this part, but I think I said something to the effect of "Don't scream", or whatever. Then I noticed she had these big scissors in her hand, which shocked the hell out of me, and I lunged at her with the screwdriver ... and my motive at this point, realising that I'd been found on the premises and there was a fight ensuing, was that I wanted to quieten her down as quick as possible to get off, to make my escape, so there was a fight between us where we were stabbing at each other. I don't remember all of it, but we came up against a window, I believe, and there was either a curtain or a venetian blind that fell down, which then exposed that room to the outside world which was again an alarm to me. And I think at that stage that the lady screamed. I do remember that I hit her but I don't know at which stage of it ... I thumped her a couple of times to stop her screaming. She went down on the floor. To further facilitate my quiet exit ...'

Surrey looked at the detective sergeant, but there was no obvious reaction to the bizarrely stilted language.

'... I gagged her and tied her up, hoping that she wouldn't make any more noise until I was away, and then as far as I can remember I went out — down the stairs and straight out the same way I came in, which was the front door.'

Surrey sat quietly as the prisoner and the two detectives spent five minutes discussing the medical aspects of Mrs Robbins' death. Adrian spoke in an authoritative way, and seemed unfazed when told that his victim had suffered thirty-two stab wounds.

'I caused that lady's death by two actions ... sorry, three: one, stabbing her in the lung; two, not rolling her into a coma position to clear her airway so her trachea wouldn't get blocked; and three, applying a gag which did quieten her down but also restricted her flow of oxygen.'

There was a long silence, which Surrey ended by suggesting they'd probably heard enough for one day. Scheduling the resumption for 9 a.m., the police had their prisoner taken off to the cells for the night and offered, once he'd gone, to join the solicitor a bit later for a drink in the saloon bar of his hotel. They knew where he was staying.

David Surrey was about to start his second whisky when the two homicide men, dressed now in jeans and trainers, arrived and bought themselves light beers. 'Not bad,' the detective sergeant enthused, settling into a comfortable armchair and glancing round the tastefully restored bar. 'I suppose you'll be going round to Stefano's for your tea.'

'If it's Stefano's, you'd better call it dinner,' Surrey remonstrated.

The constable sipped his beer and posed a question. 'You always brief Mr Curry, don't you? In Sydney, I mean.'

'Often as I can,' Surrey agreed, 'but I don't know if he'll do this. It might be Ms Engineer.'

'His girlfriend, isn't she?' Madden asked.

Surrey gave him a hard look. 'I have no idea, constable. It's none of my business.'

Unchastened, the policeman pressed on. 'Be a plea, won't it? He hasn't got much choice but to nod the scone.'

'Couldn't possibly say. I've never been in quite this position — multiple killings, detailed confessions. At least he's remorseful.'

'Is he?' DS Thompson interjected. 'I haven't seen any sign of that. It's all very how-ya-goin', matter-of-fact, what happened next, as if we're all working together to complete an ambo report, or something like that.'

'It does feel a bit like that, yes. I'd have to say that I'm not sure what I can do for him.'

'What do you call it?' the junior officer asked. 'A plea in mitigation? For a mass murderer?'

'I don't know how to class him.' Surrey took another pull at his drink and put it on the table. 'He's not a serial killer — they're nut cases who do it because there's some compulsion; they're driven. And I don't think you can call five murders spread over more than ten years mass murder.'

'Well, it's got to be multiple murder, at least.' DS Thompson was implacable.

'The first ones were gangland killings; Mrs Robbins was opportunistic ... what will the last two be about?' mused the constable.

'Wait and see.' Surrey thought it was time to eat.

As it happened, Surrey did eat at Stefano's restaurant that night. He'd admired and enjoyed the amusing Italian's television cooking program on the ABC, in which he articulated his fierce pride in the region's migrants and the culinary improvements they'd brought to the meat-and-three-veg wasteland of far north-western Victoria. And the meal didn't disappoint him, but he resolved not to disclose it to his wife. Eating the meal, and particularly the tiramisu dessert, Surrey wished she were there. Fine food's never as much fun when your companion is a novel, no matter how riveting. Still, it was such a pleasure that he ventured into another of Stefano's establishments — the nearby café — for breakfast. That didn't take long (muesli with dried local apricots and two long black coffees), and Surrey had been waiting on the bench in the police station foyer for twenty minutes by the time DS Thompson called him into the electronic interview room.

Adrian was wearing the same shirt as the day before. He looked as if he'd spent an uncomfortable night.

'What we're going to do,' Thompson told the other three men in the room, 'is finish off the interview, then remand Adrian in custody back to Sydney on tonight's plane. Will you be applying for bail, Mr Surrey?'

'There's a statutory presumption against it for murder,' Surrey said. 'Adrian, I'll make the application if you want. We can have a conference when the interview's finished.'

'Not much point,' the client observed.

'True.'

The station sergeant was called in to establish, in the presence of Surrey and the absence of the Sydney detectives, that the man in custody had no complaints about his treatment to that point. That done, the ostensibly independent officer left the room to be replaced by Thompson and Madden. The constable administered a fresh caution ('You are not obliged to say anything, but anything you do say is being recorded …') and the DS took a minute to organise his thoughts and his notes.

'I intend to ask you now a number of questions about the deaths of Sherry Lang and Fatima Khoury at Ashfield five years ago. I repeat that you are not obliged to answer my questions—'

'Yes, I understand.'

'—and that anything you do say is being electronically recorded and may be used in evidence.'

'I understand that.'

'You, or your solicitor, will be given an audio copy and a video copy of the interview, and once it is transcribed, you are entitled to a copy of that transcript. Are you prepared to answer my questions?'

'Go ahead.' Adrian spoke clearly, and looked intently at the wall.

Surrey leaned back in his chair, feeling redundant and conscious of a deskful of work waiting for him in Goulburn. Still, he was being paid to be here and there was nothing in the office that couldn't wait a day or two.

The senior detective spread out the pages of his open file and started to read. 'At about 7.40 p.m. fire brigade officers attended a fire at a property in Cavill Avenue, Ashfield. The property, which was a brick dwelling, was being leased by Sherry Lang and was operating as a massage parlour under the name "Sherry's Oasis". A large quantity of black smoke was coming from the building. When the fire officers entered the premises to extinguish the fire, they found the bodies of two females. One of the bodies, that of Fatima Khoury, was in a room on the right-hand side of a hallway leading from the front door. She was seated on a lounge and had been shot three times in the head and upper body. The other female, Sherry Lang, was found at the opposite end of the house. Ms Lang had suffered extensive burns to most of her body. She had a number of stab wounds to her face, neck and chest and she had also been shot several times, once through the right eye.'

David Surrey was trying not to show how nauseous he was suddenly feeling. He couldn't look in his client's direction, but Adrian, once again, seemed to be a study in calm compliance.

'Police were called and a short time later, Ms Lang's de facto, Louis Marks, arrived at the premises. His vehicle was searched and a .22 rifle was found in a carry case and it has been established that the blood found in connection with that weapon was that of Sherry Lang. Now, Mr Flowers, is there anything you can tell us about this matter?'

'Louis offered me $20,000 to kill Sherry. I'd had an affair with her a couple of years before, but that had nothing to do with it. He was antagonistic to her because, even though she was his de facto, she was in competition with his massage parlours and was keeping the profits for herself. I got Donny Watson to help me, and we did surveillance of the place. Louis told us when Sherry would be there on her own, so we went there that night.'

'Can you tell me who was present when you arrived at the premises?'

'Just the working girl, which we didn't expect her to be. She said Sherry wasn't coming in that night. We didn't believe that, so we put her in a room and waited. Donny was watching through the front window. We saw Sherry driving towards the parlour. She had a bluey-coloured Ford, and she parked in the car park across the street. I went into the room and shot the other girl. She was sitting down. I can't recall how many times I shot her.'

'Were you satisfied that she was dead before you left that room?'

'I wouldn't say "satisfied she was dead", but I was satisfied she wasn't going to cause any trouble.'

'Did you realise when you shot her you could kill her?'

'Yes.'

'Did that cause you any problems?'

'Yes, because she shouldn't have been there. Louis Marks had totally buggered it up.'

'When did Marks arrive at the house?'

'Not much after that. He wasn't supposed to be there either. A fight started, but that all sort of happened in fast forward. I fired some shots, and I got Sherry in the eye, I think. I also stabbed her. Later, I gave the gun to Detective Bruce Allen and he got rid of it, and I cleaned the knife and hid it in a box of cutlery at the Campsie St Vincent de Paul's.'

Surrey reflected to himself on the ingenuity of that move. And the all-too familiar story of police complicity.

'Did you do anything else before you left the premises?'

'I tore up the furniture to get stuff that would burn, and I set fire to the premises. I intended to destroy the evidence. Then I marched Marks out of there before the fire properly took hold, and we left in our own cars. Donny came with me.'

DS Thompson had enough to go on. After that, there were some formalities to tidy up, and the prisoner was left in a cell to await transport to the airport for the long trip to Sydney, and on to the remand section of Long Bay. Surrey realised he would be heading east on the same plane. He doubted that they would be seated together.

Harry Curry had spent most of that day driving from Erskineville down the coast towards the Victorian border, happily anticipating arriving at his newly purchased smallholding outside the hamlet of Burragate, and was just descending the hill into Narooma when the old Jaguar's phone rang. Harry let it ring, because he didn't want to spoil his favourite view — high tide rushing into the sunny estuary, the mid-afternoon shades of colour in the clean water glowing like blue and green opals. As he cleared the bridge and approached the town's shops, he pressed the hands-free button.

'It's you, isn't it, Dave? Who else would bother me at a time like this?'

'I'm in Mildura, waiting for the plane home. And what's a time like this?'

'I'm going up the hill past Lynch's Hotel in Narooma, trying to decide whether to stay in Bermagui tonight, or to push on to Eden.'

'Bella with you?'

'No.'

'She's not?'

'That's what I said.'

'Ah.' A pause. 'If you stay in Bermi, you can eat at the golf club.'

Harry looked down at the phone. 'That's why you're ringing, is it? Restaurant recommendations?'

'Of course. The Seahorse Inn's good, too, if you get as far as Eden.'

'Don't think I will, though. All finished in Mildura, David?'

'For the moment. The show's coming back to Sydney.'

'I know nothing about it. The show, I mean.'

'Didn't Bella tell you? I've already spoken to her in chambers.'

'Of course she did. You've got me, it's a fair cop. She held forth on the subject of your serial killer all the way from Ulladulla to Batemans Bay.'

'Oh, you mean she was on the phone.'

'She certainly wasn't in the car, I'm sorry to say. You've got nowhere to go on that thing, surely? By which I mean that I can't see anything you can possibly do for the man except plead him guilty. And why would you want to, anyway? Do anything else for him, I mean.'

'I am talking to Harry Curry, am I not? I haven't got a wrong number, have I? I thought I was speaking with the idealistic and highly principled defender of the children of the poor?'

'The infamous realist, Surrey. You've got a man who's killed six people in cold blood, who's confessed the lot, and who must inevitably plead guilty and be locked up until he dies.'

'Only five. Six is an exaggeration.'

'Oh, then it's quite different, isn't it? Only five murders — you should manage a good behaviour bond with a decent psychiatric report.'

'Smartarse. I want you to listen to me, for once in your life. This poor bastard had the worst childhood I've ever heard of.'

'She didn't go into the subjectives, Dave. Feel free.'

And for the next fifteen minutes Surrey set it all out. The brutalisation, the misery, the loneliness. It didn't change Harry's mind, and he said so.

'You don't want the brief, then? Private payer, you know. At least until his money runs out.'

'Urgent farm work. A dentist's appointment. Flooded in. Couldn't take it even if I wanted it, David. Which I certainly do not. I thought you knew a dead parrot when you saw one.'

Surrey laughed and took up the challenge. They knew each other to be Monty Python freaks. '"No, no, this parrot's not dead. He's resting! Remarkable bird, the Norwegian Blue, isn't it — beautiful plumage!"'

'"The plumage doesn't enter into it. It's stone dead."' Harry picked up his line on cue.

'"He's probably pining for the fjords."' Surrey was equal to the task. 'What are you trying to say? That you're an ex-parrot?'

Harry paused to overtake a milk tanker. 'Your Honour puts it so much better than I could ever have done. Ms Arabella Engineer of the junior Bar, on the other hand, will never say die. Fix her up with a psychiatric apologia from some self-medicating charlatan and point her at the barricades.'

'With any help from you, Harry?'

'Well, I love her — don't I? I'll do what I can, but I'm not going to appear.'

The idea of Harry Curry speaking of love stunned Surrey for a moment. Not that he doubted it, but he would never have expected the man to say so. The big, intimidating-looking barrister letting down his guard so readily? Who'd have believed it?

'What are you going to do, Harry — in the short term, I mean? I can understand that you might have this farm as a weekend bolt hole, but you're not really going to do the tree-change thing, are you? People don't retire at your age, unless they win Lotto.'

'In the very short term, afternoon tea at Central Tilba and then the Bermagui motel for the night. In the medium term, doing some planting in the *parterre* — asparagus, leeks, borlotti beans, some lettuces, tomatoes. Fixing some fences to keep Col's cows out, mending the pump, painting the shed, collecting eggs, cooking a guinea fowl. That's if I can catch one, let alone kill it.'

'Lucky bastard.'

'That sums up my feelings, too, Dave. Dunno why I didn't do this years ago. There's only one problem.'

'She'll come round. But you're not answering my question, witness. Abandoning her?'

'I bought her a workshirt and trousers at Lowes. You think she'll wear them?'

'It'll make a change from the Stella McCartney.'

'Hang on while I make this turn. Just pulling up in Tilba, old boy. I'll talk to Bella again tomorrow, after I've fed the chooks. See you.'

'Be good.'

When Harry pushed through the door of the reception office at the Bermagui motel, it was empty and, as invited by a plastic notice, he pressed the buzzer taped to the counter. The female half of the mum-and-dad proprietorial team hurried in with a mug of tea, which she almost spilled when confronted with the huge, besuited man silhouetted against the setting sun. Untidy notwithstanding the cufflinks and tie, shaggy-haired, massive hands resting on the counter, and a deep bass voice asking for a room in which he could smoke. Because Harry also told her he wouldn't need breakfast and would be pushing off very early, the owner asked for his money in advance.

Harry ate quickly at the golf club, walked back to the motel and slept like a log, dreamlessly. He was up early enough to reach Burragate by nine o'clock the next morning, having weaved his way past timber jinkers and the signwritten utes of tradesmen ('*For all your plumbing needs*') setting off for another day's work in the coastal villages. After driving through Burragate hamlet and turning down a farm track towards the slow-moving Towamba River, he stopped to open a gate and proceeded to a green weatherboard farmhouse that he unlocked and entered. Having opened all the windows to air the house, he changed his clothes and went out to check on the chickens, tidied up the house paddocks and mended a gate that wasn't closing properly. At five to twelve he took a cold bottle of Marlborough sauvignon blanc semillon and a glass onto the verandah, having lifted the cordless phone from its cradle and jabbed the first number on the speed dial. While he waited for Arabella to answer, the phone jammed between his cheek and his shoulder, Harry opened the screw top and was just pouring his first glass when she answered.

'What's it like there?'

'You'll have to come and see for yourself.'

'No, Harry. You're going to have to describe it to me.'

'It's pretty warm, and there was a good hatch on the river first thing today. The lemon trees are alive with bees, there's blossom on the cherries, the neighbours have taken good care of the chickens, Col's cows are spreading fresh manure on the big paddock, the bottom gate now closes properly, the river's up, and all's right with the world. Except that you're not here.'

'I wish I were.'

'I trust you will be.'

'Of course, but I'm not sure when.'

'The weekend?'

'With any luck.'

He took a drink. 'Surrey and I talked about your matter. That's quite a plea he's given you there. You seem to be a lot more sanguine about this man's prospects than I think is reasonable. Flowers, I mean. Flowers the mass murderer.'

'But you haven't read a single page of the brief, Harry. Be fair.'

'Bella, my love, nothing in the brief is going to change the fact of five murders. There isn't a judge on the Supreme Court who's going to listen to anything anyone can say for him.'

'They have to. Did David tell you about the subjectives?'

'The appalling childhood? Yes. The fact that the police had nothing on him until he spilt his guts? Yes. His willingness to name his co-offenders and to give evidence against them? Yes. But none of that's going to make a blind bit of difference.'

'But it has to.'

'Dirty dogs don't win, Bella. That's the shibboleth of self-protecting judges — which means all of them.'

'I understand that, Harry. I know why you're saying that. But this is about the rule of law, and whether the judge — whoever it turns out to be — whether the judge likes it or not, whether this man is the worst killer anyone has ever imagined in their worst nightmares, the law still demands that his level of co-operation — the confessions, the disclosures, the pleas of guilty — is of such utilitarian value, and so undeniably demonstrative of remorse and contrition, that he has to get a discount in the sentence he would otherwise be given.'

'So goes the jurisprudential theory.'

'So goes the law, Harry.'

'I'm not going to argue with you, sweetheart. At least, not with you at the end of a phone five hundred kilometres away. If you can get the psych's report and bring it down here for the weekend, we can work up your submissions on sentence. I'll help, I promise. We'll give him the best plea anybody could. But you've got to be realistic. Judges aren't going to put themselves in a pillory to be pelted with ordure by the yellow press and Alan Jones — not for this man.'

'I'm going to pray you're wrong.'

'Of course you are. Listen, I'm going to assume you'll be on Friday afternoon's plane. I'll be waiting for you at Merimbula Airport.'

'Unless you hear otherwise. All right.'

'I'll wash the sheets. I'll even hang them out to dry in the sun.'

'Have you got anything to eat?'

'I'll go into Wyndham. I'm sure the shop's got cornflakes.'

'What will you be doing until then?'

'Playing farmer. I've got you some farming clothes, too.'

Arabella laughed. 'Dolce and Gabbana?'

Harry finished his glass. 'I miss you, young woman. It's lonely here.'

'What about the wombats?'

'They're all married and they only come out at dusk. Who am I going to talk to until then?'

'I'll be here.'

The psychiatrist engaged for Adrian Flowers was a full-time medico–legal specialist, which (as Harry was fond of saying) meant that he was so incompetent, he wouldn't dare to treat real live people — instead he'd just diagnose their conditions and report on them in mystifying jargon and in such a way as would keep the work flowing from the personal injury plaintiffs' firms and the criminal solicitors. Or, if he had chosen to work the other side of the street, from the insurance companies and the Director of Public Prosecution's staff. Such men (and women) were the bane of the Supreme Court's existence — only too ready to prostitute themselves for a significant reward — and had almost driven the courts to the point of reforming the system to allow only the evidence of a single expert witness appointed by the court itself. Not that anyone thought that would be any more objective — two ratbag opinions will always be better than a single unchallenged ratbag opinion. Predictably enough, the expert chosen by Surrey quickly and solemnly produced a six-page report that was counterbalanced by a ten-page report from the DPP's man. Let the judge work it out.

Armed with copies of the psychiatric contradictions, her laptop, an elegant Panama hat and a pair of green rubber boots as hand luggage, Arabella descended on time from the Rex plane at Merimbula, to find Harry waiting on the lawn in front of the little terminal building, dressed in an army disposals shirt and dark blue Hard Yakka trousers. They kissed, collected her suitcase, and then Harry guided Arabella to the far end of the car park. She walked with the grace of a very tall woman.

Arabella was ebullient. 'I saw a whale on the way in. The pilot pointed it out to us.'

'Fantastic.'

'It is so beautiful, flying in here.'

'As I told you.' Indulgently, but gratefully.

They reached the LandCruiser and Harry opened the cargo door.

'What happened to the Jag?'

'It proved to be not entirely compatible with the exigencies of the Towamba road,' said Harry. 'I tore off the muffler on one of the gravel stretches. Couldn't hear myself think after that.'

'So have you bought this?'

'The man thinks I'm going to. I might. He's fixing the Jag, and he's lent this to me for the weekend.'

Harry threw the suitcase in the back next to a new spade and a sack of shell grit he'd picked up for the chickens, Arabella hanging on to her laptop. They headed south through Pambula village, which Arabella admired, and on to Eden.

'This is where you did the shipwreck inquest, isn't it?'

Harry nodded. 'And the bushfire deaths.' They climbed the short hill into the town, Harry pointing out the sights. 'That's the old post office, closed; that's the new supermarket — pretty good, in fact; hardware shop — classic early sixties provincial commercial; the newspaper office — the *Magnet*; solicitor over there in that two-storey Victorian house, but only two days a week; the Killer Whale Museum. We're going down to the co-op to get some mussels.'

While Harry made the purchase, Arabella climbed out of the car to admire the southward sweep of Twofold Bay. 'What's all that machinery over there?'

'The woodchip loader. It's all fishing and timber here. Don't be caught wearing anything green.'

'I understand. I noticed your outfit, by the way. Fetching.'

They picked up some wine at the Great Southern drive-through, and passed the Australasia Hotel a bit further along the main street, a sign declaring it to be under new management. 'That's where your Bega client stabbed his antagonist with a broken glass,' Harry reminded Bella. 'Maybe it won't be such a bloodhouse in its new incarnation.'

'I counted that as one of my great successes of advocacy,' Arabella said. 'Until the foreman of the jury told me that they all hated the victim anyway.'

Harry smiled. 'It's the country, and you won the case.'

'Thereby improving my career average.'

'I've always understood that they train the English to be good losers.'

'Well, we practise a lot. Losing, I mean. Except the Ashes.'

'Indeed.' And he ducked as she threw what passed for a punch at the side of his head.

Forty-five minutes later, they reached the farm at Burragate. RonLyn, the sign at the front gate said.

'Don't tell me that's an Aboriginal name,' said Arabella. 'I won't believe you.'

Getting out to retrieve the mail from the letterbox, Harry defended the prosaic. 'One of the great Australian cultural certainties is that you can deduce without too much effort the Christian names of the original owners of many a property. In this case, I'll bet on Ronald and Lynette.'

'I see. Going to change that, are we?'

'Bad luck, isn't it, changing the name?'

'Only if it's a ship.'

'Well, I have given thought to calling the place Buggerit. What d'you think of Buggerit at Burragate?'

'Not much, Harry.'

He got back into the driving seat, empty-handed. 'Okay, then — what about Bob Brown Acres, or the Jack Mundey Estate?'

'Sorry?'

He put the car in gear and drove slowly on the uneven farm track. 'Place'd be burned down the day I put the sign up, I dare say. It'd be labelling ourselves as notorious greenies and radicals. Hippies are well advised to keep a low profile.'

'I see. So RonLyn it is?'

'I think so.'

'Any doubts?'

'About selling Erskineville? Absolutely not. Should have done this years ago.'

'A bit hard, though, to run a practice at the criminal Bar from here, wouldn't it be?'

'If that's what I wanted to do. But I know someone with a big apartment at Elizabeth Bay. I keep a suit and tie there.'

They bumped slowly downhill between fruit trees and fences covered with wisteria still in flower. To the left, backgrounded by the native forest of Mount Imlay National Park, was an open paddock dotted with venerable eucalypts, blackwattles spreading around its fenceline. Big black chickens were chasing insects in the grass under a tree outside their coop. A calf from the next property looked at them from the lower paddock. To the right was the house, masked so densely by old fruit trees that Arabella couldn't make it out.

'Where's the house?'

Harry stopped the car at a small gate in a rabbit-proof fence. 'It's through here. You can't see it for the peaches and lemons. It was here when I left, at least.'

Slamming the LandCruiser doors, they passed through the gate.

'It's very nice,' Arabella admitted as she came under the pergola. 'My first Australian farmhouse, if you don't count Woolgoolga.'

'Your cousins' place? I don't. That's a banana factory, not a proper farm.' He gestured expansively as they approached the front verandah. 'Vernacular Hardiplank, three bedrooms, and you won't even need to stand on your toes to touch the ceiling. But I call it home. You can too, if you like.'

She smiled at him and waited for him to unlock the door, which proved not to be necessary. 'Burragate people don't lock their doors,' he explained, closing only the flywire and leaving the main door open for the scented breeze. 'Here's the kitchen.' He put down her bags and Arabella put her laptop on the table.

A shiny pale-yellow fuel stove emblazoned with the brandname 'Stanley'; quite modern-looking stainless-steel work surfaces; a fridge, dishwasher and new gas stove. Clean lino on the floor. A round table and three chairs.

'It's very nice,' Arabella said again. 'I was thinking corrugated iron, dirt floor and rickety furniture.'

'We can work on that. Take a look at the rest of it.'

Arabella was pleasantly impressed. Harry had painted all the walls and ceilings white, and had had the floor carpeted in a dark brown wool. There were new, empty bookshelves along one long wall of the living room. The books were stacked in cardboard cartons, waiting to be organised. An Eames chair. The rest of the furniture screamed Ikea. The slow-combustion wood-burning fireplace was freshly enamelled and a fire had been set inside it. 'Gets cold, some nights,' Harry said, 'even at this time of year.' He'd obviously made an effort in the few weeks he'd been in possession.

'Bedroom?'

He showed her. An Amish quilt on the bed — a blue-and-white bear's paw pattern. 'That's beautiful,' Arabella said. 'Where's it from? I haven't seen it before.'

'Bought it in Philadelphia, years ago, at an antique shop. You never saw it at Erskineville because I've been saving it.' He smoothed out a wrinkle. 'Not the biggest bedroom you've ever seen, but it's easy to heat in the winter. Here's the bathroom.'

Not new, but white, clean, neat, utilitarian. No complaints from the guest. Clean towels on the rail. Dahlias in a glass jug. She pointed at them and Harry affected a sheepish look.

Arabella went through the rest of the rooms: the two spare bedrooms that were still empty of furniture; a laundry cum storeroom that let onto the back yard. 'You have good taste, Harry. I hate to say it, but you've taken much more trouble with this than the Sydney house.'

'Certainly have. Good taste in my choice of partner, too.' He kissed her gently.

She smiled and threaded her arm through his, steering him back to the kitchen.

'Cup of tea?'

After a tour of the farm's boundaries, which included wading across the Towamba River at its shallowest point, their shoes left on the sand, they went back to the house and showered. They had dinner outside, under the pergola from which wisteria flowers hung. Harry had steamed the mussels in white wine and garlic and made a salad from tomatoes, avocado and steamed wild leeks that had self-seeded in the garden. There were lemon gelati that he'd bought that afternoon from the delicatessen in Merimbula and kept cold in an Esky in the back of the LandCruiser. He pointed out five — or maybe it was six — big red kangaroos that could just be seen through the dusk in the paddock on the other side of the farm creek.

'I've never seen them in the wild before. You'll introduce me to your wombats, won't you?'

'I'm too tired to walk down there now,' Harry said. 'If we get up early enough tomorrow, I'll take you. They're my favourites, of all the wildlife here. They have the funniest arses you've ever seen. And I scared a platypus two days ago, so there's got to be more than one in this part of the river.'

'Platypi?'

'Platypuses, Bella. If you want to use a pretentious plural, it'd be *platypodes*, wouldn't it? In the Greek?'

'The benefits of a classical education.'

'Well,' Harry grimaced, 'I could be wrong about that. It was only Shore.'

'What was?'

'The seat of my classical education. Robust Anglicanism, rugby and rowing. The Greek was restricted to the boarders whose families had country milk bars.'

They washed up and went to bed. Arabella remarked on the absence of curtains, and Harry asked why anyone would want them. It made sense.

The weekend went too quickly. Arabella, wearing the stiff work clothes ('They'll soften up after we've washed them a couple of times,' Harry promised), sat on the verandah with her computer, developing her submissions for the sentencing judge, showing each stage as she finished it to Harry, who would dictate amendments and improvements to parts he disagreed with, or to strengthen what he regarded as her good points. Arabella learned during the morning that there was a satellite dish on the roof and broadband access, at which she marvelled, and she was able to research case law for inclusion in the arguments she was formulating. Harry came and went from the house: gardening, pruning dead wood from trees, collecting the hens' eggs, watering the lettuces, even bringing back a bunch of wildflowers and native grasses for Arabella to arrange in a jug. He cooked the meals.

Arabella rang her mother in London and described the farm to her. Her mother responded that the reports of blue wrens tapping on the bedroom window at 6 a.m., and big red kangaroos grazing at dusk were 'charming'. 'She assumes all Australia's like that,' Arabella told Harry afterwards. 'So she didn't think it all that remarkable.'

They made love in the afternoon, and at night. Harry had never in his life been so happy, and he told her that.

'It's all a plot,' she complained. 'You bring me down here, take advantage of me with all this romanticism and wine and wildlife, and all the time you're planning to keep me barefoot and pregnant and chained to Stanley.'

'Stanley? Who's Stanley?'

'That's the name of the stove, Harry. Didn't you notice?'

'And pregnant?'

'Not yet.'

On Sunday afternoon, with the submissions as good as they could make them, Harry slowly drove the forty kilometres along the half-gravel, half-tarmac Towamba road, taking a little detour through Towamba village, then back across the bridge and on past the Model Farm, he and Arabella admiring the huge eucalypts in the state forest and the national park through which the road passed, but saying little. Delayed by the Sunday afternoon traffic in Pambula township, they turned off the highway into Merimbula Airport just as the Sydney plane made its final approach.

Harry handed her bag to the airline staff and took Arabella outside. 'I don't want you to go.'

She smiled and touched his face. 'It's been lovely. I'll be back.'

'And then you'll go again.'

'We'll talk about it when I've finished this matter.'

They kissed goodbye and held each other for a long time. Harry watched the plane out of sight and then drove home too fast. He clucked at the chickens, made an Emmenthal omelette and went to bed with Dante's *Inferno,* which happened to be the topmost of the books in the first carton he opened. Not nearly as good as Shakespeare, he decided after six pages, and turned off the light. With his head on the pillow beneath the curtainless window, he could pick out the Southern Cross in the sky above the house. He tried to remember that part of the poem, saying it aloud in the empty house.

And down by Kosciusko, where the pine-clad ridges raise
Their torn and rugged battlements on high,
Where the air is clear as crystal, and the white stars fairly
    blaze
At midnight in the cold and frosty sky …

Struggling to remember the rest, he fell asleep.

The SuperMax section of the Long Bay complex of prisons is every bit as forbidding as its name suggests. David Surrey and Arabella were kept waiting in the reception area for more than forty-five minutes before being escorted through a series of chipped-paint sliding gates, all heavily barred, the prison officer's keys rattling afresh at every stage. Arabella thought irreverently of old episodes of *Porridge*, but the picaresque charm of the comedy's inmates was lacking. Any light mood disappeared while they waited for their client to be brought into the tiny room set aside for legal visits.

A big, solid man in prison greens came through the door sideways. He wouldn't have fitted otherwise. Surrey, startled once more by Adrian Flowers' formidable bulk, introduced Arabella. Adrian took her offered hand politely before sitting. 'Pleased to meet you,' he said.

'Mr Flowers,' Arabella began — because Harry had drummed it into her that women barristers, in particular, had to keep their criminal clients at arm's length. Never use their first names, and they don't use yours. This client fixed his gaze on his barrister through tiny round wire-framed glasses that seemed, to Arabella, absurdly out of place on her hulking client.

The lawyers spent almost an hour with their client, confirming his instructions that he would plead guilty to all the murder charges, and the drug supply offences. Confirming his awareness of the certain consequences of such a plea. Given the five murders, the drug charges were essentially unimportant, and any sentence handed down for them would inevitably be subsumed within the major sentence of imprisonment. There was no prospect of finding a defence to any of the charges, homicide or drugs.

As Arabella had learned is the way with prisoners, Flowers had quickly assimilated the jailhouse wisdom about the sentencing procedure he was to face. It was possible that he'd been advised by an imprisoned lawyer (they even had their own table in the dining hall at Long Bay), but unlikely — not many legal practitioners were to be found as inmates in SuperMax; their offences were more venal than murderous. But Adrian knew that the issue could be simply expressed: he would get life with no chance of parole, or a sentence determined to be a specific period, probably twenty-five years (at the end of which time he would be in his seventh decade). His sentence might even be longer. That was what they talked about. There was nothing else to say, really.

Arabella had read and re-read the two psychiatric reports over and over, one from the DPP's tame man and the other from their own expert, and knew that there was agreement between them on at least one diagnosis — their client was a sociopath. In that Mr Flowers presented himself as utterly unemotional, even when she went over the Bodalla bus crash episode with him, Arabella could see why the psychiatrists had been able to agree on that.

'I won't be giving evidence, will I?'

'No,' said Arabella. 'We're going to rely on the psychiatric report. You told him everything about your childhood, your work history, and gave your explanation for how you got into this … ah, sequence of events.'

Surrey joined in. 'You've seen the summary of facts relating to all the murders prepared by the Crown; I sent you that and the two psych reports, Adrian. Given that the judge is going to rely on that material, and on what you told both of those doctors, is there any stuff in there that you would want us to contradict? Or are there any facts that you think they've left out that could help us to give the judge the full picture?'

Flowers took his time to think about that, and eventually indicated with a minimal shake of his jaw that there was nothing that he wanted to raise. The lawyers packed up their papers and slipped them into their bags. Surrey folded his glasses and slid them into his jacket pocket, but didn't stand. Nobody attempted small talk. Discomforted by the extended silence, Arabella took it upon herself to offer some encouragement.

'Mr Flowers, I think there's a very good argument to be submitted to the sentencing judge that your subjective factors, together with the contrition demonstrated by your co-operation with the police and your pleas of guilty, should militate in favour of a determinate sentence. I think you can be confident of that.'

'In English? Please explain?'

Surrey cleared his throat and looked at Arabella. 'What Ms Engineer's saying is that she thinks it won't, or should I say shouldn't, be life without the chance of parole, because you've done the right thing in not fighting any of the charges, plus you've named names. The fact is that none of these murders would have been solved if you hadn't 'fessed up to them — the police never had anything on you or anyone else — and the psychiatric picture's in your favour. That's what she means. Other minds may differ,' he finished, avoiding her gaze.

Adrian Flowers was taken away, and Surrey and Arabella repeated the gate-opening-and-closing process. Not much was said between the lawyers, and that remained the mood on the drive back through Maroubra, past the university and until Surrey dropped Arabella off in Phillip Street.

'See you next week.' He leaned across the car and spoke through the open passenger-side window. 'I'll let you know the judge and the court number if I hear first.'

'Thanks, David.' And she climbed the steps outside her chambers two at a time, anxious to get on the phone to Harry.

'I have to agree with Surrey,' Harry told her on the indistinct phone line from Burragate, heavy rain on the tin roof making it worse. 'I would have been less subtle.'

'You're supposed to support me!'

'And you're not supposed to give your client promises about what's going to happen to him. You can never do that. Never.'

'But I'm sure I'm right! Have you looked at section 19A of the *Crimes Act*?'

'It's a hot topic down here at Burragate.'

'Oh, Harry, you know it's all about whether the judge is going to find this to be the worst category of case. He has to do that before he can give him life. And the Court of Criminal Appeal has laid down the law that to be a worst category case, there has to be nothing mitigating it. And you also know that isn't the case here. It just isn't. And I didn't promise, anyway. I just said that the judge is bound to give credit for the utilitarian value of the plea.'

'I know that's what you believe, and I know it's not going to do your client any harm if you're passionately committed to that.'

'What are you really saying, Harry? That only an amateur gets emotionally involved?'

'I'd be a hypocrite if I did, Bella. That is — that *was* — always my great failing. Belief in my cases. But the more immediate problem, anyway, is what happens if you build up his expectations, and the judge smashes him?'

'I don't know, Harry — what happens?'

'We appeal!'

Arabella smiled, in spite of herself. She looked out her window. Rain was falling at Elizabeth Bay too, and it was getting dark. Harry's voice seemed impossibly distant.

'Anyway, my love, there's nothing you can do about it now. Maybe your client doesn't place much store in your opinion. You're only a barrister, after all, and a female one at that. You're just going to have to do what every barrister before you has done when they came a cropper. Blame the judge.'

'I haven't come a cropper yet, Harry. And I'm sorry, but — with unfeigned respect — nothing you or David have said affects my opinion on this. Yes, you're older and wiser; yes, you've done much more of this stuff than I have — but the law on this is clear. Clear and inconvenient, but any judge is going to have to apply it. A worst category of case would be these same facts, these same five murders, where the accused pleaded not guilty, put the government to the expense and inconvenience of a long and bitter jury trial — with the families having to endure that — where he offered no remorse, no contrition, no co-operation. And that's not Flowers. Ergo, this isn't a life sentence.'

'The birds got all the plums.'

'What?'

'The birds got all the plums. I was going to make jam. And there was a bloody great goanna trying to get into the chicken coop.'

'Oh. How's the river?'

'Running bank to bank. I've had the pump on, and filled both the tanks. The paddocks are so wet, I can't mow them.'

'So what are you doing?'

'Reading, thinking about you. Eating too much. Bushfire training's been cancelled.'

She laughed. 'I'll be there as soon as I can.'

'But not this weekend?'

'No. I'll spend the weekend on Flowers.'

'It's all done, Bella.'

'I know, but I want to know it inside out. I don't want to be one of those counsel who stand up and read haltingly through their submissions as if they've never seen them before. The judges are always on the next page, anyway.'

'Know who you've got?'

'Oh, yes, I should have said — and that reminds me to ring David. We drew Cohen.'

'A human being, at least.'

'Yes.'

'But also a politician.'

'I know. Aren't they all?'

'At Darlo, is it?'

'Sorry, Harry? There's terrific static.'

'It's not static, Bella, it's the rain. I was asking if you're at Darlinghurst on Monday?'

'No, at the Banco Court. The old one.'

'Well, at least it's a handsome venue in which to be condemned.'

Neither said anything for a bit. Harry listened to the country downpour at first hand, and Arabella could hear it as a hiss over the phone. The Elizabeth Bay rain was inaudible.

'Well … don't work too hard.' He was getting ready to hang up.

'I probably will.'

'Call me if you want to discuss it.'

'I will.'

Another awkward pause.

'Have you eaten, Harry?'

'Chops. You?'

'I'm going to a Women Lawyers' dinner.'

'Rubber chicken, then.'

'As you would say, more alcohol and self-congratulation.'

'At least I haven't got to worry — women only.' Harry had wondered with whom she was eating these days.

'Yes, but if you think that means there's nothing to worry about, you don't know much about women lawyers.'

'That's true of at least one of them.'

'I miss you, Harry.'

'I miss you too. You'd better go now; you'll be late for the dinner.'

And they hung up in the manner of teenagers who didn't know how to end the call.

The old Banco Court in St James Road is not just a handsome venue, as Harry called it, but the most beautiful of Sydney's colonial courtrooms. As Arabella, the first to arrive apart from the court officers filling the water carafes on the Bar table, looked around, it struck her as more reminiscent of a London theatre than a palace of justice — the sort of place in which she'd seen pantomimes as a child, when she and her sisters had been so enthralled and terrified by Captain Hook and the ticking crocodile that they were unable to look down and unwrap another chocolate. Polished brass rails, red plush, glittering lamps high on the walls, gold lettering, treacle-toned panelling, a florid carpet and, eventually, a scarlet judge who would come out to occupy the place of the maraschino cherry on top of the extravagant confection.

At five minutes to ten, the room suddenly filled up. Prison officers — no fewer than six of them waiting for this famously dangerous man to be brought up from the subterranean cells; the Director of Public Prosecution's team; the detectives in charge of the cases; and, running late and red-faced, David Surrey. Journalists arrived, too, dressed — as usual — as if they were on their way to Bunnings on a Sunday morning. Curiously, there was nobody whom Arabella could identify as a family member seeking what the facile were fond of calling 'closure' for any of the murder victims. 'Now, if they said what they were after was revenge,' Harry had said more than once, 'I'd believe them. But *closure*? What in the name of God does that mean? A licence to forget about the person forever?'

After a ten-minute delay, Adrian Flowers was brought up. He'd obviously elected to remain in his prison greens and Dunlop Volleys. Why not? Surrey thought to himself — a suit and tie won't change his Honour Justice Cohen's thinking. Gloomily he found himself assuming that the judge had already written out his judgment. As Flowers' handcuffs were removed and pocketed, Surrey and Arabella left their leather-cushioned cedar chairs and crossed to the dock, where the heavily encircled prisoner was standing. Both lawyers shook their client's hand and Arabella asked how he was. He nodded, no more than that. Before any further talk could take place, there were three loud knocks from behind the bench, and the court officer called 'All rise.' Everyone did, while Justice Cohen slid from behind a panelled door and took his seat with a nod to his tipstaff who bowed in response. Most of those present also bowed before sitting. But not the journalists, and not Flowers.

The formalities took less than a minute: the case was called, the Crown Prosecutor made his bow, and Arabella stood to announce her appearance — not, as the judge put it, 'for the prisoner', but, as Harry had insisted, 'for Mr Flowers'. Harry's approach was that he had never played the legal ascendancy's games (accordingly, he had never referred to any of his clients as 'the accused' or, after conviction, 'the prisoner', but always as 'my client'), and neither should she. When Arabella corrected him, she could sense Cohen J's back going up just slightly.

The Crown Prosecutor at the far end of the Bar table, a tall, rat-faced misanthrope (Harry's description when Arabella had rung him the previous evening and given him the name of her opponent), enjoyed such seniority in the DPP that he was able to seize for himself any murder case that might attract media attention and consequential reporting of his name. Surrey was unsurprised to find him running the case. Straightening his wig, the DPP's man stood and tendered a series of five white folders to the judge — one for each of the deceased. The drug matters were going to be shunted off to the District Court for a rubber-stamping on a date yet to be fixed.

'What are you giving me?' Cohen J asked, obviously displeased at the volume of detail he was expected to master.

'In each of those exhibits we've prepared a statement of the short facts relating to each offence, your Honour. Following that is the relevant part of the transcript of the police interview conducted at Mildura in which the respective confessions appear. The pathologist's reports are next, the victims' impact statements, the prisoner's antecedents, and the report of the psychiatrist Dr Darbyshire. We have not troubled your Honour with the police statements, because we've sought to summarise anything in them in the form of the short facts statements. Those police statements can be provided, if your Honour wishes.'

'I don't think that'll be necessary, Mr Crown, thank you. Ms Engineer, you haven't objected to the tender, I note. Do you have any evidence?'

The prosecutor sat as Arabella stood. 'I tender the report of the forensic psychiatrist Dr Reggiano, dated 11 November, your Honour.'

'Prisoner's Exhibit A. Is your client giving evidence?'

Arabella turned to look at Flowers in the dock, but her view was blocked by the gigantic bearded head of a prison officer. She turned back to the judge. 'No, may it please you.'

'I shall take a moment to read the exhibits.'

Silence fell as the judge opened the first folder and began to read. He turned the pages with surprising speed. Arabella whispered to Surrey, seated behind her. 'Can he really read that fast?'

'What makes you think he hasn't seen it all before?'

'That'd be improper, wouldn't it?' Still whispering.

'Wouldn't it, though? At least he hasn't read Reggiano's opinion.'

The court remained awkwardly silent for twelve minutes, then the judge closed Dr Reggiano's report and pushed it and the five folders to one end of the bench. Twelve minutes isn't enough for the lives of five people, Arabella thought, and the considered expert opinions of two specialist psychiatrists. A *Telegraph* journalist noted something in her shorthand pad. Had she been struck by the same thought? Arabella wondered.

Invited to make submissions as to the sentence the judge should impose, the prosecutor spent forty minutes going through the physical facts of each murder, and picked out the parts of Darbyshire's report that suited his purpose. He quoted selectively from the most draconian decisions his support team had been able to find in the records of the Court of Criminal Appeal and the High Court. His final contention was that the court had to treat the matter of Flowers as a worst category case, automatically imposing a sentence of life with no possibility of parole.

Arabella listened to it all, not making any notes and not looking at her opponent, but at her elegant hands on the brief in front of her. She wasn't admiring them, just trying to immerse herself in the comfort of familiarity — because she felt totally overpowered. Hours of working up her arguments under the critical eye of Harry at Burragate, then the past weekend spent polishing and memorising everything, so that she was never going to have to look down, so that she could do this eye-to-eye with the judge. But now it was all happening, she wanted nothing more than to run out of the court, begging for Harry to take over the matter. He wouldn't be afraid, as she was. He'd do a great job, and then they could have lunch at the Barracks. She felt as inexperienced as when she'd first blurted out her admiration for the big, defiant man in the expensive but rumpled suit and scuffed suede shoes. Was that really only a matter of months ago?

'Yes, Ms Engineer?'

She stood, remembering to breathe. Go straight to the point, she told herself. Eye contact. Surrey held his breath for a moment, looking at her. God, he thought, she's striking. How could that not help us?

'What will be exercising your Honour's mind, with respect, is a matter within a narrow compass: I will not suggest that it isn't open to the court to come to the conclusion that the total criminality of Mr Flowers' five offences constitutes a worst category case of murder, warranting the imposition of a life sentence. "Worst category", your Honour, being the statutory term used in the sentencing legislation.

'The worst category case, your Honour, requires that there be particular features of the greatest seriousness — and I cannot and will not engage in any futility about that here, your Honour — but it is also necessary that there be a total absence of facts mitigating the seriousness of the crime. Your Honour has to keep in mind the distinction.'

While Arabella was castigating herself for saying 'your Honour' too many times, the judge made his first interruption. He had not done that to the Crown. 'Life imprisonment, Ms Engineer, will be the appropriate sentence where the offender's culpability is so extreme that the community's interest in retribution and punishment demands it.' Said very coldly.

'So the appeal court said in *Garforth's case*, your Honour.'

Cohen J was impressed. Arabella hadn't had to look at a note to give him the name of the case. 'Indeed. So what do you say about the public interest here?'

'The public has no interest in crushing my client. Retribution and punishment can be achieved without his having to die in jail.'

'But what about *Milat's case*, Ms Engineer? He was given life, and the judges in appeal confirmed that. The concept of a "worst case" refers to every criminal act of the offender before me.'

'Quite so, your Honour, just as mitigation requires the court to give full weight to the subjective factors.' Arabella felt herself gaining confidence. She could feel her client's presence in the dock behind her, but didn't want to turn away from the judge.

Cohen J nodded and made a note. 'We'll come to that. But let's take these murders *seriatim*. The shooting of Ms Khoury at the brothel: that was brutal, cold-blooded and convenient. What your client had to say about that to the police was almost offhand, as if it were something that merely happened by the way. If you take that with the revenge murder of Mr O'Brien and the contract killing of Ms Lang — and I know he was never paid the $20,000 — they all amount to the worst category of case.'

'Your Honour, I'm certainly not going to contend that any of Mr Flowers' conduct in the crimes themselves could mitigate their seriousness.'

'You simply couldn't.' Cohen J looked hard at her. It was a challenge.

'But you don't get one instance of a worst category case by adding together any number of offences that would not, in and by themselves, meet that level.' Arabella's voice had an undertone of truculence.

'That's not right though, is it, Ms Engineer? Have you read *Griffiths' case*?'

'Yes. And that says that the court may consider the totality of the criminality involved in the several homicides. But it doesn't mean the sum of the parts can be greater than the whole of the criminality.' She chalked up a point for the defence, but too soon.

'Spare me the jurisprudential sophistry, Ms Engineer,' the judge scowled. Still, it was obvious to all in court that she knew her stuff and wasn't going to lie down.

'I wasn't aware that was what I was doing, and I'm sorry if you thought that.' Arabella put an expression on her face showing that she wasn't the least bit sorry. Here I am, she thought, Mrs Harry Curry. She raised her chin.

'No need to apologise. Look, counsel, I know how difficult your task is, and your client should be grateful for the effort you've obviously and very ably made. But isn't the position I must inevitably reach, if I look only at the objective circumstances of the murders your client committed — that is, the unmitigated cruelty of the things he did in killing these poor people — that these crimes were heinous, and brutal, and that he must serve a sentence of his natural life?'

'But that would be to ignore the subjective factors, and the court can't do that. Your discretion would miscarry. The seriousness of Mr Flowers' criminality is drawn back to a lesser level by a number of things.'

'Take me to those.'

'Thank you.' Still, Arabella was determined not to consult her notes. She knew what was on those pages. She held eye contact. 'First is the plea of guilty. That alone speaks volumes. Mr Flowers could have qualified for Legal Aid, and sat back through a lengthy committal hearing before a magistrate at which every possible legal point was taken. But he didn't. He could have pleaded not guilty and subjected the Crown to the expense and difficulty of five full-blown murder trials and the unimaginable expense involved in qualifying forensic witnesses, finding and calling eyewitnesses, arranging the attendance of police in large numbers, taking them away from their duties or their holidays for weeks on end, not to mention empanelling and holding on to a jury for months, as well as paying them.'

'Yes, the utilitarian benefit of the plea of guilty.' The slight suggestion of an intolerant tone in his voice. Arabella picked it up. I've got to get him back on my side, she thought. Right away. Plain talking.

'Yes, your Honour. Common sense says that, whatever my client gains from utility, it's even more important at a humanitarian level that his guilty plea spares the families of the deceased the ordeal of a trial. They don't have to give evidence, they don't have to listen to the horror of the deaths of their loved ones in all the pathological detail. It gives them what some are pleased to call closure.'

The judge frowned at that, but made no comment. She knew that he knew — because all lawyers knew — 'closure' is tosh.

'But, most important of all, the voluntary and unexpected disclosure of the offences and the pleas of guilty must be accepted by your Honour as proof of contrition and remorse.'

'Despite what Dr Darbyshire says?'

Arabella paused and looked him in the eye. I know what bloody Darbyshire says, judge. Haven't you read *our* report?

'Yes, despite his opinion which, as the court cannot have failed to notice, is resolutely and emphatically challenged by Dr Reggiano. So this plea alone is a very powerful mitigation, at all those levels. It entitles him to what has been called the public interest discount.'

'But you're not going to tell me that I'm compelled to give him that discount — that I don't retain a discretion in the sentence I impose?'

Oh … so that's what we're arguing about — your high and mighty discretion. Arabella looked down at the page in front of her and took a beat before making eye contact again. No backward steps, she could hear Harry saying. A sip of water and then, her elegant finger counting down the bullet points she'd set out in her speaking notes under the heading 'Mitigation', Ms Engineer the defender took her client's nemesis to each of them. Contrition and remorse. (Is there any difference? she found herself wondering. Safe and secure, part and parcel, kith and kin, Kath and Kim? Concentrate, woman.) Meritorious conduct unrelated to these offences. Prospects of rehabilitation in the context of his personality. Assistance he'd already given to the police by naming names. Flowers' promises of further such co-operation, and to give evidence against them. At least Cohen was taking notes of what she was saying. Or was he doing the sudoku?

'Those subjective factors, your Honour, are very significant in terms of the exercise of your discretion, despite the demands of an uninformed parliament and a number of areas in which the appeal judges, in their wisdom, have tied this court's hands.'

That last observation, Harry had told Arabella, would reflect the judge's own deep dislike of the politicisation of criminal sentencing, which he considered, with good reason, to be a pusillanimous deference to the *Daily Telegraph*'s editorialist and the cynical shock jocks of commercial radio.

'Perhaps we shouldn't be reflecting on the merits of the parliament, Ms Engineer. We must — certainly I must — defer to its wisdom.'

There was a stage whisper from Surrey. 'Let me know when you find it.'

'Did your solicitor want to add something, Ms Engineer?' The judge had little time for solicitors. When he was elevated to the bench, several of the more opportunistic had torn up his outstanding fee notes, and it would have been unacceptably unseemly to pursue the money from the bench.

'Probably, your Honour. I'll ask him later if there's anything I've forgotten. But can I refer to the death of Mrs Robbins — the third offence? The police concede that, without Mr Flowers' confession, they could not have established his guilt.'

'Against that, of course, is the fact that he only admitted to the murders of Ms Lang and Ms Khoury when he learned that the disgraced detective—'

'Mr Allen, your Honour.'

'Mr Allen. Those admissions only came when he was told that Allen would give evidence against him in each of those cases.'

'True, your Honour, but, had Mr Flowers pleaded not guilty and denied what Allen said, and if someone of the skill of, say, Mr Curry had cross-examined Allen, it would have been unlikely that the jury would have convicted. It would have been the word of a profoundly corrupt police officer against that of a man with no criminal record. Given the findings of the Royal Commission into police corruption, juries have displayed a distinct reluctance to give any credit to the bad apples.'

'Let's not speculate about juries and their reasoning processes. Or about the ability of Mr Curry, of which this court is well aware.' There was a barb in that.

Arabella realised that she shouldn't have mentioned her lover's name. She could feel her face colouring. 'No jury here, your Honour, and no Mr Curry. Still, however you view the other evidence, it's fair to say that without his confessions, the cases against my client in relation to the Misses Lang and Khoury, and in relation to Mrs Robbins, were not strong. There was little more than suspicion — suspicion that had not been acted upon for more than ten years. You have to draw some conclusions from the fact that the police never saw fit to charge my client in all that time.'

'Whatever, as my daughter is inclined to say.' The judge wasn't buying it. 'It also has to be said that these pleas, on which you place so much weight, came very late and only when your client was in custody red-handed for the drug matters, which he must have known were going to involve a very substantial sentence. You're going to have a hard job to persuade me to give that factor much weight. True it is that he has, by admitting his guilt, acknowledged his wrongdoing — but otherwise he's evidenced absolutely no contrition or remorse for what he did.'

He paused, and Arabella turned to look past the custody officer at her client, whose face showed nothing, and then at Surrey, whose expression was one of sympathy.

'Yes, Ms Engineer, this is all convenient for the prisoner and, I agree, utilitarian for the authorities, but when I put that in the balance against his overwhelming — and I could even say shameless — criminality, I can't see that any appreciable mitigation has been made out. Not that you don't get points for your efforts.'

Arabella was displeased by the last remark. So as long as you toss me a scrap of praise, I should be pleased? 'To adopt the expression that fell from your Honour a moment ago, *whatever*. I shall turn now to the discount to which my client is, I submit, entitled by reason of his meritorious conduct unrelated to these matters.'

There was the slightest suggestion of a smile from Justice Cohen. This girl's not just a pretty face. She can take it, and she can give it back. Back to business. 'This is his work as an ambulance officer?'

'It is. Your Honour knows from the account given by both psychiatrists that on the day of the Bodalla bus crash my client was not on duty, but selflessly presented himself to assist with the catastrophe. Dr Darbyshire played that down — which might not be entirely his fault, given that Mr Flowers appears to have been somewhat reticent on that subject — but Dr Reggiano emphasises the fact that he put on his uniform and rode his motorbike to the scene and laboured there for three hours, during which time he carried the bodies of dead children out of the wreckage, and the like. Dr Reggiano is quite sure that that horror had a long-term effect on Mr Flowers' personality.'

Arabella looked again at Surrey. His eyes seemed to be saying 'Let it go.' Then she saw him tighten his hand into a fist and give it a tiny shake. Fight on. Keep punching.

Cohen was still talking. 'Look, Ms Engineer, I see that as a commendable act which anyone would expect of any person following the noble calling of a paramedic. It's completely understandable that he would be deeply affected by what he saw and had to do that day, and that he will always carry the memory of it. And I note what was said about having to abandon his career because of a back injury, as I do his appallingly brutal upbringing.'

Arabella was waiting for the 'however'. It came soon enough.

'But I have to say that the psychiatric evidence doesn't persuade me that the cruelty he suffered as a child or the Bodalla episode are in any way available as an explanation, or a reasonable explanation, for these murders. Let's be practical about this.'

Despite his words, Cohen J's tone wasn't unkind. He was impressed with Arabella's strong persistence in the face of rebuttals that would have put many a more experienced criminal defender to flight, or at least wimpy surrender. As is the wont of judges, his Honour had rung around to see whether his colleagues knew anything of 'this Indian girl' whom he had been told would be representing the multiple murderer he had to sentence, and had been assured that she was 'a bit of a lightweight. Pretty, though.' Well, he thought, they got that last part right — but she also had courage.

'Is there anything further, Ms Engineer? Any more pearls to cast before me?'

Arabella smiled broadly, letting him know that his self-deprecation was not missed. 'No, your Honour. I shall hand up a copy of my written submissions, if you please, but your Honour will find that I've spoken to all the points we've made there.' She turned to Surrey to check, and he made a tiny shake of his head. All done. Her eyes went to the expressionless face of Adrian Flowers. For a nanosecond, she thought she saw a flash of hurt in his eyes, but it passed. This isn't about him, she thought. This is about the law, and the lawyers. The judge's next words confirmed that.

'You'll need a silk gown before you can refer to yourself as "we", Ms Engineer. Still, that shouldn't take too long. Your client can be satisfied that he has been more than competently represented.'

'Your Honour is too kind.'

The moment of grace passed, and the formal Justice Cohen took charge again. 'Not at all. Stand up, please, Mr Flowers.' The prisoner complied. 'Adrian Flowers, I have listened carefully to everything your counsel has put on your behalf, and most ably has she done it. She has correctly identified the central issue in relation to your sentencing as being whether you must die in prison, or whether you are to be allowed to see the light at the end of the tunnel. In other words, to be given a determinate sentence which, if I need to explain that word to you, would mean a fixed number of years, after which you can apply for parole. There are certainly factors in favour of my exercising my discretion as she contends, at least to that extent. You have pleaded guilty, which I am compelled to assume demonstrates a measure of contrition. You admitted your guilt of crimes that the police could otherwise never have hoped to prove. You have saved the government a vast amount of money and this court months and months of its time. You have spared the families of your victims the anguish and anxiety of a trial. You have given them closure, whatever your counsel thinks of that word. You can claim credit for a background of selfless service, particularly in the Bodalla catastrophe, and I accept from your psychiatrist that you endured an appalling upbringing, where violence was the only solution to conflict. You were brutalised from the youngest age, and you have suffered from that. All that is in your favour.'

Arabella turned, smiling, to where Surrey was sitting behind her. He shook his head. 'No, Bella. Now comes the "however".' Again, she thought.

'However, I am compelled to say that I find it impossible to reconcile a compassionate concern as an ambulance officer for the sanctity of human life and the saving of it with the cynical, violent and cold-blooded destruction of human life involved in the five homicides to which you have pleaded guilty, and, thus, I am unable to attach any weight to that component in mitigation of the penalty I must impose.'

Arabella couldn't bring herself to look across at her instructing solicitor, much less her client, and kept her eyes fixed straight ahead at the coat of arms on the courtroom wall. Had she looked at Flowers, she would have found him still expressionless. The judge paused there and shuffled through the papers in front of him, and pulled out a number of pages that had been stapled together. He started to read what was, to all the lawyers listening, the judgment he had plainly written before he came to court.

'I cannot come to any other view than that to allow a reduction of the prisoner's sentence by reason of his so-called assistance to authorities and promises of co-operation, or any of the other supposedly mitigating factors urged by his counsel, would produce a sentence unreasonably disproportionate to the nature and circumstances of the five murders with which I am concerned. He has indicated no contrition or remorse. The submission that has been made for him — to the effect that he should be allowed to see the light at the end of the tunnel — is a reference to a light, I suppose, that can be compared to that which he extinguished so brutally in each of his victims. I am not prepared to accede to that submission.

'Accordingly, the prisoner will be sentenced to five life sentences, to commence on the day of his arrest at Mildura. The prisoner may be removed, and the exhibits will be returned on the publication of my reasons for this sentence.'

The court was adjourned in silence, and Justice Cohen retreated through his panelled door to complete the crossword he'd started at 8 a.m. Adrian Flowers was again handcuffed and led out, ignoring Arabella's and David Surrey's attempts to speak to him. Arabella flopped into her chair, her head back and her eyes closed. She waved away two journalists who wanted to know whether an appeal was planned. The police left, the prosecution team packed up, and soon it was just the court officers and the defence lawyers, alone in the elegant courtroom.

'Buy you lunch, miss?' Surrey asked.

'Why not? Give me five minutes to go back to chambers and take this motley off, and I'll see you over there.'

'Where?'

'Oh, sorry, David. Here was I, fantasising about a celebration lunch with Harry at the Barracks.'

'Will I do?'

'Handsomely,' and she gave him a kiss on the cheek. 'I know you were both right. I always knew, but I wanted to defy the odds.'

'Don't beat yourself up. Harry couldn't have done better.'

'No? Maybe I could have.'

Surrey dropped his folders into his battered briefcase. 'Maybe Legal Aid will fund an appeal.'

'I don't want to do it, David. I never want to think about this case again.'

'That's no problem, Bella. They'll probably demand that it be done by a public defender.'

'And welcome to it. Actually, give me ten minutes, will you? I want to ring Harry.'

'Be my guest.'

In the end, Arabella was twenty minutes late to lunch. She and Harry didn't discuss the case much in the phone call from her chambers, but she eventually convinced him to come up to Elizabeth Bay for a couple of days to watch her lick her wounds. 'I promise not to say, "I told you so",' he said.

'You just did, you bastard.'

*

There was an early Christmas party in full swing on the waterfront lawn five storeys below Arabella's apartment. Such parties were common in November. Coloured lights, thumping music, raucous voices, water-taxis discharging guests at the nearby jetty. Harry took a beer from the fridge, opened it and went out on the balcony, leaning his elbows on the rail. He looked down at the people and the lights and the reflections in the water below: too many inebriated men in loud shirts and women in bright dresses, too much fake laughter, too much nasty music. The boats coming and going had created choppy wakes and the yachts at their moorings were being slapped with small waves, rattling their halyards against naked masts. There had been a time when he would have been an enthusiastic member of the throng, but tonight, somehow, it made him feel melancholy. He sipped his beer from the bottle, and then, as Arabella joined him, drank it quickly until it was empty. 'Burragate calls,' he said. 'This isn't exactly me.'

Arabella looked at Harry. She had been about to go back into the kitchen and pour herself a glass of wine, but she could see there was no point in that. 'If you must. But you did say you'd stay here for a couple of days. Breakfast, bookshops, a film.'

'You understand,' he said. It wasn't really a question. 'I hate parties, even if I'm not at them.'

'Yes, I do understand. Truth to tell, I don't care for parties either. Well, not much. Family parties, yes, but not parties where lawyers tout for work, and not those Christmas parties where you stand around with insincerity and a drink in your hand and conduct the same conversations with the same people as you did last year.'

'I know,' said Harry. '"Are you going away for Christmas? Seeing anything good in the Sydney Festival? We've got tickets for the ballet. I always go to the first day of the test match. Your kids finished the HSC? How'd they do?"'

Arabella looked across towards the Bradleys Head light. 'Please stay, Harry.'

He did, of course.

That was the weekend when the subject of marriage — or something to that effect — was first hinted at. Arabella got within a whisker of using the word 'commitment', but pulled back. They woke very early on Sunday morning and were talking quietly in bed, having gently made love to each other, trying to make sense of the future.

'This is really hard, darling,' Arabella said, sitting up against the pillows. 'I know I did well in *Flowers*, but I have to face the fact that I'm never going to be a jury advocate.'

'You could be, Bella. It's just a matter of doing case after case. Losing case after case, until you find what persuades ordinary people to a view they are certainly not naturally inclined to accept. Finding your own voice. You'll get there.'

'No, Harry.'

'No? Something's coming, isn't it?'

'There are a couple of solicitors in the Women Lawyers' Association who want me to take on commercial matters for their firms. They're sick of being told to brief complacent young men from good schools who think they were born to rule. They're looking for women, and they can promise a good flow of work for insurance defendants. All care and no responsibility.'

Harry didn't respond.

'What are you thinking about?' she asked.

'The curve of your hip,' he said, and she angrily pulled the sheet over herself.

'For Christ's sake! You know what I'm trying to get to: you've suddenly decided that you want to play gentleman farmer, and conduct occasional Maoist raids out from Burragate to the criminal courts down there, playing Harry-Curry-versus-the-world games and making just enough money to keep things ticking over; and meanwhile I have to make a decision about my practice and what I'm going to do with my life. We both know that I'm not a natural as a criminal advocate, so I have to choose.'

'Meaning between playing Ma Kettle down on the Towamba River and the life of the thrusting lady lawyer with the BlackBerry and the high heels and the hypocrisy. Or, to put it another way, your choice would appear to be between a life with me and a glittering career at the commercial Bar.'

'Yes.' She had wanted to soften it, but what would be the point? He had it right.

Harry thoughtlessly stroked the curve of her hip through the sheet. 'I've never lived with anyone before, Bella. I know, that's not exactly what we're doing, but this is nothing like my old life. I managed, had a perfectly satisfactory life for a long time before you bailed me up. Or thought I had, at least. Hard work, mostly for Legal Aid money, but I won a lot of cases, saved a lot of people's liberty. Always made enough for a long holiday in Tuscany every year.'

'Harry—'

'And you blew that all to bits. Thank God. I still don't understand why you did.'

'I—'

'No, Bella, let me say it. I have great difficulty understanding all this. I don't know why you wanted to weld yourself to me, and maybe I never will. I know enough about myself to know how unattractive I am — and I'm not just talking about how I look. I won't insult you by suggesting that you're quite that shallow, or shallow at all. Ever since all that crap with the Bar suspending me and then being forced to reinstate me, I'm always finding myself wrestling with my own intolerance of everyone around me, and that can't be any sort of magnetic quality. You wouldn't believe how much time I spend thinking about it. It's a silent struggle, and it's very serious, and no one else seems to have to deal with it. Are other people like me? Do they hate people on sight? Or when they open their mouths?'

'You should be English, Harry. They'll hate anyone with an accent unlike theirs, particularly other Englishmen, as Shaw said.'

'No, there's much more to it than that. I have this thing I do when I want to judge and summarily dismiss people: I subject them to my dry-cleaner test.'

'What in the name of God is that?'

'You look at someone — particularly someone in a position of power, who society says is worthy of respect by virtue of that position. Self-promoters included. And you say: if I didn't know who he was, but was told he was a reasonably successful dry-cleaner with a small chain of, say, four or five shops, would that seem right? Would it fit? The test is: does he have the look of a self-satisfied petty bourgeois? It's even worse if he talks like one, or has the politics of one, but you don't have to take that into account. It's enough to look at his suit, his tie, his shoes. Jewellery of any sort's an absolute giveaway in a man. Think of John Howard and Bob Hawke — both obvious dry-cleaners. Unarguably so. On the other hand, there are quite a few people who don't fit that picture.'

'Snobbery, Harry?'

'Sounds like it, doesn't it?'

'I can take it that you've subjected the entire Supreme Court bench to the dry-cleaner test?'

'Not just them. The District Court, the federal cabinet.'

'What about the women judges, women politicians?'

'They're tested as dry-cleaners' wives.'

'Better keep that part of it to yourself, Harry. In fact, probably best to keep the whole thing to yourself.'

'Oh, I do. You're the only person who knows about it. I may have to kill you to keep it secret.'

'So what are you trying to say? Where's all this self-pity leading?'

'It means I'm best kept at arm's length, Bella. If I have so much difficulty understanding why my mind works the way it does, I don't see how anyone else stands a chance. I listen to other people, people who are worthy of respect — certainly not dry-cleaners — and I admire them for their generosity of spirit. I don't know how they do it. How did Nelson Mandela ever forgive those unspeakable bastards? I'll never comprehend that.'

'No one's asking that much of you, are they, Harry? I'm certainly not. Have you ever talked to anyone about it? This struggle with yourself?'

'Like who? D'you mean a psychiatrist? Never met one of them who wasn't a dry-cleaner. Or nuts.'

'Ah, I see the problem. But they're not all smug and/or deranged, surely? There have to be some good ones, someone you could discuss it with.'

'It's not that I haven't thought about it. I just can't imagine trusting anyone with it. Sometimes I feel as if I'm always walking through spiders' webs. My skin, my face, they don't feel right.'

'It's a bonnie face.' Arabella leaned across and placed her hand against his cheek. 'You trust me enough. You're talking about it to me.'

'And not very comfortable about doing it, I can tell you.'

'I don't suppose I'm much of a therapist, Harry, but we both know you can't surrender to self-loathing.'

'Don't bet on it, Bella.' He got up and went into the bathroom. When he came back, Arabella was sitting on the edge of the bed.

'Are we at a crossroads, Harry?'

'You know we are. This isn't what I want, you in Sydney and me down there, but I can't see how you have any choice but to take this insurance company work. At least try it. See if that's how you see yourself as a lawyer. They want women judges. You do another ten years of civil stuff and you'll walk onto the District Court bench. Be an ornament to it.'

She put her arms around his neck. 'I won't pretend that you're not saying what I've been thinking through. Struggling with.' She kissed him. 'You're a very good man, Harry Curry.'

'I've spent the last half-hour telling you the very opposite. Bloody women. They just don't listen.'

She pushed a pillow into his face. 'About me having at least to give myself that chance, you big goose.' And she lifted the pillow to look at him closely. 'You need a shave.'

'The chickens don't care.' He went to the balcony, naked, to watch the first light leaking up from the horizon.

'Can I ask you why, Harry?'

'Why what?' He turned back to look at her.

'Why you didn't play the Neanderthal and give me the take-it-or-leave-it?'

Harry came back to sit beside her on the bed and hold her. 'My mother,' he said, 'was a much smarter woman than her husband, eminent QC and all that he was. She read Faulkner and Patrick White and loved them, understood them. She volunteered at the Art Gallery. She played the cello. She arranged flowers. Maybe she was a bit of a snob, one of the Cheltenham McGuffickes, but she was a great girl. And she was never given the chance to do anything with her beautiful mind — none of her generation were. Not that she resented it, or ever talked about it. I think she would have been unbeatable, and I think you could be. You can't die wondering.'

He kissed her, then went to shower and dress. At 6 a.m. he was having a croissant and a short black in an early opener at Kings Cross, and by 7.30 he was on the Hume Highway, just passing the Mittagong turn-off.

Confronting the abuser

A bit more than a month after he relocated his practice (ie half a shelf of criminal law texts and a laptop) from no fixed abode in Sydney to Burragate, Harry had developed something like a routine. Most mornings, he would get up and water the vegetable garden before the fierce summer sun reached it. He might do some weeding and pick a few beans, a cos lettuce, the ripe tomatoes, enough strawberries and raspberries to make up a dessert. Three or four days a week, he'd jog the five kilometres to the Towamba bridge and then jog back. During the day, he'd plant, repair fences and attend to the chickens. He'd paint things, mend things. In the late afternoon, he'd mow the paddocks, driving the ride-on mower at a punishing speed. At least once a week, a shouted greeting would be exchanged with the immediate neighbours, about five hundred metres away across the creek, and beer would be drunk companionably. When it was too hot, he'd retreat to the living room and read, or watch the cricket. His favourite beach was only twenty minutes drive away for a run and a swim.

Once a week, he'd go in to Eden to shop at the supermarket. On most of those occasions, he'd have lunch with a solicitor and discuss a Local Court brief that had been emailed to the farm: drink-driving, a pub fight, growing a bit of dope. Stuff to keep Harry's meter ticking over. He'd pick up a kilo of mussels at the co-op before heading home in the LandCruiser that, despite his reservations, he had bought. The dealer had offered to trade in the Jag, but Harry had explained that it wasn't really his to sell; it belonged to one of his incarcerated clients, and was now gathering dust in one of the farm sheds.

Every evening he'd be out with the hose again, refreshing the vegetable garden, before a telephone call to or from Arabella, usually still in her chambers, over-preparing some commercial matter for the benefit of an undeserving bank or insurance company. Arabella would want to know the news. 'It's been a quiet day in Lake Wobegone,' Harry would always say, before telling her about bushfire training or the working bee at the primary school or his plans to collect chestnuts from the river paddock. Unless it was raining a warm, summer rain, he always sat outside to speak to her, with a glass of wine in front of him. Arabella would describe the view from her chambers window — the trees in Hyde Park darkening as the sun set, lights being switched off in a random pattern in the chambers windows across Phillip Street, taxis waiting outside for barristers whose partners were sick and tired of them missing dinner with their children. In turn, he would tell her about the kangaroos on the slope across the river, hopping out to graze as the lengthening shadows faded to dusk. Every call ended with Arabella asking what he was going to cook for dinner; Harry asking when she was coming down to the farm; and Arabella making promises she didn't keep.

Not for a minute did it cross Harry's mind that Arabella was being asked to dinner with other men, or being invited to go sailing with them at weekends, and sometimes accepting. She was flattered that these barristers and solicitors admired her, but nothing complicated resulted. Had he known, Harry might have suffered a degree of jealousy. But he never asked, preferring not to speculate, and nothing was volunteered. As Arabella suspected, that would not have been wise. For when it came to lawyers with yachts, Harry was already contemptuous, and had been known to ridicule the Great Bar Boat Race — an annual event marking the end of term, in which lawyers with yachts ostentatiously made the perilous voyage from Rushcutters Bay to Quarantine, dropped anchor there and drank until one of them, or a guest, pulled down the bikini pants of one of the women present, and reputations suffered accordingly.

Harry's contempt was for the insensitive show of wealth. 'Jesus Christ!' he said. 'Why not take out a full page in the *Herald* and announce that the persons whose names appear below are rich pricks, and want the world to know it?' His contempt was consistent; he had the same attitude to the extremely expensive artworks pretentiously displayed on the walls of the solicitors' offices, sprawled across swathes of the most expensive real estate in Australia. 'Don't any of their clients realise that they're paying for the second-rate Olsens and Boyds? And don't those philistines know that Pro Hart is a mistake if you want to be taken seriously?' Eventually Arabella explained to him that the lackeys of the big end of town enjoyed being ushered into luxurious conference rooms where they were seated, unctuously, around great slabs of mahogany in leather chairs and served petits fours by liveried waiters. They didn't mind the expense at all — it was never their money with which they were being duchessed, just the shareholders'.

Harry farmed in his inexpert way with the assistance of his long-suffering and generous neighbours, made his irregular neo-Maoist forays into the magistrates' courts of Batemans Bay, Moruya, Bega and occasionally Queanbeyan, and even once climbing up from the coast to Cooma to do a cattle-duffing case — and did well for his clients, always. Pleading them guilty when he had no choice, and getting the best possible deals on sentence; the rest of the time confronting magistrates whose lists were too long and whose patience was too short to engage in any serious consideration of the requirements of satisfying themselves beyond reasonable doubt.

On one occasion when Harry forced the beak to sit through an arcane two-hour submission about irregularities in the formal charges of larceny brought against his client, the unfortunate man made some unguarded reference to it being 'all very well' to raise such technical objections, 'but mine is a very busy court, Mr Curry'. Harry seized upon the unwise remark and wouldn't let go: 'I doubt, your Honour, that the Court of Criminal Appeal would consider that this honourable court is so busy that it could be forgiven for failing in its duty to do justice to any defendant.' The judicial officer breathed deeply for a moment and opted for self-preservation, as Harry knew he would. Although the outcome was a very satisfactory one for the client, who hadn't followed a word of the proceedings but was immensely grateful all the same, the solicitor was less delighted. 'You can head off home and forget all about this, and I'm sure you will, but I have to live with this beak for years to come,' he complained. 'And he isn't going to forget that I briefed Harry Curry to come down here and monster him in front of everyone, especially the coppers. He likes to play the high and mighty judical officer, and you humiliated him.' Harry simply didn't care, and made that plain. He knew that would be the last brief from that particular firm, and it was.

Arabella mostly kept her head down, working and reworking her proofs of evidence and polishing her written arguments. Hours of research to ensure that she hadn't missed a superior court's decision that would cut the ground from under her. Often the last to leave chambers, long after the cleaners had been through, and the first to return the next morning, having to switch on all the lights. Success in an important case brought a flow of briefs from that firm. Other solicitors watching her win cases while they waited for their matters to be reached were impressed, and directed still more work to Arabella's clerk. The Women Lawyers' mafia was looking after its new girl. 'But,' she admitted to Harry in their evening phone call, 'it's not the same as hearing the jury foreman say "Not guilty". Doesn't matter how much money I've saved the insurer. Doesn't matter how clever the judge thinks my submissions are. None of that will ever make me walk out of court ten feet above the ground.'

One Friday afternoon in May as autumn was starting to make its presence felt, she gathered her BlackBerry and laptop and a bundle of briefs and caught a taxi to the airport, buying a ticket to Merimbula when she got there. She rang Harry to say she was on her way, which delighted him, but the impromptu visit wasn't an unqualified success: she stayed inside on the phone or the computer for two days while Harry moped around the vegetables and hung a new gate. He wanted to read to her at night but Arabella begged off, saying that she had twelve medical reports to mark up for cross-examination. Her insurance company client was convinced that the plaintiff was a malingerer, and expected Arabella to persuade the judge to that view on the strength of their consultant's opinion. Harry read over her shoulder. 'Archie Stephenson! That old bastard will say there's nothing wrong with a man after he's had both legs amputated.' Arabella looked up at him and said nothing, and Harry retreated to his chair. 'Sure you want to make your career on the dark side, Bella? It can't be as much fun.'

He drove her back to the airport the next morning to catch the first plane to Sydney.

On the eastern slope of Bellevue Hill, looking out over Rose Bay, a young man sat beside his family's tennis court and watched through the tall cyclone-wire fence as a weak watercolour sun rose over North Head. There were tears running slowly down his face. He bit his lips and squeezed his eyes shut, but the tears still came. Twenty-two years old, he looked younger, especially in his distressed state.

James Logie had just buried a man's body in a shallow grave in the Royal National Park.

It was a cold morning, but he couldn't feel it. He couldn't feel much at all, except an amazement that the sun was still in the sky and the ordinary noises of suburban life could be heard all around him. He left his seat and walked past the big ficus-flanked house to the front gate. The red pebbles on the drive ground under his shoes as he bent to collect the newspapers. He headed back to the house, unrolling the broadsheet, leaving the *Financial Review* (exclusively for his father), and ran his eye over the front page as he stood in the porte-cochère. Illogical as he knew it was, he was baffled that there was no story about the crime he had so recently committed. No headline: BANKER'S SON KILLS, BURIES PREDATORY PAEDOPHILE. Did he really commit a crime? he wondered. He looked at the mock-Tuscan wall separating his family's house from the equally pretentious mock-Georgian pile on its southern boundary. That had been the home of the dead man.

James turned to the sports pages and read them doggedly until interrupted by his mother, in her dressing gown and slippers, opening the front door from within. She noticed the distress in his eyes and took him into the kitchen where she fed him Vegemite toast and made a pot of tea. Her husband — the father of James and the banker featured in the headline James had been looking for in the morning newspaper — entered the room and after a glance at the front page of the *Fin Review* poured himself a coffee. He looked at his son, then his wife. 'Everything all right?'

'Terrific,' said James. 'Never better.'

James Logie senior put down his cup. 'Anything I can do?'

'I probably need to see your solicitor, Dad. Today, I mean.'

'You want me to make an appointment?'

Anita Logie moved behind her son and put her hand on his shoulder. 'I can do that.' She had some insight into the problem, and certainly more than her husband did, but, all the same, she was going to be astounded by its seriousness. Mrs Logie was a senior lawyer with the Customs Department and, a month ago, had been confided in by her son for the first time about a secret nightmare he had been living for the best part of ten years. Her response had been to send him to the clinical psychologist consulted by her Department.

So it was that James (wearing a Bermuda jacket and jeans with freshly polished penny loafers) kept the appointment late that afternoon that his mother made for him with a partner of the firm that represented the Logie merchant bank. He silently ascended forty floors above Circular Quay in a gleaming express lift and was invited to take a seat in the sleek reception area. He chose to stand, watching through the floor-to-ceiling windows the green-and-yellow ferries creasing the water as they turned at the

Opera House or went straight across to Kirribilli. Cars with their lights on were pouring north over the Bridge, trains were rattling noiselessly beside them, the flag was flying at Admiralty House, the sun was dropping somewhere into the Parramatta River, and the city was closing down perfectly normally, as if nothing had happened.

Having endured the obligatory half-hour wait, James was shown into the partner's office. He was a nice enough man, if a little vain in appearance, with overlong grey hair, a deep blue shirt with a white collar, red braces and a yellow figured tie. James found himself thinking that in *Boston Legal* the lawyers kept their jackets on all the time. The solicitor said 'Tell me about it' in a formulaic way, having no idea what was coming, and James started talking without a moment's pause. When he finished, the partner — who had not taken a single note on the yellow pad in front of him — stood and came around the desk to take a chair beside James.

'James, this firm doesn't do crime. Sure, if the CEO of one of our clients gets picked up for a PCA or his wife is caught shoplifting (and you'd be surprised how often that can happen), we'll send one of the bright young associates out to Waverley or down to the Downing Centre to look after it. But not murder. That's horses for courses. What I'm going to do is refer you to a specialist solicitor in another firm — his own firm, actually. That's your best bet.'

James nodded.

'Okay with you?'

James nodded again, spent from telling his story. The solicitor consulted a little book and entered a number in his desk phone. A man answered, audibly, on the loudspeaker.

'John Bettens.'

'John, George Cavenagh.'

'How are you, George?'

The solicitor picked up the handset and spoke into it. 'Well, thanks, mate. John, I've got a young man with me who's going to need your help. He may be involved in the death of a paedophile who'd been molesting him for a very long period of time, and he's rather foolishly disposed of the body somewhere down south in the National Park.'

He listened for a minute while the voice at the other end responded to what it had been told, then wrote on his yellow pad. 'Okay, I'll do that. Will I send him over to you now?'

He listened for another minute and nodded. 'On his way. Oh, listen — his father's James Logie, and Logie Brothers is one of our biggest banking clients. You'll know them, I'm sure. I'll get Logie senior to speak to you about fees asap, but given the urgency you can go ahead without concerning yourself on that front. Okay with you?'

James thought he could hear the words 'Okay, thanks' from the other end of the phone as Cavenagh hung up. The partner tore the top page from his pad and handed it to James.

'Grab a cab straight over there to Surry Hills. He's waiting for you.'

James looked at his watch. 'At seven o'clock?'

'Yes, James. It's a shitty job, the law, but we get to drive Maseratis. Or some of us do. John Bettens rides a bike. You'll like him.'

By seven-fifteen, James was pressing the buzzer beside the front door of a terrace house in Devonshire Street. There was a big Moto Guzzi motorbike standing on the tessellated tiles of the front verandah. James had expected a bicycle. The door snapped open mechanically and he went inside to find a man who looked no more than thirty-five, and maybe only thirty, coming down the hall. The solicitor — for he introduced himself as John Bettens — was, to James's eyes, a very young man. He wore jeans, a white shirt, no tie.

They shook hands. 'Better come in here,' the solicitor said, gesturing to the door of what had once been the house's front room. He sat behind the desk and James took one of the two chairs facing him. 'Beer?'

'Thanks.'

Bettens got up again and took two cans from a small fridge standing against the back wall. James accepted one and they popped the ring-pulls. VB, full strength.

'James — or is it Jim?'

'James.'

'Right. Listen, James, just so you know. In case you think I'm too young, I've done probably forty murders—'

James pulled back involuntarily and Bettens laughed.

'No, not personally. I should have said I've represented forty people charged with murder, about the same number of rapes, plus uncounted numbers of big drug imports, supplies, armed robs. I've done this all a million times. It's what I do. My job is to represent you, to defend you. Not to judge you, so stop feeling ashamed of yourself. What I do is handle the police, get you the right barrister, organise your witnesses — all that stuff. Everything that can be done for you. But, I repeat, it's not my job to judge you. What you tell me, I accept. Unless it's obvious bullshit. How're we doing so far?'

'Good. Well.'

'Good. But now's the time to lay it out for me, so I can advise you what we do next. Can I assume you've had no contact from the police? No? Right. Now, it seems likely that you and I will have to go to the police tonight, and you might end up spending the night in the cells here in Surry Hills. Can you do that?'

'If I have to, I suppose.'

'Well, you might. Let me tell you, one of the most important things is alacrity.'

James looked uncertain. 'What I mean by that is that we have to move quickly, and readily. It's all about appearances. We have to be frank, and co-operative. Probably the very best thing will be if you can give me all I need to know at this stage, and I can set it out in a written statement, then we'll take that statement to the detectives on duty tonight and give it to them. I'll tell them you have nothing further to say at this stage, and we'll ask them to grant police bail. Maybe that won't happen, because they might want you to take them to wherever the body is. You're going to have to agree to do that.'

James's face showed how reluctant he was to revisit the hastily dug grave. It took him some time to reply. 'Okay.'

'Might be a long night.' Bettens pulled the keyboard in front of him closer. 'Let's get started.'

By nine-thirty, they had the story down on five double-spaced pages. Bettens ran the completed document through spellcheck and made revisions and corrections until he was satisfied, then rang a number on his speed dial.

'This is Bettens, solicitor. Can I speak to the senior Homicide detective on duty?' There was a wait of a couple of minutes before he spoke again. 'John Bettens here. Who'm I speaking to?' A pause. 'How are you, sergeant? Listen, can I bring in a young man to see you right away? We've got a statement to give you about the death of a man at Maianbar, and the disposal of his body last night in the Royal National Park.' Another pause. 'Okay. I'll ask for you at the front desk, will I?' He nodded into the phone, said 'Right' and hung up.

'You'd better sign this, James, and I'll make a couple of copies. Sign every page, I think would be best.' And James did. Bettens took the statement into the next room and made five copies. He stapled them, handed one to his new client and put the others in a manila folder with the original. 'We can walk.'

Pulling on a dark blue jacket, Bettens turned off all but the hall light as they left through the front door. They walked the short distance through the cool night to the ugly concrete bulk of the Sydney Police Centre and presented themselves at the front desk. A big man in a cheap suit that screamed 'detective' had risen from a vinyl lounge as they entered the foyer and moved forward to shake hands with Bettens.

'Sergeant Francis, this is James Logie. I've got his statement here.' The detective and James shook hands gravely.

'We'll go upstairs.' They took the lift up two floors and entered an untidy open-plan office dotted with numerous empty desks; only a couple of late workers, both on the phone, disturbed the silence. James, Bettens and the Sergeant sat around Francis's desk, Bettens handed Francis the original of James's statement, and the detective read it carefully.

James Andrew Logie
299 Mansion Road, Bellevue Hill
University student
AGE: 22
I have known Kevin Egan all my life. I grew up at the above address, where he was the next-door neighbour.

Egan was a paedophile and a pervert. Egan first
molested me when I was about 12. He offered to take me
to his holiday house at Maianbar and my parents agreed.
They were friendly with him and his wife. He molested
me in the bedroom of the house by making me take off
my shorts and underpants and masturbating me. I did
not know what he was doing. He told me that I was not
allowed to tell anyone, or I would be in serious trouble.

In the years that followed, Egan molested me more
and more seriously. He raped me anally scores of times,
usually at Maianbar, but on occasion in the pool room of
his Bellevue Hill house when his wife was away. About five
years ago, when I was 17, I told him to stop or I would tell
the police. He took out his wallet and produced from it the
business card of a member of the New South Wales Police
Board, with the police crest on it. I cannot remember the
name on the card. He said this man was his friend, and
fixed 'things' for him. He said that if I made allegations
against him, the police would prosecute me. I believed him.

My life became intolerable.

I did not tell anyone, including my parents, what
Egan had done to me until he tried it on with my friend
Justin Thomson. That night, I told my mother Egan had
been molesting me for the last ten years and now he was
trying with Justin. She told my father and he said there
was to be no more contact with Egan, but did nothing
else. I am unaware whether he spoke to Egan, but do not
believe that he did.

My mother arranged for me to see her work
psychologist. The psychologist told me that I had to take

charge of my life. She advised me that I had to tell Egan to stop, threaten to make a complaint to the police if he did not, and threaten to put leaflets in every letterbox in Bellevue Hill, naming him and saying what he had done.

I did not do as she advised. I went overseas for six weeks. When I got home, Egan pestered me on the phone. I cannot now explain why I agreed, but I went next door and he molested me again. After that, he kept ringing me up, asking me to come to Maianbar. That continued for about ten days.

I left Bellevue Hill at about eight o'clock last night and drove my utility to Maianbar in order to confront Egan and tell him it had to stop. It took me a long time to get up the courage to go there. I tried three times to go before I succeeded. He asked me in and we sat on the deck, looking at the water. We drank beer. I was there for several hours. I told him that it was never to happen again, or I would definitely go to the police and I would leaflet Bellevue Hill about him. He laughed, but he agreed to stop.

When I prepared to leave, I could not find my car keys. I called out to Egan: 'Have you seen my keys?' I then saw that he was naked in his bedroom, masturbating. This repulsed me as I realised that what he had said to me about stopping the conduct was not true, and that he was never going to stop, and that I was not going to be able to go home until he had been sexually gratified. I also realised that Egan must have hidden my keys.

I said to him, 'Where are my keys?' He said, 'Don't worry about that — you don't need to go anywhere tonight.' I became angry and hit Egan on the left side of his face. A small amount of blood appeared on Egan's mouth. I left the bedroom and continued to look for my keys, intending to leave, when suddenly Egan came running through the house. There was a further altercation between Egan and myself. He wanted me to engage in some form of sexual act with him. I told him in clear terms that I did not want to. He persisted. The altercation between us was violent, but I did not use a weapon of any kind to resist his advances towards me. We had a fight and he ended up on the floor. He seemed to be unconscious. I believe I went into a state of shock. I was confused and distraught. I did not intend to kill or cause serious injury to him. I am not a violent person by nature. I believed that it was necessary to do what I did in order to stop Egan from sexually assaulting me.

I located my keys and drove back through the National Park, heading home. When I got to Engadine, I became concerned about Egan, so I turned around and went back to Maianbar. It was well after midnight when I got there, probably close to 2 a.m. The front door was open, and I called out 'Hello'. There was no answer, so I went inside and found him on the floor. I could detect no pulse, and he was not breathing.

I panicked. I dragged the body outside and got it into the tray of the utility. Then I went into the garage and took the can of two-stroke fuel that he used for the lawnmower. I sprinkled the fuel all over the living room and set the carpet alight. I used matches that were in the kitchen. Then I closed the front door and drove back into

the National Park. After I had been driving for about ten
minutes, I turned down a fire trail and kept going until
the track ran out. I dragged the body out of the tray
and dug a hole in the sand with my hands under a log.
I rolled the body in there and covered it with sand and
branches and leaves. Then I drove home.

I did not go to bed last night. I sat in the garden of our
house, waiting for my parents to wake up. I asked them
to arrange for me to see a solicitor, and I was referred to
Mr Bettens earlier tonight. Mr Bettens typed this statement
for me, but it is a true reflection of my instructions to
him. It accurately sets out the evidence which I would be
prepared, if necessary, to give in court. The statement is
true to the best of my knowledge and belief and I make it
knowing that if it is tendered in evidence I shall be liable
to prosecution if I have wilfully stated in it anything that I
know to be false or do not believe to be true.

Signature: J.A. Logie

Dated.

Francis expelled something between a breath and a sigh and
looked up for the first time since he began reading. 'Two things,
Mr Bettens: is your client prepared to be interviewed further about
this? And is he prepared to take us to where he buried the man?'

'Yes to the second.'

'Is he prepared to have the event videotaped for use in court?'

'No.'

James leaned forward in his chair, but Bettens signalled for him
to stay still.

Francis nodded. 'What about an ERISP?'

'No. No recorded interview. The signed statement is all you're getting. It tells the whole story. Anything further, he exercises his right to silence.'

'I wouldn't necessarily agree with that, Mr Bettens, about us having the whole story. But fair enough.' He turned to the second page of the statement and read through part of it again, then laid it on his desk. 'Anyone want a cup of tea? It's going to take a while to arrange this trip.'

Francis called over one of his night shift colleagues. 'Get onto Sutherland, will you — if there's anyone there — and tell them Homicide's heading for the Royal National Park to locate a body. We don't want them to do anything except bring some battery lights and meet us at the park entrance. That kiosk thing, tollbooth. And organise a photographer. Meat wagon.'

'Video?'

'No, stills will be enough. There isn't going to be a walk-through or any interview at the crime scene. You better read this statement for yourself. This is Mr Bettens, who I think you know, and his client, Mr Logie. Detective Constable Dean.'

The second detective, a small man in a dazzling white shirt with silver cufflinks, shook hands with James and the solicitor. His suit was much better quality than Francis's.

'Are we going to have any trouble locating the place?' Dean asked, speaking to Bettens but looking at James.

James didn't answer, but bent to whisper to Bettens.

'Probably not,' the solicitor said. 'We might have to go through to Maianbar first and come back from there.' The police nodded, and Dean went off to use his own phone to make the arrangements. Francis dialled an extension and asked for three cups of tea. They arrived five minutes later, all white with two sugars.

James and Bettens sat in their chairs at Francis's desk while Dean made his series of phone calls and Francis left the room, carrying James's statement. He was away for what seemed to James a very long time. Fatigue was overtaking the young man.

Just before midnight, the four men got into an unmarked Commodore and headed south. Within minutes, James was asleep with his head on Bettens' shoulder. He didn't wake until they stopped at the locked-up National Park tollbooth where two vehicles — a station wagon from the Scientific Section and another Commodore with two uniforms from Sutherland — were waiting for them. The detectives got out to speak to the other police while they waited for the ambulance, which arrived less than five minutes later. Francis saluted its driver with a wave, and all returned to their vehicles. The convoy took off for Maianbar, its headlights picking out the trunks of white gums in the surrounding forest and the occasional skeleton of a Gymea lily looming beside the road. It had been a few years since bushfires performed their scarification, and the undergrowth was thick. James groggily thought to himself that Dean was probably going to be unhappy about getting his trousers snagged on the blackberry bushes. And the lantana.

The convoy turned around in Maianbar village, which was sound asleep except for a cat warming itself on the bonnet of a parked car. In the end, it didn't prove all that difficult for James to pick up the fire trail he had used. The cars and ambulance slowly pushed along it, headlights jerking erratically up into the canopy and then down into gullies and washes, until they could go no further. Portable lights were lifted out of the station wagon and carried to the place to which James led Bettens and Francis, wielding a huge Maglite. Dean followed, doing his best to avoid thorns.

The grave was pretty much as James had described it. Glimpses of the naked body of Egan were visible through broken branches and a blanket of thinly spread grey bush sand. The lights were set up on tripods and photographs were taken, as were measurements and other notes. (What for? James wondered. None of this could possibly matter — they had his signed confession.)

Having pointed to the body, saying no more than 'There', James was led off to one side by Bettens. They watched in silence as the police painstakingly and slowly followed their protocols. The branches and leaves covering the corpse were lifted and another sequence of photographs was taken. There were close-ups of the head and face. Samples of vegetation and bush sand were collected. Bettens asked Francis if he could take James back to the car, and permission was granted. For the first time, James started to feel the cold of the bush at night, and gratefully took a seat in the back of Francis's Commodore. After a while, Bettens joined him.

'I'm thinking Harry Curry,' he said. 'To defend you.'

'I thought you were doing that?'

'Not in court, James. We'll need a barrister, as I told you right at the beginning. I don't blame you for not remembering. But he's the best man for this sort of thing. We don't want to go in with a QC or even an SC, because that might make you look desperate, and probably guilty. He's better than most of them, anyway.'

James was silent, looking at the bright lights being moved around in the blackness behind the trees. Then they were switched off, one by one.

'What happens now?'

'Well, the first thing is that they'll arrest you and take you to, I suppose, Sutherland and charge you. Then—'

'Charge me with what?'

'Murder. That'll take a while to process. Then they'll either give you police bail, or we'll be first cab off the rank in the Sutherland Local Court this morning and make an application to the magistrate.'

'What if he refuses?'

'We make a Supreme Court bail application as soon as it can be arranged. We'll get Mr Curry to look after that, I think.'

'Will I get bail, do you think?'

'The legal presumption is against it for murder. We have to face that. My feeling is, though, that the circumstances of your case ought to be treated as exceptional.'

'Meaning that my family's rich?' James couldn't disguise the bitterness in his tone.

'No, that wasn't what I meant, but it never hurts. The fundamental issue ought to be whether there's any flight risk.'

'What's that mean, Mr Bettens?'

'It means the likelihood of your taking it on the toe. Shooting through. Fleeing.'

Suddenly, Francis and Dean appeared at the front doors of the car. Behind them was darkness through which the uniformed police were carrying the extinguished lights and other equipment. Neither James nor Bettens had noticed the men from the ambulance carrying the body past them on a stretcher.

Francis opened the driver's door and put his head in. 'All right with you if I do the arrest here? You needn't get out.'

'Fine with us,' said Bettens. Francis and Dean got into the front seats and turned to face the pair in the back. Dean switched on a small tape recorder and held it above his seat, pointing it at James.

'James Logie,' said Francis, 'I am arresting you on suspicion of the murder of Kevin Egan at Maianbar last night. Sorry, the night before last. You are not obliged to say or do anything unless you wish to, but anything you do say or do will be recorded and may be given in evidence. Do you understand that?'

James looked at Bettens. 'My client understands his right to silence and, on my advice, intends to avail himself of that right. For present purposes, he has nothing to add to the signed statement provided to police last night.'

'Can I assume that it will not be necessary to handcuff your client, Mr Bettens? I intend to convey him to the Sutherland police station where he will be charged.'

'Handcuffs won't be necessary, sergeant.'

Dean switched off the recorder and Francis started the car. He looked at his watch: 3.30 a.m. 'I trust there'll be someone at Sutherland at this hour, Deano.'

Dean used the car's radio and made contact with the station sergeant. All in the car heard the perfunctory arrangements being made for their arrival. Bettens had his client enter the family's phone number in his iPhone, but made the call himself. He spoke very briefly to Logie senior and asked him to stand by for a fuller explanation in about an hour's time.

Shortly before four o'clock, and long before the sun rose that day, the convoy (minus the ambulance which had continued north to the morgue at Glebe) turned into the drive of Sutherland police station and followed it to the rear of the undistinguished postmodern building, hard up against its counterpart Local Court. James took no notice of his surroundings, being almost out on his feet. He had to be asked twice before he got out of the car and was escorted through the floodlit car park to a door opened by Dean, punching in a code. Once inside the brightly lit building, he and Bettens were taken to the charge room and the formalities of the murder charge were executed. James was grateful that Bettens handled everything, because he was long past understanding and events moved in an incomprehensible blur. He was dimly aware of the station sergeant confirming with Bettens, on the record, that he did not wish to be interviewed in any form, and somehow understood that the police weren't going to stick their necks out and grant bail.

Bettens didn't burden James with any discussion about the bail application he would make later that morning in the courthouse next door. He told James to grab some sleep in the cells, and asked that he be given something to eat and drink. 'He's had nothing much since lunch yesterday,' he told the station sergeant and went out in the street to phone the Logies. A polystyrene cup of sweet tea and two ginger nut biscuits were sent in to James, but remained untouched beside the sleeping defendant until he was woken by the slamming of iron doors at eight o'clock. He ate the biscuits and sat on the edge of his bunk for the next hour, before being moved to a holding room beside the Number 3 court where his companion was a biker with more tattoos than James had ever seen on one person. At nine-thirty he was prodded through the door and into the court where Bettens was waiting in a suit and tie, and a magistrate was on the bench. The courtroom was busy, with six or more people moving around the Bar table as their matters were mentioned, or adjourned, or stood down until later in the morning. At least a dozen more people, armed with manila folders and large diaries and burdened further with anxious clients, were seated in the public pews.

The magistrate was looking at James as he was escorted into the dock, and the little half-door was latched shut behind him by a uniformed policewoman. 'Are you James Andrew Logie?'

James nodded yes and looked to Bettens.

'I appear for Mr Logie, your Honour. My name is Bettens, solicitor. Question of bail.'

'Presumption's against it. This is the murder at Maianbar, isn't it?'

'That's a question for the jury, your Honour.'

The magistrate, a good-looking older woman with white hair and a slash of red lipstick, chose to smile at Bettens' rejoinder. 'Quite so, Mr Bettens.' She swivelled her gaze to the other end of the Bar table, where a harried police prosecutor in plain clothes was whispering with Francis, still in last night's suit. 'Sergeant? Attitude of the police to extraordinary circumstances?'

The prosecutor looked up. 'Can I have a moment for instructions, your Honour?' Without waiting for the court's assent, he returned to his whispered conversation. His body language indicated some displeasure at what he was hearing, as did his tone when he straightened up and addressed the magistrate.

'I'm instructed that the Crown does not object to bail, your Honour.'

'You mean the police. You don't work for the DPP, sergeant. In any event, noted. But the court has still to be satisfied, sergeant, that bail is warranted. Mr Bettens, what can you tell me?'

Bettens hadn't expected this, but then few of his clients lived in Tuscan villas at Bellevue Hill. He coped well on his feet.

'Three compelling points, your Honour: strong community links — Mr Logie has lived in the same house in the eastern suburbs all his life and will continue to reside there subject to your orders; nextly, there is an insuperable situation of self-defence and thus a very weak prosecution case; and thirdly my client is prepared to surrender his passport and submit to daily reporting conditions. His father, who I have just spoken with, instructs me that he'll stand as surety for any sum the court sees fit to nominate. So that's actually four compelling points.'

'His father will put up the money, even if it's a million dollars?'

'Not a problem, your Honour.'

'Anything you wish to say about that, sergeant?'

'Surrender of passport, twice-daily reporting to the nearest police station — that would be Waverley, your Honour — and a curfew between 6 p.m. and 7 a.m.'

'Mr Bettens?'

'Could I propose once-daily reporting? Mr Logie's at university, your Honour, and wishes to continue attending lectures.'

'What's he studying?'

'Chemical engineering. He's in his last year, your Honour. I have to say he really is not a flight risk. His whole life is here in Sydney.'

The magistrate thought for a while. 'Perhaps you're right, Mr Bettens, but it is quite extraordinary to grant bail in a murder case, even with the police raising no objection. I can't guess the reason. Still, I would have very real fears for his survival in remand. I won't agree to daily reporting. I'm going to leave him reporting at Waverley twice daily — it's a 24-hour station, anyway. Once in the a.m. and once in the p.m.'

'As your Honour pleases.'

'I'll adjourn this matter for six weeks. Mr Logie, if you'll go with Mr Bettens the bail undertaking can be signed in the court office. Next matter, sergeant?'

The bail arrangements took ten minutes, with Francis standing in the background, looking not altogether happy. Bettens noted the adjourned date in his diary while he waited for the bail conditions to be typed out. Once James had signed the blue form, Bettens had a quiet word with the detective.

'What was that all about? No objection to bail?'

'Phone call from the Police Minister to my boss. Apparently old man Logie and the Honourable know each other.'

'Ah. Democracy's a great thing. The minister's door is always open.'

'Your client's not going to leave me with egg on my face, is he? If he skips on his bloody bail, it'll be me in the gun, not the high and mighty minister. He'll do the usual Pontius Pilate.'

'So far as I can judge him, sergeant, you needn't worry. But …'

'Yeah? What?'

'That's what I thought about Christopher Skase, too.'

Bettens took James outside to where the big green Moto Guzzi was waiting, two helmets locked to its seat. He handed one to his client and stowed his few papers in the pannier. James noticed for the first time that his solicitor was wearing scuffed motorcycle boots. 'Francis dropped me off at the office while you were in the cells. I did a couple of hours work before I came back here.' He put on his helmet and a pair of sunglasses as he started the bike's engine. 'On you get.'

James obeyed. The handful of people smoking outside the courthouse watched as the big bike roared off towards the highway, carrying Bettens in his unbuttoned suit, red tie streaming over his left shoulder, and a young man in a Bermuda jacket, hanging on like a limpet.

*

It took Harry two days to return the call that Bettens left on his voicemail at Burragate. One reason for the slow response was that Bettens had never briefed him before, and Harry knew how to hold a grudge. By the time he made the call, he had gathered some intelligence on the case.

'I Googled your matter, and your client's father for good measure. Looks like the sort of client to breed from,' he told the solicitor. 'I think I've got the guts of it. You're thinking self-defence?'

'Yeah. A little bird tells me that the victim might just have form for molesting boys.'

'Subpoena his record for the committal hearing, then. I hope you don't want me to do that?'

'Well, it'd be good if you could. But I'll look after it if you're jammed.'

'It's not about being jammed, John. They're all paper committals now, anyway, aren't they? Nobody asks me to do them any more, because you don't really get to cross-examine anyone. Would you have any issue with any witnesses?'

'Not the lay witnesses, no. But there might be some medical issues. There's a shitload of medical reports they want to use.'

'What's the post-mortem say?'

'Heart attack. Not a lot of help as it stands.' Bettens was speaking on his mobile phone and from the background noise Harry could picture him on a stool outside Bar Coluzzi at the Cross.

'Heart failure is the cause of death in one hundred per cent of cases,' Harry said. 'The issue is going to be what caused the heart attack. Your client a big strong bloke, is he? Does tae kwon do, or karate? Packs a good punch?'

'Not at all, pretty slight in fact. Maybe sixty kilos wringing wet. Looks like a cross-country runner, not a boxer. Never had a fight in his life. Before this, I mean.'

'You'll need a decent pathologist, then, for the trial. You're not going to get one in Sydney, because the DPP considers they've got them all on a string. I'll email you the contacts for a good bloke in Melbourne. Pricey, though.'

'I won't say money's no object, but it isn't going to be a problem. What about you? You'd better let me have your rates for the client's family to approve.'

Without thinking, Harry said, 'You'll need to speak to my clerk about that.'

Bettens sounded embarrassed when he responded after an awkward pause. 'I thought you were — um, you know — not exactly in any chambers at the moment.'

Harry laughed. 'Sorry. That's quite right. They kicked me out, as I'm quite sure you've heard, but were too polite to mention.'

'How much do you think I should get in?'

'Well, I'm going to have to read everything and confer with the defence pathologist. I'm going to have to advise you on the evidence we'll need, and I've got no idea what that will be. And the trial will take — what? Two weeks?'

'I would have thought.'

'Better get in a hundred thousand. To cover both of us.'

'That's what I was thinking. At least for a start.'

'Planning on coming out of semi-retirement, then?' Arabella's voice was amused and Harry could picture her raised eyebrow at the other end of the phone line.

'You've heard already?'

'I work in Phillip Street, Harry.'

'Anyway, I'm not semi-retired. More cloistered. Nothing north of Batemans Bay.'

'Until you're offered a murder you can't refuse.'

'As you say. This case has a lot to recommend it, Bella. It's something we could do together.'

'My criminal days appear to be behind me, Harry. There's a mountain of briefs on this desk that I haven't even opened yet.' She could hardly see over the top of them.

'All courtesy of the dykes with dislikes?'

'What?' A slight edge to her voice. 'I'm not sure I heard you correctly.'

'I'm on the cordless, walking across the paddock. I was asking whether all this work comes from your colleagues in the upper echelons of the Women Lawyers' mafia.'

'As it happens. What do they dislike, anyway?'

'You heard perfectly, then. Men.'

Arabella laughed. 'Why do I always think of you when I hear the word "unreconstructed", Harry?'

'Search me.' Six black cockatoos flew overhead, squalling among themselves.

'And the word "dinosaur".'

'That'd be because of the suede shoes. There's a common but fallacious view that they went out of fashion in the fifties.'

'The brown suede shoes with the dark blue chalk-striped suit? No, I don't think that's it, or all of it. Not everyone finds the carefully crafted Curry persona charming, darling. I do, of course, but I regret to have to say that it's not the universally accepted view in the circles in which I mix.'

'Those circles would be the same dragons who want to hit me

for holding the car door open for them or standing up when they enter the room.'

'The very ones. I, on the other hand, love it. Gentlemen are hard to find. Your mother taught you well.'

'She was one of the Cheltenham McGuffickes, you know.'

'I do know. You've told me. Had her own lawn tennis court as a gel, you said.'

'Before her family fell on hard times and had to move to Eastwood.'

'No more croquet?'

'Not a sausage, croquet-wise,' Harry said. 'No more Almond Roca for Christmas, no more holidays at Terrigal, no more Straight Eight Buicks with white-wall tyres and wicker picnic baskets in the boot.'

'But your father rescued her from penury.'

'Indeed. And the hard times were never mentioned again. She persuaded him to buy a house back in Cheltenham. Without a tennis court, sad to say.'

'I love a happy ending.'

There was a bizarre noise from the Burragate end of the phone line.

'What are you doing, Harry?'

'Just collecting a couple of eggs for my dinner. One of the hens is being a bit unco-operative.'

Harry emerged from the coop and let the gate swing shut. He was holding four brown eggs against his shirt in one big sunburned hand, the phone in the other.

'We get on very well, don't we, Harry?'

'When we're five hundred kilometres apart, yes.'

'But if you take this murder, it'll be here in town, won't it?'

'I am taking it, and it will be. Yes.'

'And you'll stay with me at the flat.'

'If you'll have me. Bettens is taking a bit of persuading to dispense with the committal hearing so that we can go straight to trial, which I reckon we should do, having read the police brief.'

'Is there much advantage in that? Tactically?'

'Certainly is. It looks as if one key issue is going to be the cause of death. We hit him, yes, but the pathology might leave it open as to whether we killed him. And I don't really want to rehearse that dispute with their experts so that they can strap them up for the trial. Better to spring it on them once and for all.'

'Sounds like what always terrifies David Surrey — Harry's carrying all his eggs in one basket.'

'Haven't even got a basket with me, Bella. These eggs are in my hand. Hang on.' And he took the phone away from his ear to open the screen door to the kitchen. He went inside and put the eggs on the sink before speaking again. 'Mushroom omelette and half a bottle of Wirra Wirra Church Block. Care to join me?'

'Need you ask? Actually, I was hoping that I could come down at the weekend, but something's come up.'

'Something?' Harry's inflection was both displeased and disappointed.

'The Bench and Bar dinner at the Hilton on Saturday night.'

'Why's that more important than a weekend at RonLyn?'

'Because I agreed to be Madam Junior.'

'You're making a speech?'

'Yes.'

'Then it's abject bullshit, isn't it, that this is something that's just come up?'

'No, Harry, give me a chance. I'm not going to lie to you. The woman who was going to do it has pulled out. Her partner's just had twins. I'm the last-minute replacement.'

'Her what? Her partner's just had twins? How could that … Oh.'

'Exactly.'

'And Arabella Engineer, a woman who knows better, a great deal better, is going to demean herself at this nasty ritual of alcohol and self-congratulation by buying an expensive dress and doing her best to deliver a knowing ten-minute address with an arch tone. No doubt amusing the *arriviste* offspring of country publicans and suburban solicitors with her oblique but hilarious allusions to their affection for cocaine and for overcharging their unsuspecting clients. That's right, isn't it?'

'You've read an advance copy of the speech, then?'

'That's what you're expected to do, isn't it?' His voice was raised. 'Charm them?'

'Are you hurt, Harry?'

'Why would I be hurt? It's your decision. It doesn't affect me.'

'If you don't want me to do it, that's all you need to say.'

'And you'll do it anyway.'

'I have to. I've said I would. I'm not doing this to betray you, Harry. I've just put myself in an impossible position, that's all.'

'Which am I? The rock or the hard place?'

She laughed. 'You're a hard man, Harry Curry.'

'Mae West said they were good to find.'

And they left it there. Harry didn't cook the eggs, but poured a barely heated tin of baked beans onto a couple of slices of buttered toast and ate them standing at the sink. After that, he ate a whole litre of ice cream straight out of the carton while he watched *Four Corners*, then went to bed. At ten o'clock, by which time Harry was fast asleep, Arabella shut down her computer and went home in a taxi, microwaved and quickly ate an anonymous nutrition package, and thought about what it might be like to have twins.

Harry had his way, and the right to a committal hearing was waived. Six months later, which was indecently fast by the standards of the New South Wales criminal justice juggernaut, Harry got to his feet in Court 6 in the neo-Gothic wing of the old Supreme Court building in Elizabeth Street to make the final address to the jury in the trial of *Regina v James Andrew Logie*. His wig was old and yellow, having been inherited from his father, Wallace Curry QC, now resident in an expensive care facility on the Upper North Shore. His gown was rumpled and had a three-cornered tear just above the hem, where he'd snagged it on the hinge of a cell door years ago. Harry was mentally and emotionally exhausted, having endured an especially bad-tempered three weeks of trial. The senior Crown Prosecutor, a man whom Harry had quite liked over the years of their conflicts, seemed to have seen this trial as his chance to square the scorecard between them, and had pulled a number of strokes for which James Logie's defender was never going to forgive him. It had been a horrible case, truth to tell, deeply dismaying Bettens, and Harry regretted his bitter exchanges with the Crown medical experts who refused to give an inch to the defence, not least because he was well aware that the confrontations had shocked the jury. Worse still were Harry's fights with the judge, a political appointee from the ranks of the solicitors' branch, for whom Harry had no respect. That much was obvious to his Honour, if not the jury, and the judge unwisely raised his grievance one afternoon after the jury had been sent home for the day. Harry, having been on his feet for six hours battling with a recalcitrant pathologist, was in no mood for it. His back ached, and the stud in his wing collar was sticking into his throat.

'Mr Curry,' Justice Oldham had said, 'you have for the past three weeks made no attempt to disguise your disregard for this court, and I do not intend to tolerate it any further. I want to hear no more of your stage whispers to your instructor, correcting my grammar and my pronunciations. Whether you like it or not, I am the judge, this is my court, and the Court of Criminal Appeal is the place for you to raise any objections you may have to my management of these proceedings.'

Harry almost snorted. 'Your Honour is quite wrong. I have the greatest respect for this court. Her Majesty's court, if I may be so bold as to challenge your Honour's use of the possessive pronoun or, to put it more accurately, the possessive determiner.'

Oldham J looked baffled, so Harry had won the right to explain. As he knew he would.

'I shall explain: your Honour was pleased to call it "*my* court", which troubled me at the time, and troubles me now. As to your Honour's no doubt inadvertent solecisms and my polite and restrained references to them, I have always seen it as my duty to assist the court, and that was all I was doing. I would dare to suggest that the court's dignity can only be enhanced by a high standard of English expression.'

'By correcting me in front of the jury.'

'Yes, but only when regrettably necessary. By way of example: if your Honour would take the trouble to consult the dictionary I can see in front of you, you will see that the word "aitch" begins with the letter "a". Not the letter "h", and certainly not "haitch", if you will forgive the circularity of that observation. If you further consult the dictionary and its definitions of the words "anything", "something" and "everything", you will find that the letter "k" appears in none of them, least of all terminally. There was, further, the occasion when I used the legal maxim — quite appropriately, one might have thought — *nemo judex in causa sua*.'

'You mocked me, Mr Curry.'

'Not at all, your Honour. I merely observed that your Honour's protestation that you did not understand Latin could not possibly be the case, given your distinguished role in a superior court. May I add this, purely in the spirit of assisting the court? Your Honour may wish to reflect on the appropriateness of the popular aphorism that it is never wise to fight outside one's division.'

'Jesus, Harry. Back off, will you?' That came from Bettens, whose face was in his hands. None of this had been what he expected, despite the famous Curry temper, but he couldn't help admiring what he saw as his counsel's destructive courage. The Logie parents couldn't believe their ears — the barrister on whom James's future depended was hell-bent on insulting his judge! Mrs Logie had certainly had reservations about her son's defence counsel when she had done some internet research into Harry and found a confusing and cryptic reference in the Bar Association records to his being suspended from practice for misconduct, but Bettens had promised that he was the best man for the job, never mind that nonsense. He'd been exonerated, anyway.

What the Logies didn't understand, and Harry wasn't going to take the trouble to explain to them, was that the decision in James's case would be made by the jury, and not the judge. All Harry had disclosed to them about his strategy was that he was going to make the jury hate the victim — Egan — not that he was going to exert such dominance over the court that the jury would identify him, and not the man dressed like Santa Claus in his scarlet gown, as the authority figure.

By the time Harry rose to make his final appeal to the jury to acquit James, the unfortunate contretemps between bench and Bar was three days old, and an uneasy peace had broken out between Harry and the judge. Lots of ps and qs were being minded on both sides. Justice Oldham had made up his mind to sum up to the jury 'right down the middle', as one of his more experienced colleagues had advised. 'Don't let Curry bait you into saying something unwise that he can flay you with in front of the appeal judges. Say what you like about Curry, but he knows what he's doing. If he can't persuade the jury to acquit, he'll blame you for prejudicing them with your summing-up.'

'Yes, but—'

His colleague wasn't to be silenced. 'In any case, why would you want this kid to be convicted? From everything I've heard, the victim was a most appalling pervert with certain inappropriate connections that do the judiciary no credit. Is it true that he'd been given good behaviour bonds three times for sexual assaults on boys, but it was all hushed up?'

'No, that is true. I looked at the certificates of conviction, Don, and every one of them was granted by the same magistrate at the same court. And after court hours, too, which is an unmitigated scandal. Curry was onto that. He cross-examined the victim's wife, and she agreed that one of his drinking mates was this very magistrate. She denied all knowledge of his convictions, and even his proclivities, but the jury didn't believe a word she said. Seemed to me that they hated her, as much as you can ever tell. As if she knew everything that was going on, even with the boy next door, but so long as it happened down at the holiday house she'd turn a blind eye.'

'Jesus, Mary and Joseph! It just gets worse and worse. Are you going to put him in?'

'The beak? Probably not. He's retired now, anyway. But I don't think Curry's going to spare him in the jury address, and the press'll pick that up and run with it, no doubt.'

'Well, that might be punishment enough, don't you reckon? But, really, getting back to the ultimate issue: is it any skin off your nose if this boy walks?'

'I suppose not.'

'Well, then. If you really want to pull Curry up, do it later. Complain to the Bar Association.'

'And what will they do? Put my letter at the bottom of a very large file?'

Harry stayed for the three weeks of the trial at Arabella's Elizabeth Bay flat. The couple settled into a comfortable routine of a late dinner together, often at a handy Kings Cross bistro, walking home to resume work on their respective cases at opposite ends of the long dining table — Harry poring over the evidence in the Logie case, and Arabella worrying at a series of one-day appearances debt-collecting in the District Court, or fighting off the undeserving but seriously injured for the benefit of the shareholders in foreign insurance companies. After the first few such sessions, Harry desisted from his anti-defendant political niggling, for which his lover was grateful. From time to time Arabella would ask for Harry's advice on the rules of evidence, or Harry would try out on her a series of questions that he was rehearsing for the next day's cross-examination. Arabella was repeatedly staggered by his command of medical matters: not just the jargon and its idiosyncratic pronunciations, which Harry regarded as essential if he was going to communicate to the medical experts the impression that he knew almost as much as they did about aneurysms and coronary artery spasm, and the significance of sexual arousal in cardiac events.

'How do you do it, Harry?'

'You keep learning, or you die. Worse still, you specialise, which is a fate far worse than death. Fact is that the vast majority of our learned friends want only to do the same case over and over again in the Equity Division, or the Dust Diseases Tribunal, or the Liquor Licensing Court. They don't want to be challenged, they want to be comfortable, and to send out the same more-than-comfortable fee note at the end of every matter. If you're game to be a generalist, you have to do medical negligence, architectural incompetence, building disputes, mining cases, professional discipline. I've even defended a surgeon on a manslaughter indictment.'

'You won, of course.'

'Need you ask? I hardly ever mention my losses. What I'm trying to say is that it looks to me that you're in danger of specialising.'

'I know.'

'Find it comfortable?'

'Not yet.'

Most nights, having agreed that they were both too tired to make love, they made love. In the mornings, breakfast in Phillip Street, conferences with solicitors, clients and witnesses until ten o'clock, and the usual unholy rush to get robed and into court. When Arabella needed to use her room for conferences, which was most of the time, Harry worked in the room set aside for visiting counsel on the ground floor of the Queens Square Supreme Court building.

It went on like that for the duration of the Logie trial, until, back in Court 6, the Crown prosecutor completed his appeal to the jury to convict James Logie, ostentatiously grovelled to his instructing solicitor by asking whether there was anything else he should have said (a shake of the instructor's head) and sat down, lifting his wig briefly to wipe his bald head with his handkerchief.

Harry stood, paused, and took a drink of water. Afternoon light was colouring the stained-glass windows that overlooked Elizabeth Street. Making eye contact over the edge of his glass with the foreman of the jury, a middle-aged woman in a print frock, he paused again. Then he hitched his gown up on his shoulders and did his best to centre his ragged wig on his head. He left his white folder on the lectern in front of him, its cover closed.

'You know,' he began, with a sweep of his right arm, the palm of his big right hand open and flat, 'all this means something. The pomp, the wigs and gowns, the formal language, swearing oaths to tell the truth, the whole truth, and nothing but the truth. They're all mechanisms of justice, not just trappings. They've evolved for centuries, and we all believe in their fairness. The fundamental purpose of all this process is justice for James Logie. It's why you're here. But the system doesn't work for you or for James unless there is respect on the part of the prosecutor for his or her role — and that role is to strive for the truth. Our system of justice won't work if it's prostituted by opportunistic and cynical misrepresentation of the evidence in the vindictive pursuit of a guilty verdict. I'm going to take you to some of the more effectual misrepresentations and misleadings that have been foisted on you in due course, but perhaps the most meretricious of them needs to be highlighted right now, at the outset.

'The Crown opened a case of premeditated murder. That's what he said he would prove. Even Detective Constable Dean gave the lie to that. "On impulse" and "spur of the moment" were the words he used when I asked him to characterise the altercation at the beach house. Later in the course of this trial the Crown made an extraordinary outburst, asserting that James Logie had not suffered sexual abuse at the hands of Egan, despite the fact that you heard Detective Sergeant Francis tell you on the first day of evidence that was accepted as true — the history of abuse — by him, the detective in charge. As if that cynicism wasn't enough, you won't have forgotten that this morning, in his closing address, the learned Crown prosecutor, no doubt thinking of his overriding duty to the truth, described James Logie and the pervert Egan as lovers. *Lovers!* And that Egan's death was the result of a *lovers'* quarrel.

'If that is not the most dishonest and opportunistic prostitution of the evidence, and if it is not rejected out of hand by you and all of you as a gross and unjustified insult, intended to create prejudice against my client, you can forget what all this is supposed to mean.' Harry gestured again at the panelled walls, the coat of arms, the judge, the daydreaming sheriff's officer. 'It means nothing. It's just window-dressing. Lip service to justice.

'Another piece of unforgivable nastiness from that end of the Bar table: the Crown again sought to insult my client when he called him "shifty". A regrettable lapse, perhaps, but what's really "shifty" here? It's the Crown's case that keeps shifting — from premeditation, to no sexual abuse, to a lovers' quarrel. That is shifty.' The prosecutor shifted uncomfortably in his chair, and the jury watched that.

'Let me attempt to put before you the unadorned facts, as proved by the evidence. You know very well that it's the facts, and what you make of them, that decide this case.' Harry now opened the white folder. 'The defence argument comes down to this.' At that point, the foreman and another juror poised their pens over their exercise books. 'You could not be persuaded by the evidence you have read and heard, least of all beyond reasonable doubt, which is the criminal standard, that: (a) it was the act of James Logie in striking Egan that killed him; and (b) neither could you be persuaded that James Logie struck Egan intending to kill him or to cause really serious injury to him; and (c) neither could you be persuaded that James Logie was not acting in self-defence.

'When we come back tomorrow, I'm going to take you to each of those points and show you why you will be compelled to agree with our submissions on each of them, but let me put it in a couple of headlines for you to take home with you.'

Harry looked down at his notes again.

'First, the evidence of the cause of death does not and cannot exclude the very real possibility that Egan's heart attack had nothing to do with James striking him in the fight. What you now know, although the medical witnesses called by the Crown were most reluctant to volunteer this, is that Egan could have had that fatal heart attack at any time, and for no reason at all. He had a very serious but undiagnosed heart condition. That amounts to a reasonable doubt as to cause of death, which is enough to stop the case.

'As to criminal intent: the only intention you can be satisfied James Logie had was to defend himself from the sickening sexual advance of this pervert. There is no basis on which you could be persuaded, least of all beyond any reasonable doubt, that my client formed any intention to kill or even injure. It was just a defensive striking out at a predatory monster.

'And the last of the headlines: the Crown had to disprove the possibility that James acted in self-defence. And it has utterly failed to do that.'

Four of the jurors scribbled, catching up. Harry looked at the clock, which stood at five minutes to four, and turned to Justice Oldham. 'I'm going to move into the detail of my submissions at this point, your Honour. Would that be a convenient moment to adjourn for the day? I can say that I believe my address will finish before the luncheon adjournment tomorrow, if that is of any assistance to the court and the members of the jury.'

The judge agreed, and sent the jury off. Once the room was cleared he looked at the Prosecutor and raised his eyebrows, silently asking whether the Crown wished to raise an objection to the excoriating opening attack Harry had just made on him. The DPP's man dropped his eyes. He knew that he deserved what he was given, and mentally chided himself for wanting to get one over Harry at any price.

Although Harry's role in the trial was far from finished — he had about two hours more of his jury address to deliver — he could now afford to relax. The balance of the defence address was already written out in the white folder in his peculiar longhand and his idiosyncratic abbreviations, and he wanted to put it aside, walk back to Elizabeth Bay, and leave final preparation for the next morning, immediately before what he hoped would be the last day of James's trial. That would depend on a short summing-up from Oldham and a quick deliberation from the twelve good persons and true.

Having changed back into his jacket, he walked out into the gritty wind in King Street, past the statues of Queen Victoria and Albert the Good, following the curve of the road around to the cathedral. Parked outside, with an infringement notice under its windscreen wiper, was a 7-series BMW that he recognised as belonging to a prominent appellate silk from Wentworth Chambers. Without bothering to see whether he was being observed, Harry removed the Beemer's parking ticket and put it on the next car along, smiling to himself. As he descended the hill to the low point of William Street, a homeless man standing in front of the Lotus/Bentley showroom tried to sell Harry a copy of the *Big Issue*, but Harry waved him back and said, 'Already bought one, mate.' True up to a point, Lord Copper, but that purchase was eighteen months ago. Harry lengthened his stride as he climbed the hill to the Cross, keen to get home and out of the wind. Well, not exactly home — Arabella's home.

Harry's mind turned to the domestic arrangements. It was certainly convenient and comforting to stay with Arabella for the duration of this trial, but he had little choice. The Erskineville house was sold, and the yuppies who'd bought it had already moved in their builders to gentrify the place. Harry had never minded the outside loo, but it plainly wouldn't do for the husband-and-wife accountant purchasers. No doubt they'd be shipping in slabs of granite, boxes of halogen downlights and acres of aged hardwood planking rescued from a shearing shed or demolished warehouse. Harry didn't care. He had never felt any emotional attachment to the house, and he'd never so much as picked up a paintbrush in the ten years he'd owned it. The profit he made on the sale was more than enough to buy the property at Burragate and to keep him in reasonable comfort for ten years without working, if he chose. And with his mother long dead and his father in a retirement facility, he had no other home in Sydney.

It was convenient and comfortable at Elizabeth Bay, yes, but staying there exposed him to all sorts of subtle pressure from its occupant. Arabella had never articulated her fear that Harry was taking her for granted, and neither had she expressed her wish to be wooed (which was how she thought of it), but Harry wasn't so insensitive as not to understand that he was disappointing her. Heading left at Kings Cross past the strip-joint barkers and the takeaways and the El Alamein fountain, dodging a melancholy couple that he easily recognised as heroin addicts on the nod, he thought it might help to take Arabella out tonight and make a fuss of her. That's if she didn't have another debt-collecting case to prepare. Harry watched himself in the windows of the little shops at the bottom of Elizabeth Bay Road and thought: big ugly bloke in a suit and tie. Fabulous. He was in a bad mood before he got to Billyard Avenue and Arabella's modernist highrise.

Arabella didn't phone, and didn't get home from her chambers until after ten, having been hard at work on an advice about the merits of a test-case appeal from a judgment of the Consumer Trader and Tenancy Tribunal. Harry was already asleep.

Bettens had asked Harry to speak to James's parents before the trial wrapped up. 'Just a bit of PR, mate,' he'd said. 'Hand-holding.' The Logies were still dismayed by Harry's confrontations with the judge and the expert witnesses (at least he hadn't had any reason to rip into the police) and wanted reassurance that the jury hadn't been alienated. The group, including James himself, met at 8.30 in the café on the fourteenth floor of the Supreme Court building. Harry spent most of the fifteen minutes staring out at the indescribable view across the Botanic Gardens, the Harbour, and all the way to the Heads. A huge white cruise ship was heading for the Tasman. 'Look,' he said, finally turning to face the banker and his wife, 'I gave up trying to predict juries, or even to understand them, years ago. They do the stupidest things, and then — for no reason I can fathom — they return a verdict of such subtlety that it staggers me. I don't have much of a feeling for this one. They're listening very carefully, and I was watching them when the prosecutor said what he did about James and Egan being lovers. They hated that. I have no reason to think they're against me. Or against James. We can only wait and see.'

The jury was waiting in the jury room, ready to enter the court and listen to Harry, by a quarter to ten. For a group of twelve who had drifted in each morning over the past three weeks in dribs and drabs and very often late, this was a major attitudinal shift. The judge was able to invite Harry to resume his address on the stroke of ten.

'Thank you, your Honour. Good morning, ladies and gentlemen.' Harry opened his folder notes and turned to a page of handwriting on which a number of phrases were heavily underlined. 'Last evening, I gave you the headlines on why this prosecution has failed, and what I'm going to do now is take you to the detail of each of those three failures, bearing in mind that if you agree with me on any one of them, that's fatal to this prosecution. And I'll start with my first point, which was that the evidence doesn't establish to the criminal standard required that it was a punch from James Logie that killed the pervert Egan.

'What my friend the prosecutor did in his address to you ...' Two jurors exchanged puzzled glances at Harry's reference to the Crown as his friend, given what they had heard the previous afternoon, '... was inexcusably selective. It was as if the cross-examination had never happened, as if the witnesses hadn't backed down, or conceded, or resiled from the evidence that the Crown would dearly wish you to believe is all you need to know. So what I'm going to do is remind you of the devastating concessions I obtained from the medical experts on the issue of what caused the death, and why those backdowns are so destructive. You'll recall that, in a nutshell, the prosecution case is that my client punched Egan, causing a brain haemorrhage which directly resulted in heart failure. Let's deal with that.

'First, I'll read the critical answer the cardiologist, Dr Yass, gave me.' Harry opened a second folder holding the transcribed oral evidence. '"If you say this man died of a coronary artery spasm, it is possible. Nobody can say it is impossible."

'Next, Egan's general practitioner, Dr King, told you this: "It is my opinion that Mr Egan may have died of a heart attack."

'Then the government pathologist gave me this answer: "If this was a brain haemorrhage, it could have been spontaneous. I have not been able to determine whether the cause was spontaneous or traumatic."

Harry looked up from the transcript he had been reading. '"Traumatic", of course, means a punch, an injury. And that pathologist went on, as you will recall, to explain that brain haemorrhages such as this one are usually caused by aneurysms and lead to heart attack. I'll read you from the transcript my next two questions and his answers:

Q: Doctor, it is obvious enough, isn't it, that as a person
    with undiagnosed and untreated coronary artery disease
    and a history of adverse reaction to stress, he was a
    prime candidate for a fatal coronary artery spasm?
A: Yes, he could be.

```
Q:  In this case, a death from that kind of heart attack
    cannot be ruled out?
A:  No, not from the findings of the heart.
```

'And I'll go back to Dr Yass, the heart specialist. This is what he told you when I asked him about the significance of sexual arousal in this man:

```
The role of sexual arousal in cardiac events is quite
significant. It causes high blood pressure, tachycardia,
sympathetic activation. With people who have underlying
disease it can bring on angina or heart attack. It's just
like strenuous exercise.
```

'Now, members of the jury, that's the evidence I was able to obtain in my stumbling and inarticulate way ...' Several jurors smiled at that, '... from the Crown witnesses. Not any defence witness, mind you, paid for his opinion, but the experts called by the people who seek through those doctors to condemn James Logie. As if their agreement with the commonsense propositions I put to them wasn't enough, you also have the benefit of the truly independent expert we called — Dr Browning, from Melbourne. Can I remind you that Dr Browning is a pathologist of unchallenged distinction and experience who worked for the Victorian government, has performed more than ten thousand post-mortem examinations, has taught pathology in universities and hospitals for thirty years, who has published numerous papers and books on the subject, and who even has the courage to lecture the legal profession on pathology. Dr Browning also has the great attribute of speaking in language that lay people such as you and I can understand. What he told you was that it certainly *could* have been a heart attack that killed this man, with or without a brain haemorrhage. That is quite a reasonable and likely diagnosis, given Egan's pre-existing heart disease — he was only getting 50 per cent of the blood to his heart that he should have had, at the best of times; given also his other heart attack risk factors; and given his stress, which can precipitate a heart attack either by coronary artery spasm or by the release of hormones into the bloodstream. This is what Dr Browning said:

> So there are a number of ways in this particular set of circumstances that this man could have died of a heart attack. We simply do not know what killed this man.

'Let me repeat that: "We simply do not know what killed this man."

'That expert opinion, which means that nobody can say beyond reasonable doubt what was the cause of death, was not challenged by my friend the Crown in cross-examination. You may take it, then, that the Crown cannot dispute the expert opinion of the pathologist called by the defence. That's an end of the matter, isn't it?

'But there's more. There's the neurosurgeon, the brain specialist, we called. The Crown, of course, called no such doctor despite its resources, which are in very real terms unlimited in cases such as this. In short, Dr McLucas's opinion was that the haemorrhage found at post-mortem was *not* indicative of a head injury case — because of its location. When you find a haemorrhage in that area, it's usually related to a ruptured aneurysm. And aneurysms aren't caused by punches.

'What the medical evidence amounts to is this: the responsible, careful attitude taken by Dr Browning — that nobody can say what killed this man — is the one you must respect. His Honour will tell you that you must not speculate, and you may not guess. Put simply, the Crown wants you to find James Logie guilty *just in case* the cause of death was a brain haemorrhage resulting from his hitting Egan in the head, leading to a heart attack — but the Crown may not ask you to do that. Theory is no substitute for hard evidence. The evidence of what killed Egan must be such an absolute moral certainty that there can be no other reasonable possibility — and the evidence makes it clear to you that the very real possibilities are that the brain haemorrhage had an innocent explanation and, still further, that the heart attack may have simply been a natural event.

'Two vital things: the onus is on the prosecutor to prove his case and, second, he must prove it to the absolute exclusion of any reasonable possibility that Egan died of natural causes. It is vital, absolutely vital, that you bear in mind that we, the defence, don't have to prove the death was naturally caused: it is the Crown that has to prove it wasn't; and its evidence is just not good enough.

'If you are against me on that submission — and, members of the jury, how could you possibly be, given the evidence? — but if you are, there is still a second hurdle that brings down the Crown in this case. You heard my friend use the Latin words *mens rea*, which means, simply, 'murderous intention'. An intention to kill Egan or to cause him really serious injury is an essential element of the crime of murder. Everyone in this court knows that the essential mental intention simply isn't established — it's not as if you don't know what James intended when he fought Egan off: you can find that in his statement — exhibit K1 — and you've all got a copy of that in your evidence folders. If you go down to the bottom of the third page, last paragraph, you'll find this:

I did not intend to kill or cause serious injury to him. I am not a violent person by nature. I believed that it was necessary to do what I did in order to stop Egan from sexually assaulting me.

'And that's our evidence — the evidence upon which it is your duty to make your finding of fact as to James's intention: no intention to kill or cause bodily harm; he believed it necessary to fight Egan to prevent a sexual assault; and he believed that Egan wasn't going to let him leave until he had been sexually gratified. James's intention was to resist the sexual attack of an insatiable, serial sex offender against boys and young men, who would never take no for an answer.

'Which brings me to the third and final hurdle that, on its own, brings down the efforts of the Director of Public Prosecutions: the issue of self-defence. This is wholly independent of the other two issues that we submit to you that this case has fallen at. The point here, and I needn't take long to set it out, is that the Crown has abjectly and totally failed to adduce evidence capable of proving that my client didn't act in self-defence when he fought off the perverted rapist Egan. Did my learned friend for all his disgraceful references to "lovers" even dare to suggest that James did not reasonably believe that it was necessary to fight Egan off? Because unless he makes that submission, and can back it up with evidence, you may not convict.

'Don't be misled by my brevity — this is a killer point, if you'll forgive me for that adjective. Every one of you would want your son, your brother, your friend's child to fight off a monster such as Egan. Any young person has that right, which might even be seen as a duty. I can't put it more plainly than that: whatever else you may think about the medical evidence, or about the state of James's mind at the very moment this man was charging at him with the intention of rape, you have to agree that the Crown cannot suggest it has disproved that James acted in self-defence. Once again, remember that we don't have to prove self-defence — the prosecutor has to prove it *wasn't* self-defence. His Honour is going to make that very clear to you, with respect, and I ask you to pay particular attention to that part of his summing-up.'

When Harry paused to take a drink from his glass, Bettens pointed at the clock, which stood at 11.35. Harry inclined his head and turned to the judge. 'Perhaps, your Honour, the jury needs a break from me.' And he sat down as Oldham obediently sent the jury out for a cup of tea. 'Half an hour, ladies and gentlemen.' Again, when the door closed, the judge looked enquiringly at the Crown, who simply shook his head to indicate that he had no objection to the further embarrassment visited upon him and his employer, the Director, by Harry's address.

James, who had long since retreated into a self-protective fatalism, was taken downstairs to the cells for the duration of the morning tea break — the 'short adjournment' as it is traditionally called — just as he had been every previous day of the trial, and at all the luncheon adjournments. Each night, he was granted bail by Oldham to go home with his parents, but not to leave the house for any purpose until he returned to the precincts of the court in the morning at such time as was required by his legal advisors.

The rest of the defence group headed outside for some fresh air. Bettens went to buy takeaway coffee in Phillip Street and brought it to where Harry and the Logies were making small talk under the arcaded verandah of the courthouse in King Street. Off to one side stood a gaggle of journalists, cameramen and photographers, a number of them smoking in a knot close to the footpath. Harry looked enviously at their cigarettes, having been emphatically forbidden by Arabella from smoking in her flat, and using that as motivation to give up. Logie senior asked Harry how he thought the jury were responding to his arguments, but, as before, Harry didn't want to be drawn on that. 'As well as can be expected, I suppose,' was all he said as he pulled off his wig and held it in his free hand.

Mrs Logie was more sanguine. 'The forewoman likes you, Mr Curry. I can see that.'

'The middle-aged ones always do, Mrs Logie,' Harry said. 'The thing that worries me is that women of her age are likely to do what the men say.'

Mrs Logie bristled somewhat and Bettens said, 'I don't know about that, Harry. How did she get to be the foreman, if she's the compliant type?'

'Good point,' Harry conceded. 'But they tell me that when the judge asks a jury to choose their foreperson, someone will always ask who's been on a jury before — and the people with experience get the job. So maybe she's not a criminal trial virgin.'

'Still,' Mrs Logie said, 'I've got a good feeling about her. And they were all listening very closely to you.'

Her husband agreed. 'Quite a few were taking notes, and they didn't do that when the prosecutor was talking to them.'

Harry finished his coffee and looked for somewhere to drop the empty cup, just as the court officer came outside to tell everyone that the adjournment was over. Harry put his wig back on, still juggling the empty cup, and headed indoors, Bettens and the Logies following in his wake.

It was two minutes before midday on the courtroom clock when the jury were brought back and settled down in their seats. Harry, conscious of his promise to finish before one o'clock, was quickly on his feet at a nod from the judge.

'Thank you, your Honour. Members of the jury: let me deal with two things that you might have thought were of some persuasive value in the Crown's submissions: first that James tried to burn down the house to destroy the evidence, and second that he buried the body in a remote place. Both of those things are easily explained — by panic, not an overwhelming sense of guilt at all. This is not a young man in control of the situation in which he finds himself. This is a young man detached from reality. All his adult life, and back to when he was but a boy, he had been in the control, literally the grip, of a sexual monster. He tried to break loose — something that took the most enormous courage. I don't want to be heard to criticise his parents, who are here supporting him, but they were no help. He was on his own, and everything blew up in his face. No premeditation, just a striking out in an attempt to repel the rapist. He goes back to the house at Maianbar out of a genuine concern, and finds Egan dead. He knows the police are going to be on to him. He knows his utility must have been seen parked outside the beach house. There's no logic whatever in trying to burn down the house or trying to bury the body. The Crown's argument that those actions prove guilt flies in the face of your understanding of humanity. It insults your intelligence. It asks you to crucify a victim, because the vicious, cynical pervert who victimised him has robbed him of the ability to think straight in a crisis — and not just any crisis, but the crisis created by the sexual abuse he suffered for so long. What we ask you to do is to understand that.'

Harry took several beats and ran his eyes over all twelve faces in the group sitting in two rows in the jury box. Each juror returned his gaze.

'Your humanity is why you're here. His Honour's going to sum up to you in a few minutes and exhort you not to be motivated by sympathy or prejudice. But he's not going to tell you to ignore your knowledge of the world, your understanding that we all do stupid things when we lose control, when we panic, when we have no idea what to do. And, for all your humanity, it may well be that the question you can't answer is why James kept putting himself in harm's way with this pervert. That, fortunately enough, is a question you don't have to answer, not here, at least, but no doubt you've already discussed that among yourselves in the jury room: why is it that the victims of child abuse don't tell? Why don't they run? Why do they go back there? Maybe the answer is in the idea of control — that the victims surrender, and can't control the situation. Certainly James couldn't. The situation controlled James.

'I've been trying to decide what to say to you about the death of Kevin Egan. "Tragic" is certainly not a word I am prepared to use, as the prosecution did. You've probably heard these words many times, from the poet John Donne. He wrote this almost four hundred years ago: "Any man's death diminishes me, because I am involved in mankind; and therefore never send to know for whom the bell tolls; it tolls for thee."'

Harry didn't have to read the lines.

'No, not in this case. Our world, you may well think, was not diminished by the death of Kevin Egan, ladies and gentlemen. It would be wrong for me to say that that man got what he deserved, and I won't say it. But it would be just as wrong to call him the victim here.'

Harry backed away from the lectern until he was standing alongside the dock in which James was sitting, and put his hand on James's shoulder. The young man kept looking down. Harry could feel him trembling slightly as he resumed his address.

'James was the victim. Ten years of the most shameful and unforgivable victimisation, from which this boy will probably never recover. I hope he'll forgive me for saying that, and I hope I'm wrong about his ability to transcend it.' Harry dropped his hand and walked back to the Bar table. Still, James did not look up.

'Tragedy? The only tragedy would be if you got this wrong, and found him guilty.' Harry capped his pen and closed his white folder. When he looked up to speak again, he was almost whispering.

'Don't do that. For God's sake, don't do that.'

The judge couldn't hear that last exhortation, but the jury did. Harry sat down, and Justice Oldham organised his papers, ready to begin his address to the jury by reading out the invariable elements of his summing-up, explaining with the iron-fisted guidance of the judges' *Bench Book* the onus and burden of proof, the essential elements of the crime of murder, the role of the jury as the judges of the facts, and the necessity of a unanimous verdict. It was a brave judge who dared depart from the form of words mandated by the Court of Criminal Appeal, and Harry could anticipate that he was about to hear a script he'd heard many times before. The interesting part would be when Oldham came to deal with the weight of the evidence of the medical experts. As the judge cleared his throat to begin and looked up, he saw that the foreman was standing.

'Yes, Madam Foreman?'

'Your Honour, I've been asked to raise with you a question about the burning down of the house and the burying of Mr Egan's body.'

'Please go ahead, Madam.'

'Well, what about those things? Is Mr Logie charged with them? Do we have to decide whether he's guilty of … what was it?' She looked at the young man sitting next to her, who whispered the answer that she then repeated: 'Arson and disposing of a body?'

'Well, subject to any objection counsel may have or any comment they may wish me to make, I'm going to say, members of the jury, that you should not consider those questions. If there are to be such charges laid against Mr Logie, they will be dealt with in another place at another time.' He paused, and several jurors nodded as if they had known that.

'Is there anything further you wish me to say on those matters, Mr Crown?' The prosecutor shook his head, half rising. 'Mr Curry?'

Harry stood. 'Yes, your Honour. That is a matter that I intended to address in my submissions and, to be frank, I forgot. With your Honour's leave?' The judge nodded and Harry turned to the jury to put to them some remarks he had prepared, and certainly had not forgotten. Rather, he had made an on-his-feet decision to drop that part of his address, having the feeling that this jury would not be concerned with the technicalities of the ancillary crimes. He turned to that page of his longhand notes, looked at them, and closed his pad.

'All I wish to say about that, ladies and gentlemen, is this: you each have a copy of my client's written statement, in which he confesses to setting fire to the house and taking the body into the bush and burying it. He is still charged with both those crimes, and I can tell you as his counsel that he will have no choice but to plead guilty in both cases. Those are serious crimes, and he will be punished for them. So, while you as the jury in his murder trial are not concerned with anything except this charge, it is important that you should know that when you acquit my client later today, that will not be the end of the matter for him. He will be sentenced in another court.'

The prosecutor looked as if he was about to explode that Harry had taken the most opportunistic free kick he'd ever heard, but the judge paid him no attention and simply turned to begin his summing-up. Bettens and Harry were later to agree that the judge's speech, which continued for three-quarters of an hour after the luncheon adjournment and avoided lengthy recitations of the evidence — 'Because I'm quite sure you'll all have it firmly in your minds' — was at worst aimed right down the middle between the two sides, and at best favoured the defence by strongly indicating that the jury should accept Dr Browning's opinion that the cause of death could not be established with any certainty.

'If they do as they're told,' Bettens said as the door closed behind the jury, sent out to consider their verdict, 'they'll stop on the cause-of-death issue, and won't have to make any decisions on *mens rea* or self-defence.'

'Does this jury look the type to do as it's told?' Harry asked. He didn't think so.

The judge had adjourned the court at a quarter past three, having established that neither side wanted any redirection given to the jury on points of law. The judge's associate had approached both counsel, asking for their mobile numbers so that they could be contacted to come back to court in the event of a rapid agreement in the jury room. 'I don't have one,' Harry had said. 'Mr Bettens will give you his.' The associate looked quizzically at Harry. 'Really? No phone?'

'I could give you my number at Burragate,' he'd said, 'but it won't be much use.'

'Yes, the judge told me you'd semi-retired to the country. Where is that, anyway? Burragate?'

Harry had looked at her pearl necklace and perm. 'Nowhere near Bowral.'

James was permitted to remain in the courtroom to wait with his parents and lawyers. Harry tried to caution him against expecting a quick result. 'If they can't come to an agreement in the next hour and a bit, the judge might send them home for the weekend.'

James looked disappointed. 'Could it take that long?'

'This judge will leave them alone for at least six hours before he asks whether there's any difficulty with a unanimous verdict. There are all sorts of possibilities — one is a quick conviction or a quick acquittal; another is that they come back at four o'clock and ask to resume on Monday; and it's even possible they'll ask to keep going this afternoon and tonight and come to an agreement, so that they can get this over and done with.'

Logie senior said, 'I've been told that if they come back quickly, it means they're going to acquit.'

Bettens took that one. 'You can't assume that. I've had juries come back and convict in complex cases inside half an hour, and I've had others that took four days to acquit. It all depends.'

'Depends on what?' Mrs Logie asked. Bettens didn't respond, but looked at Harry.

'Prejudice, usually. The jury either want you to win, or they don't. Much like judges. The jury's advantage is that they don't have to give reasons, and no one can interrogate them about how they reached their decision. Judges have to torture the evidence to make it fit the result they want. That's a lot harder, because appeal courts might look very closely at it, and they have to cover their tracks.'

'Prejudice? How?' Mrs Logie wanted to know more. They were sitting in the public benches of the courtroom, with only a sheriff's officer to overhear, and he'd heard it all before.

'As my pupil-master once said, if you're Asian and charged with drugs, you have to prove yourself innocent beyond reasonable doubt. Prejudice. The Lebanese suffer it, too, and the Islanders.'

Another thirty minutes passed, the lawyers avoiding any further depressing anecdotes about judicial incompetence and jury unfairness. James was becoming visibly affected by anxiety, despite Harry's frequent winks and his mother's constantly whispered assurances about what a great job their defender had done. For someone who thought Harry had alienated the entire jury, she had swung around totally in her belief, having concentrated on every word of his address, every nuance of his tone and delivery.

The tipstaff came out and started to prepare for the return of the judge. 'The jury might have a question,' Bettens explained to James. 'They often do.' The associate suddenly came through the judge's door, businesslike in her gown, her arms full of court files. Harry looked at her and asked a question with his eyes.

'Got a verdict,' she said, sitting down and placing the files. 'I've rung Mr Crown, and they're on their way.'

It took fifteen minutes to reconvene the court. The judge came back on the bench, bowed to the courtroom, and told the court officer to bring back the jury. There was a long pause in proceedings until the jury filed in, and everyone in court heard one of them laughing at some joke as they entered. Almost all of them were smiling, but none looked at James. The foreman's gaze was towards the back of the courtroom, and Harry turned to see Mrs Egan taking her seat there. The juror was looking at her.

The jury sat, and the room went deathly quiet. Harry's guts were in turmoil, just as they always were at this moment. He pulled the solicitor's backsheet out of his folder — it was headed *DPP v Logie, Brief to Appear*, followed by Harry's name and chambers address (an amusing fiction) and that of the solicitor himself. Down the left-hand edge in Harry's handwriting was a series of notes with the name of the judge, the Crown, and a sequence of fifteen dates in order — one for every day of the hearing. At the bottom, he had noted 'Jury out 3.15.' Beneath that, he now wrote 'Verdict 4.03.' Underneath, in capitals, he lettered the word GUILTY, a little to the right of the column. Then he poised his pen to the left of that word and waited, not looking up. This was the indescribable moment that Harry lived for. Heroin, he thought, couldn't possibly give anyone this rush.

The associate stood. 'Madam Foreman, have you agreed on your verdict?'

'We have, your Honour.'

'How say you? Do you find the accused James Andrew Logie guilty or not guilty on the charge of murder?'

Harry's right hand, holding the pen, shook. Even after fifteen years of doing this, his hand still shook.

'Not guilty, your Honour.'

James burst into noisy tears. The judge looked startled, then smiled. He said to James, 'It's all right, old fellow. You came first!'

Harry wrote NOT in front of the already written GUILTY. He leaned towards the Crown, who nodded his congratulations.

'Bit unjudicial, that,' Harry said.

The prosecutor smiled. 'I think you misjudge him, Harry. He's not all that bad.'

The jury were discharged and sent off to collect their pay, and James's parents moved to noisily embrace him, still in the dock. The judge didn't seem to mind. He established that the DPP had no objection to dispensing with James's bail on the other charges, released him, and adjourned the court. He even went so far as to thank counsel for their assistance, looking at Harry with what Harry took to be a degree of irony.

Harry packed up his law books and his brief, and turned to leave. At the back of the courtroom, on the opposite side from Mrs Egan, Arabella stood. He raised his eyebrows. A smile lighting up her face, she came down to join him, kissing him on both cheeks. 'I'm glad you're on my side,' she said.

'Always, Bella.' Harry put his books back on the Bar table and put both arms around her, lifting her off her feet. 'How did you go?'

'Not as well as you, obviously.'

Outside in King Street, the media were waiting with the usual questions about how James felt. Had the verdict gone the other way, they would have asked his lawyers whether an appeal was planned and sent their camera people to try to get a picture of the convicted murderer in the back of the prison van as it headed out to Long Bay. Bettens deflected them from his client, saying that there were other charges still to be resolved, and that James wouldn't be making any comment. The disappointed journalists, seeing Mrs Egan leaving with her supporters, started to chase her for a comment, but most thought better of it and the unashamed remainder were rebuffed with hostile stares.

Logie senior wanted them all to go out that night to celebrate the win. Bettens was keen enough, but Harry claimed a prior engagement, which was substantially true. He wanted to visit his father at his South Turramurra aged-care facility. Hands were shaken, Mrs Logie kissed him and Bettens, and Arabella watched in amusement. 'Claims managers hardly ever kiss me.'

'Not that they wouldn't want to,' said Harry.

He introduced her to Bettens. 'I've heard a lot about you,' he said. She looked quickly at Harry.

The three watched as the Logie family headed up to Macquarie Street to catch a taxi home to the heights of Bellevue Hill. 'I'll make a little bet with you,' Harry said to the others. 'Before they reach Double Bay, they'll have decided that as he was innocent all along, they shouldn't have had to pay for this defence.'

'I won't take that bet,' Bettens said. 'During that last adjournment while the jury was out, Logie senior was complaining to me about our fees, despite knowing from the beginning what it was going to cost. I've got the feeling that you might have to wait a while for your money, Harry.'

'Didn't you get it in?'

'Not all of it, no. But I told him that he had an alternative.'

'What do you mean?' asked Arabella.

'I told him that if the result didn't matter, he could have done it much cheaper.'

Harry left his papers and his wig and gown in Arabella's room and took a taxi through the Friday-night traffic across the Bridge and up the highway to see his father. Wallace Curry QC was sitting alone in his room, reading that morning's newspaper. He was dressed for the frigid air conditioning in a canary yellow sweater, checked shirt with a wool tie, and brown corduroy trousers. His brown shoes had been polished and Argyle socks could be seen under his cuffs.

Harry put a bottle of Scotch in a paper bag on the bedside cabinet. 'You look great, Dad.'

'Hello, Harry. How are you?'

Harry couldn't conceal his delight that his father was having a lucid interval. He hugged him as he sat in his chair, crushing the business pages.

'Just got an acquittal in the Supreme Court, Dad. It's a great feeling.'

'Never had it, as you know. Must have been a murder or a rape, I suppose, if it's being heard there? I've had the High Court quash a series of tax decisions that went against me in the Court of Appeal, which was spectacular vindication at the time, but I don't suppose that counts. My clients liked it, of course. So did your mother. It was always enough satisfaction for me.'

'And would be for all real lawyers, Dad, but not rough-and-tumble criminal advocates like your son. We need a less subtle degree of professional gratification.'

'I was always envious of counsel to whom people entrusted their liberty, Harry, but when I started at the Bar they still had the death penalty and, to be brutally frank, that was a responsibility I couldn't have borne.'

'I'm glad I never had to deal with it.'

'Will I read about it in the *Herald* tomorrow?'

'You might.'

'You know, the nurses here cut out the stories about your cases, whenever they see your name. I've got a bundle of them in my drawer. It's like a fan club, Harry.'

'You never told me that, Dad.'

'A lot of the time, when I try to read through them they don't make sense to me. I know I don't make much sense either, a lot of the time. I'm sorry, my boy.'

'Oh, Jesus, Dad. What have you got to apologise for?'

The old man gently shrugged. 'Well, if you're winning in the Supreme Court, all that nasty business with the Bar Council must be forgotten, I would hope?'

'The suspension? That was quashed anyway, bloody quickly. It's just that for a while I didn't know whether I wanted to keep practising.'

'You'll have to keep practising if you want to finish up with an appointment.'

'What? To the District bloody Court?'

'No possibility of anything better than that?'

'I don't think even the magistrate's court at Brewarrina's a possibility, Dad. Too many toes have been trodden on, too many egos bruised and battered. I won't pretend that I never had judicial ambition, but I decided a long time ago that I didn't want to spend my weekends and holidays writing judgments and looking over my shoulder at the judges in appeal. You never did it.'

'It was offered. Mary said we couldn't afford the cut in income — with you at Shore and your sister at PLC.'

'You miss Mum, Dad?'

'You've never asked me that before, Harry. Of course. Never a day without thinking of her lovely face.'

'Women change you, don't they?'

'This is about the Indian girl, is it?'

'She's English, Dad. And I suppose it is.'

'Am I going to meet her, Harry? I'd like to. In one of my lucid intervals, I mean.'

Harry took his father's hand. 'Any day now.'

A nurse walked past the open door, sounding a muted bell. Harry kissed his father and left.

Arabella had made a salad, and she seared the salmon steaks as soon as Harry got back. They drank Moët and spoke little. While she put the plates in the dishwasher, Harry asked to use her laptop. 'It's in the bedroom,' she said.

When he came back to the living room, Arabella asked what their plans were for the weekend. Harry looked embarrassed.

'I just booked on the first plane down the coast tomorrow.'

It was quite a cold night outside, and distinctly frosty within. Arabella went to bed early, and Harry, staying up and trying to read a magazine, thought he heard her crying. He wondered, as he tried to fall asleep beside her, whether the LandCruiser, which he had parked at Merimbula Airport three weeks before, would start.

Lennie without George

There wasn't a lot of contact between Elizabeth Bay and Burragate over the weeks following the acquittal of James Logie. Harry didn't phone Arabella because he thought there was little he could say, and Arabella didn't phone Harry because he hadn't phoned her. Both knew they were being silly.

Towards the end of the third week, and after a day of country lawyering upstairs over the bank in the main street of Goulburn, David Surrey, solicitor, having cleared his desk, arranged the next day's files in a neat pile. He washed the mug bearing the slogan "Sue the bastards" and sat down again, delaying the decision to put on his jacket, descend the stairs and walk home through the twilight. It was threatening to rain, too. He rang the Burragate number and Harry answered on the second ring. But it wasn't the call Harry had been hoping for.

'Not interrupting your cooking, I trust?'

'Procrastination is the thief of time, Dave,' Harry told him. 'Go home and face the music.'

'Not just the bloody horrible hip-hop, Harry — the dogs, the TV, the bills, the appeal from the school building fund. The dripping taps that I was supposed to put new washers in last year. Dead light bulbs. Kitchen cupboards that don't shut properly. Putting out the recycling.'

'You love wallowing in petty domesticity. Admit it.'

'It's a fair cop.' Surrey grunted as he leaned over to pull out a desk drawer and rest his ankles on it. 'What do you hear from Phillip Street?'

'A deafening silence, overlaid with reproach.'

'That's not going to keep her keen, old feller.'

'And the alternative? You tell me.'

'You have to keep talking. For Christ's sake, Harry, don't let her get away.'

'She *is* away. She's up there in the air in Phillip Street, or Billyard Avenue, and I'm down here on the ground, a million miles away and in another culture. I'm digging holes for fence posts and pleading electricians guilty to low-range PCAs, or those who can afford it, and she's chairing a Bar Council committee on non-sexist language in legislation or some such essential law reform and positioning herself for a District Court appointment with the support of the sisterhood.'

'Judge Arabella? That'd be a pretty long-term strategy, wouldn't it, Harry? I mean, how long's she been at the Bar?'

'Five years here, but she tried it for three years in London before that. So, eight years, and that's almost enough for this Attorney-General. His faction's mostly women.'

'Eight years wouldn't be enough for you or me, Harry. For men, it's fifteen years, at least.'

'For every affirmative action, there's an equal and opposite disappointment,' Harry said. 'I trust my phone's not bugged, or we could get life with no prospect of parole for having this conversation.' He took the phone into the kitchen and opened the fridge in search of ingredients for dinner. 'It was different when she needed something from me. I think she's lost all interest in crime.'

'I think you misjudge Arabella, Harry.'

'Judging isn't my strong point. It might be hers.'

'Stop feeling sorry for yourself. Give her a ring, mate.'

But Harry didn't. Instead, he pulled four chops out of the fridge and some of his own vegetables — a tomato, a big potato, a few small carrots and some snow peas — and put a saucepan of water on the stove to boil. After a minute, the flame under the saucepan died and Harry, when he went outside to check, found that the gas bottle was empty. He put the food back in the fridge and took off in the LandCruiser to dine at the Eden Fishermen's Club, and counted himself extremely lucky to be waved on by the RBT unit on his way home. Obviously, the police officers manning the unit hadn't recognised him behind the wheel.

A few days later, and with the Harry–Bella relationship becoming even more attenuated by silence, Arabella returned to her chambers after another dreary day of arguing that the costs awarded to her insurance company client should be assessed at the maximum rate. Despite her solicitor's certain knowledge that the unsuccessful plaintiff in the case would be unable to pay any costs the court may be persuaded to order against him, and never mind the accumulated interest on them, he had instructed her to make the application. Her clerk asked her how the case had gone.

'Total victory,' Arabella said. 'Splendid stuff, if you enjoy futility. Poor old plaintiff couldn't afford a barrister so he had a suburban solicitor argue the case and lost, and now not only have he and his family had their takeaway food bar burnt out, but they've been ordered to pay costs at the indemnity rate, and interest.'

'Because?'

'Because an incompetent lawyer with no idea of his own limitations couldn't persuade the judge that his client didn't light the fire himself.'

'Did he?'

'He could have.'

'No harm done, then?'

'Probably not.'

What Arabella didn't know then was that the Vietnamese man whose claim against the insurance company was thrown out of court had shaken his solicitor's hand and thanked him for his efforts, then walked from the Downing Centre to Central Station and thrown himself beneath the Granville train in front of hundreds of horrified commuters. She read about it next morning in the *Telegraph*, and felt too ashamed to go to work. She spent the day looking at Harry's family tree on internet genealogy sites, then shut down her computer and sat in the dimming afternoon light.

Her clerk, a self-possessed woman with a remarkable facility for concealing her contempt for the self-importance of barristers, rang the Elizabeth Bay number.

'I just had a call from a Mr Sherry, who says he's an old customer of yours. Wants you to do a trial for him. Criminal trial. We weren't graced with your presence today … working from home, are you?'

'Sherry. I'm trying to remember. What did I do for him?'

'Well, he was having difficulty explaining it, but it sounded as if you got him a bond on some sort of Social Security fraud.'

'Ah,' said Arabella. 'Yes. Tony Sherry. An intellectually challenged person. Pleaded guilty to masquerading as an Aborigine and obtaining benefits under the Aboriginal Employment Program.'

'Not Aboriginal, then?'

'Maltese. He did well to avoid a custodial sentence.'

'He loves you. Wants to speak to you about his next big case, but I told him Legal Aid would have to be the ones making contact. He rang you from the jail. Mr Sherry, I mean, not Legal Aid. Something about it being farmed out to a private solicitor.'

'Should I give them a call?'

'Well, you might,' the clerk said, 'but it sounds as if the right person might be hard to find. Do you think David Surrey would want it? He usually briefs you, doesn't he?'

'Question is whether I want him to.'

'Too high and mighty for crime these days, Ms Engineer? Clients a bit grubby, compared with the classy claims managers who troop in here to sit at your feet?'

Arabella coloured. 'Fair play, Margaret. I'm not much chop with a jury, or so I've been told, at least without a certain amount of guidance.'

'He hasn't called you lately, has he? At least, not when I've been near the switchboard.'

'What's the charge this time, Margaret?' Arabella ignored the question about Harry.

'Well, as I said, your Mr Sherry was a bit hard to follow. Didn't strike me as the sharpest knife in the drawer, but from what I could understand it sounded like a murder. I'll phone Mr Surrey, will I, and see if he wants to grab it from Legal Aid? Maybe he could talk Mr Curry into taking an interest, d'you reckon? In the meantime, you might like to think about working from work, for a change. We'll see you in the morning.'

When Legal Aid agreed to pay David Surrey, as a Goulburn solicitor, a daily travelling allowance at the Sydney rate, he agreed to take the Sherry trial. Despite the referral coming from Arabella, he called Harry at the farm to ask him to accept the brief. Surrey, much as he liked Arabella, wasn't the only close observer who'd concluded that jury advocacy was not her strongest suit, least of all when the charge was murder. He assured Harry that he'd have no trouble getting the videoed confession ruled inadmissible.

'When is it?' Harry asked, using the remote to mute the volume on the CD he had been playing — a Russian recording of Rachmaninoff's first symphony. He often played the *allegro con fuoco* at high volume three or more times in succession and, although his nearest neighbours were five hundred metres away across the creek, they had given serious consideration to complaining. Harry knew for a fact that they preferred Neil Diamond.

'Three weeks from yesterday. Set down for a fortnight at Darlo. Plenty of time to work it up, and they'll pay us to do three jail visits to prepare the defence.'

'Can't do it, Dave. I've got a shoplifting at Bega and undersized abalone at Batemans Bay.'

'When?'

'In what would be the first week of your trial. Sorry.'

'You can flick those, Harry. This'll be a good little earner — reading time, ten days of trial and a couple of days for sentencing. Bloody sight better money than two half-days in the magistrate's court. Billy the Pig on top. You've never had much trouble handling him.'

'Just give me a minute, Dave. Putting aside the dubious tractability of his Honour Justice William Thatcher and his consequential attractiveness as the trial judge, I want to read you something, and later I'll explain it to you. Hold the phone.' Harry put down his phone and went to the bookcase that ran along his living-room wall. He took a small black volume labelled *The New South Wales Bar Association Rules* from the top shelf. Embossed on the cover was a coat of arms, a shield supported on the left side by a kangaroo and on the right by a lion. The motto beneath was 'Servants of all yet of none'.

'Here it is: Rule 93. Headed "Return of Briefs". "A barrister must not return a brief to defend a charge of a criminal offence unless the circumstances are exceptional and compelling." Should I explain that further?'

He had omitted from his recital of Rule 93 the adjective 'serious' that came before 'criminal offence', as he had the proviso 'unless … there is enough time for another legal practitioner to take over the case properly'. The simple truth was that Harry had no appetite for full-blown trials and didn't want the brief. His dissembling efforts relied entirely on the assumption that Surrey hadn't read the *Bar Rules*. He was wrong.

'Bullshit, Harry. You don't want to do it. Just say so.'

'I don't want to do it, that's true. Give it to Arabella — if she's prepared to get her hands dirty, that is.'

Surrey wasn't sure if the last remark was snide or not. 'Will you at least give her a hand, Harry? I think she's a bit underdone for something like this.'

Harry thought for a while. It was a chance for some kind of reconciliation without capitulation. Peace with honour. 'If it'll help you, Dave.'

'Bullshit again. You know it'll help *you*. You just want an excuse to talk to her again, without getting off your high horse.'

'Okay. But I'm not going to sit in on the trial. Absolutely not. She's on her own for that. Agreed? I'll give you a maximum one week in Sydney. Someone else'll have to feed my chooks.'

'You'll confer with the punter, and the witnesses?'

'If I have to. Send me what you've got.'

Ten days later, Harry was at the wheel of the LandCruiser, double-parked in Phillip Street, waiting for Arabella to come out of her building. He was early, but so was she. Climbing into the passenger seat, she leaned over to kiss him on the mouth.

'Just as if nothing had happened,' Harry said.

'Nothing *has* happened, you big goose.'

Harry pulled loose the knot of his tie. 'You've got the address for this, haven't you?'

Arabella reached into her bag and produced a sheet of paper, looking at her watch. 'The Holy Trinity Foundation, Campbelltown Road. Due there in an hour and five minutes.'

'Plenty of time.' He U-turned with characteristic disregard for the traffic, stopping in their tracks several taxis and an Australia Post van, and headed for Taylor Square to link up with the airport freeway and then the motorway south. Arabella waited until they were on the motorway before essaying anything more than small talk.

'How have you been, Harry?'

'I've missed you, but there's nothing novel in that.'

'No, there isn't. I wish I'd called you.' Arabella looked straight ahead.

'So do I,' Harry said, flicking his eyes quickly to her face and then back to the semi-trailer he was following too closely.

'Equally,' she said, 'I wish you'd called me.'

'So do I, Bella.' He turned his head to face her. 'I'm sorry, sweetheart.' She was looking at him as he said it, and smiled sadly.

For the rest of the trip to Campbelltown, Harry — fully defrosted — regaled Arabella with news of the chickens, the wildlife, the vegetables, the news values of the *Imlay Magnet*, and the eccentric bachelor further up the track. The time went quickly, and when they pulled up in front of the old brick and weatherboard church hall bearing across its gable the sign 'Holy Trinity Foundation', all awkwardness had long evaporated. Arabella took Harry's arm as they walked up the cracked and weedy concrete path to the open front door. Nobody was inside the big room they entered, which had set out along its walls rows of old cinema seats. In one corner was a table bearing a tarnished tea urn and towers of polystyrene cups, and in the centre was a ping-pong table without a net. Across the rear of the building was an unpainted particle-board partition that stopped short of the ceiling, pierced on one side by a door through which a tall, muscular man in a priest's uniform appeared.

'Father Monaghan?' Arabella asked.

'Bruce,' the priest said, holding out his hand. They introduced themselves, shook his hand, and he took them behind the partition into his office and gave them seats. 'I'd offer you tea or coffee, but the urn's broken. We could go over to the café later, if you like.'

Harry recognised the priest as a former rugby player.

'Bruce Monaghan — Norths, wasn't it? Outside centre?'

'Guilty.'

'And New South Wales?'

'Just the once. Against Fiji, knocked out cold in the first half.' He looked at Harry, and particularly his ears and nose. 'Did you play yourself?'

'Only for Gordon. I was a couple of years before your time.'

'The Highlanders. You wouldn't be the Curry who famously flattened that bloke during the national anthem, would you?'

Arabella raised one eyebrow and looked at Harry.

'Just the once,' he said.

The meeting lasted more than an hour. Father Monaghan filled Arabella and Harry in on how he'd come to be looking after Tony Sherry.

Arabella was later to tell Harry how attractive she'd found the priest. Curly black hair and dark blue eyes. To her eye, his athletic build wasn't concealed at all by the black suit and dog collar.

'I can see why a congregation would adore him.'

'What, apart from the ridiculously good looks, mellifluous voice and easy manner?'

'Well, that and his obvious sincerity.'

Harry shook his head. 'They teach them that.'

'Sincerity?'

'You never saw Norm Gilroy, did you? The cardinal. Chrome-plated smile like the front end of a Buick.'

'Spoken like a Protestant.'

Harry smiled at that. 'No, an Anglican. In my day at Shore, the difference was important.'

But getting back to what Father Monaghan had told them …

'To put it as summarily as I can,' he began, 'Tony never had much of a chance. He's the youngest of eight or nine children of a Maltese family, and was born with a significant hearing problem. That, coupled with his intellectual disadvantage, meant his education was completely unsuccessful. He's illiterate, totally. He's always been a big, placid fellow, so teachers found it easy to ignore him, put him in the corner and keep him quiet.

'When he was a kid everything was all right at home as far as he was concerned — he was happy there, at least until his mother died. He was about fourteen when that happened. His father and the rest of the family had always put Tony's problems down to being lazy, and it was only his mother who showed him affection or any level of understanding, and then he lost that.

'The family weren't bad people. Hard-working, honest, but tough-minded — especially as far as he was concerned. His father thought Tony was worthless, and didn't mind telling him so. Mostly, though, they ignored him. You'd have to say in Tony's favour that the treatment he got didn't lead him into offending against the law. What was he? Huge, really huge — as you'll see. And practically deaf, illiterate, backward. But easygoing, non-violent, even respectful. He left home, or was kicked out, when he was fifteen.

'The Probation and Parole Service produced a report based on what Tony told them about his life after he left home. He was apparently taken in as a minder by a prostitute at Guildford, although he denies that was her occupation. This was when he was still only fifteen. She seems to have been the first person who exploited him because of his size — to frighten off unwanted customers, or keep them under control. All the jobs he's had since then have been like that — other people taking advantage of Tony's size and intimidating appearance. He thinks he's always had trouble making friends because of how he looks.

'He drifted around for another ten years or so, and spent a lot of time at Kings Cross with some woman. The way Tony tells it, they were in an off-and-on de facto situation, but I doubt it. Whatever it was, that woman's gone now. He lived up there for years, working as a bouncer at clubs, and then he went off with a circus, or a number of circuses, doing odd jobs. He enjoyed the circus work. But that folded.

'About four years ago, his life reached a disastrously low ebb. He was sleeping in a disused chicken shed at the back of a five-acre farm out past Cobbitty, living on the dole. At that stage, he started to abuse the social services system by signing up for the Aboriginal Employment Program. He'd pass for Koori, easily. Very dark complexion — much darker than lots of the Aboriginals we work with. You can be sure that it wasn't a scheme Tony came up with himself. Someone must have been putting him up to it, and probably taking much of the benefit every fortnight. He didn't get more than two thousand dollars before they caught him and prosecuted him for defrauding the Commonwealth. Convicted, of course.'

Arabella leaned forward. 'I appeared for him in that matter. A couple of years ago now. I've been trying to remember — there was something special about his good behaviour bond, wasn't there?'

'That's right. He was sent to us. The magistrate imposed a condition that he had to accept the supervision of this Foundation, and had to attend two hundred hours of literacy classes here …' Harry looked out at the empty hall and back at Monaghan. The priest smiled. 'No, not in this building. We've got an old primary school for those classes, although Tony could never fit behind the desks. He tried really hard to learn to read and write, and even after the hours were up, he kept coming to classes. I couldn't say he made any real progress, but he was certainly willing. First to arrive, last to leave. And even after the bond was over — it was for twelve months — he kept coming here and doing voluntary work. Right up to the time he was arrested for this murder and refused bail, he'd been coming here most days, helping on the trucks, going out and helping people move from place to place, picking up clothes, bringing in furniture — and doing it very successfully and reliably. This Foundation is very much a place of belonging for him, it's a place where he's trusted and is able to trust us.

'But when he's away from here, he still craves acceptance. He found it, I suppose, in some form when he was taken in by the drug dealers involved in the murder. They have a Housing Commission house at Mount Druitt and sometimes let him sleep there, so that he'd be around when they were selling their dope. They let him smoke it. He believed he was simply enjoying acceptance. They were just another bunch of bastards who exploited his appearance and compliant nature.'

Arabella had been making notes in her folder. 'Has he spoken to you about the murder?'

'Not really. I've been out to Long Bay a few times to see him, but Legal Aid told him not to talk about his case, so he won't, not even with me. He's actually pretty happy there. He's been there about nine months now, and the prison officers tell me he's been respectful, well-behaved and co-operative. They've had him working in the kitchen, which he loves. The crims push him around, of course, and dictate to him, and he thinks they're authority figures.'

There wasn't much more Father Monaghan could tell them, so they all went across the road for a cup of very bad coffee. Arabella made noises to the priest about perhaps giving character evidence for Sherry at his trial. Harry looked doubtful about that, but said nothing. Arabella wrote down the priest's mobile number to pass on to Surrey.

In the LandCruiser on the way back to town, Arabella told Harry that she'd been to a talk by a visiting American criminal trial lawyer the previous week in the Bar Association common room.

'Many people there?'

'Very few. Crime remains unfashionable in Phillip Street, and the Legal Aid practitioners were too lazy to come all the way up town.'

'It would have had to be Melvin Belli or F Lee Bailey to get me there,' said Harry.

'I believe Belli's dead, and this man was very much alive. I spoke to him afterwards, and he asked me out to dinner.'

No reaction from Harry.

'I thought the only interesting thing he had to say was about constructing a case theory.'

'What's a case theory?'

'To listen to him, you can't run a trial without one. It's the explanatory hypothesis you're going to put to the jury that will be the central point of your argument for an acquittal. But it's got to be supportable on the evidence.'

'What — like They Got the Wrong Man? Bit bloody obvious, surely.'

'No, not as simple as that — you know the Yanks. Much more psychobabble. Lots of jargon. But it got me thinking, all the same, that every case has to have an explanation for the jury. If he's really innocent, why did they charge him?'

'Criminal advocacy 101. If they'd asked me to give the talk, my thesis would have been that every accused has to have an enemy, not an explanation.'

'In what sense?'

'In the sense that in the old days, before the coppers had to tape-record everything the punter said and were free to verbal and fabricate evidence to their hearts' content, the enemy was always the detective sergeant masterminding the fit-up.'

'And now that they can't do that?'

'Oh, they can still do it. And they do. It's just that it's much harder with all the protocols they're bound to follow, and the detectives aren't as cleverly evil as they used to be. Paradoxical as it may seem, the better educated coppers of the twenty-first century haven't the wit or cunning of the previous generations. Perhaps they're still looking over their shoulders at the report of the Royal Commission into police corruption, but I wouldn't bet on it. Memories are short.'

'So if it isn't the bent detectives, the alternative enemies are whom?'

'Who. The key witness, in many cases. The complainant, the prosecutrix, the victim. The forensic experts. The prosecutor himself, if necessary.'

'And, in Harry Curry's experience, the judge?'

'Almost always the judge. Goes without saying. They're such soft targets, sitting up there in fancy dress, pretending they don't know what a tweet is. The point is that the jury has to be able to decide the case on the basis of an acceptance or rejection of the accused's enemy. If you can get them to hate a judge who's obviously trying to manipulate a conviction, they'll acquit. Same with the prosecutor, or any star witness you can discredit or, more importantly, appear to discredit.'

'What you're really saying is that you make yourself the issue. The jury have to go with you, or convict your client.'

'That's about the size of it.'

'But most barristers haven't the confidence to stand between their clients and the forces of authority. Or the courage.'

'True, but that's our role, isn't it? Or that's how I see it.'

'And Tony Sherry? Who's his enemy?'

'Dunno yet. He's given a long ERISP, Dave says, and he's confessed to bashing the man's brains out with an iron bar before his mates took the body out on the Putty Road to where they dumped it and set it alight. Not much to play with on the facts, Bella.'

'So you're saying that I'm going to have to invent an enemy?'

'I'm saying that in many ways, you're a most inventive person.'

'Are you trying to make me blush?'

With the city skyline looming larger on the horizon, Harry concentrated on changing lanes as they entered the tunnel under the airport runway. They rode in silence until the LandCruiser emerged beside the airport ponds, where Arabella could see black swans dipping their heads under the water.

'The trouble with evidence in criminal trials, it's always seemed to me,' she said, adjusting her sun visor, 'is that it's all recounted so artificially and unrealistically in the courtroom: witnesses stumble through their poor recollections in slow motion, and they get most of it wrong; then the Crown subjects everything to the most favourable construction — favourable to conviction, I mean — by such microscopic analysis as to make it unrecognisable; following that, the defence spends hours freezing the frame on the action, trying to find equivocation in … I don't know — uncertainty; and finally, the judge sums it all up, holding his own magnifying glass over tiny fragments of the truth and ignoring the evidence that won't serve his purpose. It's all so unreal, and nothing like human events.'

'Which are usually impulsive, momentary and indescribable,' Harry smiled.

'Exactly.'

'Do you think the system works, Harry?'

'Traditionally, this is the point at which lawyers say, "No, but it's the best system anyone has yet come up with."'

'Is that what you think?'

'No. Juries tend to vote for the personality they like best — or perhaps dislike least — at the end of the trial: the accused, the wife of the victim, the kind judge.'

'Or counsel.'

'Sometimes. It's a sort of reverse beauty contest.' They had reached Phillip Street, and Harry stopped the car in the loading zone outside the Leagues' Club, earning the glare of the doorman. 'In the end, though, the only thing that will convict your client is the evidence. That's always the real enemy — the evidence.'

Arabella gathered her bag from the back seat. She leaned over and kissed Harry on the cheek before leaving the car. 'You've still got your key. I'll be home by eight. I just have to plead a defence and a set of particulars.' Harry knew those processes would take a lot longer than Arabella was allowing, and that he'd be asleep before she returned. He was tempted to observe that there were no written pleadings to struggle over in crime, and neither did criminal trial preliminaries drag out for years with interminable and largely pointless conflicts over arcane interlocutory processes, but thought better of it.

At Arabella's insistence, Harry explained to her his trial preparation technique of deconstructing the police brief to expose the essential narrative of the prosecution case. 'What I do is this,' he said, 'although it might not suit you. We all have to work out for ourselves the best way of doing it — but come and look over my shoulder.' He was at his laptop, and got up an old file to demonstrate with the name Ibrahim. 'I start a new file in the computer, head it with the name of the client, and then I pick up the first statement in the bundle of police evidence — I don't even try at this point to put the evidence in any order — and I summarise it. Then the second item. And so on. The trick is to cut it back hard, and put in only the relevant stuff, only as much detail as is absolutely necessary and relevant to the elements of the offence. Once I've summarised the evidence, I shuffle it into chronological order. When I've finished, what I've got is not really the story of the crime, but the factual hypothesis of guilt produced from the police investigation, in its proper timeline. Once you've got that, you look for the holes in it — identify the inadmissible evidence, the stuff you can keep out, or that you can argue should be excluded in the court's discretion. What you're really looking for is having evidence thrown out so that there'll be a failure by the Crown to prove some essential element. And you look for the loopholes.'

Following Harry's instructions, Arabella worked up a file for Tony Sherry in her own computer.

DPP v Sherry

<u>27 January</u>

    21 Hawea St, Mt Druitt. Gold arrives at house
about midday. Mitchell, Davis and Sherry inside. Drugs
(I/hemp). Gold goes home for tea at 6pm, returns 7.30pm.
All watching TV.

    c.10pm Sherry answers front door to Blake ('Spider').
Blake (drunk) asks Mitchell for credit, told 'I don't sell
any more. Ask Tony (i.e. Sherry).' Sherry also refuses.
Blake, angry, says, 'I've got something for you.' Leaves.
Group watch TV again, smoke cones.

c.12.30am Blake at home, continues drinking with friends. Furious mood. Says he'll 'bash that fat turd'. Asks friends to help, refused. Takes steel gate peg 40cm long, L-shaped. Friends drive Blake to Hawea St in his panel van, leave him.

1am Blake at front door, calls, 'I've got the $20.' Let in by Sherry. Gate peg hidden behind Blake's back. Moves as if to strike Sherry from behind. Gold leaves house, runs across road. Sees Davis jump back fence, ride away on bike. Hears shouts from house: 'Don't hit me, don't hit me' and thuds like table falling over. Sees Sherry shut front door, then silence. Gold watches from nature strip. 10 mins later Davis arrives in brown Falcon. Gold leaves area on foot, sees nothing further.

Neighbours also hear screaming. (See witness statements for detail.) 'I've had enough. Leave me alone.' 'Stop hitting me.' 'Help me.' 'You'll kill me.' 'Frank, I'm sorry. I won't tell anybody.' Thumping noises. Crashing sound. Neighbour Sherman says screaming followed by 5 − 10 mins silence. Brown Falcon arrives, backs up drive and boot left open. Falcon leaves 10 mins later.

3.45am Motorist travelling from Windsor to Singleton passing Wheeny Creek bridge sees 'log' burning near gravel stockpile on N side of road.

11am Second motorist stops to investigate. Finds burnt body of deceased Blake.

Body identified by distinctive tattoos.

DSC Hughes observes body: heavily burnt; face gagged; contained in burnt sleeping bag; wrists bound. Nearby

finds burnt 5-litre petrol can. Resting beside body —
galvanised steel gate peg.

Initial forensic opinion: body incinerated incompletely
with petrol. Tyre marks in gravel surface leading to body
location yield no tread pattern.

29 January
PM examination report Glebe morgue: multiple severe
lacerations to scalp consistent with blows from the metal
bar (gate peg) found with body. Haemorrhaging below
dura mater, brain swollen. Extensive facial fractures
incl. eye sockets, jaw, teeth. Blood in airways. No soot
in airways, no raised CO level in blood (i.e. indicates not
alive when incinerated). Blood/alcohol 0.268.

Cause of death: head and facial injuries (most likely),
possibly still alive at incineration and heat of petrol-
accelerated fire terminated residual respiration before
soot or CO inhaled. Head trauma *possibly* inflicted at two
locations (Mt Druitt and Wheeny Creek).

Harry read through the page and a half on the screen of
Arabella's laptop, sitting at the dining table at Elizabeth Bay.
They were finishing breakfast, and preparing to travel to Long
Bay to meet Surrey and have their first conference with Tony
Sherry.

'It's good as far as it goes, but a bit thin,' Harry said. 'I see that
you haven't summarised his admissions to the detectives.'

'I wasn't sure how to incorporate those,' Arabella said. 'He
shifts ground so much. Huge self-contradictions.'

'You'd better take me through them.'

Arabella didn't need to read anything. 'Well, the first version he gave was six days later when they took him to Mount Druitt police station. This was the ERISP, all on videotape. He told them that a man, and he was referring to Blake, came to Mitchell's house to buy drugs. He told them Blake came there twice, and the second time he pushed his way in and said to Tony something like, "I've got something for you," then hit Tony with an iron bar and knocked him cold. Tony says he blacked out for seven to ten minutes. He claimed he didn't hit the man when he came to, but said he put his hands around his throat. In that first interview, he claimed he was the only one in the house at the time. He said Blake left the house the second time after they had a scuffle and Mitchell came back later from the service station with a bottle of drink. He said there was no blood in the house. Despite all that, they then charged him with the murder of Blake and locked him up. So they didn't give credit to anything he said.'

Harry dragged the brief across the table and started leafing through it. 'When's the next interview?'

'That same afternoon. Sergeant Hughes claims he saw Tony sitting in the dock having been charged and waiting for Legal Aid, mumbling to himself and whimpering. Tony started to cry when Hughes spoke to him, and said he didn't want to go to jail for something he didn't do. Hughes asked if he wanted to talk about it some more, and took him upstairs to the detectives' office. He was cautioned and gave the second interview but this time there was no recording. At that stage, he was still saying that he didn't kill Blake, it must have been Mitchell and Davis, because he left the house after Blake hit him with the iron bar, and walked home to the chicken shed.

'Then they let Tony have a toilet break, and when he came back it was a whole new story. This time, the third version he gave, he admitted that he killed Blake. The police still didn't record it — just made notebook entries. They have Tony saying, "I just went crazy, but Mitchell and Davis were there, and they got rid of the body." He said they borrowed the Falcon, and he had nothing to do with that. Didn't get into the car. Then he told the police he wanted to see Father Monaghan.

'Monaghan came, and Tony agreed to do another recorded interview with him there.' Harry was still leafing through the papers. 'Can you find the relevant bit of that transcript for me?'

Arabella took back her folder and turned pages before finding what Harry wanted. She handed it to him, her finger marking a long passage.

Q37: Can you now tell me, in your own words, the circumstances surrounding the death of Peter Blake on that night?

A: Yes, I can. He came to the house the first time and said he wanted to get on, and um, they said there was no credit and he got stroppy about it, and he was drinkin' and then he left, and then he, sorry, and then he said, he argued and anticipated, and then he finally said no, and he left. About fifteen minutes afterwards he came back, right, and he barged in the door, and he said I've got somethin' for youse. Then he pulled out this fucken iron bar and clocked me with it twice. He said I'm gonna kill you. And then I fell to the ground and he hit me with it a second time and then I come to and I overpowered him, and that's when it started. And then after that I blanked out, I couldn't remember, and then we were hittin' 'im, and Mitchell and the other guy — Davis? were kickin' 'im in the head and in the gut and I was hittin' 'im with the iron bar he used on me, I wasn't, I wasn't aware of what I was doin' at the time, I was, I was awake but I like, just blacked out. Then they, it went on for a while, and Mitchell asked the other bloke to go and buy some petrol. When he come back with the car, Mitchell said we have to kill him and then we gagged him and wrapped him up in blankets and sheets and a sleeping bag and I tied his hands and we put him in the boot, and they drove him to Bilpin, or near there, said they were gonna dump him. I didn't know they were gonna burn him. And after that, I stayed and cleaned up some of the mess and then they come back about four o'clock in the morning, not the precise time, I'm not sure, it would have been about that time. Then they started helpin' me clean up the mess and we had some more cones, then I stayed there that morning. I didn't buy any petrol or drive any car or take anybody out past Windsor. The next day when it was on the news Mitchell said the bikies are at it again, they've took a body to Putty and burnt it.

Harry looked up. 'And the defences are?'

Arabella stood, took her jacket from the back of a dining chair and put it on. 'Self-defence.'

'Self-defence isn't going to work, is it? Not given Sherry's own version. Not with the victim defenceless on the floor and the three of them giving it to him, your client with the aid of the iron bar.'

'But it shrieks automatism, doesn't it? What about with evidence of his very limited IQ? I want David to organise a psychologist to give an opinion on Tony's level of intellectual functioning. Deaf, illiterate. We should have some tests done.'

Harry shook his head slowly. 'What's the defence if it isn't self-defence?'

'I'm not writing that off yet. Anyway, if that doesn't work, diminished responsibility and/or provocation.'

'Not guilty of murder, but guilty of manslaughter, in other words?'

'Exactly.'

Harry started to tie his tie. 'We'd better get out to the jail and meet Lennie. He'll want to know about the rabbits.'

'Lennie? His name's Tony. And what rabbits?'

'You haven't read *Of Mice and Men*? This bloke's a Lennie, but he never had a George. Which, I suppose, might just make you his protector.'

'Which would entail?'

'A plea bargain … you're going to have to see if you can talk them into manslaughter.'

'What?' Arabella laughed, 'and cut myself out of the largesse of two weeks on Legal Aid at junior counsel's daily rates, no allowance for reading time or conferences?'

'Still,' Harry said, 'they pay for jail visits. Makes it all worthwhile.'

They took the marble-and-chrome lift down five floors from Arabella's apartment and walked out onto Billyard Avenue, where the LandCruiser was standing, out of its element. Overnight rain had streaked the Towamba Road dust that still clung to its flanks. After struggling to get the engine started ('It's used to fresh air, not this Elizabeth Bay miasma of cocaine particles'), Harry bullocked his way up through the Cross and pointed the big diesel-powered vehicle towards Long Bay. As they bowled along, Arabella told him about the most recent phone call from her mother, asking when she was coming home. As they slowed to pick their way through the early shopping traffic at Maroubra, Arabella's BlackBerry rang. She looked at the screen. 'It's David.' She answered and listened to him for a minute, finally responding, 'Well, we'll meet you at the gate,' before switching off.

She turned to Harry. 'David says that the prison officers are on a go-slow, and no legal visits will be allowed this morning.'

'What? This is the only chance we're going to get for a conference. We'll see about that.' With the jail walls in sight, Harry sped up. He always enjoyed a confrontation with officialdom. 'The turnkeys are all Nazis out here,' he told Arabella only half jokingly. 'Well, all Germans ... and some Indians.' That brought a sharp look from Arabella. 'They are! You'll see.'

Harry parked, and he and Arabella carried their papers across to the gatehouse with its firmly lowered boomgates, where David Surrey was waiting. He took them to one side, preventing Harry from shirt-fronting the man behind the barrier. 'Bloody-mindedness gone mad. The excuse is that there's a security scare on. I told them I've come all the way from Goulburn.'

Arabella approached the gatehouse window and spoke to someone behind the grill. Then, without looking back at her companions, she waited for the boomgate to be raised and entered the building. Harry and Surrey could see her in conversation with two uniformed prison officers, one in a turban. Phone calls were being made. It was almost fifteen minutes before Arabella came out, a slight smile on her lips.

'Special arrangements have been made. We can see him at the hospital.'

'Is he sick?'

'No, but that's where they've agreed to take him. As David said, there are no legal visits, so it's being recorded as a medical.'

Harry laughed. 'How have you wangled this?'

'As you so unkindly said, there are lots of Indians in there.'

They were delayed a further forty minutes before they got inside the prison hospital, forced to stand in a cold breeze with other lawyers displaying even less patience and forbearance than they were. It seemed to Harry, as he smoked his third cigarette, that the prison officers could hardly conceal their delight in frustrating the high-and-mighty legal profession in their suits and designer spectacles, many of them engaged in testy conversations on their iPhones. Even when they were finally escorted into the hospital, to the chagrin of those left outside, Tony Sherry's legal advisors were compelled to leave their papers, and Harry his cigarettes, at the gatehouse.

Sitting alone on a plastic chair in the hospital's waiting room was a mountain of a man. 'There he is,' Arabella said, unnecessarily. Tony Sherry would have made any Tongan prop forward look puny. He was even bigger than Arabella remembered from their brief association four years earlier, and Harry paused in momentary disbelief before resuming his approach. Only Surrey was undaunted, and he set about dragging three chairs over to where his new client was perching. The chair was far too small for him.

With the introductions taken care of — Sherry having lurched to his feet for the niceties — the four settled down to talk. Sherry's features were buried deeply in the fat of his dark-skinned face, and his mouth was almost comically small. Not much could be seen of his eyes.

'Before we get into any detail,' Arabella began, 'do you understand, Tony, what's going on with your case?'

'Not really, miss.'

Surrey decided to take charge. 'Ms Engineer's your barrister for the murder trial, Tony. You asked for her. Mr Curry's a senior barrister, and he's advising us about the matter. I'm your solicitor. Did Legal Aid tell you that I'd be coming today?'

'I got a letter, but I sort of didn't get round to reading it. I can't read very well. Sorry.'

'Doesn't matter, mate. We're here anyway.' Surrey smiled at him. 'The idea of today is that Ms Engineer and Mr Curry need to talk to you about what's going to happen in court, what evidence you might have to give, and what they need to know from you about everything that happened with Spider and the other blokes. Mitchell and Davis and Gold.'

Sherry picked his nose with some success. 'I have to go in to lunch in half an hour. I work in the kitchen, and we have to serve out.'

Harry nodded. 'You like working in the kitchen, do you, Tony?'

'Yeah. Do you reckon I can stay there after the trial's over?'

'That rather depends on the outcome of the trial,' Arabella said, but Harry took little notice.

'Probably, Tony. Depends on your classification.'

'Yeah, I know. They told me about that.'

'Who did?' Arabella asked.

'The other blokes. They know all that stuff. Classification and that.'

'This is all a bit defeatist, isn't it, Harry?' Arabella said unhappily.

'If you say so, Bella. I think you'll find Tony doesn't mind it here. It's a lot better than a chicken shed, and the company's much more congenial.'

What followed was an interview relay with each of the lawyers trying to get some assistance from Tony, but it was largely a waste of their time, and after ten minutes the men desisted and sat back. Arabella kept at it, but the big baffled man, when pressed, went from denying everything, including even having been at the house, to ambiguous but troubling references betraying intimate knowledge of the burning of the body. What he said struck Arabella as far more incriminating than the material available to the DPP's officers.

It seemed to Harry that Arabella was upset that she couldn't get the mostly uncomprehending client to deal with the trial issues in any way that assisted his defenders. Tony was treating the trial as beside the point, and she couldn't get him to focus on it.

Harry placed his hand on her forearm and spoke quietly. 'I think you'll find, Bella, that conventional ideas of criminal justice and reasonable doubt and the technicalities of sentencing law are irrelevant to Tony. I'll show you what I mean.' He turned to Sherry.

'What sort of cell have they got you in, Tony?'

'There's two of us. Khalid's a nice bloke. Drugs, and he thinks he's up for a five. Prays a lot, but.'

'Clean clothes?'

'Me? Yeah — every three days. Underpants clean every day.'

'Work okay, is it?'

'I like it in the kitchen. You think they'll keep me there? We get lots of extras. Biscuits. And ice cream on the weekend. As much as we like.'

'Nobody bothers you?'

'No, nobody. I've got friends. The screws are all right, a bit strict, but all right. We watch TV. We get McDonald's when they go on strike. I think we're having it tonight.' He looked pleased about that.

A bell rang somewhere and Tony simply heaved his bulk up off the chair and left, heading for his kitchen duties. Prison routine. No farewells, no handshakes, no discourtesy intended. The lawyers put their seats back where they came from, and negotiated the series of gates and the custodial officers' passive aggression all the way back to the car park. There wasn't much to say, and Surrey climbed into his Falcon to return to Goulburn, promising to keep in touch.

As Harry unlocked the LandCruiser, he spoke to Arabella across the bonnet. 'You see what I mean? Sense of belonging, as Father Monaghan was saying. It's a bloody sight better life behind these walls than he had in the chicken shed and being a minder for the nasty bastards with the dope business.'

She said nothing until she was in the car and Harry was turning the key in the ignition. 'You can't be serious. What about his liberty? That counts for nothing, Harry?' Arabella was ready for a fight.

'Liberty to do what? Liberty for what bloody purpose? What has liberty ever given him except being ridiculed, exploited and victimised? Prison's a better life for your bloke, bars and all. He gets medical attention — maybe not the best in the world but immeasurably better than he ever had before; he gets fed three meals a day; he has a bed and a blanket and TV and a cellmate to talk to. There's a routine he can understand and conform to. Maybe a psychologist will take an interest in him after he's sentenced. His life is going to be organised for him by people who, mostly, bear him no malice. This'll keep him on an even keel for ten years or whatever he winds up getting. Maybe he'll come out of here able to read and write.'

She was shaking her head. Harry stopped in traffic and glanced at her. 'Look, Bella, hard as it is to accept, Tony's a person whose life in prison is vastly superior to freedom, or what passes for freedom for a bloke like him.'

Arabella thought about that as Harry drove to the Maroubra shops, where they parked and had a sandwich in a café. People at the other tables were speaking French. 'Something of an enclave out here,' Harry explained. 'They've even taken over the local school as a *lycee*.'

'Do I detect the suggestion of pride in your voice?'

'I'm trying to impress the urbane Englishwoman with our cosmopolitan sophistication.'

'That's all right, Harry. I'm from North London.'

Finishing her coffee, and feeling there was nothing more to be usefully said about the murder, she finally brought up the subject she'd been avoiding, unsure of how to deal with it.

'I didn't just hear from my mother — I've had an email from my sister. Diana. There's a fellow we know from London, a solicitor, over here for a visit.'

'To visit you, I assume?'

She paused. 'Yes.' She paused again. 'View matrimony.'

'What?'

'That's what the adverts say. You know: man, such-and-such age, such-and-such occupation, seeks woman, GSOH, VM.' Harry looked blank. 'Good sense of humour, view matrimony.'

'Is the GSOH an attribute of the advertiser, or a prerequisite for the prospective wife?'

'The latter, I assume.'

'Do you have to tell him a joke to prove it?' Harry signalled for the bill by writing in the air when a waitress looked in their direction.

'I would imagine one has to laugh at *his* jokes. That'd prove it.'

The bill arrived and Harry looked at it, then dug twenty dollars out of his wallet and stood up. 'This isn't exactly something that just came out of the blue, I assume?'

Arabella picked up her bag from beside her chair. 'No, not exactly.'

Nothing was said as they walked to the car. Underway once more, Harry said, 'You are not obliged to answer any questions. You have a right to silence.'

'None of this is my idea, Harry. Diana emailed me and said that Sanjay — his parents are friends of my parents and he's always been a bit keen about me — was on his way to Sydney via the Great Barrier Reef and Ayers Rock. A budget holiday package. He's pretty tight with his money, as I recall. Anyway, he was married-with-children, but I gather that ended in tears not very long ago. According to Diana, he can't have had much luck in London, so he decided to have a holiday here and look me up.'

'Has he made contact?'

'We haven't actually spoken, as yet. A string of texts from Queensland. I told you he was cheap.'

'Is he in Sydney now? You're going to have to ask him round, you know.'

'He arrives this afternoon. I think he was looking for a bed somewhere not a million miles from Elizabeth Bay, but that hasn't been offered. I'm sure his package includes a budget hotel in the Haymarket.'

Harry smiled. A red light stopped him at the pedestrian crossing outside the university at Kensington, and scores of students poured across to the bus stop. 'Look at all the budding lawyers,' he said.

'They look more like IT engineers to me,' Arabella said. 'Not a white face among them.'

'Is that a politically approved remark?'

'What's wrong with it? The Indians all work as prison guards, as you pointed out, or in petrol stations and convenience stores, and I'm merely observing that the South-East Asians are all technogeeks.'

The light turned green and Harry drove off, deliberately scattering a couple of stragglers. He grunted. 'I thought I was supposed to be the intolerant one.'

'You are, Harry. But that doesn't give you a monopoly in that area.' Arabella turned on the radio, but got only static. 'What's wrong with this?'

'It's tuned to the ABC station in Bega.'

'Of course it is. Silly of me.' Arabella jabbed the button and silenced the radio. 'So? Are you committed to the hillbilly life? Had enough time to make up your mind about your professional future?'

'Don't change the subject, Bella.'

'What was the subject?'

'Sanjay who needs a bed.' Harry swung out to avoid a taxi that had suddenly halted in Anzac Parade to pick up a passenger outside Sydney Girls High and leaned on his horn as the LandCruiser passed the driver's door.

Arabella reached across and put her hand on Harry's cheek. 'Don't worry, you big goose. You're still sleeping with me tonight.'

'That's all right, then. Should we invite him out for dinner?'

Arabella took out her BlackBerry and looked at the screen. 'I already have. I don't think you should come this time, Harry.'

'My presence might be perceived as a challenge. Is that what you mean?'

'As intimidating.' She sent an SMS, switched off her BlackBerry, gathered her bag and brief from the floor of the car and put them on her lap.

Harry watched, but had to return his attention to the traffic as they headed down a crowded Oxford Street to turn right beside the park at Whitlam Square.

'When you said I shouldn't come *this* time, doesn't that imply that there will be at least one other such occasion?'

'He's in Sydney for four days and three nights, Harry. He knows no one else here, so I have to show him around a bit. My family would expect it. God knows what Sanjay expects from me, but the first thing I'm going to tell him about is you.'

Harry stopped in the construction zone on Macquarie Street adjacent to the Supreme Court building. 'Yes, but exactly *what* will you tell him about me?'

Arabella opened her door and got out. 'Please, Harry, Sanjay is not significant, and you needn't make this any harder than it has to be. I'll see if I can organise something for us all to do at the weekend, and you two can meet then.'

'Does he like rugby? There's a Tahs game on Friday. We could all go.'

'I'll ask.' And she shut the door. Harry sat in the stationary car until a hard-hatted worker emerged from the building site and waved him on his way. He hadn't thought how he was going to spend the afternoon, so he drove north in Macquarie Street, considering his options, until he turned at the Conservatorium and continued over the Harbour Bridge and all the way up the Pacific Highway to his father's Upper North Shore retirement facility, arriving there shortly before three o'clock. He parked and went inside, asking at the front desk whether his father was in his room.

'No, Mr Curry. He's gone on the outing to Bobbin Head,' the big Islander male nurse told him.

Harry found that hard to believe. 'Really? Is this one of his good days?'

The man grinned. 'Mr Curry wouldn't go in the bus if he was having a good day,' he said. 'But if he's away with the fairies, he doesn't mind. Same with the singalongs.'

'You're not going to tell me that he joins in, that he sings? "Beautiful Dreamer", and all that?'

A broad smile. 'He certainly does. He seems to like it.'

Harry turned to go, but thought to ask whether his father was dressed for an outing.

'We put on his Burberry jacket before they went, and a tweed cap. But the bus is heated, Mr Curry, and they don't get out. The staff get them ice creams, and then they come back.'

Harry thanked him, exchanged a few words about an impending rugby match, and left the building. He sat in the LandCruiser and tried to picture Wallace Curry QC in a tweed cap, contentedly eating an ice-cream cone in a mini-bus crammed with ten or twelve other geriatrics, parked next to a lavatory block. He just couldn't picture it. He decided to go back into the nursing home and leave a note for his father. He borrowed a pad and pencil and sat in the reception area, neatly printing a reminder to the old man that he was now living on the far South Coast and couldn't get to Sydney as much as he'd like, but would call in again for a cup of tea and a talk as soon as work permitted. Harry put the note in an envelope and asked that it be handed to the old man when he got back. Maybe he'll read it during one of his lucid intervals, he thought.

As he started the engine and clipped his seat belt, he wondered if he'd ever bring Arabella to meet his father. And then he thought about Arabella and Sanjay, all the way back to Elizabeth Bay. Harry didn't know if his feelings amounted to jealousy, because he'd never known that emotion, but he rather suspected they did. He tried to be rational about it, to be fair. Grown up. Arabella might be carving out a busy commercial practice, and positioning herself for a judicial appointment after an appropriate interval, but didn't they — women — all want hearth and home? Children? There had been a time when Harry wanted all that, too … wanted to stand on the touchline at Shore's playing fields at Northbridge, watching his sons scrumming down in the second row (because they'd be big, like him, and not too fast), or applauding as they came back to the rowing shed pontoon in the school eight, everyone grinning because they'd just won the Riverview Gold Cup by three lengths. Daughters hadn't figured in those distant dreams. Dreams as distant as his first years at uni, when he had a girlfriend and an old VW.

Billyard Avenue was all parked out, and Harry circled several times before finding a space a long way from Arabella's building, and then only when a builder's van pulled out. As he walked to the flat, a thin man in a denim jacket and beanie tried to sell him drugs. 'Fuck off,' Harry told him. 'I'm a detective.' The man ran away, surprisingly fast.

Inside the flat, Harry changed out of his suit into football shorts and a sloppy joe. He put on Classic FM and made a plunger of coffee. He drank the coffee leaning over the balcony rail, watching a workboat take something off one of the yachts moored in the bay. He looked frequently at his watch, but it seemed stuck at five o'clock.

At seven o'clock, just as Harry was about to turn on the TV to watch the news, the phone rang. It was Arabella. 'I've just met Sanjay at his hotel, and we're going across to Dixon Street to have a quick dinner.'

'He's staying down there, is he?'

'Like I said, a hotel in the Haymarket.'

'See you later, then. Don't drink too much.'

'Okay.'

Harry turned on the news, having missed the headlines and the first story. No better than Channel Nine, he told himself as he watched a report on what the ABC was pleased to call 'another Middle Eastern gangland shooting', this one at Greenacre. He recognised the former detective, now promoted and with pips on his shoulders, expressing his frustration at the taciturnity of the many witnesses to the killing, not least the family of the victim. He was an officer Harry had cross-examined with some vigour on more than one occasion, and had no time for. 'You couldn't care less,' Harry told the man on screen, 'as long as it's only crooks killing each other.' Harry didn't care much either. There probably wouldn't be a brief in it for him. The Lebanese lawyers would have it sewn up.

The rest of the bulletin passed without arousing much interest. The sports reporter was concerned that the Waratahs' fullback was in doubt for Friday night's game with a corked thigh, which elicited a grunt from Harry and made him think again about Arabella and Sanjay and the outing he'd selfishly suggested. He took more interest in the weather map for the far South Coast than he had for anything else in the news, noting the temperatures and conditions for Bega and Merimbula, and killed the set before 7.30 took its turn on the screen. He crossed to the phone to call David Surrey in Goulburn, but for once the solicitor had gone home in time for dinner. No one to talk to, nothing to do. Arabella had a stack of *New Statesman*s on the coffee table, having diverted her subscription to Sydney five years ago to keep in touch with what passed for left-liberal thought in England, but Harry leafed through the last few editions without finding anything he wanted to know more about. The weatherman had promised a fine night in town, so Harry headed out for the Cross and their usual restaurant without an umbrella. A heavy shower soaked him before he got to the El Alamein fountain, putting him in a black mood and forcing him to drink two more glasses of house red than he had intended. He left a big tip because he'd been surly to the waiter, not because he enjoyed the lasagne. He hadn't.

He was in bed, reading, when Arabella came home. 'How'd it go?'

'I'd forgotten what a funny man he is,' she said. 'It was nice. Much better than I'd expected.'

'Lots of do-you-remember?'

'Lots.'

Harry grunted uh-huh, thought so, and went back to his book, but wasn't taking in a word of the long passage on the page in front of him. He didn't want to hear any more about the nice, funny family friend from London. Arabella could tell as much, and said very little before joining him in bed. They made love with the light still on, but Arabella's eyes were closed and Harry wondered who she was thinking of. That made him hate himself.

Out at Long Bay, Tony Sherry was lying on his side in his bunk, trying to engage his cellmate in conversation on the subject of quarter-pounders. 'Shut the fuck up, you stupid bag of shit,' his cellmate said, encouragingly.

Harry decided to stay up in Sydney for the whole weekend, wanting to remain until Sanjay was safely on his flight back to London. Arabella was well aware of his motive, and mildly encouraged by it. Sanjay hadn't wanted to go to the rugby match, whether or not the Waratahs were at full strength. He told Harry, when he came to Arabella's for a drink before dinner on the Friday evening, that he followed QPR because he lived at Acton. Harry nodded as if he understood, but he didn't. Arabella was quietly amused by the bull elephants bumping their tusks against each other, and ushered them out to dinner at Le Pelican near Taylor Square. Harry had booked that restaurant because its Basque cuisine bore no resemblance to Indian. Over the meal, Harry politely asked Sanjay about his work as a solicitor, but lost interest quite quickly when the answer was all about mergers and acquisitions. Arabella and Sanjay then went off on shared memories of London, families, *The Kumars at No. 42*, school, holidays and university, laughing a lot, and Harry became truculent.

'You haven't said much about your children, Sanjay. Live with their mother, do they? That can't be easy for them.'

Sanjay looked embarrassed, and Harry congratulated himself. And they reckon sledging went out with Ian Chappell? The guest tried to change the subject, but the dogged cross-examiner wouldn't let him. 'What are their names, mate? The little one, she's Indira, did you say?'

At first, Arabella was reasonably tolerant of Harry's needling, but when he insistently pressed Sanjay on the subject of the expense of the children's school fees and his access rights, she called a halt. 'If we're going up to the Blue Mountains in the morning, Sanjay, you'd better be getting back to your hotel. It's an early start.'

'First I've heard of it,' Harry said. 'What time are we planning to leave?'

Arabella looked into his eyes and shook her head. 'It's a small guided tour, and Sanjay's already bought the tickets. Two tickets.'

'Sounds exclusive. Literally,' Harry said.

He let Arabella pay the bill, which he knew was mean-spirited of him, and they walked back to Oxford Street to find a taxi. Predictably, the late Friday night footpath around Taylor Square was swarming with excitable and demonstrative persons who, as Harry would have put it had he been asked, bowled from the Paddington end. Sanjay's eyes were out on stalks. 'I suppose you don't get over to Soho much, Sanjay? It's a long way from Acton,' Harry smirked.

Once they had dropped their guest at his hotel and the taxi had aimed itself at Elizabeth Bay, Arabella let her feelings be known. 'I didn't expect you to disappoint me like that, Harry. I thought you were a bigger man than that.'

Fair enough, Harry admitted to himself. 'I'm sorry, Bella.'

'No plea in mitigation, Harry?'

'Nothing to say, your Honour.'

'Surely not. Not nothing.'

'Well, jealousy's something of which I have had no experience, so I don't handle it very well.'

'Maybe you should go back to Burragate tomorrow while I do the tourist thing with Sanjay.'

'What else have you got in mind?'

'Oh, you know: the Opera House, Manly ferry, the zoo. Bondi or Balmoral. The fish markets on Sunday morning for breakfast.'

'You really want me to go home?'

'No, I don't. But even less do I want to start disliking you.' She studied her hands, resting on her bag, as the lights in Darlinghurst Road flicked across them in the back of the moving cab. She looked out her window in a detached way at the three police officers wrestling a bare-chested youth to the footpath and found herself trying to decipher the tattoos on his back, taking no interest in the zeal of the constables.

'Okay, Bella. In the morning?'

'Of course in the morning.'

The lovers, in bed together that night, politely avoided any return to the obvious subject. Harry had shaved, showered, packed and driven off before Arabella woke. Or before she gave any sign of being awake, at any rate. Harry cursed himself for the whole journey, and the LandCruiser radiated an assertiveness that other motorists carefully avoided.

Sanjay and Arabella had a very pleasant time in the mountains on Saturday. They held hands as they strolled around the Katoomba shops, the Three Sisters and Leura, but that was as far as it went. The tour guide had them back in Sydney in time for Arabella to cook spaghetti carbonara that night, but it wasn't a success, and Sanjay was unwise enough to make some passing reference to his ex-wife's culinary skill. Even stupider than Harry to do that, Arabella thought when she phoned for a taxi to take him back to his hotel. On Sunday, she rented a car from an agency in William Street, and took her visitor on a tour of Bondi, Double

Bay, Paddington, Bennelong Point and across the Bridge to Manly. They didn't have time for the zoo, because Sanjay had to be at the airport by five o'clock. She drove him there and after he checked in his bags they sat in a coffee lounge and talked about Harry.

'May I ask if you're going to marry him, Arabella?'

'The subject has never come up.'

'People don't marry in Australia?'

'Oh, they do. Harry doesn't, I think. Well, he never has.'

'And children? You want children, don't you? I'm thinking there must be some obstacle.'

'Five hundred kilometres is a fair obstacle, Sanjay, but it isn't a geographical thing. I think the problem is that we're coming at our careers from diametrically opposed directions. If we're ever to make anything of it, one of us has to relent.'

'Ah, I see. Then it won't be you, will it?'

'Why would you say that, Sanjay?'

'Only because I know you.'

She pushed him on the shoulder and pointed at the screen where 'Go to gate' had started to flash beside his flight number. 'They want you.'

'They're the only ones who do.'

'Self-pity's very unattractive in such an attractive man, Sanjay. Get back on the horse is my advice. Just don't rush your fences.'

'How very English of you to say that, Arabella.' They stood and she walked him to the point of departure. A quick kiss and he was gone.

Harry spent the weekend taking part in the Burragate volunteer bushfire brigade's fuel-reduction burn along the fringes of Mount

Imlay National Park. At smoko, they quizzed the new boy about his work in the criminal justice system.

'Yeah, but how can you defend someone who you know's guilty?'

'I'm not the judge,' Harry tried to explain. 'My function is to represent the client as if I were in his shoes. As if I were him. It's the jury's job to judge him, not mine. It's hard not to have an opinion about guilt, but I try never to do that.'

'Sure, sure. But most of the time, you must know bloody well that they did it.'

'Well, whether they did it is hardly ever the question. It's more often why did they do it.'

'Spoken like a bloody lawyer,' said the brigade captain.

'Don't worry, skipper,' said Harry, 'I'll still represent you when they catch you for all those fires you started, just so's you could put on your yellow suit and go roaring down Towamba Road in the big red truck, with the lights flashing and the siren going, playing the hero.'

Harry's jibe might have amused the volunteers, but not the one at whom it was directed. Another smartarse remark, another enemy created, he admonished himself. Well done.

Still, as the crew was rolling up the hoses, one of the local men approached him and asked if he could come round later to talk about a custody wrangle he was having with his ex-wife. Harry, who would normally have evaded the request, agreed to see him the next morning. I'd better do something to repair the damage, he thought.

Arabella was briefed to appear in the Central Criminal Court at Darlinghurst on Monday morning, to finalise what Justice

Thatcher called 'housekeeping matters' that needed to be cleaned up before the matter of *Regina v Sherry* started a week later. She arrived half an hour before the appointed time and sat outside the court entrance drinking a takeaway coffee and waiting for Surrey. When he hadn't shown by five to ten, she rang him.

'Are you nearly here, David?'

'Nearly where, Arabella? I'm in Goulburn.'

'But Thatcher's got a readiness hearing in five minutes. I'm up here. I thought you'd been told. Sherry's in the cells, and the court officer's been out to tell me he wants to see you.'

'They're not paying me to come up to Sydney for a ten-minute mention, Bella. You'll be right and, anyway, the client doesn't need to see me today. It's not as if you'll have to run a *voir dire* or anything, is it? I mean, there's no preliminary hearing on objectionable evidence, or not to my knowledge, there isn't. Has Harry told you to make any applications?'

'No David, but that's not the point. I'd rather not be hung out to dry like this.'

'By whom? Not me, I can assure you.' He sounded a bit miffed.

'I suppose it's Harry's help that I need, really. I've never had one of these procedures before, and I don't know what they're going to spring on me.' Arabella resented having to mollify her solicitor. Counsel should never appear uninstructed.

There was silence for a while. Arabella calmed down somewhat as she waited for a response. When it came it was an anodyne assurance that from Surrey's perspective the defence case was all ready to go, in terms of witnesses and documentary evidence, and she could be sure the judge was unlikely to grant any favours to a prosecution that had already undertaken that there would be no impediment to a timely start for the hearing. She was just having an attack of cold feet, Surrey said. 'Give me a ring and let me know how we got on, will you?'

Counsel had not been required to robe for the administrative callover, which meant that Arabella's court presence was even more striking than usual — blue-black hair pulled back off her face, subtle makeup, a black Armani suit over a *café au lait* blouse. Very high heels. Justice Thatcher was impressed. The prosecutor was less concerned with the aesthetic attraction of those at the Bar table, which in his case was just as well, than with the question of what he called 'the nature of the tribunal of fact'.

'You mean, do you, Mr Crown, that you're going to apply for a judge-alone trial? At this late stage?'

'Quite so, your Honour. The Director instructs me that he considers the interests of justice and of the community favour dispensing with the jury in this matter, and I do make that application. Subject, of course, to my learned friend's consent.'

Thatcher J knew better than to articulate, at least not in open court, the objections he had to the profoundly different workload a judge-alone trial would impose on him. 'True it is,' he later complained to his associate when she brought his morning tea on a tray with two Monte Carlo biscuits, 'that I don't have to spend all that time directing the jury, and sending them out while I hear arguments and decide points of law that always come up during the trial, no matter what counsel promised today, or cooling my heels while they fight the verdict out in the jury room, but it also means that I've got to spend a couple of days writing an appeal-proof judgment to a tight deadline giving reasons to justify every bloody finding of fact I make, and identifying every relevant scrap of evidence and every adverse credit finding I make against any witness. And even then some bloody equity practitioner who never did a criminal matter in his life, sitting in the Court of Criminal Appeal, God help us, will pick apart whatever I write to give the world the benefit of his coruscating legal intellect.'

'Yes, judge.'

'I only took this job in a moment of weakness, you know. My wife still bitches about the loss in income.'

'I thought she liked being Mrs Justice Thatcher. At Royal Sydney. That's what you said.' Obviously, judge and associate were close.

'Yes, at first. Now she's always on my back about me spending the holidays writing reserved judgments and us never getting to Paris any more.'

'Yes, judge.'

Taken by surprise by the prosecution's application that Tony Sherry should have his fate decided by a judge on his own, with the jury box left vacant, Arabella's own feeling was that she should consent. She reasoned to herself that the emotional responses would be removed from the case — photographs of the fire-blackened corpse would no longer represent an insuperably prejudicial factor, and all the evidence about her client working as a minder for drug dealers, plus his obvious propensity for changing his story, would be much less significant in the decision-making processes of a judge than of any random cross-section of the Sydney community pushed together into a jury box. So, unable to obtain instructions from Surrey or guidance from Harry without requesting an adjournment for that purpose, she committed the defence to a non-jury trial.

*

'Jesus! They sandbagged you!' Harry was struggling not to shout on the phone. 'Why didn't you ask for time to obtain instructions?'

'From a cretin, Harry? Go down to the cells to ask him? Wouldn't my judgment be preferable to his?'

'Everyone knows it isn't your client who decides these issues, Bella: you had to talk to Dave and me before you fell into that trap. And I certainly would have said no.'

'Why? Be fair, Harry. A jury would have hated this fellow the minute they laid eyes on him. One look at him in the dock would be enough to terrify them, and that's without hearing about him telling lies to the police, beating the victim's head in with the iron bar, or seeing the photographs of the body. Plus we have the benefit that Thatcher will have to write a very careful judgment about provocation, which, if it doesn't work for us, you can run an appeal on.'

'What an attractive strategy — waste my time arguing an appeal in front of a court where everyone knows one of them's already written the judgment, and the other two see their job as ridiculing anything they don't like the sound of, whether they understand it or not.'

'And why was it a trap that I fell into, Harry? Why couldn't judge-alone favour the defence?'

'Because if the bloody Crown want it, you don't. They're scared of a sympathetic jury. By definition, it's a trap. And the whole strategy of identifying the enemy simply won't work without a jury.'

'Q.E.D.?'

'Precisely.'

Neither said anything for quite a long time. Harry was sitting outside the Burragate house on the verandah, with the sun descending quickly behind the mountains to his left, no warmth left in it at all. He watched a small group of black wallabies grazing on the other side of the river, raising their heads to check for danger, hopping slowly to a new patch of grass and grazing again. The biggest of them turned its head to watch a rusa deer come out of the tree line. From somewhere deep in the national park a large-calibre rifle crashed a single echoing shot, and the animals fled back into the trees.

'That bastard's shooting again. I got the National Parks out here, but they stood around with their ponytails — they were blokes, I mean — and solemnly told me that they've spoken to him, and he said he's only shooting vermin.'

'Which they accepted without further enquiry?'

'As you say. Bloody useless.'

'Well, what'm I going to do, Harry? Shall I have David put it back in for mention and tell the judge that my instructions have changed, and Tony won't consent — that he wants a jury?'

'No.'

'No, I suppose not. My fault.'

'All you can do is run a bloody good trial, Bella. If you haven't got a jury that you can make fall in love with you, you'll have to settle for his Honour. Shouldn't be all that hard. Billy the Pig used to fancy himself as a bit of a pants man.'

'According to you, Harry, they all do. So your strategy would be not to make an enemy of the judge? I'm not going to flirt with him.'

'Course not. Still, you must never seek to alienate the tribunal of fact — judge, jury or magistrate. Sometimes it happens, but it's never an advisable objective. How could it be?' Harry paused momentarily. 'Well, hardly ever. I can see it as a valid tactic when you know the case is lost, you're on a hiding to nothing, and you want to push the judge way over the top and make him vulnerable to appeal. Then it could happen.'

Arabella laughed. 'A bit Machiavellian for me, Harry, although I wouldn't put it past you.'

'It may have happened on rare occasions. Meant I couldn't do the appeals, of course, which suited me.'

'Why wouldn't you want to see your own matters through?'

'Because apart from the waste of time, the appellate judges love to criticise counsel as a way of saving the unwise judge's face. So you get someone else to appear, and he just wrings his hands like Uriah Heep over all the regrettable bits, and they eventually have to bite the bullet and order a new trial, or reduce the sentence, or whatever, however much they dislike doing it.'

'"He", Harry? I understand they let women appear in the superior courts these days.'

'If they do, it's most unwise of them. Tony Sherry can testify to that.'

'Next time I see you, I intend to introduce your private parts to a cheese grater.'

Harry laughed and drank from the beer he had fetched from the fridge while they spoke.

'Cool here today.'

'But you're sitting outside. I can hear the birds.'

'Not for much longer. It's getting dark.' A pause, during which Arabella could definitely hear kookaburras. 'You ready to go?'

'As I'll ever be.'

'Then you could come down here for a bit.'

'I'm not that ready, Harry.'

*

Regina v Sherry progressed unspectacularly through its first week. For the most part, the hearing was low-key, unemotional, matter-of-fact. Horrible in its particulars, but a quotidian murder involving persons who were of little interest or value to the rest of the community. Justice Thatcher watched carefully the video recordings of the accused's police interviews, marked up the transcripts with coloured highlighters (red for incriminating factors, green for exculpatory), and duly noted the important parts of the police witnesses' oral evidence. He heard from the DPP's pathologist, and watched Arabella try to make a case with her cross-examination of the expert to the effect that it was possible the cause of death was not the head injuries, but the immolation — for which Sherry could not be proved responsible in any degree, because there was no evidence that he even attended that event.

A few days into the trial, Arabella found herself relatively comfortable about not having to persuade a jury. The case felt more like one of her civil matters, in which advocacy wasn't the crucial factor. As Harry suspected, the judge found Arabella attractive, and sought in some degree to ingratiate himself with her.

'Let me give you some indication of my preliminary view on this point, Ms Engineer,' he said, 'because it may be useful to you and the prosecutor to know how I'm thinking. It wouldn't be in either party's interest to allow the issue of what killed the man Blake to bedevil this trial.' Arabella stood. 'No, please sit. As the evidence stands, Dr Horowitz's report gives a direct answer as to the cause of death, as you know. Exhibit A3, which says it was the head and facial injuries, and that the totality of them was inevitably fatal. And you heard him, Ms Engineer, when he said that in his opinion death would have occurred from that combination of injuries in minutes rather than hours. He was very clear about that.'

Arabella stood to make a point, but the judge waved her back down again. 'Yes, he did agree with you that in particular cases people have survived far more profound head injuries than these, but he stuck to his guns on the cause of death. Fairly and squarely, Ms Engineer, Dr Horowitz rejected what you've been putting to me about the possibility of the death being caused by incineration. My note is that on his examination, he found no soot at all in the airways and no elevated carbon monoxide in the blood, so incineration wasn't the cause of death. Yes, there was swelling of the brain, and that can be induced by heat, but again he found no evidence — this is what my note says, and please correct me if I've got it wrong — of any heat damage to the face or scalp. Not just that. When he looked at the brain under the microscope, nothing he saw indicated that the swelling of the brain was caused by heat.'

Arabella stood once more and this time got a word in edgeways. 'Let me be frank about my objective, your Honour: all I need is that the evidence raises a real possibility that although my client may be proved to have inflicted the head injuries, death could actually have been caused by the other men pouring petrol over the victim and setting him alight — which Mr Sherry had nothing to do with. I don't have to prove that the immolation caused the death, only that it's possible.'

With any other advocate, Thatcher J was likely to have made some ironic rejoinder about the bleeding obvious, but he resisted that. 'The pathologist, Ms Engineer, has to be given great respect. He saw the body up at Wheeny Creek and its immediate appearance, didn't he? And he did the post-mortem. I think you have to accept that he was particularly well placed to conclude that Blake died from the combined effect of the head injuries, and that he did die in a matter of minutes.'

Arabella was still standing. 'Your Honour will not have prejudged the issue, though, given that we have informed the court that we shall call the contrary opinion of another pathologist.'

The judge didn't take that as a rebuke. 'Of course not. My mind remains open.'

Arabella smiled winsomely. 'Your Honour's eventual finding of fact will be subject to a number of significant qualifications, with respect.'

'Namely?'

'Well, the first is that the pathologist can't say whether all the head and facial injuries were inflicted at the same time. He did concede that some of them could have been inflicted two or three hours earlier than the others. Which is relevant to the idea that Blake was further beaten at Wheeny Creek, when my client wasn't there.'

'And the second qualification?'

'If, despite Dr Horowitz's opinion, Mr Blake was still alive when he was incinerated—'

'For the sake of argument?'

'Quite. And your Honour has not closed his mind on the possibility of a mechanism, consistent with the post-mortem findings, by which that could have occurred. Then Mr Sherry isn't proved the killer.'

'Third qualification?'

'Dr Horowitz's opinion was that most of the left lung had been burnt completely away. What follows from that is that death from an injury to that part of the body, such as stabbing, can't be excluded on pathological grounds. And there was a knife found on the burnt corpse.'

Billy the Pig looked up from a textbook he had been checking. 'It's a valiant effort, Ms Engineer, and one can only be impressed by your persistence, but this little colloquy has been to let you know that my present state of thinking is that it would be fanciful to suppose that at Wheeny Creek further blows were inflicted on Blake with the iron bar, or that any other trauma was inflicted to his body apart from the burning of it. Look at it this way: clearly the other men intended to incinerate the body, or they wouldn't have taken a can of petrol with them, and if Blake wasn't already dead when they pulled him out of the boot of the car, that incineration would have killed him. So what would have been the point of inflicting any further head wounds on him? Unless your pathologist is, on some basis that I can't imagine, able to persuade me that his opinion is to be preferred to Dr Horowitz's, who observed the body at the scene *and* performed the post-mortem, I'm highly likely to accept without any doubt the Crown's evidence that the head injuries were the cause of death and that death occurred within minutes of them being inflicted. I want to be as fair to the defence as I can about this.'

Arabella looked at Surrey, who shook his head almost imperceptibly. She bowed and sat down.

David Surrey took Arabella to a café in Oxford Street when the court rose for the day. She was feeling defeated.

'He was pretty fair with us, Bella. It's nice of Legal Aid to bring Dr Beattie down from Brisbane to theorise about possibilities, but we're supposed to have the ability to read the writing on the wall.'

'Meaning that we should have left Beattie in Queensland?'

'Not at all. We'll still adduce his evidence, and Billy the Pig's still going to have to take it seriously and spell out in his judgment why he believes he can push it aside and make a finding of fact that Blake wasn't burnt to death. If he goes wrong there, Sherry'll get his acquittal on appeal.'

'You criminal lawyers have a funny orientation, David. It's as if eventually succeeding on appeal means your poor client didn't have to spend nine months, or a year, or whatever it is, rotting in a cell while the system gets around to acknowledging that the conviction was unsafe or unsatisfactory. No one gives him back the time he's served, and he gets no compensation for it.'

Surrey finished his coffee. 'You're right. We do concentrate on the verdict. I suppose it has something to do with intellectualising the conflict. Still, better nine months than twenty years hard.'

'Or just the opposite. Don't you oversimplify it? We won, never mind the client's ordeal?'

'You know how to hurt a man, Arabella.'

'It's my job.'

'Speaking of which, how is the gentleman farmer?'

Arabella was looking out at the street, and apparently hadn't heard the last question. 'If the judge is as good as his word, it's all downhill from here, isn't it?'

'We concentrate on reducing murder to manslaughter, do you mean?'

'All we can do. Harry says raising self-defence would be ridiculous.'

'Speaking of whom, how *is* the farmer?'

'I heard you the first time, David. Do you think we can run both provocation and diminished responsibility?'

'Certainly do. I reckon he'd be interested in that, and either one will do. The psych can come at two hours notice.'

'The Crown says he'll close his case tomorrow afternoon. You'd better get her to come on Monday morning.'

'Okay.' Surrey went to the cash register and paid. Returning, he gathered his briefcase and pushed his chair back under the table. Arabella did the same.

'I'd suggest we have dinner tonight, David, but I've got to settle a big set of pleadings in a bank guarantee case. It's hard to keep my other matters running while I'm locked up in a trial like this. I'm getting way behind.'

Surrey nodded. 'And you're worried that I'd want to talk about you and Harry, aren't you? Which you don't want to do.'

She looked at him, about to say something, then her BlackBerry chimed. She took it out and looked at the screen. 'Conference in ten minutes, which I'd forgotten about. Same time tomorrow morning, then?' And she flagged down a taxi. Surrey grinned to himself and walked down Oxford Street towards his budget hotel. It was all the Legal Aid rate would cover. Chinese meal tonight, obviously.

As promised, the prosecution case wrapped up on Friday, although a little earlier than expected. His Honour didn't want to start immediately on the defence evidence, and asked Arabella whether she wouldn't prefer to kick off on Monday morning. 'I'm indebted to your Honour,' she said, with a smile that some judges might have found encouraging.

Surrey had made friends over the course of the trial with the court officers, and had talked them into letting him park his Falcon in an unused judge's space, so he was able to make the most of the early mark and was back in Goulburn in time for dinner with his family.

Arabella, meanwhile, emerged from the lift at Elizabeth Bay at five o'clock, juggling her briefcase, handbag and three folders of papers, and was trying to dig out the key to her apartment when the front door opened to reveal someone dressed as a farmer with a glass of wine in one hand.

'No, thanks,' Harry said. 'We're on the sewer.'

They kissed, and he stood back to let her come in.

'What? I don't get it.'

'One of my father's jokes,' Harry said, 'and it would take too long to explain. They don't have dunny men in Golders Green, do they?'

Arabella dumped her things on the dining table. 'I object to answering the question on the grounds that I don't understand it,' she said. 'Is there another glass of that?'

'You take this one. I haven't really started on it yet.' And he went into the kitchen and poured himself another. Arabella stepped out of her high heels and sat on a Barcelona chair.

'This is a surprise, Harry. To find you here.'

'A nice surprise?'

'Of course, a nice surprise. To what do I owe it?'

'Loneliness.' He sat and sipped the wine.

'Yours or mine?'

'Good question, Bella.' He took another sip from his glass. 'Heard from Sanjay?'

'No, Harry, and I don't really expect to. What would be the point?'

'Not even a Christmas card?'

'We'll leave Sanjay out of it, Harry, will we?'

'Sorry again. Yes.' They both drank in silence for a while. 'So. Are you in your case yet?'

'Prosecution case closed this afternoon. I don't have to do my opening until Monday, and I've already written that, so I was intending to catch up on my civil stuff over the weekend.' She looked across at the briefcase and papers on the table.

'It'll keep. You know, when I came to the Bar, seriously, solicitors used not to complain until you'd had the brief for six months and hadn't sent back the advice they were after. With email, they're chasing you for it the next morning.'

'Really, Harry? In crime?'

'Yes, Arabella, in crime. Don't be condescending.' He looked a bit hurt.

'My turn to apologise. Let me change the subject: I think our trial's lost.'

'Well, as I think I told you, that depends on your objective. Set yourself a realistic target and you can hit it — manslaughter, and a much less onerous sentence. Five years instead of twenty. Not that I think that's necessarily in this particular client's best interests, but I've said all I intend to on that subject. The point is, an acquittal is something Sherry was never going to get — judge or jury.'

'That's certainly true now. Thatcher has very kindly spelled out to me that I can call a hundred pathologists, but he's still going to accept what the Crown's man says.'

'And he says you killed him with the iron bar, not the fire.'

'Not I, Harry. I had nothing to do with it.'

'That's how criminal lawyers talk, Arabella. We identify with our accursed. Don't they do that in London?'

'I wasn't in a criminal set of chambers, Harry, as you know. It was mostly Chancery, all affidavits and robust disputes over financial rights, and I think they only took me on to pretend they were something other than an Anglo boys club. But the clerk directed all the irritating little criminal stuff to me and one of the other beginners. It wasn't enough to live on, and I wasn't much good at it. And I never even got to run a jury trial. I kept my head above water by devilling paperwork for solicitors, charging less than it would have cost them to have their employees do it.'

'First time you've told me that last bit.'

'I didn't want you to know how unaccomplished I am. I wanted you to think I was … what is it judges always say when they're going to sink you, despite your best efforts? Able. I wanted you to think I was able.'

'I trust you're not fishing for compliments. The self-condemnation must be all about failing to dazzle Billy with your ingenious arguments.'

'"Ingenious". That's the same as Sir Humphrey's "courageous", I suppose?'

'Yes. When they call you "able", and your arguments are "ingenious" or "novel", you've lost. I should know. I wouldn't bother calling the bloke from Brisbane, if I were you. Save the taxpayers his fare. They'll be grateful.'

Arabella crossed the kilim that separated them and sat on Harry's lap. She put her arms around his neck and kissed him.

'If I promise not to work all weekend, do you promise to take me out to dinner and the pictures?'

'What dinner and which film?'

'I'll ask the question again, witness, and I wonder if you'd be so kind as to give me a straight answer: do you promise to take me out to dinner and the pictures?'

'I promise.'

'Thank you.' She kissed his cheek again.

'But not George Clooney and not Japanese.'

Arabella put her hands around Harry's neck and choked him.

At nine-thirty on Monday morning, Harry dropped Arabella in Oxford Street opposite the Darlinghurst courthouse, and turned left at Taylor Square, pointing the big car south. She waved goodbye and waited for the pedestrian light to turn green. Surrey was waiting for her on the other side of the road.

'I didn't know the Burragate peasant farmer was coming to town.'

'Just came up for the weekend. And before you ask, yes, it was a lovely weekend. We saw the new George Clooney film, and we went to Tetsuya's.'

'I went there once. Racehorse trainers, car dealers and their bimbos. Charming clientele.'

'There is that, but they don't cook the food, do they? And you don't have to talk to them.'

The courtroom they entered was empty. 'The Crown are usually here by now,' Arabella said.

'Once they've called all their evidence, they lose interest. It's not as if you're going to give them much to cross-examine on. I don't suppose Mr Crown ever thought he was going to get his hands on Tony. That would have been a bloodbath.'

Arabella set out her papers on the Bar table, and Surrey went back to the doorway to greet a middle-aged woman who had just arrived. 'Dr Evans?' She nodded and shook his hand, and Surrey brought the woman over to Arabella. 'This is Helen Evans, Arabella, our psych.'

'How do you do, Dr Evans?' Arabella almost subconsciously noted that the expert witness's mannish suit was two sizes too small. Like the Prime Minister. 'There's an interview room just outside. Can we have a quick word about your report?' Dr Evans spent the next ten minutes explaining some of her jargon to Arabella, who made notes in the margin of her copy of the report, and then the court officer knocked on the door to say that his Honour wanted to come on the bench. He was waiting when Arabella returned to the Bar table.

'My apologies, your Honour. I lost track of the time.' Which was true.

'That's all right, Ms Engineer. Are you ready to proceed?'

Uncharacteristically forgiving, she thought. 'I am.'

'Mr Crown, anything more before the defence opens?'

'No, your Honour.'

'Ms Engineer?'

'May it please your Honour, I seek your leave to call first an expert witness, our forensic psychologist, Dr Evans, and to open our case after that. Dr Evans needs to get away.'

'Normally, Ms Engineer, I would want you to tell me what your evidence was going to be before you called it. But I suppose I've been given a pretty good idea of the issue here.' He paused and seemed to consider. 'Very well, let's hear from Dr Evans. Have you been served with a copy of her report, Mr Crown?'

'Yes, your Honour. We don't object to it.'

'One of the advantages of a judge-alone trial, counsel, is that we don't have to give expert evidence in oral form. Neither will you have to explain the good doctor's terms of art to me, I hope. Do you tender the report, Ms Engineer?'

'I do, your Honour. The report of Dr Helen Evans, dated 2 June this year.'

'Accused's Exhibit 1,' the judge's associate said, stapling a marker to the top corner of the document and handing it to the judge. Thatcher J read the six-page report with remarkable speed, the witness was sworn in, and Arabella had her elaborate on her qualifications and publications, then asked her to explain several technical references in the report before concluding her questions by seeking to summarise its effect.

'Would this be a fair summary for the layman of what your report concludes, Dr Evans? That Tony Sherry suffers from retarded mental development, that he is of subnormal mental capacity by reason of that retardation, and that the level of his mental functioning is so low as to amount to an abnormality of mind?'

The prosecutor was on his feet. 'I object to the question.'

'Yes, Mr Crown?' The judge looked up from the note he had taken.

'Leading, your Honour.'

The judge sighed. 'Yes, Mr Crown, it is indubitably a leading question, but one asked of an expert. As you ought to be aware, the jurisprudential rationale for disallowing leading one's own witness is the temptation to put words in her, or his, mouth.'

'Yes, your Honour.'

'As you would also know, or as you *should* also know, jurisprudential theory is that an expert cannot be led.' He glared at the prosecutor, who blushed. 'I'll allow the question. Do you need it read back, doctor?'

'No, your Honour. The answer is yes. In my opinion, and for the reasons set out in the exhibit, Mr Sherry is entitled to claim diminished responsibility as provided in section 23A of the *Crimes Act.*'

Surrey leaned close to Arabella and whispered. 'Oh dear. She just waved a red rag at the bull.'

He was right. Despite his famously porcine visage, Justice Thatcher bridled, or did whatever it is bulls do. Snorted. 'If it's all right with you, Dr Evans, I'll reserve the right to myself to decide whether the mental state of the accused meets the statutory standard.'

'I apologise, your Honour.'

'As a matter of interest, doctor, are you familiar with the statutory provision governing the defence in a murder case of diminished responsibility?'

'Yes. I also have a law degree, your Honour.'

'In which case, let me remind you that what is required to reduce murder to manslaughter by reason of diminished responsibility, is that the accused should adduce evidence that—' and here Billy the Pig picked up his copy of the *Crimes Act*, '"At the time of the acts causing the death charged, the person was suffering from such abnormality of mind ..." and you would say, doctor, one arising from a condition of retarded development, "... as would substantially impair his mental responsibility for the acts." Am I correct?'

'Yes, your Honour.'

'And that the consequence of my being satisfied of that substantial impairment, which the legislation gives me no further assistance with in relation to its degree or even how I form my appreciation of its degree, is that this man, in this situation, is liable to be convicted instead of manslaughter?'

'Yes, your Honour.'

'As for your role, doctor, the subjects on which you are entitled to express an expert opinion are: first, whether this accused suffers from an abnormality of mind—'

'Yes, he does.'

He didn't appreciate the interruption. 'Thank you. And, second: does that arise from a condition of arrested or retarded development of mind—'

'Yes, it does.'

'Yes, thank you, doctor. And, third: at the time of the acts charged, did that condition substantially impair his responsibility for his acts?'

'The answer to that would depend on how you interpret the word "substantially".'

Arabella, unable to take control of her witness, could see that Billy the Pig was getting close to the end of his tether. That's enough, judge, she thought.

'Indeed it will, doctor. And that's a matter for me, isn't it? Does that complete the evidence in chief, Ms Engineer?'

Arabella was still standing, as she had been since the judge took over her witness. 'It does.'

'Mr Crown, cross-examination?'

'Thank you, your Honour.' The prosecutor stood and faced the expert, standing in the witness box with her notes spread in front of her, and looked at the first question written out in his notebook. 'Dr Evans, the validity of your opinion rests entirely on the correctness of your assertion that the level of the accused's mental functioning is so low as to amount to an abnormality of mind, isn't that so?' He was obviously very pleased with the question he had crafted.

'Yes.'

'It is certainly below average?'

'Yes, it is.'

Mr Crown studied the next note in his book, keeping his eyes down. 'And was there a time frame in which you placed him for the purpose of forming your opinion on the consequential impairment of his mental responsibility for his attack on the deceased man?'

'Yes. I looked at the whole of his life history as he gave it to me, and as it was documented in the other material that's annexed to my report.'

The Crown looked somewhat triumphant, and the judge's expression indicated that he knew where this was going. Arabella wasn't sure.

'So, doctor, what you admit you didn't do was make your judgment as at the time he was hitting Mr Blake with an iron bar?'

Arabella heard the penny drop: this is all about ignoring Tony's general intellectual status so that they can isolate out the fatal blows, she realised. Is the law that unrealistic? Or is it just the rationale for a crushing sentence?

Dr Evans could tell from the cross-examiner's expression and his use of the word 'admit' that she was in trouble. 'Well, to be fair, that was an element of the time frame I considered.'

The judge took over. 'As I read the law, doctor, and that, too, is exclusively my province notwithstanding your law degree, the time frame you *should* have considered, and considered exclusively, was the period when he was beating the man's brains in. That's not to be averaged out with periods of lesser or greater impairment, for whatever reason.'

'That, as you say, would appear to be a matter for the court.' The witness was almost mumbling, but Thatcher J could hear her perfectly well.

'Nothing else, is there Mr Crown?' A hint of mutual self-congratulation in his question, which was not really a question.

'No, may it please you.' The prosecutor sat, going into a happy huddle with his instructing solicitor.

'Re-examination, Ms Engineer?' A hint of a challenge this time.

'If I may have a moment, please, your Honour?' Arabella and Surrey bent their heads together.

'You can't save her now, Bella. Let it go.'

'I fear you're right, David. Bugger it. He's just going to ignore everything she said. We wasted our time, hoping for humanity.' Feelingly.

That caused him to raise his eyebrows. 'We've still got provocation.'

Arabella stood and waived her right to ask further questions in an attempt to save as much as she could of the witness's credit. The judge told Dr Evans she was excused, and took the short adjournment. The psychologist fled the court without a backward glance. Law degree or not, she looked totally uncomprehending of the criminal justice system's intolerance for the pitiful man in the dock.

As Arabella took off her wig, she turned to see her client being taken downstairs by the prison officers who attended with him every day. She felt ashamed, and took hold of Surrey's upper arm through his tweed jacket. 'My God, David, when's the last time either of us spoke to Tony in this trial? Or thought about him as a human being, rather than an exhibit on which we're trying to focus statutory definitions? As far as we're concerned, he's just a thing, like the iron bar. We stand up here with our backs to him, calling him retarded and subnormal and abnormal and challenged. We didn't ask his permission for any of that. We didn't explain to him why we had to do it. They wheel him in every morning, and take him down for a cup of tea or a sandwich twice a day, and then they wheel him back to Long Bay every night. What must he think of us?'

'Don't beat yourself up over it, Bella. It's what we do. Anyway, Sherry slept through all that evidence this morning.'

'No, David, no. It isn't "what we do" — or it shouldn't be. Harry wouldn't have treated him like this, you know that. Harry would have told him jokes, and called him "mate", and asked him about the jail. Tony would've loved Harry.'

Surrey shrugged. 'We can still have a coffee, heartless bastards as we are.'

At twilight the following Friday evening, Harry was leaning against the bull-bar of the LandCruiser, parked at Merimbula Airport, watching Arabella's plane on its final approach, its landing lights ablaze. She was the first passenger off, carrying a small overnight bag and nothing else. Her long hair had been coiffed into a precise bob, and she was wearing faded jeans and a lime green cotton jumper. Harry stopped breathing for a moment as he watched her. As she strode through the gate, he saw that her shoes were soft red leather.

Harry walked into the little terminal building to meet her.

'No luggage?' They embraced.

'Nope. Let's go home.' They were on the highway less than ten minutes after the plane landed. Arabella gazed out the window as night fell across the green fairways of the Pambula golf course on the western side of the road.

'You've had some rain, then?'

'Too much. The chooks are getting morose.' Harry lifted his hand off the wheel, greeting a neighbour from Burragate heading north. 'What'd he give him?'

'Eleven years.'

'Whack. Non-parole period was what?'

'Six years. I've brought the judgment and the sentencing remarks for you to read.'

'I'd prefer Elmore Leonard.' They rode in silence and Harry concentrated on giving a wide berth to the empty timber jinkers lit up like Christmas trees, barrelling along in both directions on the highway. He even let one overtake the LandCruiser, which struck Arabella as radically out of character, although she didn't mention it.

'Still, you got provocation. You got him acquitted of murder. Something to be proud of.'

Arabella felt no pride. 'Let me read you what he said about diminished responsibility.' She unzipped her bag and took out two sheafs of white pages and turned on the cabin light. As she flicked through them, Harry turned right at the Eden roundabout, following the big green sign to Orbost.

'Here it is: "I reject Dr Evans' opinion as to his intellectual capacity. I am not satisfied that the level of his mental functioning is so low as to amount to an abnormality of mind. On the contrary, I am satisfied that his level of functioning is in the normal range albeit, I accept, below the average." For heaven's sake! In the normal range! He can't even tie his laces. He has to wear Velcro shoes!'

'Imagine what Billy the Pig would have found if he hadn't been in love with you.'

'In love with me? What in God's name are you talking about?'

'I had frequent reports from Dave. He says Thatcher's tongue was hanging out so far, his associate had to roll it up. He gave you provocation, after all is said and done.'

'That was never in doubt. Let me find that bit.' She turned back a couple of pages. '"Mr Blake's conduct when he came back to the house and violently struck Mr Sherry over the back of the head without any warning, coupled with his grossly abusive and threatening language and his earlier conduct towards Mr Sherry that night, was such as could have induced an ordinary person in Mr Sherry's position to lose self-control. I am wholly unpersuaded that the Crown has established beyond reasonable doubt that the fatal blow or blows struck with the implement were not struck by Mr Sherry under provocation." That's it, Harry — two sentences after two weeks. What a brilliant victory for Ms Engineer!'

Harry turned right off the highway at the sign that said 'Scenic drive: Burragate 34k'. His headlights picked out the reflectors on the roadside posts, and revealed a black wallaby grazing in the green pick at the side of the road, ignoring the LandCruiser as it passed under heavy acceleration. 'We won't quite make it home before it's fully dark. That was a fixation of my mother's — children have to be home before dark.'

'It's just as well she didn't live in London. In winter, it gets dark at three-thirty.'

Harry slowed as they hit the first gravel section of the road. 'Could you ever go back to that?'

'If I had to, I could. Of course. It's London. But I'll tell you what I cannot do: another murder trial. Never, ever again.'

They both thought about that as Harry pushed the big car hard through the twisting road — now gravel, now tarmac. The trees met overhead, the dark canopy of the huge eucalypts shutting out the vestiges of the distant sunset. 'One of the locals came to see me and said that given I was the big city lawyer, I should be able to get them to seal this whole road.'

'What did you say?'

'I told him I like it as it is. I don't want a million tourists jamming everything up.'

'And how was that received?'

'Badly.' A goanna swung its head to glare at them before scuttling into the bushes. 'I had hoped not to make any enemies down here.'

'What's your score to date?'

'Three, I think. That road petitioner, one of the bushfire brigade and the phantom shooter from the village. I called the authorities about him again.'

'Oh, Harry.'

'*Vedremo*. I'm working on it.'

She chuckled. 'I'll bet you are. How long can I stay, Harry?'

'Forever. How long *can* you stay, Bella?'

'There's a notice of motion in the District Court on Thursday. I'm booked on the plane back on Wednesday night.'

Harry turned in at the gate. The RonLyn sign reflected the car's lights for a second as they swept across it. 'Five days,' he said as he pulled up next to the house. 'I trust you won't be bored.'

'Just so long as you stop complaining about my haircut.'

Harry opened his door. 'I haven't said a word,' he protested.

'Precisely.'

The shaken baby

David Surrey, seated at a round marble-topped table outside La Gerbe d'Or in Paddington, looked up as Harry approached and joined him at the table. 'Ah,' he said. 'The blind man with a machine gun.'

Harry threw a heavy weekend newspaper on a vacant chair and sat down. 'The what?'

'That's what someone called you at the Law Society dinner last night. You want a coffee?'

'And an almond brioche, if they've got one.' They had, and it was the last one.

Eight o'clock Saturday morning in late November. Harry had caught a cab over from Elizabeth Bay to Five Ways and bought his newspaper before breakfasting with the solicitor, who was making one of his rare visits to Sydney. For once, Surrey wasn't playing the part of the Goulburn lawyer, but was dressed in sunglasses, shorts, boat shoes without socks and a pink polo shirt with a small animal stitched on the left breast. Harry, on the other hand, carelessly affected the appearance of an impecunious but big, fit and strong builder's labourer — faded T-shirt, football shorts and Dunlop Volleys, also without socks. His hair, as usual, was unruly to the point of unmanageability.

'Adopting a Double Bay persona, Dave?'

'When in Rome.'

'You staying up here for the weekend?' Harry tore a piece off his brioche and ate it.

'Not if I can help it. After this, it's back to Goulburn in time for lunch with the family. Last night's mandatory rubber chicken appearance was a punishment imposed on me for my sins as the president of the Southern Tablelands Law Society.'

'Just make sure you change the pink shirt before you go home, mate.'

'You have an unnecessarily jaundiced view of my town, Curry. We're very progressive.'

'So you say. I'm here for the conference. So confer with me.'

'Arabella not joining us?'

'Not at this hour, old boy. And to whom should I credit the remark about me and the machine gun?' He finished his short black in one gulp.

'As if you care, Harry. As Oscar said, the only thing worse than people talking about you at Law Society dinners is people not talking about you at Law Society dinners.'

A polychrome gaggle of cyclists arrived and leaned their bikes against the railing along the edge of the raised footpath, the cleats on their shoes making loud metallic noises as they fussed about, hanging their helmets from handlebars and stepping up to take the table next to the two lawyers.

'Mammals,' Surrey observed, or that's how it sounded to Harry as the solicitor finished his bacon and eggs and laid the knife and fork parallel on his empty plate.

'Aren't we all?'

'No, they're called MAMILs. Middle-aged men in lycra.'

Harry smiled. 'You'd better let me have the fact situation, Dave.'

Surrey finished his coffee and waved his hand to order another. The cyclists were consulting the breakfast menu and talking about granola, which caused Harry to shudder involuntarily.

'We've got the son of one of my oldest clients. Good family from down near Crookwell. The boy's twenty-four, only child, tennis professional. He didn't quite make it here — runner-up in the state titles, or came third, that sort of thing, but never a serious prospect for the pro circuit. He wanted to give it a go in Europe, though, and got himself a good job coaching at an upper-crust London club, not Hurlingham but pretty good nonetheless, who let him play minor tournaments on the Continent. He did reasonably well, made a bit of money, but came home about eighteen months ago — he's been at a bit of a loose end. Doing some coaching, trying to get a job as sports master at a decent private school.'

'There's no such thing.'

'As you say, Dud. About a year ago, he took up with a woman a bit older than he is, with a little boy. They had a flat at Dulwich Hill. Our boy, Hamish, was crazy about the kid, who was just three. Loved him and looked after him much better than the mother did. The mother, in fact, is a bit of a waste of food, according to Hamish's father. But very attractive and sexually adventurous, or so she told the police.'

Harry tore off another piece of his brioche. 'We'll come back to sexual adventures later. Do I note that you speak of the child in the past tense?'

'Very. The mother, name's Angie, got herself a job as a waitress to help with the rent while Hamish looked for a decent job. On her first morning at the café, Hamish drove her to work and then looked after the boy at home until it was time to go back and collect Mum. Angie was only doing the morning shift — three hours. Hamish says absolutely nothing untoward or unusual happened at home; he'd watched TV and played with the child and read to him. He was fine when he put him in his car seat, yet when they got to the café he was having some sort of spasm in the back of the car. The café people called an ambulance and he was rushed off to the Children's Hospital, but he died the next day.'

'Cause of death?'

'Brain trauma. They found a subdural haematoma at the post-mortem.'

'Ah.' They both lapsed into silence, looking out at the traffic passing in the sunny street. Young people in open cars and on motor-scooters were heading for Bondi, beach towels around their necks. Harry finished his breakfast and Surrey consulted the messages on his phone. The waitress collected their plates. A solicitor they both knew walked past with a small boy riding on his shoulders, and they all said hello to each other. Customers went in and out of the patisserie.

'So the charge is murder?'

'It is. They want you, Harry, and they'll pay for a junior. Will Arabella want it?'

'We can only ask. She hasn't touched a criminal brief since Sherry, though. She says that's her last ever, but I think she meant murder.'

Surrey nodded and wrote in the air, asking for the bill, which was speedily produced. People had started to queue for the tables.

'This baby thing sounds like sad stuff. Not to be too crass about it, Dave, but what's the defence?'

'He didn't do it. Never struck him, never shook him.'

'Police are relying on what? That he's the only one who could have done it while the mother was at work?'

Surrey put two twenty-dollar notes on top of the bill and stood up. 'Got it in one, Harry. They've got a medical opinion that the fatal injuries were inflicted in that period. That they must have been.'

Harry shook his head slowly. 'Have we got anything to go on?'

'Well, the child was physically self-destructive. Had a history of self-harm, and was even under psychiatric treatment.'

'Aged three?'

'Yes, since the age of two-and-a-bit, I'm told.' He pointed west. 'Goulburn calls.'

Harry inhaled hard and let out a long breath. 'You're going to have to stop giving me these easy briefs.' He picked up his newspaper, still folded, and put it under his arm. The two men walked to where Surrey's Falcon was parked in a side street and Harry accepted the solicitor's offer to drive him back to Elizabeth Bay.

'What was the child's name, Dave?'

'Jarrod.'

'Of course it was. And the client's name?'

'Hamish Sommerville.'

As Surrey pulled the car up and double-parked outside Arabella's modernist apartment building, Harry asked him about his earlier reference to Angie's sexual adventurousness, and what relevance it had to the murder charge.

'It seems that when the police searched the flat at Dulwich Hill, they found all these knotted sheets tied to the rail in the wardrobe and asked her what they were for. She said, "So I'm sexually adventurous — so what?"'

'So that hasn't got anything to do with anything, has it?'

Surrey shook his head. 'Not as far as I can see. Tends to prove what I told you — that she's a waste of space.'

'Actually,' Harry said as he got out of the car, 'you said she was a waste of food.'

'Both.'

Arabella was still asleep when Harry entered the flat, so he took the paper to one of the Barcelona chairs in her sunny living room, and read it through. Didn't take long. He did half the cryptic crossword, then impatiently gave up, muttering at an impenetrable clue. He dropped the pen and paper on the carpet, then walked over to look at Arabella through the open bedroom door. Still asleep, the curtains closed, her hair tangled in the pillows and her long brown legs uncovered by the sheet. Harry took the stairs down five levels, coming out onto the buffalo-grass lawn between the building and the seawall. He spent twenty minutes dead-heading the hibiscus bushes and weeding beneath them.

'What are you doing? I'm calling security.'

Harry straightened and looked up five storeys at Arabella's balcony, where she was drying her hair with a white towel and smiling at him. 'Be up in a minute,' he called.

She was standing in the kitchen in a bathrobe making toast when he returned, and spreading it with jam. He made tea for them both, and they sat at the dining table. Arabella had retrieved the *Herald* from the floor, and was reading the headlines on the front page. 'No news, I see.' Harry grunted and stole a piece of toast.

'How was Mr Surrey?'

'Want a junior brief in a murder, Bella?'

'After all this time in civil? Do I get to know the particulars?'

'Not yet. You're just a cab on a rank, young woman. You don't get to pick and choose the nice clients and the nice crimes. You know that.'

'What? I'm just supposed to say, "Yes, please" and take whatever I'm offered?'

'That's the ethical rule, yes. You can't refuse a brief that's in your field of practice.'

Arabella took a sip of her tea. 'I can if it's beyond my capacity, skill and experience.'

'That would hardly apply to a junior brief, Bella. You're not going to get out of it as easily as that. And you can't say that you prefer to stick to insurance work. You hold yourself out as a criminal lawyer, or you did the last time I Googled you.'

'Too late to amend my profile on the chambers' website, I suppose?'

'Far too late.'

'I may be otherwise engaged.'

'That won't work. The date hasn't been set yet, and David'll be sure to find something mutually convenient.'

Arabella leaned over and put her hands around Harry's throat. 'It must be pretty bad, this case you two want to force on me.'

'Somebody killed a baby.'

That silenced her. She removed her hands and sat back in her chair. Harry licked the tip of his finger and picked up the crumbs and a swirl of jam from Arabella's plate. 'It's obviously very complex. Lots of medical issues, even child psychiatry. We should get the brief next week, and meet the client and his family the week after that. Lots of hand-holding with the parents, I fear. You're good at that.' He ate the crumbs.

'Being a woman.'

'Just what I was thinking.'

'I would have a great deal of difficulty in putting my heart and soul into the defence of a baby-murderer, Harry.'

'Even if he's innocent?'

'Is he?'

'So we are instructed.'

'And that's good enough for you?'

'It certainly is. I'm briefed as his defender, not his judge and jury. You, too.'

The weekend over, and with Harry on his way back to Burragate, Arabella was in her Phillip Street chambers by 7.30 on Monday morning. Harry had spent the past week with her, and they'd been to a concert, an art gallery opening and a film. Three restaurant dinners. Despite the pleasure of his company, Arabella was relieved to have her time and her home to herself, because her inbox had filled up over the week and she had yet to deal with it. Hundreds of pages of attachments. The insurance companies' solicitors were trying to clear their decks before Christmas, which meant that they were hell-bent on briefing out their litigation for February, March and April to their panel of compliant, client-approved barristers and washing their hands of it all, at least in the short term. To a woman, the solicitors planned to have January to themselves, and to arrive back at work at the beginning of the new law term to find that counsel had brought everything up to date: comprehensive advices on their clients' prospects of successfully defending the claims; advices on what evidence had to be gathered before the cases could be run; drafts of subpoenas to be issued and lists of expert witnesses to be engaged in search of that evidence; advices on what it was going to cost their defendants if they lost; and advices that the all-too-obviously hopeless cases should be the subject of rent-a-judge mediations at which modest but craftily tempting compromises could be offered to plaintiffs who, truth to tell, would get a great deal more from the judge if they had the resources and the courage to fight their cases. Even from a notoriously mean judge.

And then her clerk's assistant knocked, opened Arabella's door, and wheeled in a three-decker trolley stacked with two dozen bulging folders of evidence in a building case. Variously labelled Plans, Photographs, Scott Schedules, Engineers' Reports, Architects' Reports, Geotechnical, Damages, Liability. Arabella opened Volume 1, labelled Observations and Pleadings, and read the first five explanatory pages. Then she rang Harry, grateful that he'd finally agreed to use the mobile phone she'd bought for him — albeit grumbling that there was no reception at Burragate, and he'd only be able to use it on his forays into what others may be pleased to call civilisation. She caught him in the car on the freeway, passing the Buddhist temple at Dapto.

'A building case, Harry! I've never even seen one before, and there are at least twenty volumes of evidence. Nine plaintiffs and four defendants.'

Harry asked her to wait while he stopped the car and plugged in his new phone's hands-free connection. That done, he resumed his trip down the coast, passing soon the burgeoning and treeless Shellharbour village, and Arabella kept him talking for the best part of an hour, reading from the brief.

'Now you can summarise it for me, Bella. It's not so easy to concentrate in this traffic.'

'As you wish, master. In a nutshell, it appears that these nine homebuyers bought into a new estate at North Richmond five years ago, all getting practically identical three-bedroom brick-veneer bungalows — what's brick-veneer, Harry? You'll have to explain — and now they find the houses were all built on clay that won't keep still and the unstrengthened floor slabs are buckling, their walls and ceilings are cracking, the doors won't shut, the plumbing leaks. The solicitor for the plaintiffs — a notorious ambulance-chaser — says they all want new houses. The best part of three million dollars! I've never done anything as big as that.'

'You should be able to persuade them to give you a leader, Bella. It's a big case.'

'No, Harry, I don't want to be led. I'd like to do this on my own. You're not angling for it, are you?'

'God, no. Building cases get very messy, Bella. Very technical. Architects, engineers, geotechnical experts.'

'How do you know all this, Harry?'

'I used to be in chambers in the next room to a bloke who did nothing else. Made a fortune. Most building cases get sent out to a referee — an engineer, or a retired judge. The court hates them because they tie up resources for months, and flick-passes everything it can. All day, every day, there were experts trooping into this fellow's room with great rolls of plans and models and drill cores.'

'This one's been farmed out, too. The referee's an engineer, I think. I'll look at that again later. It's exciting, isn't it? My solicitor says there's a month in it — a really big case.'

'Nine cases all being heard together? At least thirteen counsel, unless you get some silks briefed, which could take it up to fifteen. Can't see them all announcing their appearances in less than a month, so you'd better make the estimate at least twice that long. You'll have no problem paying the rent for quite a while, Bella.'

'It's an ill wind that butters no parsnips.'

'Couldn't have put it better myself. Who's your client?' A red light went on in the fuel gauge, attracting Harry's attention.

'We insure the local council. The claim is that its building inspectors approved substandard work and/or incompetent engineering designs and thereby caused or permitted the defective construction. The other defendants are the architect, the builder, and the developer. They're all sued for professional negligence or breach of contract.'

'So it'll all be about apportioning the blame between defendants. Your people might not have to carry much of it.'

'You'd assume so, but my solicitor's summary says we might be the last man standing. She's pretty pessimistic.'

'What do you mean by that? Hang on, just coming into Nowra and I have to get diesel. Can you call me back in ten minutes?'

'Couldn't you call me?'

'No, you do it, Bella. You can afford it better than I can.' And he hung up. Arabella replaced her handset and looked at it, mildly surprised. This parsimony had to be attributable to Harry's late-onset conversion to Burragate subsistence farming. When she duly pressed redial, she could hear him crunching up the wrapper of what proved upon enquiry to be a large Cherry Ripe he'd picked up at the service station cash register. Having chided him for the self-indulgence ('You'll spoil your lunch'), she returned to the building case and its difficulties.

'The problem, as I understand it, is that the architect's bankrupt, the developer's in liquidation and the builder can't be found. The council's insurer may well have to wear the whole three million.'

'Poor old insurance company. Wait till I get my handkerchief out.'

Arabella laughed. 'I know, I know. The council might have to put a penny on the rates.'

'It's so different, isn't it, Bella? So much less stressful appearing for defendants in civil actions. Counsel have a duty of all care, but no responsibility. In crime, we win or we fail.'

'Not everyone thinks that way, Harry. You and I know lots of Legal Aid hacks who consider that they win with every day they can drag the trial out and charge another fee. Guilty or not guilty has very little to do with it.'

'I can assure you it won't be like that in the Sommerville case,' Harry said. 'We're expected to win, and it'll be an unmitigated catastrophe if we don't.'

'Sommerville?'

'Hamish the baby-killer.'

'Don't let anyone else hear you say that, Curry. It could have repercussions.'

'Have you heard what the solicitors are calling me, Bella?'

'I've certainly heard some of the things they call you, but I take it there's something new?'

'"Blind man with a machine gun", according to Dave.'

'Not bad.'

'Yes, I quite like it.' Harry chuckled.

He slowed the LandCruiser to negotiate a narrow bridge.

'Where are you, Harry?'

'Just going past the Jervis Bay turn-off. Millions of pelicans flying over. Should be home in about three hours, maybe a bit more, depending on the prevalence of grey nomads on the road. Looks like rain, too.'

'Will you be working on the murder?'

Harry blew the horn at a garbage truck that crossed to his side of the road without warning. 'No wonder you're a garbageman,' he yelled, but the LandCruiser's windows were all up and the air conditioner was on, so Arabella was the only person who heard him.

'*Comme d'habitude, mon coeur?*'

'*Come al solito, bella mia.*'

They talked about a session — 'What to Do When Things Go Wrong' — in the Bar Association's series of continuing legal education lectures that Arabella said she felt compelled to attend that afternoon. Harry had quite a bit to say about the necessity for lawyers to stand on their own two feet and fight their own battles without the nannying of counsellors or psychologists. Arabella was inclined to argue with him, but given Harry's poor record in dealing with the professional misconduct complaint that had led to his recent-enough suspension, when he only aggravated his alleged offence by over-assertive engagement with the tribunal, she thought it impolitic to endorse the warm fuzziness of their professional body.

'Now, a lecture on the hazards of cocaine abuse — that'd be more to the point.'

'No doubt, Harry. Look, about Hamish—'

'Well, I haven't got the brief yet, so I can't work on it. The chooks will need some attention, and then the vegetables, and then the pump — because I think the top tank's got to be close to empty. But I hope to break the back of it over the next week or two, if Dave can send it down. At least I can make a good start before we head off.'

'Head off? To where?'

'Where? Toscana, of course.'

There was a sharp silence. The LandCruiser's tyres thumped over patches in the highway.

'You didn't tell me about this.'

'We talked about it.'

'When, Harry? When did we talk about it?'

'Last winter. I was bemoaning the fact that I hadn't got away for summer in Lucca, and it was the first time for years. You said it'd be a change to go at Christmas, when there wouldn't be the crowds. You said it was a good idea. You must remember that.'

'Yes, but that was all it was. An idea. You said nothing about actually doing it.'

'I'm saying it now.'

Another long pause. Harry crossed the Burrill Lake causeway and changed down in anticipation of the hill to the south. Black swans on the water ignored him.

'And me? You mean we're both going?'

'Yes, I assumed that. Have you changed your mind?'

'My mind's got very little to do with it, Harry. Of course I'd want to go, but I have just now — literally just now — got landed with this huge building case. You haven't forgotten that? It has to be ready to go by the start of term — and there's obviously weeks of preparation to do over Christmas. Most of December and all January. There's no way in the world I could get away.'

Harry started to speak, but Arabella cut him off. 'I'm upset, Harry. I don't want to talk any more. Not now.' And she hung up.

Harry drove angrily, exceeding the speed limit and shouldering aside caravans with displeased drivers, until he stopped in Moruya for a sandwich and a cup of coffee at an outdoor table. A convoy of four-wheel drives towing aluminium boats drove north, fishing rods in their holders, and Harry's thoughts turned from the impenetrability of women's moods to early mornings on the river at Bibbenluke, watching the sun rise and trying to put a dry fly in front of a brown trout. His rods and reels and flies and waders were somewhere under the Burragate farmhouse in a jumble of unclassifiable items that had been brought down from Erskineville in cartons and left for later organisation. The good thing about trout fishing, he'd told Arabella, wasn't the relaxation — it wasn't relaxing but quite intense, in truth, stalking fish; you had to concentrate on what you were seeing and doing, to the exclusion of all else. Crawling through the grass, looking for rising fish, trying to second-guess them with the right fly selection and then tying it on the leader and somehow casting it from beneath a willow without hooking one of its branches. Harry thought of the champion angler, long dead now, who'd made his best rod for him and sprayed it with dull camouflage paint so that his casts wouldn't flash in the sunlight and spook the prey. He grinned as he recalled the old man's story of taking the war-hero former state governor fishing on the Monaro, and how his guest had produced a bottle of Chivas for the anglers at morning tea, throwing the cork into the river and saying, 'They tell me that's how you do it here.'

The bass note of a huge semi-trailer decelerating split the air, and Harry returned to the here and now. Home in time to feed the chooks and get the pump going. Not much water in the house tank. There were some sausages in the freezer and some tomatoes in the garden. As he unlocked the LandCruiser to resume the trip south, it was starting to rain.

At three o'clock that afternoon, the insurance company's solicitor had arranged a conference for Arabella with their consultant architect and engineer. The three crowded into her room and the engineer, who had intended making a weak joke about the coincidence of the barrister's name and his own profession, took one look at Arabella's harassed expression and thought better of it.

'The idea,' said the solicitor, whose name was Virginia and who wore a severely tailored suit, 'is for Ms Engineer to get a quick overview of the technical issues before she starts her serious reading of the expert reports. You know, so she can concentrate on the real issues.'

There was a good deal of nodding, adjusting of spectacles, uncapping of pens and opening and shutting of folders. Arabella took her time to find the architect's report of some sixty pages in Volume 12 and read quickly through the conclusions set out in the last two pages. 'Would I be right, Mr Rudder, to understand that your opinion set out here in detail is that there's nothing fundamentally wrong with the buildings' design?'

'Subject to the engineer's view about the edge beam of the slabs, that's fair enough.' The architect, obviously, had never been concerned with anything as humble as a three-bedroom brick-veneer at North Richmond. His pale linen suit was by Armani, and he wore a startling Gene Meyer tie over a dark olive fine-wool shirt. His spectacle frames were circular tortoiseshell. 'These are cheap, functional houses of no particular merit. Equally, they have no particular faults, unless you object to the flushing loo and the washing machine and the TV all being audible in every room of the house, given the flimsiness of the internal walls. It's all standard lowest common denominator stuff. The developer probably found the designs in a catalogue and paid a licence fee. Or didn't,' he sniffed. 'I would guess that no architect was paid to supervise the builder's work. One wouldn't expect that with this sort of development, at these prices.'

'Have you read the other parties' architects' reports?' Arabella asked him.

'Yes. We all come to the same conclusions, fundamentally, and everybody defers to the engineers on the question of the slab being the cause of the cracking. It probably is.'

Arabella turned to the civil engineer. 'So it looks as though you're going to carry the burden. I've read your report, Mr Gutteridge, but I won't pretend to understand it all. It seems to me that you're a bit lukewarm on the design of the floor slabs.'

The engineer looked more like a bank manager in a grey suit from Fletcher Jones and a maroon tie over a plain white shirt. Stout and uncannily like Ronnie Barker. 'Well, they could have been better. Given the movement you're going to get on clay, they should probably have been stiffened with decent edge beams. Under-engineered, yes.'

'And you'd have to say that if you were asked in cross-examination?'

He nodded to Arabella. 'I would.'

The solicitor wanted to contribute, and turned to Arabella. 'Then in terms of legal liability the lion's share of the blame, and of the damages, has to be attributed to the design engineer, doesn't it?'

'Not exactly, Virginia. If the developer just bought off-the-shelf designs and plonked them down without regard for the environmental conditions — by which I mean clay soil that was going to shrink in the dry weather and swell when it rained — I don't see how you can rope in the design itself. This is all down to local conditions.'

'Well,' the solicitor persisted, 'our client's the council. The slabs were poured before our inspectors came out, and they couldn't see the state of the edge beams when they were buried.'

'Not as simple as that,' the architect said. 'Everyone's going to agree that the inspectors should have signed off on the footings —

or not — before the concrete was poured. They'd seen the plans and specifications. It hardly matters that they were too busy to get to the site in time. I'll leave it to the lawyers, but that's evidence of negligence, isn't it? Failure of the duty of care?'

'In any event,' said the engineer, 'there's not much point attributing the big share of the damages to a defendant who's broke, is there? The council looks to be the last man standing, and I wouldn't be able to say under oath that they're blameless. Might have to wear the lot if it's the only party with a bank account.'

'Or an insurer who'll stand behind it.' The solicitor looked down at her file, then at Arabella, her eyebrows raised.

'Don't look at me, Virginia — at least, not yet. This is my first briefing, and I'm going to have to master all twenty volumes of paper you've delivered before I stick my neck out.'

What she didn't say was that she wanted to run it all past her own counsel before she stuck her neck out. Arabella was well aware that it would have been professional suicide to make any such disclosure in front of this solicitor, whose surname was Fairfax and whose father was a District Court judge with whom Harry had frequently clashed in criminal cases. On one occasion at a country circuit dinner Fairfax J, somewhat disinhibited by overindulgence in free alcohol, had confided to Harry that 'What the judges don't like about you is that you try too hard.' Harry, unaffected by drink but uninhibited as always, responded by asking whether the judges felt the duty of the Bar was to put on a show for their clients' benefit, but ensure that the guilty were, nevertheless, convicted.

As he stepped down from the LandCruiser to swing open the farm gate, Harry noticed that the ground under his shoes was already saturated, and now the heavy showers that he'd driven through since leaving Moruya were gathering strength and becoming a storm, complete with a flash of lightning and thunder to go with it. Harry quickly closed the gate behind him and dropped the short chain over its priapic fastener, the RonLyn nameplate banging against the pipe, and climbed back into the LandCruiser, out of the now heavy rain. As he bumped slowly down towards the house, resisting the jerking steering wheel, he looked at the water that was starting to flow freely in the wheel tracks in front of him, washing small pebbles ahead of it. Ten past three, and the closed-over sky was dark and the high branches of the tall gums were whipping in the wind. He parked under the spreading black wattle, retrieved his bag from the back seat, and ran through the house gate to the verandah. Inside, he turned on the kitchen light, took the sausages out of the freezer to thaw and went to his bedroom to change into shorts and a work shirt. He rang the neighbours to say he was back, leaving a message on their machine and asking them over for a beer later in the week. Picking up his gumboots and a hat from the verandah, he fed the unhappy chickens roosting in their boxes above the wet ground and walked downhill to the river to start up the pump. Much of the fence to one of the lower paddocks was lying on its side.

The Honda pump caught well enough on the third pull of the cord, but coughed and cut out as Harry was on his way back to the house. Investigating, he found the petrol tank dry, and cursed himself for forgetting to pick up any fuel in Eden. Siphoning diesel from the car's tank would be no use. Oh, well, he thought, I'll get petrol in Eden in the morning when I go to the supermarket. Won't be enough water in the tanks for a shower tomorrow. Standing in the warm rain and wiping his wet face with his hand, Harry looked across the river. The sand, wet from the rain, had darkened in colour and the stream was flowing faster and deeper than a week ago. The tough bushes growing on the sand islands were starting to be pushed and pulled by the strengthening current as it rose and reached them.

In the vegetable garden, Harry collected a big handful of beans, a lettuce and some ripe tomatoes. Letting the screen door bang behind him, he stood in the kitchen and stripped off his sodden clothes, then draped them over a clotheshorse on the verandah. He changed the bed linen and tossed the old sheets and pillowslip into the washing machine, together with the dirty clothes he'd brought back from Sydney. When he started the machine, the kitchen lights momentarily dimmed, and he wondered if another blackout was imminent. They'd become more frequent in recent weeks. The phone rang and he picked it up.

'You're speaking to a naked man.' Harry ran a hand through his wet hair and went into the bathroom to fetch a towel, still carrying the phone handset.

'And that's supposed to excite me?' It was Surrey.

'I thought it was Bella calling. Sorry. It's pissing down here, Dave, and the phone doesn't like it — keep your voice up.'

'You could use the rain, couldn't you? It's been a pretty dry spring, up here at least.'

'Yeah, it has. But it looks like it's been raining solidly here for the past few days. I don't need a flood.'

Surrey laughed. '"We'll all be rooned,' said Hanrahan." You're sounding like a cocky, old mate.'

'You rang up to insult me, did you, you supercilious townie bastard?'

'No, to ask whether you want me to send the Sommerville brief down. The police papers have just arrived here. I can put copies of everything in the document-exchange satchel tonight, and it should be with Hugo in the morning. You can collect it from him.' Hugo was an amiable Bega solicitor with a branch office in Eden.

'Yep. May as well. I won't be able to do much else here if this rain sets in — the grass needs cutting, which'll take a couple of days to do, and the kangaroos have knocked over a fence, so I've got to rebuild that, and there are a lot of vegie seedlings to plant, but none of that's going to happen until it dries out.'

And then the phone, which depended on a satellite link, went dead. Harry looked at the handset, shrugged and replaced it in its slot before dressing in dry clothes. Not yet six o'clock, but he made himself dinner. Despite the storm, it was still light enough to walk down to the river at nine, which he did with the benefit of an umbrella, a yellow slicker and bare feet. The stream had doubled in width, spreading out across its coarse sandy bed, and was perhaps half a metre deeper than when he'd arrived home five hours earlier. In the paddock bordered by the creek feeding into the river, one of the chestnut trees had split in half at the thickest part of its trunk, which saddened Harry. He wondered what wombats did when the entrances to their burrows were under water.

Back on the verandah, Harry pulled a leech off his ankle and squashed it with a loose river stone from the garden. He hung up his wet-weather gear and went inside to try the television, but the signal wasn't penetrating the downpour. Nor would the radio work. He put on his *Magic Flute* CD and looked for a suitable book to read, but could find nothing, so he lay on the sofa and listened to the Queen of the Night competing with the wind and the sound of the rain on his tin roof. The quince tree was banging its branches against the guttering.

At six the next morning the electricity was off, the rain was still thundering onto the roof and the view from Harry's bedroom window between the stout trunks of the ribbon gums, their branches still whipping in the strong wind, was of the river running a banker one hundred metres wide, with no sand visible. Harry could see that the bottom paddock was under at least a metre of dark brown water, and the river was rushing by at great pace, its surface crowded with white foam, logs and fencing debris. He guessed that the power poles where the cables crossed the river near the Towamba bridge had been swept over, and it was going to be some time before a crew came out from Eden and restored the power supply. He went downhill to check, and saw that the river had risen well above his pump, and the fallen chestnut. Maybe the pump had been carried away. Flooded, but not enough water in the house to take a shower. He decided to get away while it was still possible. Quickly dressing and packing all he needed to get back to Sydney, Harry locked up and climbed into the LandCruiser but then got back out to fill the chicken feeder, trusting that it would suffice for a week, or until he could ask the neighbours to look in on the hens. If the neighbours could cross the creek, that is. He put out some old dishes to catch rainwater for the chooks to drink.

He drove out of the property and stopped to padlock the gate. The creek was over the road one hundred metres east, downhill from the gate, but to no great depth — yet — and he pressed on. At Towamba, the long low bridge on the side road south to the village and its school was so far submerged as to be invisible. Maybe it wasn't even there any more. Cars were stopped on both sides of the river, with people out of them, yelling across to each other.

School-aged children in raincoats and sou'westers were smiling, confident that Towamba Primary would be closed for some considerable time. Harry stopped for a word with his neighbours, saying that he was going to try to get to the highway before things got any worse, and they wished him good luck. 'See you back here in ten minutes,' one said.

Harry drove slowly east, over gravel sections of the road that were heavily corrugated, and getting worse. In many places, torrents of water spread across the surface from little white waterfalls descending from higher ground. About ten kilometres from the highway, a big gum had fallen across the road and its wet black trunk stood cantilevered on one large branch that had speared vertically into the softened surface. Harry stopped and tried to calculate whether the LandCruiser could squeeze beneath the tree. As he considered the dimensions of vehicle and obstacle, a white utility truck from the council arrived, flashing its yellow light, and its driver, in full wet-weather gear, walked under the fallen tree to discuss Harry's options with him.

'I reckon you'll be right,' he said. 'Anyhow, if you don't get past now, you're going to have to wait a couple of hours until we can get the chainsaws here and cut it up. We're pretty busy. Look, just go slowly and I'll give you a yell.'

With the council man watching and encouraging him, Harry inched the big vehicle forward. At the last moment, the man shouted to him to stop. 'There's only an inch in it, but you'll scrape the roof if you keep going. What a bastard.'

Harry got out to look. 'Gee, it really is only an inch, isn't it? What do you reckon about me letting the tyres down?'

Just then, a larger truck signalled by more flashing yellow lights arrived with four men aboard, and lots of ladders and ropes and chainsaws and hazard triangles and Road Closed signs. The crew got out to enjoy Harry's dilemma. 'Bloke reckons he can get through if he lets his tyres down,' said the first man.

The foreman looked at Harry. 'Not as dumb as he looks, is he?'

Harry laughed. 'I couldn't be,' he said. 'It's either that, or get you bastards to lower the road.'

Deflation worked. The crew whistled and waved as Harry slipped under the tree, blew the horn, and headed for the highway and a service station with an air hose. He topped up the fuel tank out of gratitude, and from there he drove to a café in the main street of Eden and ordered the full-scale cooked breakfast. Three fried eggs, bacon, tomato, two sausages and toast. He had to make do with reading the *Imlay Magnet*, no *Sydney Morning Herald* having made it so far south through the storm, until the solicitor's office opened for business and he could collect the Sommerville brief.

At nine o'clock, the receptionist opened up, handed the papers over and let Harry use their phone to call Surrey, who said, 'Why don't you come up here to Goulburn? You can stay with us and work the thing up in the office here. I've got everything you need. When the water goes down, it's a much shorter drive home for you. It'll only be a couple of days. The girls would love to see you.'

They discussed it for a couple of minutes until the eavesdropping receptionist interrupted to tell Harry that he wouldn't be able to get up to Goulburn. 'Brown Mountain's closed on the other side of Bemboka, and so's the Kings Highway up from Batemans Bay through Braidwood. Landslides on both of them. There's only the Princes Highway.'

Harry relayed that news to Surrey. 'Well,' he said, 'the ABC's saying the highway's cut at Bega, so maybe you're not going anywhere.'

But he got through. The river flats south of Pambula were flooded, and the police were only waving through large trucks and proper four-wheel drives. North of Pambula, the road was clear and he made good time. At Bega, everything was saturated but the sun was shining and Harry eventually picked his way through the residential streets indicated by Detour signs, bypassing the flooded low-lying areas to the north of town and rejoining the main road. After that, it was pretty plain sailing, but the farm fences he bowled past were festooned with debris that indicated the depth of the flood earlier in the day. Harry was certain that Burragate and Towamba wouldn't recover so quickly, and listened to the ABC's reports from Eden. Still raining down there, rivers still rising, bridges out. Emergency declared.

Somewhere south of Wollongong, he was lamenting the loss of the Jaguar with its on-board phone when he suddenly recalled that he now had a mobile in his bag. Harry stopped to retrieve it and called Arabella in chambers to bemoan his fate and tell her that he was heading for the smoke.

'The phone's out at Burragate, so I missed your calls.'

'I didn't make any.'

'Be that as it may,' Harry said, 'I'll need a bed for the night. Yours isn't occupied, is it?'

'Indomitable and incorrigible,' she responded. 'It's just as well you're coming. I need to ask you about edge beams.'

'They speak of little else at Burragate,' he said. 'I'm your man. Be there in ninety minutes.'

It took some hours for Harry to thaw out Arabella that night. They both tiptoed over the eggshells of Harry spending Christmas alone in Tuscany, never actually addressing the subject.

Harry made dinner — a risotto — and regaled her with a grossly exaggerated account of his narrow escape from the Burragate flood. Arabella was unfamiliar enough with the extremes of the Australian climate not to disbelieve most of what he told her, and listened in while he phoned his neighbours to obtain an update on the river's condition. Relating to Arabella what they told him, he exaggerated even more.

'Robert says the river water's going to be undrinkable and unusable for a couple of weeks. They're okay over at their place — they've got a back-up rainwater tank — but mine's rusted out, and it's going to be a problem.'

'I see.'

'I was thinking I'd get Dave to organise some conferences in the Sommerville thing while I'm up here.'

'Probably a good idea.' Thawed out, but not warm.

When they got into bed, Harry stayed on his side. All night.

Harry spent the next day, having contacted Surrey about organising some conferences with the client and his witnesses, in bookshops and record stores, restocking Burragate's library for the coming months. Arabella rang him on the mobile, which she had insisted he should carry in his pocket, to say that someone in chambers had tickets for *La Bohème* that night that they weren't going to be able to use.

'Would I like it, Harry? Bollywood's more to my taste.'

'In that case, and assuming it's the Baz Luhrmann production, you'll love it. Totally Bollywood, as young people would say. It's a young person's opera.'

It wasn't the Luhrmann production but Gale Edwards, and they both loved it. At the interval, they strolled with other audience members on the Opera House broadwalk, looking across at The Rocks and the lights of the Bridge and drinking domestic méthode champenoise priced as if it were Billecart-Salmon. Assertive little ferries pushed aside the glistening velvet-black water, and an empty train rattled noisily over to Milsons Point on its way up the North Shore. The office buildings surrounding Circular Quay were all lit up, but deserted except for the cleaners.

Harry finished his drink. He praised the singing and, especially, the acting. 'That girl playing Musetta — she's going to be huge. How often do you see a singer as beautiful as she is?'

Arabella put her arm around his waist. 'Is this an attempt to make me jealous?'

'Only if it works.'

'You can't avoid Tuscany forever, Harry.'

'Are you referring to the place, or the topic of Christmas?' He took her empty glass, and the bells started ringing. The audience headed back inside, carrying them with it. Harry returned the glasses to the bar, grateful that there wasn't time to continue the conversation.

David Surrey had been able to arrange for his consultant forensic pathologist in the Sommerville trial to fly down from Brisbane at short notice, to confer with counsel in Arabella's chambers the next afternoon, even if he couldn't himself attend.

The doctor was late, phoning from the airport to say that the taxi queue was a kilometre long and that he'd be there as soon as he could. Arabella was somewhat uneasy about holding a conference without a solicitor being present.

'The Bar Rules don't allow it, Harry.'

'That's about self-protection for barristers, Bella. It's so you don't see a criminal client on your own who'll later verbal you, if he thinks it will help him. You know: "I wanted to plead guilty and show how remorseful I was, but the barrister wouldn't let me." Hardly applies to an expert witness, and I've got you to corroborate my version of whatever may be said, anyway.'

'Perhaps. Makes you a bit sorry for solicitors, though. No protective rule for them.'

'Solicitors are big girls. They can look after themselves.' Harry looked at his brief, which was one-twentieth the size of the brief in Arabella's building case that loomed in one corner of the room, still stacked on a trolley. 'I don't know this pathologist. Never had him in a case, which is hardly surprising, his being from Queensland.'

'That'd be the usual problem, wouldn't it? Sydney pathologists not wanting to contradict each other?'

Harry snorted. 'Bloody medical profession.'

Arabella looked out the window at the chambers building on the opposite side of Phillip Street. 'And how easy would it be to get a Sydney silk to give evidence of professional negligence against one of his learned friends, Harry?'

'They'd line up. Do it for nothing. Wouldn't even charge a fee.' He continued looking at the report in front of him, turning pages then backtracking. 'There's a funny gap in this bloke's CV. Did you pick that up? We'll have to ask him about it.'

'Suspicious, do you mean?'

Harry tapped the document with his finger. 'There's a faint bell ringing in the back of my mind.'

'Do you want me to Google him?'

'Dunno how we ever managed without it.' Harry, who had taken Arabella's chair, yielded it and she pulled her keyboard forward and typed 'Dr Craig Bonaventura' into the search engine. Harry looked over her shoulder at the page of results. He jabbed one entry on the screen with his finger. 'Let's have a look at that.'

Up came a judgment of the Queensland Medical Tribunal. Harry pulled over a chair and sat, and they read the screen together, quickly scrolling to the relevant part.

[1] The Tribunal convened to undertake a formal hearing into whether Dr Bonaventura had engaged in professional misconduct, in that he was found guilty by the District Court of Queensland at Brisbane of:

(a) five counts of the indictable offence of obtaining property by deception, committed between June 2007 and March 2008, in relation to obtaining a monetary advance from five different financial institutions on the security of the same vintage motor vehicle; and

(b) four counts of the indictable offence of perjury, committed within the same period, in relation to four statutory declarations given by him to financial institutions in which he falsely claimed that he was the legal and beneficial owner of the vehicle.

[2] A series of matters was acknowledged by Dr Bonaventura:

(a) He obtained a Bachelor of Medical Science with Honours in 1978 and a Bachelor of Medicine and Bachelor of Surgery in 1980, from Queensland University.

(b) He specialised as a Forensic Pathologist.

(c) On five separate occasions between June 2007 and March 2008, Dr Bonaventura approached financial institutions seeking to obtain a monetary advance on the security of the same vintage motor vehicle which he claimed he had recently purchased for $95,000 from Historic Cars of New Farm.

(d) In support of his applications for finance to the various financial institutions, Dr Bonaventura provided documentation in the form of a receipt from Historic Cars of New Farm and a statutory declaration falsely swearing *inter alia* that he was the registered owner of the vehicle and that it was not subject to any charges, liens or other encumbrances.

(e) Dr Bonaventura never paid for the vehicle and it remained in the possession of the dealer.

(f) In particular, on 27 June 2007 he got a receipt marked 'Paid' from the son of the proprietor of Historic Cars of New Farm after assuring him that his father knew all about the transaction. Dr Bonaventura gave a personal cheque for $2000 to the son but this was dishonoured a few days later. The receipt was provided to the National Bank and Cookabundy Finance Pty Ltd and he entered into agreements with them and they advanced him the stated value of the vehicle.

(g) On 28 November 2007 he obtained a further invoice from the dealer describing the vehicle and indicating the price of $95,000. This document was later altered by having the word 'Paid' written on it and it was provided to Bendigo Bank Limited and he entered into an agreement with them and they advanced him the stated value of the vehicle.

(h) On 9 January 2008 Dr Bonaventura obtained a further receipt marked 'Paid in full' from the dealer for the vehicle on the strength of his indicating that he wished to trade in another vintage car, a 1926 Alvis 12/50, and providing a personal cheque for the balance being $29,000. On this occasion, he instructed the dealer not to cash the cheque for several weeks. This receipt was provided to Advance Bank Australia Limited and Delhi Finance Limited and he entered into agreements with them and they advanced him the stated value of the vehicle.

(i) The total amount received by Dr Bonaventura from the five different finance companies by deception was $418,817.09. He made intermittent repayments to the finance companies and the total loss sustained was $385,839.25.

(j) Dr Bonaventura was declared bankrupt in September 2008.

(k) Dr Bonaventura was found guilty of five counts of obtaining property by deception and four counts of perjury, committed between June 2007 and March 2008.

Neither Harry nor Arabella said anything for some time. Both kept looking at the computer screen and then Harry crossed back to the other side of the desk.

'And he's to be our star witness? God help us.'

'But it wasn't his professional expertise that was at issue in the tribunal.' Arabella sounded doubtful. 'David says he's the best there is on paediatric cerebral injuries.'

'No doubt. But he'll be eaten alive. They can portray him to the jury as a disgraced and dishonest man, struck off the roll. Just a mouth for hire who's so desperate for a quid that he'll say whatever he's paid by the defence to say. Zero credit.'

The phone rang and Arabella answered it, said, 'Thanks, ask him to wait,' and hung up.

'He's here.'

Harry thought for a while. 'You'd better let me handle this, Bella. Maybe he can still be of help.'

'It's all yours, Harry, and welcome to it. Will I get him sent round?'

Harry nodded and they again exchanged places, Harry behind the desk and Arabella sitting to one side. She buzzed her receptionist and asked for Dr Bonaventura to be shown to her room. He knocked and entered, carrying a very expensive-looking briefcase and carry-on bag. Harry invited him to sit, they exchanged names, Dr Bonaventura produced a business card, and Harry turned the screen of Arabella's computer around to face the consultant. Recognising the words he was confronted with, he pursed his lips. Harry returned the screen to its original position.

'That's our problem, as you can well imagine. Is Mr Surrey aware of it?'

'I have no idea. He certainly didn't raise the subject with me.' The doctor tugged at a cufflink.

'And you obviously didn't feel the need to disclose it to him.'

Expensive suit, expensive luggage, expensive haircut, but bankrupt, Harry thought. Fur coat and no knickers, as the cockneys were fond of saying. Not my problem. My problem is that I can't expect a jury to accept anything you say. It occurred to Harry that this man had probably already extracted from Surrey, at the Sommerville family's expense, a business-class ticket for his flights, and a night at the Hilton before he returned to BrisVegas. He certainly looked the type.

'Well, Mr Bonaventura—'

'Doctor.'

'No, *Mister* Bonaventura, in your case "Doctor" would be a courtesy title. You don't have a doctorate, I note.'

Sullen silence from the other side of the desk. Harry wasn't finished yet. 'I'd better get this other issue straightened out, as well, or it's going to nag at me: what sort of car was it?'

'Car? I don't know what you mean.'

'The one you fraudulently claimed to have traded the Alvis in on. What was it?'

'Oh. A Ferrari. 1969 Dino.'

Harry laughed. 'For $95,000? Are they all stupid?'

Shamefaced. 'It wasn't a very good one. No engine, and it needed a new gearbox. Someone had put a Ford V8 in it. Some question about its authenticity.'

Harry smiled and shook his head. 'Only in Queensland,' he said. 'I know.'

Arabella thought it best to intervene before the exchange ended in tears. 'Now that's out of the way, can we decide how you can help with this, if at all? Dr Bonaventura, Harry believes we can't put you in front of the jury because of the fraud. Have you been giving expert evidence in Queensland without any problems?'

'Not since I was convicted and struck off. This will be the first time.' He seemed grateful that she, at least, persisted with use of the courtesy title.

'No,' said Harry, 'it won't. Call me old-fashioned, but I want to win this case.'

'Look,' Bonaventura said, with what Arabella heard as a note of desperation in his voice, 'I *can* help. This prosecution case is a molehill of bullshit pushed into a mountain by a bunch of second-raters who think they can make money out of being experts on child abuse. I can give you the ammunition to blow them out of the water, even if you're not prepared to call me as a witness. If you're willing and able to do the homework, you won't need any expert witnesses.'

Harry closed his folder and sat back. 'Tell me more.'

'The prosecution are entirely dependent on this group of doctors from a backwater private hospital, who think they can carve out a niche for themselves, and attract a fortune in consultation fees and grants and government funding, by setting themselves up as consultant forensic child-abuse experts, as if they're the font of all wisdom.'

'Fount of all knowledge,' Harry corrected him.

'Whatever. The point is that they've never been seriously challenged, and it's high time they were. In fact, they've done bugger-all by way of original research, and just parrot off the literature — or the literature that suits their cockamamie theories. They turn a blind eye to anything that doesn't suit them. They have a superannuated neurosurgeon in this case who hasn't been in an operating theatre for fifteen years. He's a professional joke. They're very vulnerable to a well-briefed attack, I can assure you.'

'And I can assure you,' said Harry, 'that we'll do the homework. Anything you assign to us, within reason. But I'm going to hold you to your promise that you can brief us into a winning position. So, how's this: we'll read and understand everything you tell us to, and we'll plan all the cross-examination with your guidance and approval. If you're satisfied that we're on top of it, and that the attack is as good as it can ever be, are you prepared to stake your fee on our success?'

'You mean ... I'm only paid if there's an acquittal?'

'That's exactly what I mean.'

Arabella started to form words of protest, but Harry held up a hand silencing any dissent. Bonaventura was thinking. He sat in silence for what seemed to the lawyers to be a very long time.

'All right.'

Harry nodded. 'I'll tell Mr Surrey. Seeing you're down in Sydney, you can spend tonight and as much of tomorrow morning as you need to print out a list of the essential literature for us to master and where we can find it. That's the first step. There's no point in Ms Engineer doing her own internet medical research, because we can't discriminate and you can. And you can also give us as much dirt as you can come up with on these self-appointed geniuses, or at least tell us where to find it. Email it or bring it all here by two o'clock tomorrow, if you can. After that, we'll meet again in a week or so to prepare the cross-examinations, individually. We'll need two or three days for that.'

'All right.'

Harry stood and held out his hand to Bonaventura for the first time. 'We'll be seeing you.' They shook, the doctor turned and shook Arabella's hand, and left.

'You're a hard man, Harry Curry.'

'Can I come up and see you some time?'

'You still have the key, don't you?'

Dinner that night was at Le Pelican at Taylor Square. When Harry decided on the entrée of *girolles*, he asked to speak first to the chef. 'I didn't know anyone grew *girolles* in Australia,' he said.

'No, they don't,' said the Frenchman. 'They're flown in. Would you like to see them?'

Harry said he would, and the chef returned to the kitchen and came back with a small open cardboard box in which the tiny orange fungi were lovingly packed. 'One hundred and forty dollars a kilo,' he told them.

'I'm celebrating,' Harry said. 'Do you think you could have them send us out a Mercurey? The 2006, I think.' He was in a good mood, having successfully used the force of his personality to put Bonaventura exactly where he wanted him.

When the chef left to despatch the wine and supervise preparation of their *onglets de boeuf*, Arabella tackled Harry about his treatment of the unfortunate ex-pathologist.

'What, exactly, are we celebrating? The poor man's mortification, do you mean?'

'More a matter of motivation than mortification, I would have said. He was a very naughty boy to commit that sin of omission with Dave, and you have to ask yourself whether he would ever have voluntarily disclosed it to us. Yes, I know he's in professional *extremis*, but that's never going to justify an attempt to sting the

Sommervilles for a shameless fee, expenses at the top of the range, and then almost certainly cop a total discrediting at the hands of the Crown in front of the jury, with catastrophic consequences for the young man facing the murder charge.'

Arabella tried the wine and liked it. Very much. 'Harry, I don't accept for a moment that he was going to keep it a secret, and neither do I think he's a cynic or an opportunist, as you seem to believe. Be fair. He's suffered destruction of his reputation to such a degree that his expertise is now judged to be of no account. You and I could have no idea of his feelings. He must loathe himself. He's hardly going to compromise all he has left — his expertise.'

'You're probably right, although the haircut might indicate a certain self-regard.' Harry finished his entrée. 'In any event, maybe he'll take the opportunity to rehabilitate himself with the assistance he can give young Sommerville. If the prosecution's experts are as unimpressive as he says, it has to be possible to discredit them. He'd be performing a service.'

'About that medical evidence preparation,' Arabella said, pausing while the waiter removed Harry's entrée plate. 'I can't be much help there, because I've still got that building case to get on top of.'

'I appreciate that. One day it's geotechnical controversies, the next it's paediatric neurology. Never let it be said that the Bar doesn't offer us challenges. It's the best thing about what we do, I think.'

'I'm not sure that most of our learned friends would agree with that.' Arabella poured some water into her second glass.

Harry drank deeply, and then held his glass up to the light to admire the wine's colour. 'There was a bloke in my old chambers who did nothing but injured applicants' cases in the compo court for maybe twenty years. Didn't stop him vomiting in the loo every morning before he put on his wig and gown.'

The *onglet* was every bit as good as the *girolles* that preceded it, and as the *millefeuille* that followed it. Harry didn't have to stay on his side of the bed that night. It probably helped that he confided, as he calculated the waiter's tip, that he'd cancelled the trip to Lucca. Hadn't actually booked it, not yet.

Arabella's building case, having been referred to an eminent retired engineer for the arbitration process, convened not in a courtroom but in a large room at the Dispute Resolution Centre, in order to deal with the preliminaries before the presentation of evidence commenced. As Harry had predicted, the many interested parties all had their own legal representation, and there were almost thirty lawyers jammed around the squared-off tables or standing behind them. The referee looked daunted at the array confronting him, and the process of noting appearances took almost half an hour.

'I have arranged,' he then told the lawyers, 'for us to view the subject properties next week, on Monday. Your experts have all been out there, of course, and I trust that this will be the last time we need to inconvenience the householders. If the parties agree, I was going to see if the court can arrange a couple of mini-buses to take us there.'

There was an audible sniff from one of the Senior Counsel who had assertively placed himself next to the referee. It was well known at the Bar that this man, universally disliked and mysteriously nicknamed 'Deborah', had recently leased for himself a new Maserati Quattroporte — confirming his learned friends' assessment of him as a pretentious *arriviste*. 'Jumped-up' was the more commonly used epithet. There was no way that Deborah was going to travel in a mini-bus, not when he could cut a swathe through the far western suburbs in a car worth roughly twice as much as any of the bungalows at issue in the proceedings. 'Some of us would prefer to make our own way out,' he told the referee.

'Suit yourself,' was the reply. In the end, the communal transport option was abandoned and by the time the day's formalities were completed, Arabella's solicitor had agreed that the referee could travel out to the site with the council's representatives.

'Isn't that a bit improper?' Arabella asked later, as they drank coffee at Society Caffe in Phillip Street. 'I mean, shouldn't the arbitrator keep his distance? Justice has to be done and it has to appear to be done, as they say.'

'We're not going to worry about it,' said Virginia. 'It's not a secret arrangement — he asked me for a lift in front of everyone, and they had their opportunity to object, so they can forever hold their peace. Anyway, he's not a judge or even a lawyer, so I don't consider that those rules apply.'

Arabella felt and looked sceptical, but decided not to make an enemy by arguing about it.

'And it'll give us a chance to make friends with him,' the solicitor grinned, discomfiting Arabella even more. Australians were always doing things that took her by surprise.

When Arabella got home at nine that night, Harry had already eaten and was sitting at the dining table, engrossed in a document on the screen of his laptop.

'Sorry,' she told him. 'The Women at the Bar Committee wouldn't get to the point.'

'I shall refrain from making the obvious comment,' Harry said, flicking his eyes up from the screen for no more than an instant.

'No, go ahead. You couldn't possibly say anything I haven't already thought.' She hung her jacket in the bedroom and walked back out to the kitchen. 'Did you leave any of that quiche?'

When Harry made no reply, she went back to where he was sitting, still reading. 'Harry? Is there anything to eat? And what's so fascinating, anyway?'

'It's an article from the *Journal of American Physicians and Surgeons* about the shaken baby syndrome.' Harry pushed back from the screen and looked up at her. 'You're going to have to read it, but I think it may well be the complete answer to this case. Bonaventura put this at the top of the list of the literature he wants us to master, with a string of asterisks against it. I can see why.'

'I'm not going to read it on an empty stomach.' Arabella headed back to the kitchen.

'There's still half the quiche and a takeaway salad in the fridge. And some sauvignon blanc, I hope, because I want a drink.' Harry joined her by the fridge and volunteered to organise her meal while Arabella changed. 'Hurry up — *Boston Legal*'s on in half an hour.'

Arabella, surprised, paused at the bedroom door. '*Boston Legal*? Since when did you watch that?'

Looking slightly sheepish, Harry confessed that back in the Erskineville bachelor days, it was one of his viewing compulsions. 'Nothing if not unpredictable,' she noted as she sat on the bed to remove her shoes.

'Oh,' he called, 'and I forgot to say: Dave rang this afternoon. We've got a judge, and it's set down for the last week of term.'

'What? Sommerville?'

'Sommerville. The family's all in favour — they want to get it over and done with before Christmas.'

Arabella left her clothes on the bed and pulled on running shorts and a tank top. They won't be in such a hurry if it's a loser, she thought. Walking into the bathroom to wash her face and hands, she asked Harry what he thought about such a sudden start.

'Fine with me,' he called from the kitchen. 'As long as we can finish it in a week. I don't think the jury would be happy to have their turkey dinner at Darlo, either.'

Arabella reappeared in the living room. Very long legs and elegant bare feet, Harry thought — not for the first time. She looked troubled. 'But the judge'll adjourn it for Christmas if it runs over, surely? Who is it, anyway?'

'Rathmines. Not a bad draw, in fact, if a bit obsessive about his own brilliance. Maybe he'll give us a day or two off, but that's all.' Harry took the quiche out of the microwave and put it on a plate with the salad. Arabella collected a knife and fork out of the top drawer and took her meal to the dining table. Harry poured two glasses of wine and joined her.

'Do you know Rathmines personally?'

'We were in the same chambers for a couple of years, up to the time he was appointed to the Supreme Court. At his send-off, he gave a speech about how little time it was going to take to convert him from a judge-hating barrister to a barrister-hating judge.'

'Is that what he is?'

'No more than anyone else. They tell me he watches *Judge John Deed* on cable TV and identifies with him. All the same, he's always been reasonable to me.'

'I don't know how much use I'm going to be,' Arabella said. 'We've got a view in the building case at the start of next week, and I'm going to have to prepare for that. Presuming that's all we have to do before the end of term, that'll only give me six days to work on the shaken child.'

Harry finished his drink and poured himself the few cc's left in the bottle. 'Should be enough. I'll see if I can carve off some particular issues for you, or at least one particular issue, and I'll do the rest.' He looked at his watch, then located the remote and turned on the TV. Alan Shore and Denny Crane appeared in the uniform of the US Coast Guard. 'I've seen this one,' he complained.

'But I haven't,' said Arabella, bringing her glass to the sofa and making herself comfortable. 'Where do you think they get their stories?'

'*Halsbury's Laws of England*, probably. Either there, or Disneyland. Not that I mind.' He turned up the television's sound with the remote, and they watched in silence for five minutes before Harry said, 'I think this is the one where the judge is caught with his pants down in a public lavatory.'

'More of a documentary, then,' Arabella said.

The weekend was spent by both barristers in reading and making notes and thinking, sometimes out loud. Harry spent almost as much time consulting the online medical dictionary as he did reading the expert reports. 'This'll go down a treat with the jury,' he called out on Sunday afternoon. '"An injury threshold for neural tissue must be the product of mass and acceleration and is related to the inverse of the mass of the individual brain raised to two-thirds power." I've always said that, haven't I?'

'How are twelve laymen and laywomen, none of them smart enough to get out of their jury summonses, going to handle that?' Arabella asked, looking up from her folder. 'Just as well they don't have juries in building cases. Most of this stuff's equally impenetrable, and the trouble is that their experts seem — at least to me — to be just as logical and just as persuasive as our experts. It seems so silly when you have an expert referee. Why can't he decide on the basis of his own expertise? Thirteen parties, more than twenty experts … what a waste of money!'

Harry wouldn't agree. 'A waste of time, Bella, certainly. But let no lawyer say it's a waste of money.'

'I see your point. Afternoon tea?'

Harry closed the lid on his laptop. 'I thought you'd never ask. Let's get some fresh air.'

It was a beautiful early summer afternoon, and they strolled to the Elizabeth Bay shops where they chose a café and sat outside to drink coffee and eat *biscotti*. A homeless man came by and asked for money, which Harry gave him. A five-dollar note. 'It'll get you into the Matt Talbot tonight, if you want,' he said.

The man studied the note in his hand and nodded.

'You all right, mate?' Harry asked.

'I won't tell you,' the man said. 'It'd only upset you.' Harry laughed, and the man walked up the hill towards Kings Cross. A couple and their two children, riding scooters and wearing Roosters' jerseys, gave him a wide berth.

Harry borrowed Arabella's BlackBerry and phoned his neighbour at Burragate. Arabella listened to one side of the conversation.

'G'day, Robert. It's Harry. How's everything?' A pause. 'He didn't lose any, did he?' A longer pause. 'Thank Christ for that. How are your fences?' A short pause. 'Listen — I'm thinking of coming back down tomorrow night. You reckon that'd be okay?' A medium-length pause. 'Good on you. You want me to bring anything from town? You sure? Okay, I'll be over for a beer before tea.' A short pause. 'See you then.'

Harry switched the phone off. 'The news from Lake Wobegone is that the water's gone down a lot and the power's back on. Half Col's cows are stuck on the other side of the river, but he didn't lose any of the calves. My chooks have been fed, but they've stopped laying.'

'Who could blame them? The way you described it, they were probably expecting to be taken aboard by Noah. Did he say anything about the road, or the bridge?'

'I forgot to ask, but he would have said. Gives me something to look forward to when I get down there.'

'Did you get an invitation to dinner?' She stood up and retrieved her BlackBerry.

'Tea. Dinner's the midday meal in the country.'

Arabella studied Harry's face to see if that was a joke. 'Seriously?'

'Seriously. You get used to it.'

'You love it, don't you? Floods and droughts and wombats?'

'And tea at six o'clock. There wouldn't be a single person in a twenty-five-mile radius of Burragate who could tell you the name of the Chief Justice of the High Court.'

'Including local solicitors?'

'Them most of all. There's even a barrister lives down there who's forgotten the name.'

'No bad thing.'

Harry put money on the table and covered it with the sugar bowl, took Arabella's hand, and they walked back to her flat. The further they walked, the tighter he held her hand. Eventually, he let it go and put his arm around her waist. She followed suit, and they walked, smiling, in silence. No more work took place that afternoon, or that evening.

On Monday morning, Harry took off in the LandCruiser after breakfast, the papers for the murder trial in a cardboard carton on the seat beside him. Arabella came out to the street with him to say goodbye, carrying her briefcase. After he'd gone, she stayed on the footpath and waited for Virginia, the council's solicitor, to pick her up. She was right on time, in the latest model Volvo four-wheel drive. 'For the dogs,' she explained when Arabella commented on the size of the car for a single woman. They picked up the engineer-referee in town (Arabella had to be reminded of his name — Haskins), in front of the arbitration venue, and headed for North Richmond, where all the parties' lawyers were to assemble at 10.30. There was a narrow amplitude to their conversation en route, all three studiously avoiding anything that hinted at the facts or the merits of the case with which they were involved. The Vietnamese market gardens they passed along the Windsor Road at Vineyard were the subject of exaggerated interest and observation. There were a few hostile looks from the other legal teams as the three descended from the car at the *locus in quo* in Bowen Mountain Road, but nobody voiced their antipathy.

The claimants' houses were arrayed on either side of a short cul de sac — five down each side, with a turning circle at the western end. There were two floor plans evident: the double-fronted bungalows either oriented with the front door and living-room picture window on the left or right-hand side, both styles featuring a narrow overhung verandah parallel to the street. Behind the houses were open paddocks, awaiting the next stage of Sydney's urban sprawl and another developer's gentle touch.

Mr Haskins bustled off to gather the lawyers together and agree on a plan of inspections, with Arabella and Virginia following at a distance suggestive of non-alignment.

Virginia paused and turned on her high heels through 360 degrees. 'God, what a depressing place. And it's going to rain.' The gunmetal clouds had been building all morning, and seemed to back up from the Blue Mountains, preparing to open their swelling bellies.

Arabella was forced to agree with her instructing solicitor's opinion. Most of the houses looked practically abandoned. In two, derelict cars occupied what should have been the front gardens. There was a caravan beside one house, obviously occupied by several people. Children emerged from its door to stare sullenly and silently at the men and women in suits. A trio of obese young women in tracksuit bottoms and too tight tops gathered in the turning circle. Children did wheelies on their bicycles, riding as fast and as close as they could to the interlopers. Arabella looked over the fence of the last house on the northern side of the road and saw a horse restively pacing in soft mud, its hoofprints everywhere. Not a blade of grass remained, and a bale of hay, split open, was scattered across the back yard. The horse circled a Hills hoist with babies' clothes pegged to its wires. It was already humid and getting hotter. The male lawyers were removing their jackets and carrying them.

Mr Haskins announced that they'd start at the first house on the northern side, and led the lawyers (in what appeared to Arabella to be their order of seniority) through the first front door. The inspection went slowly, with the householders — they all seemed to be women, most with little children around their feet — wanting to point out cracks in the walls, not all of which were evident to the naked eyes of the solicitors and barristers, who frequently glanced at each other in silent corroboration that there was little to be seen. As the legal caravan progressed from house to house, more and more of the lawyers dropped out, not needing to see or hear any more. Arabella stayed the course, listening to the aggrieved women for whom she was having difficulty feeling any sympathy, and least of all when they demanded that someone buy them new homes. They all said 'home', not 'house'. The referee dutifully kept making notes on his clipboard, which carried the nine checklists he had prepared before leaving the city.

When the inspections were finished and all the complaints had been duly noted, the first drops of rain fell. There was hurried agreement that the view was over, and people climbed into their cars. Deborah's Maserati chirped its back tyres as it took off under unwarranted and ostentatious acceleration, exposing the words 'wash me' that some boys had lettered on its boot lid in smears of the local yellow clay, quite unjustifiably — because, until they got their hands on the car, it had been perfectly clean.

The heavens opened, and Haskins, Arabella and Virginia ran for the Volvo. As they fastened their seat belts, the referee pointed through the wet windscreen at the one house they hadn't visited. 'Those can only be the people who aren't part of the action,' he said.

Arabella, from the back seat, looked closely at the house. 'It's the only house in the street with a garden.' Which was true. Bright yellow dahlias blossomed in front of the low front fence, and behind it were well-tended beds of tall sunflowers, cosmos daisies in several colours, grevilleas and callistemons. Against the brick-veneer walls of the house's facade was a narrow bed of camellia bushes, and geraniums in flower. There was a recently mown lawn of couch grass and a concrete path leading to the front porch on which a brightly painted tricycle had been parked out of the now thundering rain. 'Do you think it would be all right ...'

'Do we think it would be all right to what?' Virginia turned to ask.

Mr Haskins also turned and smiled at Arabella. 'I think she's asking whether we could visit that house. Complete the set.'

Virginia looked doubtful. 'Everyone's gone,' she pointed out.

'Not everyone.' Mr Haskins smiled again. 'We're still here. Why not? They haven't got lawyers. They're not suing. It's just a friendly visit. Fact-finding.' And before the two lawyers could look at each other, he opened his door and climbed out. The women did the same, and they all hurried through the house's open gate and up the path, sheltering under the overhanging eaves while the engineer knocked on the front door. It opened almost immediately.

'Come in,' the young woman said. 'It's shocking out there, isn't it?' Her invitation was accepted. As soon as they were inside and the door was shut behind them, Arabella and Virginia, looking at the interior, removed their shoes. 'You don't have to do that,' the householder assured them, but Mr Haskins also noticed the light-coloured carpet, which was spotless although dotted with plastic toy cars and dolls, and bent to remove his own shoes.

'Sorry to burst in on you like this, but we've been inspecting your neighbours' houses—'

'For the court case, you mean?' the young woman asked.

'Yes, for the court case,' continued Mr Haskins, 'and I couldn't help but be curious about why you haven't joined in. I mean, the houses are all off the same plans and they're all on the same soil and the same floor slabs, so you must have had the same problems the others did.'

'Well, that's true. We did.'

At the owner's urging, Arabella moved from the little entrance area into the living room. There was a low bookcase with an *Encyclopaedia Britannica* and a number of Reader's Digest condensed books on the shelves. There were photographs of children, printed on canvas, on the walls. There was an entertainment unit against the back wall, with a TV set, a DVD player and a CD system. CDs and DVDs were stacked neatly in their boxes on top of the unit, alongside a cluster of gilded sporting trophies. The furniture was somewhere on the modest side of Ikea, but well kept. A boy and girl who looked to be about seven, and twins, were playing a card game on the carpet, and looked up at the suited but shoeless strangers with polite interest. They didn't speak.

Virginia turned to their mother, who was wearing the tracksuit-and-top local uniform, though in her case the combination was not ill-fitting. 'Would you mind telling us, seeing you've had the same problems, why you didn't sue? Didn't your walls crack like the others?'

'Oh, yes, they did. In fact, we had worse cracks than most of them.'

'Can you show us the damage?' Mr Haskins asked.

'Not really, no. It's fixed.' She raised both hands for a moment, then let them fall to her sides.

'How do you mean?' He was looking at the cornice, where a repair was visible, but barely. 'I can see that one's been filled.' He pointed.

'My husband did it. He did them all. It was quite a big job, took him all weekend to do the lot, all the cracks. That was the winter before last, and we haven't had any more trouble.'

She took the three visitors to see the repairs in the laundry and bathroom, and into two of the three bedrooms. The third bedroom, she told them, had never suffered any damage. There might be a bit of a crack behind the kitchen cupboards, she said, but they'd never bothered to look because you wouldn't see that anyway. Arabella asked whether her husband was a plasterer by trade, and she laughed. 'No, he works at Bunnings as a storeman. So he got the Polyfilla at staff discount. Polyfilla Villa, he calls this place.'

Mr Haskins wanted to know more. 'He must have done something else,' he said, 'because the clay under your house swells and shrinks depending on the weather. I'm surprised the cracks didn't open up again when there was movement. The others have trouble closing their doors.'

'My uncle's a brickie, and he told Graham to run the hose around the footings when it's very dry. The idea's to keep the clay at a fairly constant wetness, he says. So we do that, and it seems to work all right.'

'Well, thanks very much for showing us,' Haskins said.

'No worries. Would you all like a cup of tea?'

'No thanks,' said Virginia. 'We'd better get on the road. We appreciate the offer.'

'You have a lovely home,' Arabella told the householder. 'You must be very proud of it.'

The woman beamed. 'We love it. I'm pleased to meet you all.' They put on their shoes, and she showed them out into the rain, which hadn't let up.

Not much was said for a few kilometres. Then the referee turned from the front seat and spoke to Arabella. 'Polyfilla and a garden hose.' They all chuckled.

'No new houses, then?' Virginia was bold enough to ask.

'This conversation never took place,' Haskins said firmly, 'but I would be very surprised if, after all the barristers have talked themselves to a standstill over the next six weeks, and all the solicitors have rendered accounts that would defy anyone's imagination for shameless creativity, and the experts have all staked their reputations on proving that black is white, I didn't sign off on a report that limits the damages awards to no more than five thousand a pop. And that would be bloody generous, I must say.'

'Well,' said Arabella, 'I can only say how glad I am that the conversation never took place.'

'Aren't we all?' Virginia concurred, and Mr Haskins simply looked out the window and smiled to himself. After all, he, a retired man, was being paid for every day of hearing over which he presided. $2500 a day. Not as much as Deborah and the other Senior Counsel were charging, but a great deal better than a poke in the eye with a burnt stick. And all the better if it wasn't a difficult contest to resolve. They're all entitled to their day in court, aren't they?

Harry spent the week at Burragate, maintaining a strict schedule of farm work in the mornings — principally rebuilding the fallen and flood-damaged fences and overhauling the pump — and trial preparation in the afternoons and evenings. He felt much better, stronger, for it, carrying heavy fenceposts up and down the hill, using a borrowed auger to dig out post-holes by hand, straining the wires, and rehanging gates. Honourable, physical effort. From time to time he rang an old client in Canberra, a neurosurgeon who owed him a big favour as a consequence of a hotly contested coronial inquest into a surgical death, and took tutorials in intracranial bleeding and its aetiology. As he fed the chooks on Friday afternoon, Harry was telling himself that with the assistance of Bonaventura and the ex-client, he knew as much as he was ever going to be capable of assimilating about inflicted paediatric head injury. When Arabella rang him to apologise for being otherwise engaged than on the matters he had assigned to her, he had spared her any admonition.

'You may not believe the titles of some of the papers I've had to read,' he said. 'One of the best was "On the Theory and Practice of Shaking Infants". I swear I'm not making this up, and there's another one here I've got to read to you; it's "The Whiplash Shaken Infant Syndrome: Manual Shaking by the Extremities with Whiplash-Induced Intracranial and Intraocular Bleedings, Links with Residual Permanent Brain Damage and Mental Retardation". You're probably familiar with the authors — Duhaime, Gennarelli and Thibault?'

'The three gentlemen of Verona, aren't they? You have my undying admiration, Harry. But I've read the client's statement — and he's absolutely categorical that he has never shaken the child, isn't he?'

'Sure, but that remains the Crown's case theory. The child misbehaved while Hamish was babysitting him, and he shook him so hard that he caused the brain haemorrhage. It's a kind of formula that they apply to every infant death case — it's the stepfather/mother's boyfriend syndrome, and that amounts to child abuse. Usually works, too.'

'They don't seem to have paid any attention to the psychiatric picture, Harry. Jarrod was obviously not a well child.'

'They've paid attention to it all right, but so far as they're concerned it only confirms their angle of attack — the little bloke was so disturbed as to be uncontrollable, provoking Hamish to shake him in frustration. There's no doubt that there was a subdural haemorrhage, so they're fixated on this opinion from a single quack that the injury was not only caused by shaking but was definitely suffered in the three hours Hamish was babysitting him.'

'Sounds as though you're well on top of it, Harry. Is there still something you want me to take charge of?'

'Yes — this whole question of the time of the injury that caused the death. If we can introduce some doubt about it necessarily occurring during that period when Hamish had sole charge of the baby, all the better.'

'Do I ask Bonaventura for a separate briefing on that — the time, as opposed to the cause?'

'Well, it might be useful for you to get in touch with another expert as well. I've got an old client in Canberra — a neuro — and I'm going to ask him to speak to you. I'll email you the phone number and a time when he's able to talk. Belt and braces, I think. Avoids unforeseen embarrassments.'

'Are we going to win this, Harry?'

'We'd better. Not only would the client go to jail for a very long time, but his parents will lose their house.'

'Why?'

'They've mortgaged it to pay for his defence. And, even if he's acquitted, there's no great likelihood of him being awarded costs.'

Eventually, Harry thought to enquire about progress in Arabella's building case.

'The view out at North Richmond proved most valuable, Harry. I don't think that's going to be a difficult matter.' She chuckled lightly.

'Is that just a feeling, or is there something you're not telling me?'

'It's not just a feeling.'

'What are you trying to say?'

'All I'm prepared to disclose at this time,' Arabella said, 'is that I anticipate having a great deal more time to work on Sommerville than I previously imagined.'

It was just as well that the building case load had suddenly lightened, because it gave the Sommerville defence team sufficient time to complete their trial preparation — split, as they were, between Phillip Street, Goulburn and Burragate. They regrouped in Sydney on the Friday before the last week of term, and spent several hours with their client (and later, his parents), explaining the strategy Harry intended to implement, starting Monday.

Hamish listened intently to everything he was told, but confessed that there was much he didn't understand. 'But don't try to explain it all again,' he said. 'I have confidence in you.'

'Good of you to say so, Hamish,' said Harry, 'and probably the best way to go. I'll ask you to bear in mind a couple of things as the trial progresses, though: first is that we're going to lose some battles, but that doesn't mean we lose the war.'

'Then what does it mean?'

'In any trial, the defence and, for that matter, the prosecution, make objections to certain evidence being put before the court and also raise various other purely legal issues. The jury gets sent out, and we have an argument, and the judge makes a ruling. We're going to win some of those arguments, and we're certainly going to lose others. I don't want you getting in a mind-set that, if and when the judge rules against us, we've lost something. That's not how it works. I have the objective of making it very hard for the Crown to put evidence suggesting you are guilty before the jury, and I'll be pushing every reasonable objection to the limit. And winning an argument doesn't mean that we win the case, either. It's all tactical, it's all technical, and you simply have to leave all that to us and try not to worry about it. You will worry, of course, but at the end of every day I'll do my best to explain where we are. Okay?'

'Okay.'

'Good man.' Harry looked at him and registered, yet again, how readily clients surrendered to the need to believe in their defenders. Hamish, at least, wasn't fearful.

'And what's the second thing, Mr Curry? You said there were a couple of things.'

'Correct. The second thing is about your part in this trial. What we have here is a team: Mr Surrey is the solicitor, and he briefs us to defend you, he organises our witnesses and he's found the expert to brief us on the medical picture. And he's done a good job of it, but now he steps back. Ms Engineer and I run the case in court — we deal with the judge and the prosecutor, we handle the witnesses, I do the cross-examination, and the two of us address the jury at the end. So in this team the lawyers do everything for you, except the one thing we can't do: and that's give your evidence, and be cross-examined. Your job in the team is just to concentrate on your evidence, to read it and read it and read it—'

'I've already done that.'

'Yes, and you'll continue to do it. Don't concern yourself with the medical issues, or with which witnesses are telling the truth or lying. Just make yourself so familiar with your proof of evidence that you could give it in your sleep. And let me tell you a secret that not many lawyers know: you're much more likely to win this case if the jury likes you.'

'How do I make them do that?'

Harry turned to Arabella and let her respond. She dwelt on the agreeable, boyish face of her client and balanced it against the indictment confronting him and the jury's first-blush assessment of him. The police don't charge people unless they're guilty, right? Best to give the boilerplate response. Once size fits all.

'Well, first of all, you don't behave like a clever dick. No pulling faces, no silly play-acting, like laughing at a witness who you want them to disbelieve or looking triumphant when you think we've kicked a goal. Just keep still, keep serious, treat them with respect. They're your judges, and they'll be watching you all the time. So don't pick your nose in front of them.'

'I wouldn't!'

'She doesn't mean it literally, Hamish.' Harry took over. 'And when you're being cross-examined, keep your answers short, simple and truthful. Don't, under any circumstances, try to argue with the prosecutor. Just listen to the question, answer it in your head, then repeat the answer out loud. It's not an exam, and you don't get points for answering quickly. Think before you say anything, and remember this: if the answer's no, say no. If it's yes, say yes, and if you don't know the answer, say so. Don't guess. Never try to puzzle out why he's asking that question, or where he's going with it. No second-guessing. That's *our* job. Think of it this way — we'll have covered every possibly relevant issue in your evidence in chief; that's when you're answering me. Your job is to keep all your answers the same, never mind who's asking the questions. The truth isn't dependent on the identity of the questioner, is it?'

'No, it's not.'

'So I don't want to hear anything in your answers to the Crown that you haven't already told me. Because it's the truth, and it isn't going to change. Okay?'

'Okay.'

'The thing to remember is that you don't answer in such a short way that you sound evasive. But you're a good-looking young man, you're a bit of a sporting hero, and you're very likeable. Just bear all that in mind, and that you have the ability to win this jury with your honesty. You'll be fine.'

'Easy for you to say, Mr Curry.'

'No, Hamish, it's not. Nothing glib about it. But I've done enough of these cases to know that what I've told you is the best advice I can give. We're a team, and you are as well positioned to play your part as you could possibly be. So are we. We're certainly better prepared than the Crown.'

David Joncs's windows in Elizabeth Street were attracting young families, even at 9.30 on a hot December Monday morning, to listen to the carols and look at the moving dioramas of Father Christmas, elves, cute toyshops, even cuter puppet families, snow and shining parcels under the tree. The Sommervilles followed Hamish's solicitor and his bewigged and begowned defenders out of Arabella's chambers, down the short distance in King Street and around the corner to the Supreme Court entrance diagonally across from the big department store. The entranced infants pressed up against the windows took no more notice of the young man as he climbed the stone steps to the court foyer, about to go on trial for the murder of a three-year-old, than the young man took of them.

Inside the court, Hamish was placed in the dock by the court officer and given a glass of water. To dilute his panic, Arabella stood beside him and reminded him of his role in jury selection: if he recognised anyone on the panel — whether hostile or sympathetic — he was to indicate to her. Friends could stay, enemies would be challenged. Hamish turned and studied the faces of the jury panel, waiting in the public pews and staring about them until their numbers were called. As it turned out, and always seemed to turn out in trials in the city, the entire array were strangers to the Sommervilles, and Hamish merely shook his head at Arabella.

Harry, meanwhile, greeted the unfriendly prosecutor as he set out his books and his folders and made small talk about how long the case would likely run. 'It can't go past Christmas Eve,' the gloomy little man whispered. 'My wife's booked us in at Noosa.'

A couple of journalists took their seats. The judge's associate came through the judge's private doorway and took her place, reading over the words that she would be required to recite at the start of jury selection and shaking the small wooden lucky-dip box that held the jury members' identifying numbers. The barristers sat, spread open their notebooks, arranged their monographs, and uncapped their pens. The solicitors sat behind them and did much the same. The tipstaff knocked on the far side of the judge's door, three times, and the court officer shouted 'All rise.' It was a moment Harry always found released a rush of adrenaline into his bloodstream.

Out came his Honour Rathmines J, solid in his scarlet gown. Straight down to business, having the case's name called, the prosecutor announce his appearance, Hamish plead to the charge (an almost inaudible 'Not guilty'), after which Harry announced his and Arabella's appearance 'for Mr Sommerville' (not 'the accused', of course).

The preliminaries were completed and the jury had been selected well before 11 a.m. The judge gave the jury an early morning tea adjournment in which to introduce themselves to each other and choose their foreperson. Harry winced at the word. Because Hamish had been granted bail at an early stage of the matter, he was permitted to remain with his lawyers and drink the coffee his parents had fetched from Bar Coluzzi across the road. They needed something to do, and there wasn't much to be said — nothing had happened, yet — so they talked about the weather. It was obviously going to be a very hot summer. When they went back in, the Crown would be called upon to open his case to the jury.

'Remember,' Harry told his client, 'this is as good as the prosecution case gets — the opening. Don't be overborne by it. The evidence is never as strong as they tell the jury it's going to be.'

'Does that apply to us, too?'

'Oh, no. I always understate the defence case. That's if I open at all. Sometimes I make the judgment that it's better just to put you straight into the box to tell them the true story. That's what they usually want to hear.'

'And in my case, Mr Curry?'

'We'll have to wait and see.'

The Crown's opening was as underdone, underpowered and unimpressive as the man himself appeared to be. He stumbled in his delivery, lost his place frequently, mispronounced names and misplaced documents from which he intended to read. He had hardly reached the halfway point in his notes before the judge, whether through sympathy or impatience, interrupted to suggest that he call his first witness — the police officer in charge of the case. The judge's intervention was a blunder, because it robbed Harry of the opportunity to follow the Crown's speech with a short opening of his own that would have taken the form of a powerful anticipatory rebuttal. Arabella tugged Harry's sleeve and asked whether he didn't want to ask for the jury to be sent out, and things put back on the rails.

'I don't think so, Bella. Let's just see how this plays out.'

'But what about the psychiatric evidence? Shouldn't the jury be told about that right from the start?'

'Maybe not. Maybe we can make it look as if the Crown's hiding it, and flog them for trying to keep the jury in the dark.'

She thought about it but was unconvinced. 'You're in charge, of course.'

'Got that right.'

Harry had had David Surrey write a long letter to his counterpart at the DPP, offering to reach agreement on a statement of facts to be read to the jury covering all the uncontroversial matters, instead of plodding through a roll-call of formal evidence. That had been achieved, and Surrey had signed off on a four-page typescript that had been through several revisions, as advised by Harry.

'The benefit of that,' Harry had explained to Arabella, 'is not just that it avoids something like a dozen witnesses or even more being trooped through the witness box to give evidence or produce documents that aren't in issue, with nothing for us to cross-examine on. It also serves to reduce the sheer heft of the Crown case. It never seems anything like a balanced process when they have forty witnesses and we have one, or maybe two.'

So the detective sergeant in charge became the prosecution's first witness. After he was sworn and had given his name, rank and station, the judge interrupted the Crown and directed a remark at the jury.

'Before we kick this off,' he said with an ambiguous look, 'let me tell you how you *don't* decide this case: you don't decide it on the basis of which side you think has the best barrister. Or barristers.' He paused and looked across the faces at the Bar table. 'Yes, Mr Crown. Go ahead.'

Arabella leaned forward and looked past her leader at their opponent. It seemed to her that he was about to cry. Harry stared fixedly ahead.

'Umm, sergeant, have you prepared a statement of the ... umm ... facts?'

'Yes.'

'Your Honour, my understanding is that Mr Curry has no ... umm ... objection to the statement being ... aah ... read out.'

Rathmines pursed his lips. 'No objection, Mr Curry?'

'None, may it please you.'

The judge couldn't hide a sceptical look. 'Go ahead, then, sergeant.'

The policeman wasn't a much better reader than the Crown, and had just as much difficulty with some of the names of the *dramatis personae*.

'"On 27 May—"' he got that part right '"—the Ambulance Service attended a call to a Dulwich Hill café to assist a child then aged three years and two months, Jarrod Machado, who was suffering some sort of spasm in the back of the accused's car. He was admitted to the Sydney Children's Hospital suffering from a number of injuries, but significantly an injury to his brain which was the probable cause of a subdural haemorrhage which led to brain swelling and death the following morning. In the three-hour period before he was seen to be suffering from the spasms, the child had been in the sole care of the accused, Hamish Sommerville, then the boyfriend of Jarrod's mother, Angela Machado. Ms Machado had begun part-time work that morning at Effie's Espresso Bar at Dulwich Hill, and before the accused drove her to work, she had looked in at Jarrod and checked on him while he was still asleep. The accused drove Ms Machado to the café, leaving the child asleep in their flat. After Jarrod died, the accused was interviewed by police and told them that when he came home, Jarrod had woken up and he got him up and dressed him. They watched television together during the morning — *Play School* — and, he said, he noticed that the child's speech was somewhat slurred, but at 11.15 a.m. he rang Ms Machado and Jarrod spoke to his mother on the phone. There was a short coherent conversation between the mother and Jarrod in which the mother suggested that he get his crayons and draw a picture, and Jarrod asked the accused to get the crayons to do this. Half an hour later, the accused put Jarrod in the back of the car, in the child seat, and drove to pick up his mother. When the accused got to Effie's Espresso Bar he went inside and was introduced to the people in the café and they walked back to the car together. It was at that stage that they noticed Jarrod in the back of the car apparently convulsing and the ambulance was called. The child was in the sole custody of his mother and the accused on 26 and 27 May. He was in the sole custody of the accused from about 8.30 a.m. on the 27th until 11.40 a.m.'"

The witness put the pages from which he had read his evidence on the ledge in front of him and the Crown spoke.

'On 15 June, did you interview the accused at the Sydney Police Centre?'

'Yes, sir.'

'And was that interview ... aah ... electronically recorded?'

'It was, sir.'

'Do you produce the original of the recording, the ... umm ... ERISP — for the benefit of the jury, that's the Electronically Recorded Interview with a Suspected Person — and a transcript of it?'

'I do, sir.'

The prosecutor asked the judge for permission to play the DVD of Hamish's interrogation, and it was granted. The jury sat in silence, with only the foreman taking notes, as the forty-five-minute recording played out on the big screen opposite them. In it, the detective sergeant in the foreground could be seen reading a series of questions from a clipboard, with Hamish, a small and indistinct figure in the centre of the screen at the distant end of the table, answering him. Responding to what he was asked, he told the story of his meeting Angie Machado before she separated from her then partner, Jarrod's father, and, after the separation, seeing progressively more of her until they ultimately set up house together five months before Jarrod died. When asked if he had ever struck the child, Hamish heatedly denied it. At one stage, he raised his voice.

'If you want to know, I was really the only one who cared about him. It was me that took him to the doctor when he got sick, and it was me who made sure he took his medicine. It wasn't Angie, it wasn't Jarrod's father. When he hurt himself falling off his bike, I took him up to the hospital and got him X-rayed and checked out. I loved him. I never even smacked that little boy when he was naughty.'

The recording showed that, having vehemently responded to the question, Hamish calmed down and gave the rest of his answers about the events of 27 May in a flat tone. The detective sergeant then told him he was under arrest, and would be charged with Jarrod's murder. Hamish, despite the small image of his face on the courtroom video screen, was obviously stunned.

The screen went black. The prosecutor told the judge that was the evidence in chief, and Harry rose to cross-examine. He took a long time before he looked up from his papers and locked eyes with the policeman.

'Given what our client told you — that he had never, in his life, laid a hand on the child — will you tell the jury what inspired you to charge him with his murder?'

'Information from Dr O'Brien.'

'What information?'

'That all the circumstances pointed to him. That he was the only one who could have caused the injury in that three-hour period.'

'Of course, you knew that Dr O'Brien had nothing to do with treating Jarrod?'

'Yes, that was at the Children's Hospital. He doesn't work there.'

'No, he works at a place he's pleased to call the Child Abuse Trauma Centre Incorporated.'

'Yes, I think that's the name.'

'Why was he ever involved in this matter?'

'You'd have to ask the DPP that.'

'I'm asking you. You're the officer in charge.'

'Operational policy, then. We send all these cases to Dr O'Brien's Centre.'

'Was he paid a fee, to your knowledge?'

'I object.' The Crown surprised Harry with the speed of his intervention.

The judge glared at him. 'I'll allow it.'

'You'd have to ask the DPP that.'

'Dr O'Brien's fee doesn't come out of your budget, then?'

'Not to the best of my knowledge.'

Harry turned to address the judge. 'I call for access to all records of any payment made to Dr O'Brien or the Child Abuse Trauma Centre Incorporated in relation to any report, advice, memorandum or like communication concerning the death of Jarrod Machado. My instructing solicitor has given notice that we would make the call.'

'Not produced.' The Crown half rose to say the words, then sat.

The judge glared again. 'And when will those records be produced, Mr Crown?'

'If they exist, does your Honour mean?' This time he stood.

'Don't try my patience, Mr Crown. Of course they exist.'

'Tomorrow, your Honour.' Somewhat cowed. His attempt to win favour from the team behind him was looking to have been counterproductive bravado.

His Honour looked to Harry to put the court's time to some good purpose. 'Have you any other questions for this witness, Mr Curry? I don't want to adjourn while the documents are found and produced, and lose the rest of the day.'

Harry took a moment to think about his answer, then he asked Rathmines to excuse him while he took instructions from Surrey. Having said no more to the solicitor than 'Enjoying this, are you, Dave?' to which the response was 'Certainly am', Harry turned back to face the bench.

'In fact, may it please your Honour, we think we could move on to the next witness for the prosecution. I have as much as I need from the sergeant, and I believe we'll be content to use the documents he's going to produce later, when we hear from Dr O'Brien. But may I reserve my right to recall this witness if the need arises?'

'Very well. Members of the jury, we'll take lunch now. Adjourn the court.' And he left the bench while the court officer was still in the process of commanding all to rise.

The trial settled down, and the prosecution, by calling witnesses over the next few days, fumbled together the building blocks it relied upon as the foundation for the proof of Hamish's guilt beyond reasonable doubt: the pathologist detailing the cause of death that he had established at post-mortem (head injury involving a subdural haemorrhage, swelling of the brain and retinal haemorrhages); Dr O'Brien giving his opinion as a child abuse expert that — because Jarrod had a coherent telephone conversation with his mother at about 11.15 a.m. — the fatal injury was caused by shaking and must have been inflicted between 11.15 a.m. and 11.40 a.m., establishing the time of its infliction as within the period when Hamish was in sole custody of the child; and Mr (he insisted on being addressed as Mister, not Doctor, because he was a surgeon) Griffiths, the retired neurosurgeon on Dr O'Brien's medico-legal payroll, telling the jury that the brain injury arose from injuries to the forehead which occurred as a result of repeated severe blows, and not by shaking. Mr Griffiths had his own theory, and wasn't much concerned to make it dovetail with O'Brien's.

Harry managed to get into evidence the invoice eventually produced by the DPP solicitor, showing that Dr O'Brien's corporate consultancy was to be paid $15,000 for giving the evidence. The jurors' eyebrows shot up as, one by one, they read their passed-along copies of the bill on the letterhead of Child Abuse Trauma Centre Inc., now entered as an exhibit by Rathmines J with a degree of alacrity. Surrey remarked that the invoice alone ought to be enough to discredit O'Brien. Mr Griffiths, it emerged from Harry's questioning, thought the post-mortem report's mention of a bruise on the little boy's forehead was strongly corroborative of his theory.

Angie Machado was also called by the prosecution, to prove that Hamish had, indeed, been the only person who could have laid hands on Jarrod during the three hours she was working at the café. She was pretty, certainly, but otherwise unlikeable (if not exactly a waste of food or space), and plainly reluctant to give evidence against Hamish. Hamish never took his eyes off her in the witness box, or as she walked out of the courtroom when her evidence finished.

The Crown's expert witnesses were all cross-examined with what the judge was later to describe in his summing-up as 'considerable vigour', with Harry and Arabella sticking closely to the script prepared in reliance on the advice of Dr Bonaventura. Each evening after court, they had, with Surrey present in Arabella's room, a telephone conference with Bonaventura to check progress and to update their approach, given the evidence adduced that day. As far as the barristers were concerned, it was all going according to plan, but Hamish and his parents were becoming more and more pessimistic, despite daily conferences that accentuated the positive. Harry assigned Arabella the task of taking their client through his evidence statement, again and again, to ensure that he was confident about what he needed to cover and more than aware of the likely issues upon which the Crown would cross-examine him.

After considerable thought and debate within the defence team, cross-examination of Angie was assigned to Arabella, in the belief that the jury wouldn't respond negatively to her posing questions that might have suggested bullying if Harry put them. It worked well, and Arabella was able to have the child's mother confirm that Hamish had, if anything, been a better and more caring parent to Jarrod than had she. Perhaps even more importantly, she accepted Arabella's invitation to detail Jarrod's psychiatric problem, and the self-harm that manifested it. The women on the jury were visibly upset by what they heard.

By Friday, the last day of the law term, the Crown was ready to close its case. When the defence team met in Arabella's chambers to schedule their evidence, Arabella reported to Harry and Surrey that Hamish was as ready as he was ever going to be. 'He's terrified of what he calls "trick questions", but I think he'll do well.'

'Maybe he won't have to. I'm thinking of making a no case to answer submission this morning,' Harry told them.

Surrey sat up straight in his chair. 'Are you sure? Wouldn't that mean that if the judge is against us, we can't call any evidence?'

'No, Dave, it doesn't. Why do people believe that? I reckon we've got a respectable argument and — you never know — maybe Rathmines will jump at the chance of finishing this before Christmas. Even the Crown's wife wants it to end quickly.'

Arabella thought they were hopelessly unprepared to argue that the prosecution case didn't reach the *prima facie* standard. 'We haven't even prepared an outline of submissions, Harry.'

262

'Perfectly true,' he said. 'But I have marked up the transcript and put the documents in their proper order, and I'm game to give it a fly. You'll have to help, of course.'

'How, exactly?'

'We're going to take Rathmines to the highlights of all the exculpatory stuff we got in cross-examination. We're going to read it to him.'

'Yes, but—'

'By which I mean I'm going to read out my questions, and you're going to read the answers we got. Liven things up a bit. Give the judge a show.'

Which they did. At ten o'clock, the prosecutor wearily closed his case, and sat down. The judge asked whether Harry intended to open the defence case to the jury, or start in on the first witness, '... who I assume will be the accused?'

'If your Honour pleases, we wish first to make an application in the absence of the jury.'

'Some substance to it, is there, Mr Curry?'

'So we believe, your Honour. It may be best to ask the jury to come back at two o'clock.'

The jury were given four hours to do their Christmas shopping in town. As the door closed behind them, Harry rose to address the judge, who opened his book and poised his pen above an empty page.

'No case to answer, Mr Curry?' The judge's tone was obviously intended to convey a don't-waste-my-time rebuke.

'So we submit, your Honour.'

'Seems like a tall order.' Rathmines appeared to relish the prospect of dismissing the argument.

Harry ignored that. 'I apologise that we have not had time to prepare a written outline for the court or my learned friend, but perhaps that won't be such a disadvantage. Your Honour, with his extensive background on this side of the Bar table, will understand the exigencies under which all counsel work in a jury trial.' In fact, Harry doubted that the former barrister presiding over the trial had ever had the responsibility of defending the liberty of a subject, but a little flattery never went astray.

Rathmines J was apparently not altogether pleased at what might be regarded as a regrettable lack of assistance to the bench — no written outline of argument — but grunted his assent. Harry took hold of the lectern that stood on the Bar table in front of the prosecutor, and moved it to a point between himself and Arabella, who remained seated.

'I'm going to ask Ms Engineer to assist me with the evidence, your Honour.' Harry took a moment to place beside the lectern the folders containing the transcriptions of the trial evidence, and told Arabella to open the folder of documentary exhibits at its index.

'May it please your Honour: our client having pleaded not guilty to the charge of murder, each ingredient of the crime of murder must therefore be established by the Crown beyond reasonable doubt. That being the case, the first thing the prosecution must prove beyond reasonable doubt is that it was the act of the accused that caused the death. The Crown is relying here on two heads of the legal definition of murder as a possible basis for the return by the jury of a verdict of guilty: the first is that Hamish Sommerville caused the death by shaking or — somewhat embarrassingly, given Mr Griffith's contradiction of the evidence of Dr O'Brien — by striking the child, both requiring a concurrent intent to cause really serious bodily injury; and the alternative is that, if that specific intention is not proved, he acted with reckless indifference to human life.

'If the prosecution can't prove either head of murder, it's theoretically still possible for a verdict of manslaughter to be returned, if the Crown were able to prove to the requisite standard that the act of our client causing Jarrod's death was unlawful and dangerous, and that would have required proof to the criminal standard that the act was one that any reasonable person must have appreciated would subject the victim to a risk of serious injury. But Mr Crown confirmed to me this morning that he is instructed that your Honour is to treat this as murder or nothing. No compromise.'

Rathmines J looked incredulous. 'Can that be right, Mr Crown? Murder or nothing? Your masters won't have a bar of manslaughter?'

'So I am instructed.'

'On their heads be it. Is that what you mean?'

A nod was as far as the troubled little man was prepared to go. He sat, and Harry got back to his feet and resumed his argument.

'The charge in this case arises out of the death, as your Honour knows, of Jarrod Machado, a three-year-old boy, on 28 May. The evidence extracted from the prosecution witnesses by the defence in the course of cross-examination — and it is evidence that the Crown, in our respectful submission, sought to evade and even to conceal from the jury's consideration — discloses that Jarrod Machado was no ordinary little boy. He was subject to severe behavioural problems in the months before his death. Let me highlight that.'

Harry lifted the heavy transcript folder onto the lectern and turned a page. 'Page 49, your Honour, at line 23. I asked the child's mother this: "Ms Machado, isn't it true that Jarrod had engaged in various forms of self-destructive behaviour over the period of several months before May this year?"'

Arabella stood and put her finger next to a highlighted section of the transcript beneath Harry's question, which she then read.

'Yes.'

Harry's turn with the transcript. '"And what form did this self-destructive behaviour take?"'

Arabella: '"He bit his own tongue, he pulled out his hair, and he banged his head against the table and the windowsill. He ran at the wall and the refrigerator, head first."'

Harry motioned with his hand and Arabella sat down. 'The court also has as Exhibit 2 four photographs taken at Jarrod's third birthday party, clearly showing bruising to the centre of his forehead. Your Honour will be aware that the expert evidence supports the submission that this self-injurious behaviour probably had its origins in the fact that Jarrod felt insecure following the break-up of the somewhat turbulent relationship between his mother and father and his father's replacement by Hamish Sommerville. The evidence also establishes that Ms Machado sought counselling and treatment about the behaviour and the child was seen by a psychiatrist, and there were ongoing arrangements for further treatment right up until the time of his death. The evidence of the self-destructive behaviour was further corroborated by Mrs Sommerville who had minded Jarrod on occasions, when she spoke to the investigating police. Jarrod's father, Peter Lowing, said in his evidence in chief that he hadn't witnessed any such conduct, but the fact is that he had had nothing to do with his son immediately before the 27th of May and he agreed that he'd been advised by Angela Machado of Jarrod's problems. Similarly, your Honour heard evidence that Ms Machado had advised the staff at the preschool Jarrod attended of the nature of his problems, she had discussed them with her own mother, and she had mentioned it to the neighbours in the block of flats in which she and our client were living.

'The defence submits, your Honour, that there can be no doubt at all that the evidence establishes that Jarrod did engage in self-destructive behaviour. He was being treated for it by a psychiatrist. In the months immediately prior to his death, he exhibited injuries to his forehead indicative of the fact that he had been banging his head against hard objects. The clear establishment of these facts obviously gives rise to the question as to whether it can be shown that the act that caused Jarrod's death was inflicted by someone other than himself and, of course, that must be proved by the Crown beyond any reasonable doubt. If there is any reasonable possibility that the operative cause of death was occasioned by an act of Jarrod himself, this prosecution cannot succeed.

'The Crown has based its entire case on seeking to establish that the injuries that caused the death were inflicted while the child was in the sole custody of Hamish Sommerville. As to that, what is it that the evidence establishes? Well, we know that Angela Machado went to work at the café on the morning of 27 May. We know when she was driven to work by our client the little boy was still asleep. Next, we know that at about 11.15 that morning back at the flat, Jarrod was able to conduct a logical conversation with his mother on the telephone and they discussed him doing a drawing. To go back to the transcript of Ms Machado's evidence ...'

Harry turned another page and read. 'Page 51, top of the page: "Had there been any sort of an incident of Jarrod banging his head on 26 May?"'

Arabella stood and took her turn to read from the same page. "Yes, like I told the police, he hit his head very hard on the fridge that day; I told the neighbours about it.'" Arabella sat down and Harry took over again.

'That evidence was corroborated by the neighbour, Mrs O'Leary.' Harry opened another folder and put it in front of Arabella.

She stood and read out the next highlighted passage: 'At page 111, your Honour, line 8, Mrs O'Leary said this: "Angie came across the hall and she looked upset, so I asked how Jarrod was and she told me he'd been banging his head again. Angie just sort of raised her hands in despair."'

Harry spoke again. 'So the court has a consistent picture of Jarrod's self-destructive head-banging, which was a serious problem and so well established that he was under psychiatric care. I don't wish to be unduly critical of the Director of Public Prosecutions, but it may well be thought that that was a matter worthy of deep consideration before our client was subjected to the indescribable fear and stress of a murder trial.'

Rathmines J looked up from his notes and gestured with his pen at the empty jury box. 'The jury's not here, Mr Curry. No need for the advocate's flourishes, is there?'

'As your Honour pleases. The point I'm trying to make, flourishes or not, is that — and this had to be achieved under cross-examination, which was unfortunate — Ms Machado's evidence, which must tend to negate any assertion that the cause of death can be attributed, beyond reasonable doubt, to any person other than the deceased child himself, had to be dragged out by the defence, when the Crown's duty, as the Court of Criminal Appeal has repeatedly emphasised, is to search for the truth, not to seek a conviction at any price.'

He looked down and turned up another page of the transcript for Arabella to read out.

Arabella stood. 'Ms Machado at page 55, line 18, your Honour: "About three weeks before he died, I went back to the flat and heard loud banging noises, and when I went in I found that Jarrod had been hitting his head on the windowsill and had smeared himself with faeces. He had hurt his forehead and it was red raw and Hamish and I discussed taking him to the doctor, but we put that off because he already had an appointment with a psychiatrist for the following afternoon. After we cleaned him up and put him in clean clothes, I talked to my mother on the phone and while we were doing that Jarrod was banging his head on the coffee table and I had to hang up."'

Arabella sat down, and Harry deliberately waited before getting back to his feet, to allow the judge to complete whatever note he was making in his book. Harry glanced across at the prosecutor, who had his eyes closed and his head back. When the judge's pen stopped moving, Harry stood. 'In Exhibit B, the record of interview conducted with our client, he told the police that on the morning of the 27th when he was babysitting Jarrod at the flat, there was a further incident when he was speaking on the telephone to a friend. The child banged his head again, just before Mr Sommerville left the flat to go and pick up Ms Machado. It has to be remembered, your Honour, that Mr Sommerville made unequivocal denials and there is no direct evidence that he ever caused any injury to Jarrod. The Crown case, such as it is, depends entirely on circumstantial evidence, and that being so, the law provides that the circumstantial evidence must point to no other reasonable conclusion than the guilt of Mr Sommerville.

'Let me turn next to the issue of proof to the absolute criminal standard of the cause of death. We accept, as the court must, the pathologist's opinion that the head injury caused the child's death and that the mechanism of death was the swelling of his brain. The controversy is not as to that issue, but with Dr O'Brien, who asserts that the head injury would have prevented Jarrod from having any sensible conversation after it had been inflicted. He wishes to persuade the court that the head injury must have followed the coherent phone call at 11.15 and preceded Mr Sommerville's arrival at the café with the child, already suffering spasms, about twenty minutes before midday. And that's what he can't do. Let me go to his answers in cross-examination.'

Arabella stood and read: 'Dr O'Brien is at page 121, line 6: "I cannot preclude the possibility of a head injury occurring earlier than 11.15 a.m."'

Harry: 'True it is that Dr Griffiths, the neurosurgeon, was adamant that the injury did not occur earlier, but that expert witness is more of a problem for this case than an asset. We'll come back to him a little later. The pathologist, Dr Finlayson, on the other hand, told the jury this ...'

Arabella, still standing, read the passage: 'Page 202, foot of the page: "The injury might have been inflicted as much as days before, and a person suffering such a head injury might be able to conduct a lucid conversation."' She looked at Rathmines as she sat, and he made another note.

Harry took a beat. This is under control, he told himself. Going well. 'I then asked him about the significance of the drowsiness and slurred speech described by the proprietor of the café, who stood beside Mr Sommerville's car while they waited for the ambulance and watched the child after the spasms abated.

Arabella: 'Dr Finlayson at page 203, line 14: "I consider that his sleepy appearance and the problems he was having speaking were consistent with him having previously suffered the injury. As much as days before."'

The muttered conversation between the prosecutor, now very much awake, and his instructing solicitor at the other end of the Bar table was getting louder, attracting the attention of the judge, who frowned.

Harry kept going. 'On the basis of that evidence, then, this court can't say and a properly instructed jury couldn't be persuaded that it can be established satisfactorily that the injury must have occurred after 11.15 a.m. on the 27th of May. For that reason there remains the real possibility that it occurred on the day before that. The significance of that, which will not have been lost upon your Honour, is that very significant incidents of head-banging occurred the day before — on the 26th. It will also be necessary, with respect, to bear in mind that if the injury to Jarrod that caused his death did occur on the 26th, then it might well have occurred at a time when the child was in the custody of both his mother and Mr Sommerville, or for that matter in the custody of his mother alone.'

Surrey stage-whispered 'Half past eleven' at Harry's back, and he and the judge looked at the courtroom clock.

'Convenient moment, Mr Curry?'

'Certainly, your Honour.'

'Just to check with you, though,' the judge said, 'and I won't be holding you to it, but do you think you'll be finished in time for the Crown to respond by one o'clock so I can bring the jury back at two?'

'It may take a little longer than that, your Honour.'

'Oh well,' the judge said, 'I don't suppose the jury will mind. Only four shopping days to Hanukkah.' And it was time for morning tea. Twenty minutes, the associate told the legal teams. Harry and Arabella pulled off their wigs and dropped them on the table, then draped their gowns on the backs of their chairs. The privileged prosecution team headed off for their room and its electric jug, affecting a complacently long-suffering attitude and muttering that the defence argument was more appropriate for sideshow alley at the Royal Easter Show than the heights of the Supreme Court. Waiting for their lawyers in the foyer, the Sommervilles intercepted Surrey, the first to emerge, and asked how it was going.

'Okay, I think. But it's a hard row to hoe — judges always take the position that, if there's *any* basis for a conviction, that's enough for a *prima facie* finding, and they should leave it up to the common sense of the jury.'

'But the jury's not on Hamish's side,' his mother pointed out. 'Did you see those women at the back crying when Dr O'Brien gave his evidence on Tuesday?' Surrey had seen it, and it worried him.

Harry and Arabella passed with a wave, and left the building to stand in the sun in Elizabeth Street. Neither had much to say, although Harry told Arabella how well she had picked up on the question-and-answer readings.

'Sorry I didn't get time to rehearse it with you. But it's going very well — keep it up.'

Arabella squinted in the bright light. 'More the sort of thing you'd do with a jury, isn't it?'

'I don't know, Bella. I've always wanted to do transcripts two-handed. Nobody else does it. It seems to bring it to life, and, whatever may be the conventional wisdom, I've found the majority of judges share the same emotions as the majority of human beings. Not all of them, I must concede.'

'And Rathmines?'

'Who knows? He was always the life of the party at chambers dinners. The most I can say is that he's interested, but for all I know his interest may be in no more than looking at you.'

Arabella shook her head and focused on a harried mother on the other side of the street, pushing a stroller carrying two children and trying to juggle big bags of festive purchases.

A television news station wagon pulled up and its crew started unloading camera gear. Arabella asked Harry if they were there to film Hamish.

'No. Some other poor bastard.' And he headed back into the courtroom to prepare to resume their plea for the liberty of his client.

The hearing reassembled right on 11.50 a.m. and Harry was back on his feet, waiting for the judge's nod. When it came, he made a minuscule bow and moved on to the next heading on his pad. 'The second issue on which we contend the prosecution does not achieve a *prima facie* case is that of the agency of the fatal injury. Dr O'Brien expressed the clear view that the head injury was unlikely to be self-inflicted. Dr Finlayson, the pathologist, agreed with that. But unlikelihood isn't certainty, and what the Crown must prove in this case, your Honour, is not simply that it was unlikely or even highly unlikely that the injury was self-inflicted. What the Crown must prove beyond a reasonable doubt is that the injury was *not* self-inflicted. Looking at that test, this was the relevant evidence of Dr O'Brien.'

Harry opened one of his folders and turned the pages, then put his finger on a highlighted passage as Arabella, feeling quite confident in her role now, stood. 'Here,' he murmured.

She read the passage. 'Dr O'Brien at page 127, line 11: "The bruising of the child's forehead would, in my opinion, have required multiple impacts. His head striking the windowsill in the room, for example, could have produced the injuries to the head if it were done with enough force, yes, but it's most unlikely that this child could do that himself without any intervention.'

Harry interposed. 'Lower down on the same page, Dr O'Brien did make this concession.'

Arabella read the words that Harry indicated: '"Quite obviously, I couldn't say that it's impossible. I am aware of studies which indicate that subdural haemorrhages can be caused by relatively small applications of force, particularly one Japanese study."'

Harry turned a page of his planned address and looked at Rathmines, who pushed his glasses back on his nose with the tip of his middle finger. He used to do that at chambers meetings, Harry recalled, when he was angry. So? 'And I asked him to admit that this was an area of medical controversy.'

Arabella: 'Dr O'Brien at page 127, line 33: "Yes, it is."' At a subtle indication from her leader, she resumed her seat. The judge made another note and Harry waited for him to finish and look up before he spoke.

'While Dr O'Brien was of the view that the injuries were consistent with what he was pleased to call "shaken baby syndrome", he again had to concede that the effects on a child's brain of shaking remain a matter of some medical controversy. The court is aware that his views were expressed as a result of his own experiences — which proved to be minimal — and a reading of medical literature. Those minor experiences of Dr O'Brien's own did not, of course, involve dealing with a child who had a history of self-destructive behaviour, including severe head-banging, which has been documented as existing in this child.

'Dr Finlayson was also of the view that it was unlikely that the injury to the brain was self-inflicted, although he, too, had to acknowledge a lack of experience in dealing with a child with a history such as that of Jarrod Machado.'

Harry cued Arabella with a sideways glance.

'Page 224, your Honour, line 27, still in the cross-examination of Dr Finlayson: "I'm aware of a French study that indicates it's highly unlikely that a child can inflict upon itself a subdural haemorrhage by head-banging."'

Harry took over. 'That was a little less than frank, as it turned out. I followed that question up by asking whether a recently published Japanese study hadn't shown that one child in ninety-one had in fact done so.' The judge noted this. Again, Harry let him finish, then went on. 'When I showed Dr O'Brien, and for that matter, the other medical experts called by the Crown, the paper from the *Journal of American Physicians and Surgeons* by Dr Uscinski in 2004 — Exhibit 7 in the documents folder' (Arabella turned it up) — 'each of them conceded the validity of the author's primary point.'

He turned to Arabella, who was still standing beside him with the highlighted document in her hands. 'Second paragraph, your Honour,' she said, and picked up the quote:

... shaken baby syndrome became widely accepted as
a clinical diagnosis for inflicted head injury in infants
after the publication of hypotheses in 1971 and 1972.

However, in 1987 and again in 2003, careful laboratory
investigation of the biomechanics of head injuries
showed that human beings cannot achieve the necessary
accelerations for causing intracranial injury in infants by
manual shaking alone, but that impact is required.

Harry had his mouth open to speak again, but the judge, head down
and writing fast, held his left hand up in a stop sign. Harry was
happy to wait. All this note-taking had to be a strong indication
that he was listening to the argument. Harry was counting the
dead light bulbs in the ceiling fixtures when Rathmines cleared
his throat to prompt resumption of the defence submissions.

'What it amounts to, your Honour, is this: experts such as
Dr O'Brien have nothing but medical literature to go on, and the
medical literature is, by definition, hearsay. It cannot, again by
definition, be based on anything but the histories, or confessions,
or lies, that the authors or researchers or medical practitioners or
police have been told by the persons who caused the head injuries
to the children. The doctors' mistake is accepting as true the self-
serving accounts given by the baby-killers — men, for the most
part — who couldn't bring themselves to tell the shameful truth,
which must have been that they punched the child or otherwise
struck its head on or with some object. They all claimed that
they had done no more than shake the baby, believing that was
somehow a lesser and more easily understandable offence. I'll
leave your Honour to consider that paper in its entirety, but would
simply ask Ms Engineer to remind the court of Dr Uscinski's
conclusion.'

Arabella read it out to a silent courtroom, many of whom were
noticeably registering shock at Harry's use of the words 'baby-

killers'. Hamish was squeezing his hands together and trembling, and Surrey gave him a hang-in-there look as his junior counsel read from the American journal.

> While the desire to protect children is laudable, it must be balanced against the effects of seriously harming those who are accused of child abuse solely on the basis of what is, at best, unsettled science.

'Or, we would say,' Harry added as Arabella resumed her seat, 'bad science, too willingly adopted by an undistinguished doctor more concerned in carving out a forensic niche for himself and the financial return associated with it than he is with the truth.'

The judge's face displayed a mixed reaction to what Harry had just told him. He took off his glasses and looked at them as if he expected to find the lenses cracked.

'In all the circumstances, Mr Curry, it might be best if you withdrew that criticism. It really has no place in a no case to answer application, which has to be confined to objective legal argument and not matters of credibility or imputations as to a witness's motivation.'

Harry bowed a little more deeply than on the previous occasion. 'I withdraw the personal criticism, if your Honour pleases.' His Honour nodded and Harry went on. 'Which brings me to the evidence of Mr Griffiths, the neurosurgeon, about which I can hear my learned friend muttering to his instructor. As the court heard, Mr Griffiths thought the brain injury arose from repeated severe blows to the forehead, and not from shaking. At least on that, he didn't support the child trauma expert, and is plainly correct. And there's an even more important concession made by Dr Griffiths ... I'm sorry, I should have said *Mr* Griffiths, on page 88.' Harry sat to make Arabella's next reading even more telling.

'Your Honour will find it at line 36: "Yes, the lesions on the child's forehead could have been caused on the 26th of May. I can't argue with that."'

There was much more to it than that, of course. One of the things Harry and Arabella did was get the judge to look again, closely, at the exhibited birthday photographs. Rathmines shuffled back and forward through the poignant pictures in silence. Despite his earlier undertakings to the court, Harry didn't finish until almost three o'clock. The judge told the sheriff's officer to hold the jury in their room, and that he'd speak to them before four.

The prosecutor was confident that the trial would proceed and that Hamish was going to be called upon to submit to his cross-examination, and showed it in the compendious way he emphatically dismissed the defence arguments in short order. Half an hour, in fact, and much more confidently than he had begun the case. Aware of Rathmines J's track record — which would tend to indicate that he would much prefer that a jury did his work for him by finding guilt or not, rather than impose on himself the task of researching, drafting and delivering a judgment covering a difficult area of law and exposing himself unnecessarily to the risk of reversal by the Court of Criminal Appeal — Mr Crown expressed the view to Harry, the judge having given himself ten minutes to consider the opposing arguments, that it was a lay-down misère that he'd leave the final issue to the jury. 'You're probably right,' Harry conceded.

Harry and Arabella spent the rest of the judge's thinking time with their client and his parents, reminding them of his previous assurance that losing this argument would mean no more than that Hamish may give evidence on Monday. 'We won't have lost anything but a technical legal argument,' Harry said. 'It was almost a spur-of-the-moment thing, anyway, because it seemed to me that the weaknesses in the medical evidence were even more obvious than we first thought. And we all have to thank Dr Bonaventura for that.'

'Will he be giving evidence, then?' Mr Sommerville wanted to know.

'Can't see that it's necessary, can you, Harry?' Surrey asked.

'I agree, Dave. There's nothing he can say that we haven't already got from the other side. Griffith's a bit of a problem, but I reckon we can skate over him.' Harry had never explained to the family the problem with Bonaventura's professional misconduct humiliation, but Surrey now knew and was displeased.

And then the court officer called them to return. Once all were seated inside, the judge came back on the bench and asked for the jury to be brought back. It was five minutes to four. Harry whispered to Arabella. 'He's against us. He can only've brought the jury back into court so that he can send them home and tell them we'll be in our case on Monday morning.'

Arabella looked shattered. She hadn't been taken in by Harry's anodyne family-comforting words. 'I thought you had him, Harry.'

Rathmines started speaking, so she said nothing more, and prepared to make a note of the impending judgment dismissing their legal argument. He turned in his chair, his focus on the jury box. He smiled and paused to take a sip of water.

'Members of the jury, I apologise on behalf of the legal representatives for your having to wait. It's been necessitated by one of those legal arguments about which you were warned on Monday morning when we commenced this case. But I've brought you back now so that you can hear what I have to say about this case and where it goes from here. Now, normally we don't do this, but I've been sitting up here for long enough to have some sort of understanding of how juries feel when they reckon someone's keeping them in the dark. What happened while you were in the jury room, or off shopping, was that Mr Curry and Ms Engineer, the counsel, as you know, for the accused, made an application to me to stop this trial on the grounds that the prosecution evidence is insufficient to be left to you to make a decision as to whether Hamish Sommerville is guilty of the murder of this poor child. Now please don't think that's a reflection on you, or your intelligence or capacity to understand the medical evidence. It's not, not for a moment. In fact, this sort of application is a very severe criticism of the Crown — *if* it succeeds. What, in reality, the defence is submitting to me is that this charge should never have been brought.' Most of the jurors were leaning forward in their seats. He had their full attention.

'Now despite what you may think — or the *Daily Telegraph* or Alan Jones may want you to think — judges and lawyers live in the real world. Just as you do. We all know that this has been an upsetting case. It distresses all of us. A defenceless child suffered such terrible brain injuries that he died. It's terrible. If that was done by the accused, he cannot be allowed to walk free. But there's an old saying, and a very true one, that it's far better for a hundred guilty men to go free than for one innocent man to be condemned. We must, none of us, ever forget that.' Rathmines paused. For effect, Harry thought.

Arabella leaned close to Harry. 'What's he doing?'

'Good question.' Harry looked back at Surrey, who shrugged.

The judge continued. 'Members of the jury, this is the only case I am aware of which has come before criminal courts in this state where the deceased child has had a well-documented history of self-harm. That's important because in the ordinary course of events, such an assertion would not be given great weight whereas in this case it must be considered very carefully as a possible explanation of the injuries involved.

'The next point is that this is a case where there is no evidence to suggest that the accused had physically abused the deceased child on any previous occasion. Indeed, all the evidence is that he was a caring person who had shown a real interest in looking after the child and helping him overcome significant problems. You have read the report of the child's psychiatrist in which he says that it was the accused who followed his instructions for holding Jarrod when he became difficult. He said the accused showed appropriate concern for Jarrod and he carried out the doctor's advice because the mother was not able to. Further, the Sommerville family's physician for many years, who knows the accused well and to whom he took Jarrod when he was ill on two occasions when he was taken down to Crookwell, described the accused as a caring and generous individual and was strongly of the opinion that violence towards a small child would be entirely out of character for him. That doctor also said the accused had discussed with him methods of helping Jarrod because he was concerned about his behaviour. He said he didn't doubt that the accused loved the child. Apart from being a noteworthy feature of this case, this evidence would also raise the good character of the accused and he would be entitled to have you take that into account in the trial — if it went any further — not only on the question as to whether he committed the offence, but also as to whether he is telling the truth when he denied to the police having committed the offence.

'Looking now from a judge's standpoint at the evidence as to whether Jarrod might have inflicted these injuries himself, I must weigh the prosecution's argument that he could not have done so against the evidence of Dr O'Brien that he cannot say it is impossible. I also take account of Dr Finlayson's evidence that, though very unlikely, it is true that a small degree of force can produce a subdural haemorrhage. The child's psychiatrist also said he could conceive of head-banging causing serious injury.

'Against the background of that medical evidence, this case is one where there is documented evidence of head-banging by the deceased child which had resulted in noticeable injury previously. The evidence must be accepted that the head-banging by Jarrod was of a most unusual kind and that there had been a serious episode of that on the 26th of May and, as the accused told the detectives, another incident on the morning of the 27th.

'The Crown's case must depend on the evidence being capable of proving beyond a reasonable doubt that the deceased could not have caused these injuries to himself, and that they were deliberately and intentionally caused while he was in the sole custody of the accused. To prove both those propositions the Crown relies on the medical evidence. The only doctor to give that evidence in such a way as to prove those propositions was Mr Griffiths, but he is contradicted by Dr O'Brien and by Dr Finlayson and to some extent by the psychiatrist. It is accepted by all the experts that this area of medicine is a controversial one, and indeed Mr Griffiths, under cross-examination, has changed his own view about one significant aspect of the evidence he gave:

he admits the bruises on Jarrod's forehead could have occurred earlier that week.

'That being so, I hold that it would not be possible for you, the jury, to base a finding of guilt on the medical evidence as it stands. If the Crown cannot prove beyond reasonable doubt both those propositions, that it was the act of the accused that caused the fatal injury and that the accused committed that act with the requisite mental intention, then the evidence is incapable as a matter of law of establishing to the very high standard that applies in every criminal charge the guilt of the accused.'

Harry's back straightened, and he looked across at the jury's faces. They seemed to agree with what the judge was saying, which wasn't the response he'd been expecting from them. At least, not yet. Arabella put her hand gently on Harry's forearm, and he lowered his eyes and smiled. Surrey was smiling too. The Sommerville parents were clinging to each other, and Hamish, in the dock behind his lawyers, had his head in his hands as the judge finished his remarks.

'So it comes down to this: on the evidence adduced I hold that there is no case for the accused to answer. I enter a verdict of not guilty.'

The judge dismissed the jury and sent them off to be paid their pittance. Harry made an application that the DPP pay the defence's costs, and, after a brief and unenthusiastic response from the prosecutor, the order was made. 'So the parents get their house back,' Harry told Arabella, and Surrey showed profound relief because he had warned the Sommervilles not to count on it; that costs orders against the DPP were as rare as hen's teeth. The Crown congratulated Harry, something he hadn't expected, and Mrs Sommerville kissed Arabella and then him.

'I'm not sure that he's right,' Harry said to Hamish, whose father was alarmed. 'I think there probably was a *prima facie* case for you to answer. He got caught up in the emotion and the time of year.'

'Does that mean the prosecution will appeal?' Sommerville senior was still fearful.

'They can't,' Arabella told him. 'Hamish has been acquitted. They might seek some sort of advisory ruling from the appeal court, but why would they take the trouble? And, given the failure to establish a *prima facie* case, they've no chance of appealing against the costs order, either.'

'But it's all over? We can take him home?' Mrs Sommerville wanted to know. 'How did you manage it?' she asked Harry.

'It's Christmas,' was all he said.

'In Tuscany, too,' Arabella told Surrey. He grimaced, but Harry pretended not to have heard.

The fisherman who hated the sea

'Yes, Mr Curry?'

Harry took some time to get to his feet, but nodded to the judge and slowly gathered his brief, the folder of copies of the documentary exhibits, and his glass of water, stood as if his thoughts were elsewhere, and walked the length of the Bar table to take the prosecutor's position at the end closest to the jury. Court 1 in the Wollongong Supreme Court boasted a beautiful red cedar Bar table, with chairs to match. The building, at the top of a hill, was something of a spectacular Victorian Italianate wedding-cake folly, but recent, less admirable, additions had cut its aesthetic value down to size.

The DPP's local prosecutor looked miffed, glancing over her shoulder as if to ask what the defence counsel was doing at the Crown's end, but she had been warned that it was Harry's invariable practice at this point of a trial to usurp the strategic position closest to the jury box. Harry took the prosecutor's place so that he wouldn't have to address his final speech to the twelve citizens over the heads of a Crown trying to look bored, and a fidgeting, paper-shuffling solicitor. The prosecutor, something of a tyro (it was her first-ever murder trial), gracelessly yielded and moved to the remote end of the table. Patiently, Harry arranged his papers on and around the lectern and waited for her to settle before he looked up from his notebook at the jury. His client, seated in the dock behind him and guarded by a policeman, kept his anxious gaze on the jury box as his counsel began his final address.

'Ladies and gentlemen, the first thing you want to know from me is how long I'm going to be. Well, I promise to be finished by lunchtime. Of course, that's a lawyer's promise, and you know what they're worth.' The foreman and a couple of jurors smiled, but the rest were keeping their expressions noncommittal. Harry had learned long ago that counsel won points from judges and juries if they could give fair warning of how long their addresses were going to be, and he was always surprised when his opponents failed to pick up on juries' watch-consultings and other indications of increasing restlessness. That had happened again in this case, with the Crown's address, just completed three minutes before Harry was called upon.

'The next thing you want to know from me is why my client didn't plead guilty. Why I'm standing here, setting out to persuade you that you should acquit him, despite everything you've heard in the last two hours.' An older woman in the back row of the jury box nodded. Harry had earlier identified her to his instructing solicitor as one of the 'Well, he did it, didn't he?' types.

Justice Temple, the most recent of the female appointments to the Supreme Court and previously a salaried Public Defender who firmly believed that she'd seen it all (and who may have been an impressive lawyer in the eyes of the Court of Criminal Appeal, but had never been particularly persuasive as a jury advocate), took off her reading glasses to give herself a sharper view of Harry. She'd never seen him in action before, but was well aware of his take-no-prisoners reputation and had expected much more in the way of incendiary and objectionable cross-examination during the evidence phase of the trial. In fact, the case had run pretty smoothly.

'You might remember — I certainly hope you do —' Harry continued, 'that my first words to you on Monday, when I made my brief response to Madam Crown's opening, were these: "Michael Stanich did not murder Rudolfo Ponti."'

At that point, Harry paused and the six men and six women on the jury looked behind him at his client. The accused looked terrified. His large, dark eyes were downcast and his shoulders, in an ill-fitting suit (the first he had ever worn) were unnaturally high. A man of about thirty, utterly out of his element, utterly isolated and caught up in a system he didn't understand or have any hope of understanding. Beside him on the shiny wooden pew, polished by the backsides of thousands of desperate men and hundreds of women over more than a century, were a school exercise book and a biro that Harry had provided in which he could make notes of things he'd want explained during the court's adjournments. After four days, the book was still blank.

Harry's voice brought the watchers' attention back to him. 'There is no dispute that it was my client who killed the deceased. There's been no argument about that, and there's not going to be any. But murder, as her Honour will instruct you when she directs you as to your legal duties, as well as being the most serious offence in our criminal law is not just about a fatal act. There must also be a murderous mind.' Harry's description of the victim as 'the deceased' was deliberate: don't use his name any more than is absolutely necessary — don't constantly remind the jury that he was a person, a father, a husband. Make it all clinical. Formal, not emotional. Keep the emotion on your client's side of the ledger. Never call your client 'the accused', and use *his* first name whenever you can.

'And the Crown has not proved that Michael Stanich had a murderous mind.' Harry let that one sink in for a while, panning his gaze across the front row, watching them think about it.

'What the Crown had to prove, and to prove all of it beyond reasonable doubt, were three things: the first was that my client killed the deceased. That, at least, has never been in issue. We've admitted it from the start, from his very first interview at the Eden police station. The second thing that the Crown had to prove was that when Michael fired the fatal shot, or shots, he did so with the intention of killing the deceased, or causing him really serious injury. And that's the first point at which this prosecution failed. The Crown has failed entirely to prove intention — least of all to the very high standard the criminal law imposes: beyond any reasonable doubt.'

At this point, the DPP solicitor started keeping count of the number of references Harry would make to 'beyond reasonable doubt' — the standard of proof required to convict Stanich. His experience was that the more the defence flogged this issue, chanting the mantra, the weaker their defence must be. So much was that tactic the central part of Harry's jury submissions that all he had written on his notepad were the capital letters BRD.

'The defence case is that Michael had no such murderous intention — in truth, he had no intention at all, because he was in a state of total panic. If you think it's a reasonable possibility that he had no murderous intention, that he really was in a state of panic and wasn't thinking straight, or at all, then he cannot be found guilty of murder. He might be guilty of manslaughter, and her Honour will explain that to you when she sums up, but he is not guilty of murder.

'The third thing which this prosecution, by the evidence it produced in this trial, had to prove, and the other fatal flaw in their case, their inability to do so, was that there is no possibility that my client, when he pulled the trigger, believed it was necessary to do so in self-defence. I'll have more to say about that later.'

The foreman was busily making notes in his book. 'You don't have to take my word for it.' Harry made eye contact with him when he looked up from the page. 'Let me take you to the evidence of what Michael did intend. And there can be no better evidence than for you to watch and listen to what my client told the police not much more than an hour after the shooting. You know what he said, because you have seen the DVD of his interview with Detective Sergeant Alchin and Detective Constable Davidson. You also have the benefit of knowing *how* he said it, and I shall talk to you more about the absolute sincerity of his explanation. But I'm going to have my solicitor play the DVD for you again now, or at least the relevant part. Exhibit 15, your Honour. The part I want to show you, on this question of my client's intention, begins at answer 53, after Detective Sergeant Alchin asked him: "Tell us in your own words what happened, Michael."'

Harry turned and nodded to his young and nervous solicitor, a Legal Aid lawyer who, like Madam Crown, was engaged in her first-ever murder trial. As she picked up the remote control for the DVD player and pressed the PLAY button, the jury's eyes turned to the big screen bolted to the wall opposite them. Harry took over the remote and remained standing at the lectern, watching with them, the judge, and everyone else present in court as his client appeared on the screen, seated at the far end of the table in an anonymous room at the Eden police station. The fixed focus of the video recording placed Harry's client in the centre, but furthest from the camera — so far, in fact, that his eyes were indistinct. On either side of the table, with papers in front of them, could be seen the profiles of the arresting detectives — both big, bearded men whose manner was noticeably gentle, but formal. They had their protocols, and they were going to observe them to the letter. Too many murder prosecutions had been thrown out of court because police hadn't dealt fairly with persons-of-interest in custody.

The 'tell us in your own words' question having been asked, Michael Stanich could be seen taking a moment to think. He was obviously in a distressed state. He sniffed constantly, mucus streaming from his nose, and he thoughtlessly wiped it from time to time with the sleeve of his sweater, which had large holes in it. On the screen, Stanich bunched up his face, put his elbows on the table, and clasped his hands together. Without looking up, he began his answer. The judge and the lawyers were able to follow his words on transcripts prepared by the prosecution, but the jury were not permitted by the rules of evidence to have copies. That was fine with Harry, who wanted the judges of the facts, his client's jury, to concentrate on the humanity of the man they were to judge, and not on words typed on a page.

```
I went there to see Rudolf 'cause he's suing me. I was
going to try to talk to him about it. What I thought was
I'd scare him into maybe dropping the case against me.
    I just wanted to scare him. Maybe he wouldn't sue me.
I can't afford to be sued. Got no money as it is.
```

Harry, now in charge of the remote, thumbed PAUSE. 'Just to remind you: Michael's referring there to the fact that the deceased, his landlord, had commenced an action against him in the Small Claims Court for $3320 over damage to the tiles in the cake shop Michael had leased from him at the Eden shopping centre.' He buttoned the picture back into life, and Stanich was speaking.

When I didn't sleep last night, I thought about it —
putting the gun down there at the parking lot. Getting
it out when he came to work. Letting him see I had it.
I could see him saying 'I'm sorry. I won't do anything.
I'll stop.' It was the only thing that I could think of him
saying. What else could he say? If he's seen a gun, he'll
get scared. 'I'm sorry.' I thought he'd be scared.
    I picked up the gun and ran towards him — I don't
even know why. He turns, and I thought he'd say 'I'm
sorry — I'll drop the case.' I might scare him into
dropping the case.
    He was coming towards me and I was backing away
from him. I didn't expect him to do that. I expected him
to run.

Harry again pressed PAUSE. He looked at the jury, and waited for them to turn from the frozen image and give him, waiting patiently, their attention.

'That last answer, incidentally, gives the lie to the Crown's attack in cross-examination on my client that he had recently fabricated the evidence that he expected the deceased's response to be "Sorry — I'll drop the case."' Harry pressed PLAY again and once more Stanich's voice was heard.

As soon as he came at me, I pointed the gun down. I
didn't aim it at him. After he swung at me he just kept
coming forward, and I was backing up. He just kept
trying to grab the gun, so I ended up pointing it at him.
I pointed the gun at him because I thought he was going
to grab the gun and shoot me. I was backing away. He
grabbed the gun and pulled towards him. That pulled the
trigger and shot him in the belly. I just couldn't believe it.
I hadn't pulled the trigger. I couldn't believe it.

He didn't fall down.

I did back away ... Even into one of the wheelie bins.
I wanted to run. I was scared of him. If he grabbed the
gun, I thought, he was going to shoot me. If he grabs the
gun off me now, he's going to kill me for sure. I said to
myself: if he gets it, I'm going to die.

He got hold of the gun. He grabbed the gun again and
I thought he's going to kill me for sure! I just pulled the
trigger as fast as I could. I didn't have it lifted up, using
the sights of the rifle. I didn't aim, nothing. Just pointed
it towards him. I didn't even see where the bullets hit.

He didn't fall down, and I just kept pulling the trigger.

Harry killed the picture and returned the remote to his solicitor.
Some jury members were still writing notes, and he waited for
them to finish. 'Of course, you have all the exhibits available to
you in the jury room, including your own copy of Exhibit 15, and
you can play that as often as you wish. If you want to refer to the
transcript that we lawyers all have, it can be read out to you.

'The next thing that I want to show you is the DVD made by
Detective Constable Davidson when Michael was taken to the scene

of the shooting to do a video-recorded walk-around. Might I have access to Exhibit 17, your Honour?' The judge's associate handed it to the court officer, who handed it to Harry. 'I'll ask my solicitor to play it for us.' He passed her the disc and the remote and she complied. Harry waited for the picture to come up, looking at the faces of the jury until it did, trying to see how they were taking this.

'Okay — we'll play you the part of this recording in which Michael was asked about what he had in his mind at the precise moment of the shooting.' Harry nodded to his solicitor who sped the image to a predetermined point on the counter and froze the frame. She handed the remote back to Harry.

'This begins with Michael being walked around the car park at the Eden shopping centre where the shooting took place, and filmed by the police. And you'll recall that earlier in this recording, he pointed out the place where he hid his rifle in the garden bed, the place where he sat in front of the hydrangeas waiting for the deceased to arrive for work, and the point to which he had walked with his rifle, intending to throw a scare into the deceased, before any shot was fired.' Harry pressed the PLAY button and this time his client could be seen being escorted in handcuffs in the centre of the picture, then stopping to stand with his hands down in front of himself while he answered questions from an off-camera voice. His answers were uninflected, strikingly similar to his earlier interview responses. Then he stopped by a row of wheelie bins, looked around, and addressed the camera directly.

```
When I got here, he's pulled the gun forward, trying
to get it off me. I'm pulling, or he's pulled — we both
pulled — then it shot him, and I was standing here in
shock. He said to me, 'You shot me, you dickhead!'
```

Harry, still standing, killed the picture. The jury's eyes turned away from the black screen. The foreman raised his eyebrows as if asking Harry to comment on what they had just seen.

'Well, that's the account he gave on the very day of the shooting. Twice. Totally frank, totally honest, totally spontaneous. My client, quite obviously, had no sense of self-protection or even self-awareness when he answered the detectives' questions. To put it in a word, he was unguarded. You saw it at the police station when he wiped the snot off his face with the sleeve of his jumper — you can't get any more unaware of yourself than that. That man on the screen, this man here, was giving his answers, absolutely unconcerned with how they were going to sound here in court. The idea of these events being examined in a court hadn't even occurred to him. He was telling the truth. He wasn't thinking how to put a spin on it. If you're going to do something as sophisticated as that, so considered as that, you don't use your sleeve as a handkerchief.' Harry paused to give them some time to think about that.

'But his explanation didn't end there. I anticipate, with respect, that her Honour will direct you when she sums up the evidence and gives you directions of law about how you approach your job, early this afternoon, that my client had no obligation, no duty, no responsibility to get into the witness box and give evidence in his own defence. Under our system, no accused person is under any obligation at all to prove his or her innocence. Guilt must be proved entirely by the prosecution's evidence. The prosecutor would not have been entitled to criticise my client for not giving evidence on oath, or for merely leaving his explanation to the things he told the police on the day of the shooting. But he hasn't hidden behind his legal rights. Fully aware of his right to silence in this court, Michael took the oath on the Bible and told you the truth. By doing that he exposed himself to cross-examination by a skilled and determined prosecutor who — you can be quite certain — would have found any contradiction or weakness in his evidence and flogged him with it. My learned friend, the very able Madam Crown, got nowhere.' Truth to tell, Harry had not been at all impressed with the prosecutor's skill, and was indeed grateful for her inexperience. But he'd learned very early from the veteran criminal defenders he'd closely watched that the more you praise your opponent's fearsome forensic skills, the more you can praise your client's ability to withstand them. This Crown wasn't taken in. She knew what he was doing, because she had been warned by the senior prosecutor that this was a classical defence tactic.

'True it is that my client was giving evidence long after the events of which he spoke, and he's had a long time in which to prepare himself. And I won't pretend he hasn't had the assistance of lawyers in organising his thoughts. But only one man could give his evidence. Only one man knows what was in Michael Stanich's mind on the day the deceased grabbed hold of his rifle and fought him for it. This is the man.' And he turned away from the judge and jury to face his client, who looked up into Harry's face with an expression suggesting gratitude, then back down at his hands.

'May I ask you just, for a moment, to take your minds back two days to when my client was in the witness box? Certainly, he was nervous. That's not his element, and you won't hold that against him. We lawyers may be confident and even glib, some of us —' (a sidelong glance at the prosecutor, not lost on the jury foreman) '—but you as a cross-section of the community will well appreciate how terrifying it must be to be on trial for murder, and have to try to explain yourself to a jury of strangers who already know that you did kill the man with whose murder you are charged.

'It is also important for me to acknowledge that my client appears before you wearing a suit and tie with his hair combed and his shoes shone. Here, he's in a very different condition from that he was suffering on the day of the shooting. But you can see past all that, and past all the formalities and legal language and bowing and scraping, and you can see into all those indications of sincerity. They can't be faked.' At this point, Harry scanned the faces and knew he had the undivided attention of every jury member. There wasn't a sound in the courtroom except for Harry's voice. Deep, confident, committed. Harry Curry in his element. He'd read somewhere that a survey had established that people thought tall men to be more intelligent than small ones. Harry didn't believe it for a moment, but he hoped the jury did.

'You, ladies and gentlemen, are judges, just as is her Honour, but you are the judges of the facts. Her Honour has no opinion on my client's guilt or innocence, as she is bound to tell you, and you should ignore any indication you may think she gives on that subject. Her only role here is as the judge of the legal questions.' Justice Temple's face seemed to say that Curry was right, of course, but why did he take it upon himself to raise the matter? He certainly knew that any judge had to give a direction in the same terms to the jury, but plainly she was severely displeased at his implication that she might otherwise have attempted to impose her own views on the jury's decision.

'It is you and you alone who judge my client, and you do that by employing your knowledge of the world and the affairs of people such as yourself. My client is a person such as yourselves.

Like you, he's not a judge or a lawyer. Like you, he lives in the real world. He has the same dreams, the same hopes, the same fears, the same prayers. He prays that you will understand what was in his mind and in his heart, and he's done his very best at all times to tell you what it was. Let me read to you the relevant part of the evidence he gave you on oath, starting, your Honour, at page 121, about halfway down.' The judge turned to the page in her folder of the trial transcript which was, again, not something that the jury were entitled to have. Harry put his hand on the page and said to the jury: 'I had just asked him the question: "What was in your mind when you were thinking about taking your rifle to the shopping centre?" And this was his answer.'

Even while he was saying those words, Harry was telling himself that he'd been right to take the — for him — highly unusual step of putting his client in the witness box. He'd done it in the belief that, in this case, the jury would punish the accused man for hiding behind his barrister. Of course it exposed an inarticulate and terrified man to the mental minefield of cross-examination, notwithstanding the inexperience of his adversary. But Harry judged it unavoidable and, schooled by his counsel and having read the skilfully prepared proof of evidence (obscenities and solecisms included for authenticity) scores of times as he sat in his cell at Silverwater, Michael did himself proud.

I came to two conclusions about what could happen if I took my rifle and confronted Mr Ponti with it. I thought he would either be scared and beg for his life, say he was sorry and agree to drop the case; or the only other thing I could imagine was he would call the police, and if they came after me I would shoot myself.

But it didn't go according to plan. Nothing did.

He didn't drive into the car park the way I had pictured it, but he came from the opposite direction. That threw me straight away. He didn't park his car where I thought. He got out of the car and started abusing me, and I hadn't expected that, either. I was just sitting there on the edge of the garden bed with the blue and pink flowers.

He walked towards me. I wasn't angry at all — I was just feeling threatened by what he was saying, because I wasn't doing anything. I hadn't thought that was going to happen. He walked off, and I turned round and got the rifle out of the garden and ran after him. I just thought of scaring him.

He was calling me 'dickhead', 'idiot' and 'stupid'. 'Why aren't you out fishing? That's all you're good for.' I stopped and he got to within three metres of me and as he got closer, I was walking backwards away from him. He was saying, 'Give me the gun,' and I wasn't expecting him to do that.

I had the gun behind me, pointing away from both of us. I was fending him off with my left hand, but he didn't stop coming forward, getting close. He threw punches at me. He just kept trying to grab the gun. I backed into the garbage bins. They stopped me.

He got hold of the gun. Grabbed it by the end of the barrel. We were wrestling with the gun. I pulled it really hard. One of his hands let go of the gun, which swang it towards him. That's when I shot him in the stomach.

I was in shock. I couldn't believe it. I think I said to myself I am in big fucking trouble now.

Harry stopped reading and looked up, making eye contact with a young woman in the back row of the jury box. She hadn't smiled at any of his pleasantries, or shown any sympathy for his address to this point, so he knew he'd have to work on her. And not just her.

'You will recall that I began my address to you by referring to my client having no intention at all; to his being overcome by panic. You can't doubt the truth of that. This is how he put it when he gave his evidence to you.' He turned a page and started reading from a brightly highlighted section of the transcript.

I was petrified. He'd been—

The judge interrupted. 'What page, Mr Curry?'

'What?' Harry's head snapped around.

'Where are you reading from? What page of the transcript?' The judge's tone was very slightly apologetic.

'The next page from where I was, your Honour. This follows on.' Harry looked angrily at her. Judges aren't supposed to halt the flow of counsel's final jury address, and she should have known better. As far as Harry was concerned, he was addressing the jury, not her, and her job was to keep up or keep silent.

'Here it is, members of the jury.' Harry looked down and began reading again.

I was petrified. He'd been shot — it was an accident — but I thought: now he's going to get the gun off me and shoot me. He's going to kill me for sure. It's all I could think of him doing. I was scared. I pulled the trigger as fast as I could to stop him getting the gun. There wasn't a pause in the nine shots.

Harry paused and looked at the jury, but heard the sharp, insistent tap of the judge's pen on the bench in front of her. He turned.

'I notice the time, Mr Curry. Were you intending to take a break soon?'

Harry looked at the clock: 11.40 a.m. — he'd gone past the usual morning tea adjournment. 'Yes, your Honour, thank you. Would that be a convenient moment?'

And the court was adjourned.

Harry completed his address to the jury just before the luncheon adjournment, as he had promised. He pointed out to them that he had reached the finish, and seven minutes before his estimate. Then he closed his pad, pushed his law books together, and put the cap on his pen.

'Just one last thing,' he said. 'This death was a tragedy. Maybe the deceased was a hard man, even an unkind man, and someone we wouldn't ordinarily like to associate with. Maybe that's wrong, maybe I shouldn't say that, but it doesn't matter. To lose his life like that, bleeding to death on the ground in a parking lot, is dreadful. But it would be just as dreadful to destroy another life — Michael's life — by finding him guilty of intentionally, or even recklessly, killing this man when that simply isn't what happened. This whole thing is a tragedy, but you shouldn't make it any worse. Whatever you decide, my client will live with this for the rest of his life — with this awareness that he took another man's life. It's not as if he's ever going to forgive himself. But he's young, and he's hard-working, and he's a good person. Your decision will save a life, or it will destroy one.' He looked along the faces of the back row in the jury box, and then swept his eyes along the front row, stopping with the foreman. Harry realised, with amazement, that there were tears on his cheeks. 'My client thanks you.' And he sat, leaving his tears where they were until the jury had been taken out. I'm tired, he thought. And I'm sick of all this.

After lunch, the judge took over proceedings, her eyes fixed firmly on the *Bench Book of Jury Directions*, opened at 'Murder', and spent an hour directing the jury about how it should approach its job, turning then to summarise the evidence and arguments on both sides. Harry made notes of how one-sided the summing-up was: three or four times as much attention to the Crown case as to the defence evidence. New judge, same old trick. Just before three o'clock, a woman juror held up her hand and said that she wasn't feeling well, so Temple J adjourned, asking them all to be back in the jury room by 9.30 on Monday morning.

Saturday afternoon, just after lunch, and Harry and Arabella, in the LandCruiser, drew up to the kerb outside Wallace Curry QC's South Turramurra high-end care facility. When they got inside, Harry found that the nurses had the old man dressed in his alpaca jacket and linen trousers, ready to go out in the Sydney heat. Smiling, he stood as the couple came through the automatic glass doors.

'Punctuality, Harry. *La politesse du roi.*'

Another lucid interval, then. Harry was pleased, having anticipated that the long-arranged introduction of Arabella followed by a drive and afternoon tea would be meaningless, or would even have to be called off.

'Dad, may I present my learned friend, Arabella Engineer?'

Curry QC took her hand and looked at the tall young woman, dressed in a paisley-patterned silk shirtwaisted dress and sandals.

She removed her sunglasses. 'Enchanted,' he beamed. 'But I rather think there's some other relationship than that of colleagues.'

Arabella bowed her head and smiled almost shyly.

'Not a criminal lawyer, surely?' He kept hold of her hand.

'Not really, not any more. I'm trying to concentrate on civil work, Mr Curry.'

'Which would make you a civil Engineer!' He obviously thought that hilarious. 'And, in any event, if you're at the Bar, you can't call me Mister. It's Wallace.'

'Thank you.' Her hand was released with a certain amount of reluctance. In his day, Curry QC had a bit of a reputation.

Harry gestured towards the doors. 'Where are we off to, Dad?'

'Afternoon tea, boy, and a view of the old stamping ground. As agreed between the parties, or had you forgotten?'

'Of course not, but I thought you might have changed your mind.'

Wallace took Arabella's elbow and steered her through the doors. 'What he means is that he thought I might be on some other planet.'

Harry didn't see any point in pretending. 'And we're very happy that you're not.'

'As am I, boy. It's not very pleasant there.'

Arabella insisted on taking a back seat in the car. 'So that your father can see better, Harry. I'm fine back here.'

Curry QC was not entirely impressed with the LandCruiser or its robust suspension. 'Something happened to the Jaguar?'

'*Hors de combat*, Dad. I've been using this for some country work. You know I'm living down the South Coast.' Too difficult to fully explain about Burragate and the semi-retirement it represented.

302

'And I read in the *Herald* that you're doing a murder somewhere down there, didn't I? It'd have to be Wollongong, wouldn't it? That's as far south as the Supreme Court goes.'

'There's always Goulburn,' said Harry, 'but maybe even that's just District Court trials now. But yes, it's in the Gong. Should get the verdict on Monday.' He stopped suddenly for a red light that he would have run had his father not been in the car. 'The judge has just about finished her summing-up, but a juror wasn't feeling well, and we lost an hour on Friday afternoon.'

'You'll win that, will you?'

'Well, hardly. My bloke did it, but I'm trying to make them think I'm going in hard on self-defence to get them to compromise on manslaughter.'

'I got that impression from the newspaper. You fellows and your criminal strategies. You're as bad as common lawyers. Give me a nice, clean tax appeal any day,' he said, turning to look at the other passenger. 'Do any tax, do you, Arabella?'

'Not even my own, Wallace, I'm sad to say.'

'Ah.'

They drove in silence for a while with the old man attempting to take in the new landscape that presented itself as they travelled up the Pacific Highway towards Hornsby, then turned south-west. Probably just as ugly as he remembered, Harry thought, but different.

'I suppose it's the self-indulgence of a silly geriatric,' Wallace said, 'but I wanted to see Cheltenham again before I die.'

'You don't intend to die soon, do you? I think I should have been told.' Harry looked at his father.

'Not particularly, but I thought it best to come back to the old stamping ground while it still means something to me.' He turned in his seat again and spoke to Arabella. 'We brought the children up at Cheltenham. There wouldn't be any place better, we both thought. My wife grew up there, you know, in a big family with a lawn tennis court. Not that our son appreciated it. Harry got sick of catching the train to Shore, of course. Never stopped complaining.'

'He has that tendency.' Arabella was starting to enjoy the Harry-bashing.

'Used to complain that he was the only Shore boy on the platform at Beecroft. In his boater. You remember that bully who knocked your hat down onto the railway line, Harry?'

'Vaguely.'

'"Vaguely", he says. Narrowly avoided the Children's Court, truth to tell.' Harry's father was amused at the recollection.

'What?' asked Arabella. 'As the offender?'

'Yes. Knocked the boy's front teeth out. Big boy, and older than Harry. Went to King's, of course, and hardly in any position to make fun of another school's uniform. Do they still wear that chocolate soldier outfit?'

'No idea, Dad.'

'The police attended, but only momentarily. His parents wanted me to pay for new teeth, but I had one of the big city firms who briefed me in those days write them a splendid letter threatening to sue their thuggish offspring for common assault on my sensitive defenceless son, and that was the last we heard of it.'

'I'd agree with sensitive, but you might have a little difficulty finding a witness to corroborate your assertion of defencelessness,' Arabella said.

'I wouldn't even agree with sensitive,' Wallace said. 'But perhaps you know my son better than do I.'

Harry brought the car to a halt. 'If you two have had your fun at my expense, we're here.'

'Where, boy?'

'Beecroft shops, Dad. Do you want to get out? Find a café?'

They climbed down from the car and spent twenty minutes walking the footpaths of the streets adjoining the railway station. The old man was obviously disappointed that there was little or nothing he could recognise. He didn't like the look of any of the cafés that remained open.

They came to an unpleasant postmodern facade and Wallace stopped in front of it. 'Dr Terrey's house has gone, then. He took out my wife's appendix, Arabella. GPs used to, in those days.' They walked further down the hill towards the station. 'Barber's gone. Dutchman, nice fellow. Had a sign that said "Be like Robinson Crusoe — get your hair cut by Friday."' They came to the intersection. 'No chemist. It's not even called Railway Parade any more. D'you remember, Harry? You and your friends tried to sell the chemist the wings from Black Prince cicadas that you caught one summer? They faithfully believed that chemists would pay them five dollars for each wing, Arabella. Supposed to have special properties.'

Harry smiled at the memory. 'Suburban childhood myths, Bella. Surely you had them in London?'

'Never saw a cicada in Hampstead, Harry. We used to believe you could get drunk on Coca-Cola with an aspirin dissolved in it, though. Does that count?'

Curry QC crossed the street and stopped in a car park. 'There used to be a hardware shop here that Harry bought his mother's Christmas presents from. A plastic butter dish with a lid that said Butter. Remember that?'

'I've still got it, Dad. Mum gave it to me when I moved to Erskineville.'

'She was never happy about your choice of suburb, boy. She was—'

'Yes, I know. One of the Cheltenham McGuffickes.' Harry put his arm around his father and hugged him for a moment. The old man was never tall, but had shrunk with age and didn't come much higher than Harry's shoulder, or Arabella's, for that matter. Still the neatly clipped moustache and luxuriant grey hair. A silk tie on Saturday afternoon in the suburbs. All bounce and bullshit, one of his closest learned friends had said.

'Not much to see here, Dad. D'you want to take a look at the house and go on somewhere else for a cup of tea?'

'Yes, boy. Let's do that, eh, Arabella? And we'll show her the tennis club — Harry spent all his holidays there. Homework was studiously ignored. Drove his mother to distraction.'

They headed back to the car. Arabella cautiously asked whether Wallace missed his wife. 'Every day. I think of her every day. I know our Harry thinks she was a terrible snob, but he's wrong. She died and her hair was still not grey, you know. Women of her generation, Arabella, never had a chance. She would have made a much better barrister than I did ...' He stopped and slowly looked around the streetscape. A train pulled out of the nearby station, sounding its horn. 'She would have loved to travel, but I was always too busy with my cases. And she couldn't have gone on her own. Women didn't.'

They got into the car and his father asked Harry about his own travelling plans. 'You didn't go to Italy this year, boy?'

'No, I didn't. Bella had a big building case at the last minute, so we didn't go. Maybe in the summer.'

'The *European* summer,' said Arabella. 'I'll try not to hold my breath.'

They drove past the Beecroft Public School, and a late Victorian building on the opposite corner. 'That was Wilson's Store,' said the old man. 'Maxam Bakeo, Kinkara tea, Reckitt's blue bags. Broken biscuits.' Arabella had no idea what he was talking about.

Five minutes later, Harry pulled up outside the former Curry family home in Cheltenham. A quiet street. No inner-city joggers to clutter the landscape. Tall eucalypts on the neatly mown nature strip; high boxwood hedges. 'There it is, Dad. Number 15.'

The old man peered at the dense shrubbery. 'Can't see a thing. We didn't have that hedge — there were camellias and sasanquas, and a low brick wall. You should have seen them in autumn, Arabella. My wife was a wonderful gardener. Knew the names of everything.' He spoke proudly.

The view of the house was, indeed, obscured. All that could be seen was the slate-tiled roof and the tops of the cotton-reel Federation joinery along the underside of the verandah awning. A Mercedes in the gravel drive blocked any view in that direction. The old man was visibly disappointed. Harry bent low over the steering wheel to look at the house, but his view was no better. 'They say you can't go back.'

'In which case, they're right. It doesn't mean one doesn't want to.' Curry QC paused. 'Why do people have to live in fortresses? It wasn't like that in our time — the gates were left open, and the children were always out on their bikes, riding into each other's places. Harry used to play cricket in the street. His mother had a postman's whistle that she blew when it was time to come in.'

Harry made no comment, and Arabella didn't know what to say. The old man sighed and looked straight ahead through the windscreen, which Harry took to indicate that he should drive off. Arabella leaned forward from the back seat. 'You seem a bit tired, Wallace.'

He didn't reply, and Harry abandoned plans for afternoon tea.

'Will I drive past the tennis club, Dad?' Harry looked back at Arabella. 'Dad and Mum used to play croquet there.'

'No, boy, I don't think so.'

There was no further conversation, and the old man slumped in his seat, held back by the seat belt. Twenty minutes later, they were back at South Turramurra, outside the no-expense-spared care facility that had been Curry QC's home for more than five years. He made no move to leave the LandCruiser, and Harry got out and went around to the passenger's door, which he opened. His father swung his legs out and prepared to climb down.

'The nurse can take me in, doctor. I'm sure you need to be getting back to the hospital.'

'The nurse, Dad?'

'This very pleasant young woman.' Curry QC tilted his head towards Arabella in the back seat.

'Right. Look, why don't we both come in with you, and organise a cup of tea?'

With Harry on one side and Arabella the other, Wallace Curry walked slowly down the brick path to the automatic doors, which hissed open. Harry looked over the top of his father's head at Arabella, who smiled sadly. When they had him back in his room upstairs, seated beside the bed and with the cup of tea Arabella had fetched, Curry QC looked content. He thanked them both. Harry kissed his father goodbye, and Arabella put her hand on top of the old man's and squeezed gently for a moment. He looked up at her and bowed his head twice. Harry had seen him make that gesture in court. It meant then that he'd completed the submissions he wanted to make, and there was nothing more to say. The decision was out of his hands.

They drove most of the way back in silence. As he parked at Elizabeth Bay, Harry asked whether Arabella was going to spend Sunday in chambers.

'I wasn't planning to. The building case's pretty well under control, and there's nothing that can't wait. Did you have anything particular in mind?'

'I want to write out some notes I made about Shirley Temple's summing-up. That's all.'

'Does she know you call her that?'

'Everyone's called her that since she first came to the Bar. For the moment, I can't remember what her real name is.'

'Are you going to be asking for redirections?'

They caught the lift up to the fifth floor. 'Am I ever! She's going for my bloke, well and truly. The Appeal judges won't listen to me if I don't raise every objection with the judge herself.'

'Maybe it's her way of levelling the playing field. I pity that baby prosecutor, trying to face down Harry Curry in full spate.'

'It's not the judge's job to compensate for incompetence. Anyway, she wasn't that bad. The Crown, I mean, not Shirl. Just a bit wet behind the ears.'

Arabella unlocked her front door and they went inside. Harry slid open the balcony doors, and she went into the kitchen to put on the coffee. Harry threw himself down on the Corbusier sofa and closed his eyes.

Arabella returned and sat opposite. 'Anything in particular that gave offence?'

Harry looked at her and took a beat before speaking. 'It started out like every other summing-up you've ever heard: explaining her role, the jury's own role, the onus of proof, the standard of proof, the elements of the offence. All straight out of the *Bench Book*. Unanimity, ignoring anything they saw in the media, all the boilerplate. Then she made some reference to "taking the emotion out of it" and gave them a really heavy-handed rev-up about sympathy for my client playing no part in their deliberations.'

'Meaning?'

'Something to the effect of "Mr Curry's spent a great deal of time on his client's background, and you might think unnecessarily — the fact that his brothers are all fishermen, that he wasn't really cut out for that occupation because he could never get over his seasickness, and that's why he was leasing a shop from Ponti. That has absolutely no bearing on the issues you have to decide." Then she went on about the only possible relevance of the trawler work Michael used to do being that it was the reason he owned a semi-automatic rifle.'

'Why did he, may I ask?'

'The boats all carry them. They shoot the sharks that get caught in their nets. When he gave up fishing and opened the cake shop, he took his gun home and forgot about it. It was really a last-minute brainwave to take it with him when he went to the Eden shopping centre to have it out with Ponti. But to listen to Justice Shirley Temple, you'd think it was the greatest premeditation of all time. Never mind that the coppers didn't think so, and told the jury that.'

'Only when you cross-examined them, I presume? I'll bet they didn't volunteer it.'

'Naturally not, but it was never a real issue. She was trying to dilute all the effort I'd made to evoke some degree of empathy with my bloke — his feeling that he let the family down, which only became worse when he couldn't make a go of the cake shop and had to toss it in, and then the ultimate nastiness of the landlord twisting the knife over half a dozen cracked bloody tiles at the back of the shop counter. Sued him in the local court. My whole strategy was to have the jury develop some understanding of the overbearing accumulation of failure, the personal disgrace, and then that appallingly stupid and vindictive claim for three thousand dollars, which he didn't have. Michael's no great intellect — he didn't know what to do. He couldn't ask his brothers for more money, and there was no one else. Most people would have snapped, and he certainly did.'

'Most people wouldn't have taken a loaded gun and pointed it at their landlord.'

'Whose side are you on?'

'Oh, Harry!' An indulgent but pitying look.

Harry started to make a heated response, but pulled back. 'I'm sorry, Bella.'

She went into the kitchen and retrieved two espressos. They sat in silence for a while, listening to kids playing outside and the distant hum of marine motors. There were shouts and a loud flapping noise as the mainsail of a yacht returning to its mooring was released from the masthead, just outside the sea wall beneath them.

'But what can you do? To counteract the anti-defence summing-up, I mean?'

'I'm thinking about it.' He stood up and walked out onto the balcony to watch the yacht. 'You know what I was wondering on the way back from dropping off Dad?'

'I thought you were depressed about his little show of senility.'

He turned to face her. 'No, not that. I accept that. I'm pretty happy when he knows who I am and where we are. No, I was trying to get to grips with the sad fact that, every trial I do, I make an enemy. It isn't always the judge, let me say, but it will be, this time. And she's a good hater. People in the Labor Party always are.'

Arabella put her cup and saucer on the side table. 'You surprise me, Harry. I thought conflict was just another tactic. It's served you well.'

'The only case that matters is the one you're doing right now. The question is whether she's poisoned the jury, or whether they're committed to me.'

'Any indications?'

'Oh, I think I've got the foreman and a couple of the older men. The women are a bit harder to pick, and there's at least one who doesn't like me one little bit.'

'I'm sure you're right — but I've never been able to do that, to read the jury. I've never had the time or the self-possession to try, even. Did anyone teach you how to do it?'

'No, it's something I've made up for myself. I tell them a joke at a few stages in the trial, and in my address, and I look for the ones who don't smile. Then I work on them.'

'What's that supposed to mean? Work on them?'

Harry came back into the room and sat down next to her. 'You make eye contact, and there's a little contest over who's going to look away first. I'm not trying to make them uncomfortable, but to persuade them of my confidence in a viewpoint they don't have. I'm asking them to put aside their prejudices for a moment. I'll tell you a good little trick you can use for that.'

'Yes?'

'Invite the jury to cross their arms. You say: "You don't have to do this, but just humour me for a moment, if you'd be so kind — and please just cross your arms." Most of them will do it.'

'And?'

'And then you say to uncross them and re-cross them the other way.'

'What does that do?'

'It makes anyone surprisingly uncomfortable. Physically, I mean, even if only momentarily. Everyone crosses their arms in one particular way, and when you're forced to change, it feels really strange. But it also usually makes them smile. And when they do that, you say to them: "You see how different it feels to do some everyday thing in an unaccustomed fashion? Well, that's what you have to do here … put aside your prejudices. You're predisposed to assume my client's guilty, because the police thought so, and arrested him and charged him; and the DPP thinks so, because they indicted him and want you to convict him. But don't just do the comfortable thing of following their lead. It might feel strange, but it's important to see things from a new perspective. It's not so radical, it's just crossing your arms, after all." '

'That's very interesting, Harry. I've never seen it done — by you or anyone else. Do judges let you do it? Do they ever stop you?'

'It's usually too late before they think to pull you up. It's already happened.'

'But what does it prove?'

'Nothing at all, but it gives you an opportunity to dictate, ever so gently, to the jury. It puts you in charge of their thinking. Sometimes.'

'Did you do it in Wollongong?'

'No. If I had, maybe it would only have been another thing for her Honour, Lady Justice Shirl, to have a whinge about on Monday morning.'

'Another thing for you to ask for a redirection on.'

'Not in this case. But I've got others.'

'Which will, no doubt, sufficiently inflame her.'

Harry turned on the television in time for the news. 'No doubt at all.'

Sunday was spent reading books, going for a walk together down through Rushcutters Bay and around the mansions of Darling Point, and having dinner in Dixon Street. From time to time, Harry would make a note on a piece of paper, and put it in his pocket. By the end of the day, he needed two pieces of paper. On Monday morning, he left Elizabeth Bay in the LandCruiser at first light, and had his breakfast in Wollongong close to the courthouse, writing out his scrappy notes in the form of an application he intended to make to the judge. Making such an application — for what were known as redirections to the jury — was predicated on the assertion that the judge had been in error in her summing-up. Never an easy argument to make.

At ten o'clock, counsel and solicitors were at the Bar table, and Michael Stanich was back in the dock, waiting for the trial to resume. After ten minutes, the judge's associate came out to inform the lawyers that the sick juror had improved somewhat over the weekend, but was at her doctor's and hoped to make it by eleven. The associate passed on the judge's invitation to counsel for tea in her chambers. The barristers removed their wigs and gowns and followed the associate through the judge's door, and along a corridor. The associate knocked on a door and showed them in. Harry was carrying his handwritten notes.

'Good morning, judge,' said the Crown.

'Morning, Madam Crown. Morning, Harry.'

'Shirley.'

'I wish you wouldn't call me that.' She gestured to the chairs on the opposite side of her desk. 'I've got a new nickname now.'

Harry asked what it was.

'Judge,' she said, curtly.

There was a frosty silence until the associate took their orders. Harry wanted another black coffee.

'Have you got much longer to go with the summing-up?' he asked.

'Half an hour. That is, unless you want to argue about redirections.'

'I don't want to argue.'

'Good.'

'But I do want you to redirect.'

'On which points?' Obviously displeased.

'If I had my way, I'd put it on the record that you should withdraw the whole of your summing-up and start again.' Harry said it in a mild tone, but it was a massive insult, as he well knew. The prosecutor didn't know where to look, but she knew enough to maintain her silence.

'But you're not going to do that, are you, Harry?'

'No, Shirley, I'm not.' Still not calling her 'judge'. 'The CCA would only have a transcript of your remarks, and they wouldn't get any sense of the tone in which you spoke them, so I'd be pushing it uphill. I'll just ask for a few specific redirections —

five, at last count. But you're not finished yet, so I'll reserve my position on the number of points I'll raise.'

Harry took a sideways glance at the prosecutor as she was handed her cup. She was, he thought, taken aback that counsel — and junior counsel, at that — would speak to a Supreme Court judge so disrespectfully. Tough, he thought. She'd better get used to it. And what have I got to lose, anyway? Shirley's not going to make it any worse, and maybe she'll even water it down in the final things she has to say in the hope that we won't appeal. If we lose, that is. No need to appeal if Michael's acquitted, however reprehensible the judicial performance.

After that, morning tea was a tense affair, and didn't last much longer. Harry spent twenty minutes on the courthouse steps, smoking and fuming, and at ten to eleven the court officer came out to tell him that the missing juror had arrived.

Temple J began by telling the jury that she intended to recapitulate her summing-up and directions of law, given that the weekend had intervened and they may have had other things on their minds. She then ran through a sort of *Reader's Digest* version of what she had told them on Friday afternoon, but without the anti-defence flourishes and antipathetic tone. Harry was pleased, and thought the change would be very beneficial, but he wasn't going to forgo his client's rights.

Finishing, and telling the jury that they would shortly go back to the jury room to consider their verdict, the judge turned to the Bar table.

'Was there anything, Madam Crown?'

The prosecutor half rose. 'No, may it please your Honour.'

'Mr Curry?'

Harry stood. Temple didn't have to invite his criticisms in the presence of the jury, and he thought her foolish to do so. Maybe she thought he'd baulk at a confrontation in their presence, but if that was what she believed, she didn't know Harry.

'Five matters, your Honour: The first concerns your address to the jury on Friday, which I respectfully submit was not fairly balanced. By my watch, you spent fifty-two minutes summarising the Crown case, and considerably less than thirty minutes on the defence.'

'Second point?' Frowning, hand moving to straighten her wig.

'I ask you to redirect on the *mens rea* element so far as it involves recklessness. The law is, clearly, that recklessness has to be explained to the jury as meaning that the accused is proved to have been aware of the possible consequences of his action, but decided to go ahead anyway.'

Temple J thought for a minute. 'Yes, Mr Curry, I think I should make that quite clear. Will you go on to your next point, please?'

Harry smiled to himself. Curry 2, judge nil. 'I ask your Honour to redirect the jury on self-defence. With the greatest of respect—' (Harry had earlier explained to his young solicitor that 'with respect' means 'You're wrong, judge'; 'with great respect' means 'How could you get it so wrong, judge?'; 'with the greatest respect' means 'The Court of Appeal will crucify you for that'; and 'with unfeigned respect' means 'How did you ever get to be a judge? Are you having an affair with the Attorney-General?') '—your Honour is bound to tell the jury that self-defence is something that in this case must be disproved, beyond reasonable doubt, by the prosecution's evidence. The way your Honour laid down the law was capable of indicating to the jury that we had some onus of proof, which is certainly not the case.'

Temple J was quicker this time. 'No, Mr Curry, my direction was in conformity with the law. The jury understand that. Anything else?'

Harry paused. His last two points weren't as good as the self-defence objection. If there had to be an appeal, it would rise or fall on that issue, and a couple more minor quibbles weren't going to make any difference. He was happy that he'd protected his client's best appellate argument, and he decided that enough was probably enough. 'I think not, your Honour. Just the three matters, it seems.'

With Harry back in his seat and making a note, her Honour told the jury that they shouldn't place any weight on the longer period she'd spent summing up the Crown case than she had on the defence, because the value of evidence was a matter of quality and not quantity; and then moved on to correct what she had said about recklessness. She even put in a comment that, because Michael Stanich had given sworn evidence that he was so confused and upset that he never turned his mind to the possible consequences of producing the gun, that evidence — if they thought it was credible, and her tone suggested she didn't — must decide the issue in his favour. And then she sent them out just before one o'clock, saying that sandwiches would be taken in to them. To the disappointment of Harry and his solicitor, she ordered that the accused be held downstairs in the cells while the jury were deliberating.

'She didn't need to punish Michael just because she dislikes you, Harry.'

'How very perceptive of you,' he said.

Harry caught up with the judge's schoolmarmish associate as she was checking off the exhibits from her list and handing them one by one to the sheriff's officer to take into the jury room — DVDs, the post-mortem report, photographs of the scene of the crime. At least Harry had persuaded the judge not to enter into evidence the appalling photographs of the bullet-riddled body. Too prejudicial. He gave her a scrap of paper on which his solicitor had written her mobile phone number.

'There's our number, Madam Associate. We're going to have a cup of tea, probably over at David Jones. I don't suppose this's going to be quick, but if you don't call us, we'll come back at quarter to four.'

'Thank you, Mr Curry. I would have thought they'll still be deliberating tomorrow, wouldn't you?'

'Hope not. But I defer to your greater experience.'

She smiled for the first time. 'Yes, I suppose I've sent out more murder juries than even you. We did ten last year.'

Harry removed his wig, gown and jabot but kept his Bar jacket on. His solicitor — her name was Renata, he remembered with difficulty — stood with one hand on the courtroom door until Harry joined her, and they strolled downhill from the old courthouse to the big department store, and took a table in its café. She took out an iPhone and sent a text message while Harry ordered tea for both of them.

'So, Renata, how do you like murder?' Harry rearranged the napkin holder and the salt and pepper shakers and looked at her. Pretty girl, unattractive spectacles. He'd taken in the very high heels and tight pencil skirt as they walked downhill.

'Much better than child sex. We get a lot of that down here.'

'And drugs?'

'Of course. Boring bloody lists of precursor chemicals and laboratory equipment, endless certificates of analysis. Reams and reams of indecipherable telephone intercepts. And never an acquittal.'

'Sounds to me like you're not long for the criminal justice system.'

The teas arrived and she waved away the milk and sugar. 'Port Kembla girls aren't much in demand at Allen Allen and Hemsley.'

'What?' said Harry. 'Not even the very smart ones?'

'Not even university medallists. I couldn't get an interview.'

'University medal? I'm impressed.'

She sipped her tea. 'Don't be — it was Wollongong Uni. A Macedonian surname's not much help, either.'

He asked her about her family, because he was genuinely interested, and she could tell that. They spent an hour in which Renata told the story of her father arriving in Sydney on a ship and starting work in the Port Kembla coke ovens the very next day. Twenty-three years there, and never a sick day, until he was hurt in a car accident and never worked again. Ripped off by a local solicitor who mismanaged his personal injury case.

'Is that why you did law?'

'Bullseye.'

Harry paid, and they walked back to court.

There was no verdict by four o'clock, and the judge had the jury brought back into the courtroom.

'Mr Foreman, please don't think I'm attempting to hurry you, but would you prefer me to adjourn now, and you can come back tomorrow and resume your deliberations?'

The foreman didn't need to consult any other jury members, but informed the judge that he thought they were close to agreement, and would all prefer to remain and see if their verdict could be reached later in the afternoon. So they went back to their room.

Stanich had been brought up from the cells, and this time was allowed to remain with his lawyers until the verdict was brought in.

'I know this is bloody hard for you, Michael,' Harry said. They were sitting in the public benches, with a policeman keeping an eye on the prisoner. 'It's the hardest part of any trial, the waiting.'

Renata looked as nervous as her client. 'What do you think, Harry?'

'I don't try to guess. I think we've still got the foreman, but the rest are giving me very blank stares.'

Michael was clasping and unclasping his hands. Harry didn't think he could last much longer without breaking down. He put his hand on the younger man's shoulder. 'Bertrand Russell said that when you're facing a catastrophe, you should plan what you're going to do if the worst comes to the worst, make a decision, and stop worrying about it.'

Stanich lifted his head. 'First of all,' he said, 'I've never heard of that bloke. Russell. And second of all, what would I plan? To sit in a jail cell for the rest of my life — that's not much of a plan, is it? I've already been there since I was arrested, and it's terrible. I hate it.'

Harry looked rueful. 'Good point, mate.'

They sat in silence for about twenty minutes, and then the message came out. 'We've got a verdict.'

The accused was placed back in the dock under guard, and Harry put his wig on and sat back at the Bar table. Renata leaned forward and said to him, 'I've heard that if the jury are smiling, you're going to be acquitted.'

'Yes,' said Harry, 'I've heard all those theories too. The other one is that if they walk in and avoid looking at your client, he's been found guilty. I don't believe any of it.'

The judge came back on the bench and gave the nod to the court officer, and the jury filed in. Some were smiling, and some were looking away from the man in the dock. Harry's guts, as usual when a verdict was impending, were fizzing.

When the court had settled, and the foreman had been called upon to stand and announce the verdict, he looked at Harry.

The associate stood.

'How say you? On the charge of murder, do you find the accused guilty or not guilty?'

The foreman took a breath. 'Not guilty.'

'And as to the alternate charge of manslaughter, do you find him guilty or not guilty?'

The foreman kept looking at Harry. 'Guilty.'

Harry nodded at him almost imperceptibly and whispered, 'Thanks.'

Temple J thanked the jury, and discharged them. They were taken off to be paid, and to return to their far less interesting jobs on Tuesday.

'Madam Crown and Mr Curry, I'm going to stand this over for sentencing. Four weeks?'

'Suitable, your Honour,' said the Crown, making a note on her pad.

'Mr Curry?'

Harry pulled a thin diary out of his Bar jacket side pocket and turned some pages. 'That would be the Monday, your Honour, and I'm starting a matter on that day in Sydney. Would it be possible to make it the Friday?'

The judge looked at her own diary. 'It would have to be in Sydney, Mr Curry.'

That was what Harry had been after. 'I have no objection to that, your Honour. My client will be out at Silverwater anyway, and my instructing solicitor won't object to a trip up to the big city.'

'You're not seeking bail for your client at this stage?'

'No, your Honour. He'll obviously be given a custodial sentence, and he may as well keep serving it. It may not be all that substantial, and he's already been in custody since the day of the offence.'

Temple J looked puzzled. 'Not all that substantial, Mr Curry?'

'Oh, your Honour won't be aware of this, but Madam Crown will agree that, on my advice, my client offered to plead guilty to manslaughter right from the beginning. The DPP wouldn't agree to the plea bargain, but manslaughter's all he's been convicted of.'

'So?'

'So he's entitled to the maximum discount. Twenty-five per cent. Your Honour is going to have to sentence him as having pleaded guilty at the first opportunity, demonstrating his remorse and contrition. He's also a person of good character, with very strong subjective factors affecting the exercise of the court's sentencing discretion. That is, if the politicians haven't so circumscribed it as to make the concept of judicial discretion an oxymoron.'

The judge couldn't have agreed more. 'Who are we, Mr Curry, to question the wisdom of parliament?'

'Indeed, your Honour. Mere labourers in the judicial vineyard.'

'Friday the thirtieth, then. Bail is refused. Madam Crown, can the Probation and Parole Service do a pre-sentence report by then?'

'I believe so, your Honour. I should just confirm that Mr Curry's quite right about the early plea.'

'Yes, but let's not jump the gun. Sentencing's in a month.'

'As your Honour pleases.'

And that was it. The judge retired, handcuffs were produced, and Michael Stanich was taken out of the dock and manacled. Harry stood close to him. 'Congratulations, Michael. You did a great job.'

'No, it was you, Mr Curry.'

'Well, as I told you, it's a team effort. Now, they'll send a parole person out to Silverwater to interview you for this report to the judge. Just tell them the truth, and don't leave anything out. Tell them all about how Ponti drove you nuts over the rent and sent you broke when the shop failed. And tell them all about being sued over the broken tiles, and how that made you feel. If you do yourself justice on that, the judge will get it all.'

'Okay.'

'You do understand that jail time's involved, don't you?'

'Yeah, but how much?'

'If I had to guess, I'd say another two to two-and-a-half years, if she wants to be decent about it. You get credit for the time already served, and the extra month before sentencing, plus however long she takes to hand down her decision.'

Michael thought about the time in jail. 'She's not going to make it any heavier because she doesn't like you, is she?'

'No.' In some cases, Harry would have been bound to say yes, but he knew that Shirley Temple was made of better stuff than that.

Harry and the solicitor shook hands with Michael, and he was taken downstairs to wait for the jail truck. Harry changed his clothes in the barristers' robing room, and joined his solicitor outside the courthouse. She was looking relieved, and perhaps not a little pleased.

'We got a result, didn't we?' She took off the glasses.

'Certainly did. Something to remember, for your first murder.'

'Funny about his family, though.'

'Meaning?' asked Harry.

'Well, I've never had a case before, not a trial, anyway, where nobody ever came along to support the accused. It doesn't look good, does it?'

'I really don't know. I rather gather that his brothers think he disgraced the family name. I can tell you this, though: I was doing a sentence for an Aboriginal man out west, and the whole courtroom was filled with the relations — old people, babies crying and kids misbehaving, everyone there that the solicitor could think of. The judge — one of those District Court misanthropes — said to me: "All right, Mr Curry, I've seen the family. They can be shown out now." Maybe that tells you something about the usefulness of manifesting the support network.'

A taxi pulled up beside them and Arabella got out, to Harry's patent amazement. The driver took her overnight bag from the boot and put it on the footpath.

'What are you doing here, Bella? I should have been gone by now.'

Arabella greeted the solicitor. 'Hi, Renata. How did it go?' She handed the driver a note and waved away the change.

'Really well, Arabella. Not guilty of murder, guilty of manslaughter. Sentencing at the end of the month. Mr Curry scores again.'

'Well done, you! Both of you. And tell me, Renata, did he behave himself?'

'Yes. Not well, though.'

Harry interrupted the amusement at his expense. 'I didn't know you two were acquainted, let alone involved in an anti-Curry cabal.'

'You never asked,' said Renata. 'Arabella and I are on the same committee of the Women Lawyers'. Have been for six months.'

'And we've been in contact by SMS all day.' Arabella punched Harry's arm. Then she kissed his cheek. 'Are we going to Burragate?'

Harry shook his head from side to side, but he meant yes. 'You could have told me,' he grumbled, 'before I made a pass at her, or something.'

Both women dissolved in laughter.

With the benefit of daylight saving, they made it to Burragate before it was fully dark. The hours it took to drive south from Wollongong had been spent, first, with a blow-by-blow account of the final day of the trial, including the confrontation at morning tea, and then they turned to personal matters. Arabella's still-burgeoning civil practice, and Harry's struggle with a reduced income — the consequence of his preference for subsistence vegetable gardening and fence-mending to defending drug supply and sexual offence trials at Penrith or Campbelltown.

After they had both showered and changed clothes, and Harry had put his *Magic Flute* CD on at reduced volume, he took a chicken out of the fridge ('Her name was Muriel, and I cut her head off and plucked her the weekend before last'), stuffed it with an onion and some breadcrumbs from a packet mixed with fresh herbs from the garden and put it in the oven in his mother's old black baking dish, surrounded by his potatoes, carrots, pieces of pumpkin and more onions. 'Sixty minutes should do it. You're in charge of the wine.'

She took a cold Margaret River white and a bottle of mineral water out onto the verandah, and lit the mosquito coils. Harry put together a bowl of almonds and dried apricots. Neither said anything as they worked their leisurely way through the aperitif, Arabella sticking to water, and they both watched, without comment, a small family of red kangaroos grazing in the gloom in the bottom paddock.

'This is what they call in books a companionable silence,' said Arabella.

'Except for Mozart.'

'Yes, except for Mozart. Just the three of us.'

'Counting Mozart, do you mean?'

'Well, no, not actually. I was referring to the baby.'

There was quite a long silence. 'You were referring to the baby?'

'Yes, I was.'

'My baby?'

'Yes.'

Thanks

To:

John Bettens, solicitor and friend, for the use of his name;

Dr Ronald Uscinski MD, for the use of his name and for permission to quote from his paper 'The Shaken Baby Syndrome', *Journal of American Physicians and Surgeons*, vol. 9, no. 3, Fall 2004;

Peter Lowing, solicitor and friend, for the use of his name.

Read on for a preview of the next collection of
Harry and Arabella stories from Stuart Littlemore

Harry Curry: Rats and Mice
Avaliable 2013

A personal injury paradox

Queen's Square in Sydney isn't really a square, but the intersection of Macquarie Street and St James's Road. Albert eyes Victoria eternally across the passing traffic from his plinth of Moruya granite while she stares off, unheeding, in the direction of Parliament House. Rarely is either spared a glance by any of the solicitors or barristers hurrying into the Supreme Court building as if they were iron filings attracted to a magnet.

Harry Curry — big, rangy of limb and crumpled of beautifully cut suit — unfolded himself from the front seat of his cab in Macquarie Street, slammed the door a little too firmly, and, carrying his overnight bag, strolled to the barristers' café opposite the Supreme Court steps. He'd caught the early flight up from Merimbula, and would meet Arabella Engineer of junior counsel in her chambers in half an hour. Harry detested Phillip Street. It was where the New South Wales Bar Association concentrated its power, a power its governing Council had abused by suspending Harry from practice not so long ago for unsatisfactory professional conduct. Specifically, for using an obscenity to a judge, when all he did was quote — somewhat ambiguously — what his client had told the police. Phillip Street was where Harry's father (the once-eminent Brylcreemed

QC Wallace Curry, now resident in a luxurious North Shore retirement facility) introduced him to the Bar by buying him the right to occupy a room on his old floor at a cost of $350,000, over fifteen years ago. Ancient history, that — Harry was now a displaced barrister of no fixed professional abode. With considerable justification, Harry never felt welcome in The Street, and avoided the legal faubourg whenever possible.

With those fifteen years under his belt, Harry would ordinarily have been entitled to expect appointment as a member of the Inner Bar — a Senior Counsel. No more QCs, of course. Republican sentiment in the State Labor government saw to that, twenty years ago. The view from the President's chambers was that the prerequisite fifteen years had to be racked up while junior counsel kept his or her nose clean and, admiring of Harry's super-robust advocacy as many of his learned friends were, none would seriously contend that his record was without blemish. Never a silk, always a stuff. As if he cared.

Harry took a table at the back of the café and put his bag down. He sat facing the street, so he could keep an eye out for Arabella's arrival across the road, and for lawyers he would not welcome to his table. There were plenty about, but none approached him. Harry ordered eggs on toast, bacon, tomato and sausage with a long black and hadn't long to wait before it arrived. As it did, he saw the former New South Wales Attorney General arrive and occupy another table. The Attorney and his government had been thrown out of office by the voters ten days earlier and, while previously the first law officer had always breakfasted attended upon by his barrister acolytes who could be imputed to be hoping for some crumbs from his table (judicial appointment, a brief in a Royal Commission, or at worst a magistrate's job), he was now alone and unfeigned-upon. Harry concentrated on the plate in front of him. He had no reason to feel any affection for this Attorney.

His plate clean and his coffee cup almost empty, Harry looked up from the newspaper the waitress gave him to catch a glimpse of Arabella climbing the steps into Wentworth Chambers. He smiled. Head-turningly tall, elegant in a short black jacket, silk dress and high heels, carrying her laptop slung over her shoulder and a bunch of flowers in her hand. She always had flowers in her room. The woman he loved, almost from the moment she had marched up to him after his disastrous disciplinary hearing and tentatively proposed to him a professional alliance in which he would be the strategist and she the mouthpiece. At first, Arabella was happy to have Harry's guidance in winning minor criminal trials (on Legal Aid), but the Women Lawyers, already admiring of her exoticism, noted her growing confidence and started briefing her in seriously rewarding commercial matters. A better class of client, they assured her, than those deadbeats she'd been looking after at Darlinghurst and the Downing Centre emporium of justice. It was plain to Harry that the Women Lawyers wished to take possession of the striking import from the London Bar, and he didn't blame her for accepting the better-paid work. Together in court from time to time, they still managed to look after the criminal clients of David Surrey, Harry's longstanding and longsuffering confidant and work-provider, and run a number of other worthwhile cases involving the liberty of the subject. Harry said the real deadbeats were the CEOs on five million a year.

The personal alliance between Harry and Arabella developed very soon after the professional one. It was all her idea, but it hadn't been easy for either of them. Harry confessed to sexual and social awkwardness, but it didn't take her long to overcome both. Then Harry's increasing disenchantment with the profession had thoughtlessly put 500 kilometres of distance between them: he was now resident on 12 hectares of riverfront farmlet down near the Victorian border at Burragate, appearing in bread-and-butter matters in the southern provincial courts, and Arabella remained in her *Vogue Living*-style apartment overlooking Elizabeth Bay. When Harry came to town, he slept there. They still loved each other, and she was pregnant.

Harry drained his cup and left money on the table to cover his meal and a generous tip. As he left the café, he paused beside the ex-Attorney General's table. The man — resembling nothing so much as a bluetongue lizard in a new suit and tie — kept his bald head down, reading the *Herald*. He didn't acknowledge Harry's presence, keeping his eyes on the paper. Harry flicked the back pages with his second finger, as if brushing away a fly.

'You'll find Positions Vacant at the back,' he said. The redundant politician removed his glasses and looked up but said nothing as Harry smiled pleasantly, turned and strolled with his athlete's gait across the road to catch the lift to Arabella's floor.

The receptionist rose and tried an 'Excuse me, sir...' as Harry, still smiling, emerged from the lift and headed down the corridor without submitting to her authority. A senior junior barrister (one of Harry's contemporaries, if not his friend) who was loitering nearby with a coffee in one hand and a tabloid newspaper in the other explained to the young woman that it was all right. 'That's Mr Curry, Natalie. The boyfriend. Never been known for his manners.' Natalie sniffed. 'GPS school, of course.'

The door to Arabella's small room was open, and Harry entered without knocking and sat in one of the clients' chairs opposite her. Arabella had been reading her emails. Other floor members walked to and fro outside in the corridor, some heading off to court in their wigs and gowns, clients and attorneys in their wakes.

'*Cosa c'è di nuovo?*'

The elegant woman looked up and smiled. 'Not much.' She stood and they both leaned across the heavily laden desk to kiss. 'Did you sleep in that suit?'

'Little plane, big bloke. You know how it is.' But he was acutely and admiringly aware that on Arabella's too-infrequent trips south, she always emerged from the plane looking like a model ready for a photo shoot. Even her jeans were elegant. He had no idea how she did it, because she was almost as tall as he, and no better suited to the cramped aircraft.

'You're not in court today, Bella, are you?'

'No. Doctor's appointment at eleven.'

He frowned. 'What's the matter?'

A pitying look from Arabella. 'Nothing's the matter. The obstetrician, Harry. Once a month.'

Abashed. 'Yes, sorry. Of course.' A pause. 'You look terrific. Radiant, as they say. Blooming.'

'I feel terrific. It agrees with me.'

'Don't tell me you two are already conversing?'

Arabella looked to one side and spoke over her shoulder. 'I'm just looking for some pink tape to strangle you with.' She turned back, leaned across the desk, and touched his cheek. 'We have to talk about this, you know.'

'I do know. That's really why I've come up. That and to have a talk with the Bar Association.'

'About what?'

'They're unhappy about me claiming the farm as my chambers.'

'Is there supposed to be something wrong with that?'

'No. I could practise out of the boot of my car, like the Lincoln Lawyer, if I wanted to. What they don't like is me giving my professional address as Ned Kelly Chambers, Burragate. I'm going to offer them some alternatives — Christopher Skase Chambers or Marcus Einfeld Chambers.'

'Do you think that's wise, Captain Mainwaring?' She raised her eyebrows. Arabella's Anglophile father, a London GP, never missed a re-run of *Dad's Army*.

Harry shrugged. 'They had no problem with naming chambers after Garfield Barwick or Edmund Barton. Ned wasn't even a politician, let alone a tax evader. They tell me there's a university named after Alan Bond, and it's alleged to have a law school. I rest my case.'

'If it's a boy, I hope he'll be as fearless as you, Harry. I just want him to know the meaning of restraint.'

'A much overrated quality, if you ask me. Just think how destructive the banks would be if Jesus had restrained himself with the money-lenders in the temple.'

Arabella laughed. 'I fear you've been on your own down there too long, my love, talking to the chickens. You need a bit of time in the city, with people.'

'Also overrated.' He picked up a folder from her desk and flicked through its pages. 'That's about enough avoiding the subject, isn't it?'

'Yes it is. But can we go for a walk? I don't want us to talk about the baby in here.'

It being a beautiful spring morning, they decided on the Botanic Gardens. Crossing Macquarie Street at the Hospital and turning left, Harry asked whether Arabella's reference to the child being a boy was an informed one.

'No, and I don't intend to find out before the birth.'

He nodded. 'But we have to think about names.'

'Harry, we need to debate *surnames*.' She looked through the railings at a Parliament House attendant hoisting the State flag.

'Yes, we do.' They strode on in silence past the Public Library, and beneath the statue of Matthew Flinders, overshadowed by the Port Jackson figs. At the signals controlling traffic coming up from Woolloomooloo, Arabella's attention was attracted by a highly decorated red bus whose open upper deck was occupied by smiling tourists (to whom Sydney was something to be experienced entirely through their digital viewfinders) and their guide, pointing toward the Opera House with an outstretched arm. The lights changed in the couple's favour, and they crossed to enter the gate to the Gardens. Joggers brushed past them. Sydney on a spring morning. After walking the meandering, freshly hosed paths in silence for five minutes, they found a bench and sat. The Harbour coruscated in the distance, and there was bright new growth on the trees. Gardeners were planting annuals from trays and watering them. Harry pointed to the purple buds that were starting to appear on the jacarandas.

'They used to say at Sydney Uni that if you hadn't done the work by the time the jacarandas were in flower, you'd fail your exams. They even said it in my father's day.'

'And in your own case?'

'Proved to be true.' He paused and looked at his hands. 'Is marriage one of today's topics?'

'Yes.'

'Are we discussing it romantically, or as lawyers?'

'As lovers, Harry. As parents.'

'But I've always wanted—'

'No Harry, don't leap to conclusions. I'm not asking you to marry me. At least, this isn't something that arises because I'm pregnant. The baby's practically irrelevant.'

'Let me think about that for a minute.' It was obvious from Harry's expression that he was struggling with it. He took off his tie, rolled it in a ball and put it in his jacket pocket. Then he stood up, removed his jacket and dropped it onto the grass. 'Okay, I'm a dinosaur. I would have assumed that the pregnancy was a relevant consideration in deciding about our future. I just don't know what you're telling me: we've never spoken about marriage. Love, yes. Marriage, no. If you'd ever asked me, at any time since we became lovers, I would have said that of course I want us to marry, but it never came up. Until now. I didn't buy the farm and sell Erskineville because I wanted us to live apart — it was because I didn't want to work in Sydney any more. To be more accurate, I didn't want to work in the law any more, or no more than I absolutely have to. Still, what else can I do? I've never learned to lay bricks. I've never tried to persuade you to come and live our lives at Burragate, have I?'

'No, you haven't.'

'That's always been up to you, and I agreed you had to give the commercial work a good hard try.'

'Yes, you did.'

'And it's going well?'

Arabella put her hand on Harry's. 'It's going very well. Not that I delight in being a damages-minimiser and debt-collector.

But it pays a lot better than crime, and my lifestyle's not cheap, even without the baby. Nannies don't come cheaply, either.'

'You plan one of those short maternity leaves, then back to work with a stranger raising our child in an apartment? When there's a farm and a river and air so clean that the fruit trees get those growths that die in city air?'

'You haven't told me about those.'

Harry became enthusiastic. 'I went to the nursery in Eden and showed them a branch I broke off one of the cherries. It has this fine growth on it like coral that I thought was a fungus, and I wanted a spray to deal with it. They told me it's not a problem, and that it only grows where the air is really pure. They thought it was great, Burragate. The locals call it Buggarit.'

'You love that place, don't you? It's important to you.'

'Yes, and for all that I'd sell it at the drop of a hat if you wanted me to come back up to Sydney and live with you, married or not.'

She put her arm around him and kissed his cheek. 'Do you want to apply for the job of nanny, Harry?'

'No. For the job of father.'

Arabella found herself needing to do something with her hands, but hadn't brought a bag or even her handkerchief. 'Let's get a cup of coffee.' They stood, Harry picked up his jacket, and they walked downhill to the kiosk, where they took a table on the deck overlooking the pond. Birds were arguing in the trees and a primary school excursion was threading its way along the path, pushing and shoving and yelling.

Harry gave their orders to the waitress and waited until she left. 'The job's not taken, is it?'

'You're the father, Harry. Nobody can deny you that.'

'It's the *job* of father I'm talking about, not the biological fact. It's an executive role.'

'So it is.'

'Is it in Elizabeth Bay, this position?'

'Not in the long term, no. Not necessarily. But my mother insists on coming over before the birth, and I have to assume for a while afterwards.'

'Fine with me, Bella. I'm not applying for a position as grandmother.'

'What I hoped was this, Harry: that you'd stay with me for the period immediately before the birth — going up and down to the farm if you have to — just be there when my mother comes to Sydney, and be there at the birth, but let her have the run of the place for a month or so after the baby arrives.'

'And after that?'

'After that we make our decisions.'

'On what subjects?'

'Nannies, marriage, domicile.'

'Name? Names?'

'The surname's Curry. You may imagine that my mother might think that's a trifle unfortunate, but I told her it's not negotiable.'

'Christian name TBA?'

Arabella laughed. 'Who said anything about my child being a Christian? Neither of her parents is.'

'As you say. I shall, being suitably chastened, politically correct myself: first names TBA, then?'

The coffee arrived. Later, they walked down the sun-dappled path to the sea wall, holding hands. When it was time, Harry walked Arabella back uphill to Macquarie Street and sat in the obstetrician's waiting room during her consultation, rapidly solving the quick crossword in the *Herald*. Arabella came out smiling and introduced Harry to the doctor, a woman. She looked both of them up and down.

'Probably a very tall baby,' she said.

They both laughed.

'Dr Rose says it's due in six months, Harry.' The doctor nodded.

'Pisces, then,' Harry said.

Arabella looked mildly shocked. 'Harry Curry, you don't?'

'I do. They're hopeless dreamers, Pisces.'

The women looked at each other, exchanging mock-sad looks.

Harry spread his hands and opened his eyes wide. 'What? I got that from the crossword.'

Harry had left his overnight bag in Arabella's room, perhaps unsubtly, yet as he accompanied her back to chambers no invitation was issued for him to spend the night at Elizabeth Bay, and he chose not to raise the subject. Arabella had been waiting for him to do so, and when neither referred to it they parted with both feeling unhappy, Harry carrying away the offending item of luggage. She had a series of conferences with witnesses lined up for her case next month, at half-hour intervals for the whole afternoon.

The Vice-President of the Bar, into whose very expensive chambers Harry was shown immediately upon his arrival at the reception desk, was pleasantly surprised that Harry was so easily compliant with the Association's request that he find another name for his professional address. In fact, he'd never had any intention of naming it after Ned Kelly. That was just a bit of mischief he'd inserted in the Law Society diary's contact list of counsel. She'd always been told that Curry was abrasive and hard to get on with, and for that reason had equipped herself for a confrontation by placing a copy of the Bar Conduct Rules front and centre on her desk, but all he asked her was whether she had children and how she and her husband managed as working parents. In fact, she took to him and thought she was beginning to understand his attractiveness to her junior colleague Engineer. No, not exactly attractive — those close-together eyes, broken nose and untamed hair — but he certainly had something magnetic about him. A confident strength to him, or maybe a strong confidence. The unexpected ease between them made the next part of her task even harder.

'Having dealt with that so amicably, I'm also expected to talk to you about the disadvantages of your practising one-out down there on the far South Coast, far from the immediate assistance your colleagues can provide.'

'Ah, well done — "Immediate assistance". I like a good euphemism.'

'All right — far from disciplinary oversight.'

'Why did you get the short straw, Ruth?'

'The rest of them are scared of you, Harry. Especially Frosty, ever since the Ethics Committee stuffed up your suspension. I don't think he could face you, having been your father's pupil and everything that implies. Embarrassed is hardly the word. Mortified would be closer to the mark.'

'To think that a stellar panel of equity silks could purport to rub me out, having denied me procedural fairness or natural justice or whatever this year's trendy cliché might be! Unimaginable. And I suppose that what you're supposed to negotiate, with fearful Frosty hiding beneath your skirt, is that I'll keep a low profile somewhere south of the Illawarra, not insult the learned magistrates and highly regarded political hacks — sorry, esteemed dizzo judges on circuit — and generally keep out of trouble. Or so I infer.'

'It's a powerful inference. You do have a chequered history with judicial officers of the District Court, Harry — even you would have to admit that. Never mind the magistrates, most of whom believe you hold them in contempt.'

'Neither my clients nor I admit anything. I make it a rule of practice.'

The Vice-President sighed. 'This isn't going to become a problem between us, is it? We were doing so well.'

'I'm going to be a father in six months,' Harry smiled and folded his arms.

'So Arabella tells us. Well, obviously, you'll be a reformed character. Mellow, even.'

'Got it in one, Ruth.' They smiled at each other. 'And Arabella's already broadcast the news?'

'Tell one Woman Lawyer, and you've told them all.'

'You're not telling me you're a Woman Lawyer, surely? I thought you were heterosexual.' She threw the Bar Rules at him, but missed. 'Ah. You certainly throw like a girl.' Harry stood and took a last look around the room. 'I've got a plane to catch, Ruth. Maybe you'd be interested in giving an after-dinner speech at the Bermagui Institute some time?'

The Vice-President raised one eyebrow. 'The Bermagui Institute?'

'An occasional symposium of intellectuals, retired to the South Coast.' She frowned. 'And their wives,' he added. She scowled.

'Get out now, Harry Curry, or I'll have you up before PCC 1.'

'That'd be the industrial-strength Professional Conduct Committee? We've met before.'

'No. It's the Political Correctness Committee. Constituted entirely of women with short hair and boiler suits.'

'Very good, Ruth. Frosty says you've got no sense of humour, by the way.'

'I already told you to get out, I believe.' So he got out, with a wave.